Ian Robertson

The Hags of Sickle and Bow

"Typical Robertson,

grippingly different"

Dedicated to Milly Muse who, with the machete of her mind, hacked through the jungle of my grammar.

Ian R.

Life is short; live longer; buy a step ladder

*WELL DONE
HAPPY NEW EYE
TEST
o HCRAS

Ian*

The Hags of Sickle and Bow

Copyright © 2017 by Ian Robertson
Published by Ian Robertson

~~~~~

Createspace Edition
ISBN: 978-1542819077

~~~~~

Ian Robertson asserts his right to be identified as author of this work in accordance with the Copyright, Designs and Patents Act 1988.
All rights reserved.

~~~~~

Without limiting the rights under copyright reserved above, no part of this publication may be stored in a retrieval system or transmitted or published in any form or by any means without the prior written permission of both the copyright owner and the publisher of this book. This book must not be sold or distributed for commercial purposes by any person or persons other than the seller or sellers authorized by the above author and publisher nor be circulated in any form of binding or cover other than that in which it is here published and without a similar condition including this condition being imposed on any subsequent owner.

~~~~~

This is a work of fiction. Names, characters, places, brands, media, and incidents are either the product of the author's imagination or are used fictitiously.

~~~~~

Prepared for publication by Popsible Press

Edited by Alec Hawkes
Cover art by Janey Slater

~~~~~

Ian Robertson is 52 years old and works successfully as a chef at the seventeenth century manor house, Llancaiach Fawr in the Taff Bargoed valley. He is a native of the Welsh valleys and this immersion feeds his creativity and obsession with its culture and people. His work although based in reality has a surreal, carnival quality.

~~~~~

Thanks to Alec and the Team for their dedicated work, and to my lovely kids Georgia and Jay for all their help and support.
Ian R.

Contents

THE OTHER CHILD	1
AND THE DOG WAS DEAD	4
THE TROUBLE WITH PRAYER	9
NO PLACE FOR MAGGOTS	19
THE TROUBLE WITH MEN	28
THE BREW OF A FOUL WIND	36
RUFFLED FEATHERS AT THE ROAST DUCK INN	40
WILDFIRE	54
A BLOOM OF WORRY AND BOILS	58
WHAT YOU WISH FOR	66
ON THE SIDE AND UNDER THE TABLE	74
THE MARCH OF OMENS	80
THE NIGHT OF THE WEASELS	84
THE CHAINS OF FORGIVENESS	96
OUT OF THE ASHES	102
THE TURN OF BLAME AND GAIN	106
THOUGHTS OF SMOKE	115
OLD AS THE HILLS, MA MUGS	118
FOR THEIR SINS	126
HAPPY NEVER AFTER	132
THE NON CONFORMISTS	136
A CLEAN KILL	142
WHAT SALLY SAID	148
THE LOCK HORNS	152
A PARTING VISIT	163
A DRINK OF BLOOD AND BONE	170
COMETH THE GREAT DAY	177
A PLACE FOR FLIES	180
THE EVE OF REVELATIONS	187
HORNS DAY	192
HORNS DAY - THE BLODGER BROTHERS	208
HORNS DAY - THE HARDY BROTHERS	214
HORNS DAY - THE BEAST OF MORRIS BEVAN	228
THE ETERNAL HANGMAN	240
SOLACE IN AMBER	255
LIFE'S TOO SHORT	261
FOUR MOONS HAVE PASSED	270
THE REVOLT OF THE SILENT KETTLES	276

THE HAGS OF SICKLE AND BOW

THE OTHER CHILD...

It was a time before man had claimed the moon. It was a time when science hadn't completely dismissed the word of God, but was inching in for the kill. It was a time when the wonder of the world arrived in our living rooms at the flick of a switch, and pylons replaced temples as objects of wonder. But this overhead-powered Earth still held mystery, dark corners still clung to life, ready to pounce on the unexpected. It was a time when childhood tales still threatened and chilled young hearts with the thrill of superstition, and monsters and demons still had their place, in a world that was not yet... completely discovered.

There was something other about the child, just the sight of her nagged and unsettled, stirring a blood-lust of emotions. Clans of the mean-minded soon took notice and clawed together, pointing mean talons towards her whenever she passed... And the gossip swarmed. '*She favours the night*', they'd say, '*no child of mine*', they'd snub, '*there should be a law and the church should know bette*r.' But the child would pass the gaggle and shrug and, with a flick of her hair, shake off the narrow-minded tar and feathers.

Her father had strived black and blue to beat the Lord in, and the Devil out. But still she favoured the night and its whispers, its shroud and its kin. Her Mother tried to love her, but the emotion never sat right. A kiss would shy short of its mark, a hold would crush then quickly slither, so the child grew bare of touch, in the care of stone.

The church, ever conscious of revolt, proclaimed her a pandemic, a plague capable of catastrophic mutation, a blight and a curse and a swill of free thought. So night and wood became her nurture, and a feast of mystery dwelt darkly there in. She could translate in owl and slither in snake and hop and learn ugly like toad. She learnt root and herb of harm and healing, fungus of illusion and the soothe of balms, and the child grew and the wild grew with her. Her hair was a flame of autumn fall, her eyes the depth of amber, her lips as red as berry poison, her skin the shine and shadow of moonlight. And with the rise of her beauty grew the seeds of envy, a green mist that choked the homely wives and fuelled the gaggle to a frenzy.

No man, it seemed, was safe from this devil of beauty; no church blessing sacred, while the taint of her presence soured the faith. But she revelled in the rumour, proud to be crowned their wicked tempest, and flaunted her mischief till the gossip roared.

Away from the closed walls of village eyes, she found the open minds that dwelt with the stars, and travelled to the moon, a community that never took root, their home, always the far reaches of the horizon. And with them came the knowledge only people without borders could bring. The lore of oceans, hills and dreams, travelled and gathered with them, a roll of wisdom they spoke, borrowed from their history and an ancient craft of time. With them she found her soul, they who treated all as one; they who worshipped love and freedom, above the cult and God of men. They showed her the earth and she prospered, they showed her the will of the Great Mother and the power to wield her nature, and she purred in magic and felt at home.

"For the best!" said her Father, waving farewell to family and shame. Her Mother choked, but still the tears would not show, but she well rehearsed some words of sorrow, shrugged her shoulders then turned her back. The streets dimmed to a shun, the night of her leaving as, without fanfare or tears, she walked her farewell. Eyes peeked behind curtains, and hecklers howled, damning her passing and forbidding return. Good riddance was the fork on every tongue, as wicked minds wished her ill, and cursed her on her way.

The town that raised and damned her now sat in the valley below her, its cold grey stone sitting like a cancer at the heart of nature's beauty. She looked back for spite, not old time's sake, at the hovel and cobbled shell of her youth. She held her head high and blew a curse to the wind.

"I take nothing from you, not a penny or a dream, nor a single memory…and all I leave is a curse and a wish of ruin!"

AND THE DOG WAS DEAD...

The town of Sickle grazed peaceful on the banks of the river Bow. Unlike the river, the town sat rooted in nostalgia, going nowhere. Life in the town seemed to idle along as the river gently rippled by, and for the world's eyes, this idyllic seemed not to have a care. Away from nature and the willowed banks, grew the concrete of man, a bizarre piece of humanity huddled together; close knit, yet worlds apart. Mortared in an embrace of terrace, avenue, grove or crescent; lives sheltered in their stone domains. In a privacy of multitudes, stone walls rise high, borders are set and family laws and standards applied. Each to their own; bolt the doors at night as darkness mutes the town. Shields are drawn and the world shuttered out, as people's lives become their own. The streets heave into silence as another day's echoes pass. The night holds its breath, as private passions and horrors unfold.

Number twenty eight Hampton Row sat gagging in its terrace, the harmony of spring-flowered boxes told lies of the winter that shivered inside. The youth of love and home had obeyed to the rust of old age and had turned stone as bone. The clock ticked spiteful as time marched cold to the grave, and this is where Norman Stubs dwelt, with a face of no nonsense and duty done. He sat rocking himself peaceful in the smug of remembers, while his dogged wife scurried under his feet, dusting and polishing and brewing the bloody tea.

Of course Norman knew his wife still held port for desire, he could sense her vibration. Her passion was now just a frustration that consumed her in rage. But Norman just smiled and folded his paper; *'Friday'*, he thought, *'lovely, fish and chips for tea'*, and as the delight was served Norman sniggered, *'she's wearing make up again'*, he smirked, *'I'll have trouble tonight!'*

Norman Stubs neatly tucked himself into bed, turned off the reading lamp, mumbled a good night to his wife and turned a cold shoulder. He was waiting for it, they'd wallowed together now for over forty years there was not a motion or sigh that did not have meaning. "Get your bloody hands off my willy, woman," groaned Norman, slapping the offending hand and dashing his wife's hopes.

"Oh please Norm! It won't take long, it never did," said his wife, bear-hugging his back in desperation. But her once Romeo just grunted and jostled to the far reaches of the bed. "How many times Gwyn? I'm sixty five years old, all I require from my bed in my old age is peace, and not to be disturbed by squelching about in unnatural geriatric buffoonery."

Gwyn fumed, released her embrace and pounded her pillow. "Oh for God's sake Norm! There's nothing unnatural about making love!"

"Nothing unnatural Gwyn? Have you looked at yourself lately? You are sixty four years of age and rising; eighteen stone and rising, you have a receding hair line that is rapidly rising and that makes my ability to rise about as bloody unnatural as you can get!"

"Oh Norman Stubs! You're a cruel, heartless man, you care nothing for me and my needs."

"Oh please don't Gwyn! Banging on about your bloody needs; for I have grafted all my life too for filling your bloody needs, this house, and every bloody thing in it. All renewed mind, again and again to keep you ahead in your eternal race with the Joneses…Ah I know what you can do Gwyn, fill your passion with the other great love of your life."

"And just what is my other great passion in life Norm? Pray do tell because it's a mystery to me!"

"In short Gwyn…Food!"

"Food? And do you honestly believe that a bag of chips can quench my desire?"

"Look at it as compensation Gwyn."

"Oh you really are a bloody pig! Compensation you say, well believe it or not Norm I cannot get passionate with a fucking potato!"

"Funny Gwyn, neither can I. Now if you don't mind, the hour is late."

Gwyn shot out of bed, now fully primed for war. Norm knew this saga well, it had re-run for the last twenty twilight years. He quickly went into survival mode and buried his head in the bunker of his pillow and whistled, chuckled, counted and braced himself for the tempest. His darling wife paced herself to a boil, her fury steaming up the room. The attack started with a point, then the dam burst and the torrent let rip.

"You…You... You useless shit faced snivel of an ungrateful bastard man, I've given my life to you! And you lie there with your big fat gob and accuse me of being pampered…….Oh, oh just tell me Norm, when you were this mighty provider, this, this, primal hunter gatherer, who raised the kids? Tell me who kept the home just the way Norm likes it, and who still keeps it the way bloody Lord Norm likes it? Oh yes, you've retired but I never can. I still cook, clean and scrub the bloody toilet…Ever diligent, mind, that Norm's dinner is served at six o'clock, while you? Oh you just potter in your garden and slip off for your well earned pint. Oh yes Norman Stubs, I think you'll find that my needs are a lot less demanding than yours."

Norm sat up in bed and folded his arms and shook his head. "Do you really think you are going to change me now Gwyn? At my time of life? Why can't you just be happy with what you've got? God knows it's more than most, and, and find some humbling that suits your years, and quit this parade of comic book seduction, those days are long gone Gwyn! I've done my duty, you've got your kids…"

"Oh I'm sorry, did I forget to thank you for that? The wonderful gift of giving birth that you so generously bestowed on me, oh how selfish of me, and as for your duty, what a fleeting watch that was…Oh yes, the writing was on the wall on our honeymoon when, after a couple of sweaty fumbles and primal grunts, you broke wind, laughed and did pig impressions all long night in your sleep. Oh God how I despised Hollywood after that night…Oh, my Mother was right it's a chain they should give you on your wedding day not a bloody ring! Oh yes, a chain to bind you to your bloody contract of servitude…… Oh it's no wonder you smiled when I signed that sheet of paper, you'd already bought the cage!"

"Oh, so this home I've sweated and grafted for is a cage is it Gwyn? Damn it woman, you've done well by me!"

"God Norm, your pathetic…" Gwyn points to her chest and head and the tears start to flow. "My heart and my mind, that's what you caged."

Norman tuts and shakes his head. "Damn it woman, I do believe you've finally lost the plot."

"Lost the plot? I've never had a bloody plot, this miserable bloody life has all been your…BLOODY PLOTTING!

Gwyn slammed the bedroom door and thundered down the stairs. She then tried slamming the living room door but it had always defied her, the ill-fitting bastard thing. His doing again; the only door in the street that opened and mowed the carpet at the same time. But the kitchen door slammed just fine, and his favourite mug smashed against the wall just fine!

Never mind, put the kettle on. And so here she was again, clutching a cup of tea, a brew that, despite its reputation, didn't make anything fucking better, and she should know! Oh, how many times had she sat lonely in a fog of tears, surrounded by the dark that seemed to take a great delight in wrapping her in grief, the only sound her bubbling self-pity and the grinding of his snores that scratched down the stairs and grated her nerves to crumbs.

A yap snapped her back to the here and bloody now, she reached down and picked up her beloved pooch. "You love me, don't you boy," she gasped, clutching him for affection, and the little dog yapped again and dribbled her face in devotion.

Gwyn finally took charge of herself, sucked in the chilled night air and felt it shudder her senses back to life. *"She knows the way of it,"* she said to her dog, as she roughed behind his ears. *"Live to the passion and beat of your heart,"* she says, *"because once that beat fails, if you are not content with the life you've lived, then you fail with it."* The sobs tried to take hold again but Gwyn defied them with a cast iron breath. *"Oh for her youth to be so wise, just to know who, and what you are before you even begin...just to have the balls to go along with the ideals of no other. She makes choice seem so easy...Leave him',* she says, *'and live the magic with me, I promise she said, we'll be free to fuck and destroy whatever we like, we could sing the day with angels or dance dirty with devils at night...and what do I always reply?"* She sighed deep and scratched the dog's ear. *"But my husband, oh yes, even as I swim in the velvet of her words I think of that leech that has been sucking me dry of hope for years."* As if in answer to insult, the snores ground deeper and the scratching became a sonic boom. Gwyn ripped at her hair in a rave of frustration. "Oh shut up, shut up, shut up!" And the tears flowed again but this time streaked with heat, boiled in the furnace of rage. "Oh I'd like to wring and wring that belching, snoring lousy bloody neck, just take my hands and twist and twist till his eyes scream red and his nose bursts blue, oh God! Oh God!"

And there she stayed, bent in exhaustion, crammed in the position that sleep unexpectedly had chosen.

The night finally let go its grip and sunrise flickered in, chasing off the shadow and revealing all. Gwyn woke, stirred by the movement of the world outside, her back and head ached, and she shivered. "Oh not again!" She groaned. She tried to rise and noticed two things. One, the snoring had abated and two, the dog was dead...She screamed.

THE TROUBLE WITH PRAYER...

The vicarage perched high above the village on a backdrop of nimbus, its faith carved in granite. As solid as God, it boasted heaven as its neighbour, its position giving awe to the faithful and threat to the disbeliever. Morris Bevan believed. He believed in the grand abode he dwelt in, that perched high and grand above his parish and he believed, like his home, that he too was ordained to perch high. His garden bloomed hymns to the sweet hum of nectar; the soil, sponge-rich, gave grace to fruit and the promise of jams. Oh yes, Morris Bevan believed that abundance was reward for the faithful. But to some, it seemed, Morris Bevan believed most of all in himself. He greeted the world wrapped in his Jesus long grey face, holding a snarl of purity, eyes that pierced you snide with contempt. Oh indeed, the air he breathed was sweeter, his eyes rose tinted and oblivious to shadow, his days were the colour of glory and never questioned. For Morris Bevan was, above all, above the words *thou shall not*, for those words belonged to peasants and not the trusted servant of God.

Grunts of pleasure and protest echoed through the teak polished home. The sound seemed not to belong to the china tea-sets, the porcelain idols, the framed biblical scenes, the embroidered *God Bless This Home* and the fine polished, oak and teak finish. Finally the sofa shuddered to silence and a cry of relief quickly howled to despair.
"Oh Lord, Lord! Look what she's made me do!" Morris Bevan dismounted and laughed and zipped up his flies and wiped the sweat of shame off his soiled brow, his lanky frame swaying above his now un-pinned wife. Sylvia Bevan dressed and hated him.
"You're the Devil woman," said the vicar, quickly clipping his dog collar on his ugly apple tree neck. His wife sneered. "Do you really think that collar can hide who you are? Just look at you, standing there choking for forgiveness, you're pathetic."

"Believe me, woman, the Lord sees you for who you are. He knows your ilk, and your power to invoke demons in a man, and believe me, I am already forgiven."

Indeed Sylvia Bevan could still invoke demons in men. Now in her middling years, her beauty, elegance and grace seemed eternal; petite with tight-curled, blonde, movie-star chic, and star blue heavenly eyes. "Oh please don't forgive him Lord, let the pervy little bastard suffer for eternity."

"Hold your devil-forked tongue woman!"

"Oh I won't, this is the only enjoyment I get out of this sordid business, seeing you frantic for forgiveness. Oh its magic, aye, just one pathetic squirt and you shrivel back down to the pathetic worm you are."

"Blast you woman, you've the Devil…"

"And you've the holy spirit, or so you claim, so it must be that which compels you to tie me up and spank me, and all the other greasy disgusting things you do." Her husband sneered, now composed, he feels fit once again to look down. "Huh, you think God would favour you over me? Oh believe me, he knows your crime and that of all your sex... The choice of Eve long ago left you with the scar between your legs and the power to possess...The abuse I claim is the justice for man."

"Oh I must say I agree there, for you certainly looked possessed at the time, head all puffed up like a boiled beetroot, panting and puffing like a truffling pig." Morris cupped his hands in prayer and paced the room. "Oh Lord, hear me now and I promise never again to harken to this harlot's call. Sylvia cupped her hands and fluttered her lashes up to the heavens. "Firstly Lord I never, I swear, call him. In fact, it's more of an ambush than an invitation. Secondly he smells, and this obsession with my backside bloody well hurts, and next time he removes his belt I pray his trousers tangle round his ankles and he breaks his fucking neck!"

"Why, you blaspheming little bitch!"

"Steady Morris, I haven't finished yet. Anyway Lord, I know deep inside you don't give a fuck so I hope one day, unaided, I can muster enough strength to break it myself!"

"Oh you really are a walking curse! And you need to mind your tongue when addressing the Lord. Or, God help me, I might break something myself!"

Sylvia held out her hand. "I tell you what? We could make a deal, I'll mind my tongue and you mind your cock."

"God help me!" Morris blasted to the heavens, then pointed a damning finger at his wife. "I never should have married you! You reeked of trouble, but I was too naïve to know the smell."

"Oh you made it your business to marry me, I was just a pawn for your ambition. You crawled up my Father's backside just so you could have your own parish...I'll give you this mind, you were good, fooled my dear old Gran. I can hear her saying now, *'ooh he's got a lovely faith, and his manner is the way of angels'*. Oh how you loved it as your little plot took hold and fooled us all...except my Mother, she had the way of you."

"And did you ever consider I was doing your Father a favour, taking the shame of you out of his home? God knows he was at his wits end, the good Lord rest his soul, it was I who rid him of his burden, and God knows I'm paying for it now!"

"Good, and I hope you pay till you're rotting in your grave."

"No doubt I shall, but there at least I will find peace in the house of the Lord."

"Huh, sure he'll want you, I would imagine sadomasochists had a better welcome down below, they certainly seem better equipped for it."

"The good Lord understands and forgives the weakness of the flesh in the nature of making love."

"Huh, you don't make love, you inflict it! Oh, believe me, I see the Devil in your eyes every time you try to bind and spank me...Oh yes its flame you'll see, not pearly bloody gates!"

"Hold that tongue woman, or I swear I'll take my hand and..." A firm knock of the door stopped Morris in his tracks; he quickly rearranged himself as Sylvia looked at him. She shook her head and laughed. "Oh good, salvation! Seems there is a God after all."

Morris scowled "We have a guest, I take it I can rely on you to act accordingly."

"Don't I always... Well run along then, it could be a very important soul to save, or better still one of your wealthy congregation with a nice big fat donation, that will cheer you up." Morris contended his mood and made for the door. Sylvia plumped cushions and arranged neat the façade. Morris opened the door. "Why, old Tom, what a pleasant surprise... My dear," he hollered, "pray, charge the kettle, I have a delightful surprise, old Tom has graced us with a visit."

Tom the Placard woke that day alive, and cursed the day for it. "Never mind, there's always tomorrow," he assured himself. The end had been nigh for Tom for the past fifty bloodless years, so he was well used to disappointment. Not even an earthquake in all that time that he could use as a sign, though true to say a power-cut that lasted several days did stir a bit of interest for the briefest of moments. Oh how he hankered for that judgement day, if not only to say I told you so. But old Tom would not give up, he'd see it through to the bitter end, he just prayed he would be still alive to see it.

Every morning started the same; he relished his breakfast as though it was his last, looked out of the window to assess any possible tell-tale damage. He washed, shaved and strived to look his best. A suit was the order of every day, for what could be more official than meeting the son of God. Next for Tom's orchestrated attention was his beloved placards, they lined the living room walls, all well constructed prophecies of doom. *But which one today*, he pondered. The choice was as vast as it was grim, he could go for a standard 'JESUS IS COMING' or for more impact perhaps 'YE FAITHFUL REJOICE, SINNERS ROAST TONIGHT'. The decision made, Tom would buff his placard to a shine of salvation. Then, last but not least was Tom's index of sinners that dwelt in the locality. This was a duty old Tom took deadly seriously, for it was his favour to the Lord, a way to cut down the workload on that fateful day, and would probably provide him with a ringside seat and a speedy exit. Tom's book of suspects was as black as the bible and heaving full of sinners, and on this particular morning Tom had, he believed, a very interesting new entry. The subject was female, the abode, Wickle Cottage. He never trusted the solitude of that address, and finally the category of suspected sin. The entry read simply, *Whore?* With the morning's ritual completed, Tom decided on his placard of the day. 'AND THE EARTH SHALL RENT AND HELL SPEW FORTH'. And for Tom, the sooner the better.

Sylvia, as her husband had expected, had quickly spruced; and Morris made their guest feel at home using his best silkworm grace. Sylvia pulled back a chair and patted the cushion "Hello Tom dear, take a seat and the world off your feet." Old Tom gruffly nodded and removed his cap, revealing a tuft of grey hair. Apart from the grey hair that spoke his age, Tom was a fit and wiry old hatchet, with a weathered face that always peered bold and proud. He gave a toothless, wrinkled grin and cracked his old back down. "Oh don't worry about my feet Mrs Bevan, it won't be long before every foot will be taken off this world; tables, chairs, feet an all, all blown to bits; flesh and wood splintered and cracked all over God's earth…Uh, they'll get no rest then Mrs Bevan. Old Nick is not noted for his comforts."

Sylvia politely smiled. "But of course Tom, though I'm sure you'll have time for a cup of tea and maybe a slice of cake, before we're blasted into bite size pieces."

Tom rubbed his hands in anticipation "Oh now you're talking Mrs Bevan, I've always said your baking was proof an angel walked among us."

"Quite so," said Morris with a joyless guffaw. Oh how Sylvia hated that forced attempt at emotion, that forced interest, that she believed could only fool an idiot. Morris took a gentle sip of his tea and smiled. "So Tom, to what do we owe this blessing of your visit?" Tom wasted no time in reply. "Well, as you are aware Mr Bevan, I concern myself deeply in the faith of our good community. Indeed, I strive for the good of every soul in your beloved parish. But as I'm sure you are aware, Vicar, some souls are not worth the flesh they are wrapped in; some souls defy the word of God and strive to corrupt those of a weaker mind and faith…And as I always say Vicar, corruption and sin are only a bite of an apple away, and I believe we have a viper among us, with a basket full of forbidden fruit."

Morris placed down his teacup. "Oh indeed Tom, and the church is forever grateful to you and your bold crusade."

"Well I'll come straight out with it Vicar, for God knows time is short!" Tom scanned the room and edged closer. "Wickle Cottage, it would seem, is harbouring mischief again…"

"More tea Tom," interrupted Sylvia. "Wickle Cottage you say."

"Yes Mrs Bevan, there's an ill wind, and it's blowing a very suspicious washing line."

"Ah, suspicious washing line?" Puzzled Morris.

"I think what Tom means is sexy underwear, but of course dear you would not be expected to know of such things," Sylvia smirked at her husband.

Morris just gave his wife a smile "Ah, but of course I see."

Tom quickly continued, eager to reveal all. "And so do I see Mr Bevan, garments laced for testosterone, devil thrilled and not a lot for the imagination; in short the attire of a whore."

Morris tutted. "Well dear me Tom."

"Oh yes Vicar, she has a very well used back door." Sylvia almost choked on her tea. "You all right Mrs Bevan?" said Tom with alarm.

"Yes fine," said Sylvia, brushing spilt tea off her blouse.

"Anyway," continued Tom. "There's a lot of men going in and out."

Sylvia chuckled. "Of her back door."

Morris shot his wife a warning glare but Tom soldiered on, oblivious of the intended wit. "Indeed, and I'm afraid I've noted some well-respected pillars of our community poking round there, men who vowed otherwise, men who share pews and prayers with us on the Sabbath, no less. Now, you know me

Vicar, I've got nothing against strangers as long as I know them...But I smell corruption!"

"So tell me Tom, just who do you blame for this supposed behaviour?" asked Sylvia as she started to clear the table.

Tom answered with no doubt "Why her of course, availability on that scale is a damning for sure!"

"Oh but of course, how silly of me to even think men are capable of corrupting themselves."

Morris spotted the rebel rising in his wife and quickly intervened. "Steady now dear, Tom has only the care of the community at heart, isn't that right Tom?"

"That's right Mr Bevan, and if I've read the signs correctly, I fear grave danger." Tom looked around the room suspiciously; satisfied of privacy, he pressed on. "I fear, Vicar, that the Whore of Babylon walks among us. Now, I've no need to remind you of your revelations, Mr Bevan."

"She's from Ireland and her name is Fitzpatrick." Sylvia's proclamation stopped the conversation in its tracks and her husband's jaw dropped. "What! You know her?"

Tom shot out of his chair. "Good God! Irish catholic, the end is closer than I thought!"

Sylvia ignored the dropped jaws and shell-shock and pressed on. "She's a lovely lady, always in the charity shop, as a matter of fact I've invited her for service one Sunday."

Morris is next to bounce out of his seat. "What, you've invited a catholic into God's church?"

Tom raised his hands to the heavens and proceeded in chant. "Oh Lord, Lord, I see it now, yes, yes, there's no time to pack! All will stand naked before the storm, the Pope and the beast are upon us, and soon the whore will bring down the temple."

"She tells fortunes," continued Sylvia calmly. "That's why men, and women, visit her. She reads palms and tarot cards."

"A witch!" Tom blasted. "Why, that's the ultimate whore, for if she courts the Devil she'll allow any beast into her bed. Good God! Now there's doom for you!"

Morris paced the room. "Never mind all that, have you any idea what a disastrous effect a catholic spinster in my church would have on donations."

Sylvia shook her head. "Oh the charity of the church never ceases to amaze me. I must have been mistaken, believing the house of the Lord was open to all."

Morris snarled back in retort "Don't be so absurd, anyone might show up."

"Well I'm sorry dear, but it's done now, I've invited her."

"Well, as head of this parish I veto the invite."

Tom reached up, clutched the vicar by the shoulders and looked him sternly in the eye. "Oh no Mr Bevan don't do that, let the pariah come. The good Lord would never ignore such blasphemy; he'll zap us for sure, and I will bear witness to the glorious bang. Oh, the end at last, I've waited all my life for this!"

Morris still stared hate towards his wife. "I think you might find, Tom, that not everyone shares your enthusiasm for premature obliteration."

Tom laughed. "Oh Mr Bevan, I think you'll find there's nothing premature about death, it arrives just at the time the good Lord bestows it, and for folk like us, rigid in faith, judgement day is a full house; all our candle blown wishes come true with an ageless eternity to enjoy them. Oh glory be, I must spread the word we're doomed, oh happy days!"

Tom scurried for his coat, panting in excitement "Well I'm afraid I must be going, it's been nice knowing you, but time is pressing and I've a word to spread." And off he scampered, slamming the door in haste.

With Tom gone, the mood soon turned back to loathsome, the façade of normality twisted in on itself to an even greater rage. Morris popped his cork and Sylvia smiled her well-rehearsed smile, perfected especially to goad her despised spouse.

Morris's index finger gnarled into her face, the knotted bone aimed at her forehead, loaded with his fury. "You really are the most bothersome bitch!" he fired. "News of your association will spread like wild-fire through the parish, and I will not have the order of my church disrupted by your borderline insanity... Huh, inviting such a creature into God's church!"

"Oh and just what sort of creature is she?" Sylvia snapped, shoving the digit out of her face. "And what makes you think the animals you mass with are any better? The councillors, bankers and all the well healed hypocrites who polish their cocks clean every Sunday, fill your coffers and get a full blessing to do it all again... Ring any bells?"

"God damn you woman, you are talking about the cream of our community..."

"Oh don't worry, Fitz has told me about all the worthy pillars of your glorious parish who have knocked on her door feigning a palm reading but pressing for a hand job, and I mean - why wouldn't they!? Single, Irish, and a witch to boot, God, she must be gagging for it!" Morris teared thin air in frustration. "I warn you woman, there's only so much..."

"Ooh I just had a thought... you haven't been there knocking, have you? I mean, she's a looker mind, right up your street, long golden curls, shapely and buxom, it wouldn't be the first time would it Morris?"

"ENOUGH! How dare you woman, you remember this; my position is the only position you have, and..."

"Oh and you remember I can topple that position any time I please, and I think you'll topple a lot further than me."

"God damn you." Morris raised his hand, and not for the first time. Sylvia just smiled, unmoving. "Go on then, but I warn you this time it won't be a fucking door!"

Morris, shaking for control lowered his weapon. "May God forgive you, you fucking abomination!"

"Well Morris, if he forgives you I reckon I'm in with a good chance!"

Morris had left the home, a Vicar consumed in the fires of hell. Sylvia relished the victory and its reward of peace. This was Sylvia's time, time to uncork the bottle and pour a far from conservative measure of blood red relief. Sylvia smiled as the tumbler filled. Next she flicked open a packet of fags, struck a flame, put up her feet on her patio table and breathed in the sunshine and hum of the garden. She'd miss the garden, it was the one place in the home that felt like hers. For it was she who tended and nursed it, the landscape was a vision of her Utopia, every clipped hedge and rowed primrose was her indulgence, her peace, her sanctuary, and soon, it would be left to him, and like everything else he touched it would corrupt and turn sour. Her husband might preach about the beauty of God's earth, but in reality he had no time for it, you could not make profit from it, and you could not gain position or power from a well kept lawn. She knew the only beauty Morris saw was his self important reflection that smirked back at the only thing Morris loved, his preened and tended reputation that was trimmed to a whisker, and sadly fooled all.

But Sylvia knew, she was his ticking time bomb, his Achilles heel. But the price of being his nemesis was costly, for she bore and carried the scars of the man every day of her waking life. Sylvia poured another glass and dreamed; not long now and she could harbour in the arms of a caring love, bathe gentle in the caress of shared emotion, and at last, at long last wash the hell of him out of her life, because when Sylvia next left home she would not return.

NO PLACE FOR MAGGOTS...

Life breathed of inspection at number forty three Primrose Drive. The abode stood to attention from sunrise to sundown. Order was king and every crumb knew its place. Not a thing evaded attention, and not a single second ever escaped. Cuthbert Combs ruled his domain unanimous, peacock proud and flint sharp. Not a drip or pin drop happened without his say so, and not a scrape or rustle would utter an un-requested sound. Every morning was six O'clock, and Cuthbert Combs woke polished, precise to the button with a matron-like determination, for this home was his ward and he diagnosed its treatment.

He looked down on wife and bed and sighed, God how he hated the mess sleep made. "Six O'clock." He waited impatient for a reply, coldly aware of the seconds wasted.

It seemed to take minutes before his wife's head appeared from under the duvet, and as always dreadfully ruffled. The delicate mouse creature emerged, her freckled face nibbling awake. "Oh morning dear," she said, rubbing her eyes to life.

"Of course," replied Cuthbert, stock still, gently adjusting the balance of his gold rimmed spectacles with minimal movement, till they sat perfect. Indeed, the man had a habit of perfection and delivered himself, always with pendulum precision, and just like a pendulum Cuthbert Combs was balanced just right. Slight of build, medium height, tucked at the edges, he moved with the grace of a whisper. "Look?" He pointed at the bed.

"What dear?" Puzzled Sally, getting out of bed, her waif frame, sandy hair and freckled face giving the appearance of a field mouse rising from its burrow."

"The mess to the bed, your wriggling seems to be getting worse, and I've noticed lately coughing."

"Oh I'm sorry dear, I seem to have caught a bit of a cold." Cuthbert shook his head and wagged a finger. "Tut, tut. What do I always say dear?"

"Oh of course, how silly of me. People don't catch colds, colds catch people."

"Sloppy! We obviously must improve our personal sterilisation."

"But is that really necessary dear?"

"But of course!" Gasped Cuthbert. "Vital in fact, do you care nothing about my health?"

Sally just smiled. "But of course I care dear, I'll go put the kettle on."

"A minute," commanded Cuthbert. "I mean! Is it not enough for you, that I risk my life daily facing the swill of this world?" Sally tries to respond but is silenced with a finger. "Oh you really have no idea of the pigs that dwell in banking, every morning they arrive infested, with their soiled suits, leaking body odour as toxic as any silo. Do you know some lift their legs? Yes that's right, Sally, just like a dog...and then, oh God, they, they sneak one out, and carry on as if nothing at all untoward has happened!"

Sally very gently stroked his arm. "Oh my poor dear, I'll..."

"And then of course there's the clients; do you realise, Sally, I broke with farmers?" Sally put a hand to her mouth in shock. "Oh heavens!"

"Yes, that's right, farmers, creatures that dwell in the bowels of the earth. God, you taste them before you see them...What we are talking about Sally is professional muck spreaders, yes that's right. Men who proudly soak everything they see in shit!"

"Oh how awful dear, perish the thought!"

"Oh believe me, Sally, it is more than thoughts that perish downwind of these beasts, and one would think, with all the money they deposit, they could afford a bar of soap. Anyway," Cuthbert looked at his watch. "Eight minutes passed, another two and breakfast would have missed the boat."

Cuthbert and Sally sat at the breakfast table. Cuthbert cracked open the top of his egg and inspected the content. "Hmm, the texture of this egg seems to be at least ten seconds over...disappointing!"

"I did three and a half, just the way you like it dear." Cuthbert threw down his spoon and huffed. "Yes, but how many times Sally…one must allow at least ten seconds for the egg to adjust to the drastic submergence into boiling fluid… time does not stop you know, Sally, for them who misjudge it."

"Sorry dear, I'll try to remember tomorrow."

"Oh blast, this really has the feel of a troublesome day."

"Try not to upset yourself dear, you'll sprout a worry rash," said Sally, quickly removing the offending egg. Cuthbert shooed, with a wave of his hand, his failed breakfast away. "Oh a worry rash is the least of my blemishes to worry about. Oh you have really no idea the tightrope of reactions I walk daily, you have never fully understood the dangers I face in this pox-ridden world. Why, the very air I breathe is plagued with vomit, oh God how I choke, in this swill!"

A knock at the door launched Cuthbert out of his seat with Jack-in-the-box surprise. "Oh my God! They will not come in!"

"Calm down dear, your rash is starting to erupt."

"Of course I'm erupting, don't you realise woman? There's someone at the door at forty three minutes past; hardly normal."

"Oh, don't worry dear, I'll see who it is and if they are not up to par I won't let them in."

"Oh believe me, Sally, someone up and about this early is bound to have hygiene issues."

"I'll go and see dear." Sally walked to the front door. "Oh, and Sally!"

"Yes dear."

"Letter-box vetting before the door opens."

Sally opened the letter box and peered out; "Hello." A pair of stained yellow, red ripe eyes greeted her from the other side. "Good morning Mrs Combs. Tom Price here, acting on behalf of myself and the church community, I urgently need to speak to Mr Combs in his official role as church secretary, and, as I'm sure you are aware, time is precarious to say the least and even more so with the news I bare, news that has driven me to intrude upon your persons at such an early hour."

"Hold on a second Tom, I'll see if Mr Combs is available." Sally scurried off back to relate the message to her waiting husband "Its old Tom dear, says he has urgent church business to relate."

"Oh God damn him and his filthy obsession with death! Oh, I suppose you'd better let him in, if you don't he'll only come back and ruin another day."

"Righto dear, I'll go and let him in." Cuthbert grabbed her by the arm before she left. "But before you do, check first that he has not had any association with those damn missionaries that have just returned from darkest Africa, bloody inconsiderate meddlers. I mean, don't they realise the third world is a melting pot of viruses that have a pandemic reputation, and an iron willed incubation period? Well go on, check, and if safe, let him in."

Tom entered the room, cap in hand. "Morning Mr Combs. Ah, sorry to intrude at such an early hour, but I bear tidings I feel are most pressing."

"Indeed, I would be lying, Tom, if I said this was a welcomed visit, but you're here now so please take a seat." Cuthbert and Tom sat at the table.

"Well Mr Combs..."

"Before you continue any further Tom," Interrupted Cuthbert, "You have exactly thirty three minutes, not a second more or less, and I'm afraid we cannot provide tea for the time, for such has already passed, and all crockery is now soaking in Milton, as is our way. And Sally..."

"Yes dear?"

"There's no need for your routine to be derailed, I mean the bedroom won't clean itself."

"Of course dear." Cuthbert dismissed her with a flick of his hand and off she scurried.

"Oh no problem about the tea Mr Combs, I've always said grave tidings are a dish best served cold."

Cuthbert smiled. "Well, Tom, as I say time is pressing, get on with it!"

"Right...It's Wickle Cottage, Mr Combs. Well, not so much the cottage itself, but its inhabitant. I've had my suspicions about the dubious reputation of the tenant for quite a while; a lady, I'd say, who gloats herself in sin. But after talking to the Vicar, the character of the tenant seems to be more dubious than I first thought. You see, there are a lot of men folk visiting her dwelling at all hours and..."

"So Tom, you are telling me this new resident of our parish is a slut? And a spinster, I suppose?"

"Exactly Mr Combs! And..."

"Oh Tom, all single women are sluts! They've either had too many men, or they still want too many men, and this town is littered with the like!"

"Good God, littered you say?"

"I'm afraid so old man, you pay so much attention to death that you miss what the living of this town get up to. Why, the back alleys of this town are arenas of alfresco debauchery!"

Tom gasped. "Well good heavens!"

"Oh believe me Tom, I see the filthy back alley skuttlers sucking and pawing each other, disposing their muck in a frenzy of viral contamination. Oh yes, Tom, our beloved community is awash with filth!"

Tom nodded his head in admiration. "Oh Mr Combs, I love your conversation; it makes the end of the world seem so worthwhile."

Cuthbert smiled at the adulation. "You see, Tom, I was born divine; I really believe that. And it is that divinity that drives me forth in my quest for purity. Some, I suppose, would see my chaste as a curse, but to me, I see it as proof that heaven is well vacuumed and dusted."

Tom slapped his thigh and laughed. "Oh praise the Lord Mr Combs, what wisdom you bestow out of those sparkling enamels, but I'm afraid there's more."

"My, my, this is getting intriguing. "

"She's also a witch! You know, tarot cards and all sorts of devilry."

"Good God Tom!" Cuthbert sniggered. "Do you really believe all that mumbo jumbo?"

"But it gets worse Mr Combs; she's Irish, and a Catholic to boot!"

"What! A dirty thieving gypsy! How do you know all this Tom?"

"Why, Mrs Bevan knows her, quite pally it would seem, and I strongly believe this whore has bewitched the vicar's wife, for she's invited her to church."

Cuthbert slammed the table with his fist. "Scandalous! Such a woman should not be allowed anywhere near our hallowed grounds, she's probably a host for the blight. But tell me Tom, where did the vicar's wife meet such a foul creature?"

"Ah, at the charity shop, she reckons."

"Charity shop?" Cuthbert stood, his face changing from pale to blood red. He walked through the room to the foot of the stairs and hollered. "SALLY! SALLY!"

"Yes dear."

"Here! This instant!"

Heeding her Master's call, Sally quickly scurried down the stairs and into the room. Cuthbert stood, *Headmaster impatient*, with his hands clamped behind his back. Sally, knowing his stance and tone all too well, bowed her head, her delicate frame all a tremble. Tom fidgeted in anticipation of his well sown mischief. Cuthbert pointed Sally to a chair. "Sit," he commanded.

"Whatever's wrong, dear? I can see you're upset, your anxiety rash is erupting," said Sally with a tremble to her voice.

Cuthbert took a deep breath "Tell me Sally, you work at that second-hand rag and bone, dustbin shop, have you encountered by any chance an Irish hag by the name of? Ah, sorry Tom, I don't believe I caught the name?"

Tom cleared his throat and shifted in obvious discomfort. "Ah, Fitzpatrick, but the Vicar's wife never mentioned Sally, Mr Combs."

"Why, she did not need to Tom. Fitzpatrick? How apt for a dirty little tinker, do you by any chance know her, Sally?

"I don't think so dear, but so many people come to the shop."

"Liar!" Cuthbert slammed down hard on the table and prowled right into his wife's face. Tom jumped and Sally shook. Cuthbert's right eye now started to twitch violently, his face erupting with lumps. "Oh you know her all right, why, you women are all the same; you feed on gossip and never miss a tell or tale. If that viper has slithered from that accursed isle and has used your so-called shop...And quite often, according to Sylvia bloody Bevan...I'll guarantee you bloody well know her!"

"Well now I think of it she has been in once or twice, but she seems very nice."

Tom put a reassuring hand on Sally's shoulder. "Well there you go Mr Combs, very nice, she seems to appear to all, surely, that's proof of her power to bewitch."

Cuthbert sneered. "Quiet, Tom I'll deal with this...In fact you can leave!"

"But I was only saying, Mr Combs!"

"And so am I Tom...Fuck off!"

"Well I never," gasped Tom, quickly rising from his seat and donning his cap. "Well umm...I'll see myself out."

"Indeed you will" said Cuthbert, still staring intently at his wife. Tom, without further word, shuffled out of the room. Cuthbert waited for the front door to close then quickly resumed his tirade. "Very nice you say, nice; I suppose like those harlots you work with. The fat one? Ah what's her name? Yes Gwyn, a nymphomaniac blob with a mouth like a sewer, and then of course there's the Vicar's wife; far too intelligent for her sex and no doubt capable of rebellion. Oh you see, I know Sally, the Vicar confides in me, and he is at his wits end with his troublesome upstart of a wife."

"But Sylvia and Gwyn are my friends, my only friends, they're very kind to me." Sally started to sob, but Cuthbert continued, unmoved. "And next, of course, the customers? The plague of poor that swarm round that shop, with their dirty little pennies out, all bartering for rags and soiled hand-me-downs...God, they're disgusting!"

Sally took a hanky from her pocket and blew her nose. "But, but surely its God's work; helping the needy?"

"God's work! Do you really think the destitute belong to the Lord? For Christ's sake, the very reason they are poor is that the Good Lord wants nothing to do with them! Do you really think he'd encourage followers with lice? I mean, perhaps we should change the scriptures to include, *'believe in me and thou will still get a giro in heaven'*. Oh I can see the carnage now, paradise littered with empty bottles of barley wine, soiled sots bothering angels and emptying their bladders over the pristine gardens." Cuthbert grabbed hold of Sally's hands and squeezed them hard. "You see, my dear, all these things I do, I do with your well-being at heart, and with that in mind, I feel it is time for you to give up the charity of others and finish at that accursed shop."

"But, but I love my work there dear. I mean, it's my time, when I meet people and..."

"Now let me stop you there dear. My time? Don't you find that statement a little bit selfish? I mean, since I so kindly accepted you as my wife should not all time be ours? I mean, those precious hours you spend at that shop surely could be better spent in the care of our home? Extra cleaning perhaps, for as you are well aware, Sally, you can never over clean, and a clean home is a safe home."

"But dear I already clean for five hours a day and I love that old shop."

"Enough! It stops now! And you'll soon realise, Sally, that all these things I do, I do to keep us, safe and healthy, and that is a duty I shall never shy from!"

Cuthbert had left for work, and Sally scrubbed and bawled. It's funny, she thought that this vigorous cleaning that drove her insane also kept her sane. Eventually, with the kitchen cleaned, the lounge polished, the stairs vacuumed, the beds aired and the toilet bleached, she slumped. Her tears had long been spent and now came that hollow empty ache, that retched void that destroyed all hope and crushed every glimmer of chance. Oh she loved her husband dearly, it was her nature. But Cuthbert denying her the shop, felt like he denied her life, and now all that was left for her was the air that she breathed.

THE TROUBLE WITH MEN...

Councillor Boris Hardy was a portly, belchy, nappy-rash-faced, humidly sticky man, with the manners and eyes of a pig. He pressed down hard on the hand that cupped the crystal ball, panting and slobbering and licking his foul, bruised-plumb lips, his bald head pulsing in anticipation. It had not taken long for the reading to turn sour, as the lady guessed it would. She had quickly concluded she did not need a crystal ball to delve in and see this man's intentions.

He held the hand firm. "What you doing, pretty? Eh, wasting your time with this hocus pocus, earning pennies? Why, with your looks you could be making some tidy money, for I'll tell you; you're the best thing in an arse I've seen around here for a long time!"

Fitzpatrick tore her hand free. "And just what would earning this extra money entail, Councillor?"

Councillor Hardy edged round the table towards her. "Well, taking me upstairs would be a good start."

Fitzpatrick laughed. "Let's get something straight, Councillor; I read palms not pricks!"

Councillor Hardy grabbed Fitz by the arm. "Now look here you little tinker bitch; life for the likes of you could get pretty rocky round here, and you'll be far better off making a friend of me... You see, I'm the sort of man who can make things all for the better... or all for the worse."

Fitzpatrick glared back. "Get your fucking greasy fat paw off me!"

"Oh, playing the hard gypsy bitch, eh? Well your pegs and curses don't frighten me, you see I don't believe in magic!" Councillor Hardy stood, puffing out the fat of his manhood, and scrunching his fist. He waved it in her face.

Fitz quickly jumped out of her chair and stared up defiant into the Councillors beady, black coal eyes. "What about pain, Councillor? Do you believe in, that?!" Fitz smirked right into his face.

"Huh, do your worse you phoney little tart, I like it rough!"

Fitz shook off his grip, grabbed hold of his shoulders and brought up her knee, ramming it hard into the Councillor's groin. Councillor Hardy choked, crumpled to the floor, wheezing for breath, puffing out half choked obscenities.

Fitzpatrick towered over the wreck that bulged and dripped guts all over her floor. She laughed. "Make things happen eh? Seems to me you can't make it off the floor Councillor."

"Councillor Hardy heaved himself to his knees, head thumping, red through the effort, saliva and sweat making a gravy streak down his chin, his piggy eyes pumping with hatred. "You'll see... fucking whore!"

"Oh I see all right! What I see is the greed and spite of the world, manifested before my eyes in the form of a vile hog who gnaws on the bones of the little people, who stuffs and stuffs till he bloats with their gore!" Fitzpatrick advanced menacingly towards the crumpled councillor, the red of her hair seeming to spread flame through the room. She now towered above him, her beauty turned gargoyle as her mood raged. Councillor Hardy rubbed his disbelieving eyes and snorted, as the so called *weaker sex* did the unthinkable and disobeyed, and attacked its better. He mustered all his strength, and with a roar heaved himself up. A punch, walloped into the side of the councillors head, again tipped him off balance. He splattered to the floor with a grunt. "You fucking Whore," spat the councillor with rage. "Oh you'll fucking pay for this, you'll see. I'm the law, and King, around here."

Fitz bent down and poked the councillor in his bulging gut. "What I see, Councillor fucking Hardy, is indeed a King. A King that feasts in a sewer! Now get your fat, dirty arse off my floor, and get the fuck out of my house!"

It was probably the quickest the councillor had moved since forced sport at school, he bungled across the room puffing and panting, fumbling with jacket sleeves and disarrayed attire. Finally his shaking hand managed the door latch, he gulped and found his voice "You'll regret this, be sure of that, this is a decent community and, and I'll make it a priority, I swear, to run you out of it!"

"Uh, you couldn't run a bath without mummy dipping an elbow," mocked Fitz.

Councillor Hardy regained his gruff authority, as he edged away from harms reach "You'll regret this, I'm a wealthy and well respected man in this community, my word carries clout, and I'll have no problem getting the likes of you turfed out! Oh believe me I know everyone that needs knowing, your landlord included. Oh yes, a couple of pulled strings and you'll swing for sure, right out of this town!"

Fitzpatrick just folded her arms and smiled, unperturbed by the hot air that fluffed towards her. "Be careful, councillor, I like a fight, born to fight in fact. You'll find no screaming damsel here, you kick me and I'll break your fucking leg!" Fitz slowly walked towards him, and Councillor Hardy hot-footed it on his legs while they were still intact, puffing out threats as he panicked away. Fitz crossed her middle and index finger and pointed them towards the fleeing councillor. "You like giving out hot air?" She cursed. "Have a belly-full, on me!"

The square of Sickle was proud, proud of its medieval veneer. Proud of its council enforced flower boxes and its litter free footpaths and its statue of Edward Cyril Fletcher, the bugle blower at the famous Hampton Charge. The Roast Duck Inn rolled next to Peter Pucks Pastries, that hugged right next to Polly Smiths Cut and Quiff, and Bill the Bulls Beef and Chop shop. Saint Martin's charity shop stood swept to the corner, out of sight of the town's grand display. Proud, had no place for charity or the beggars that used it, and although the church supported the venture, it had no time for the needy who they deemed had let themselves and the parish down. Tom the Placard had chosen this particular spot, as he often did, to picket for the Lord. His choice of doom. 'HEED THE LORD AND THE LORD WILL PROVIDE FOR ETERNITY'.

Gwyn looked out of the shop window. "Look at the old bastard, nothing to look forward to but death!"

Sylvia came to the window. "Aye, and he won't be happy then, unless he takes us all with him... meddling old goat! He came to the house yesterday, Gwyn, forecasting doom involving a certain friend of ours."

Gwyn laughed. "Fitz? It's bound to be!"

"How on Earth did you guess?"

"Oh come on Syl, Irish spinster in a cottage, tucked in the dark woods and reading tarot cards, matter of time?"

"Well actually," says Sylvia, folding and shelving newly donated shirts. "He thinks she's a whore!"

"But of course, what else would a man think a single woman was?" Gwyn shrugs. "I mean, she could be single because she just doesn't like men. But oh no! We're only ever single if we like them too much." Both smiled and went back to stacking and arranging in the cramped little shop. Sylvia put the last touches to her display. "Right, I'll put the kettle on!"

"Syl...There's something I have to tell you! I, I....." Gwyn started to sob.

Sylvia rushed over and put an arm around her shoulder. "Gwyn love, what's wrong?"

Gwyn fumbled with her hanky. "Oh nothing, nothing...Well actually every bloody thing!

I, I, Oh Syl, I killed Humphrey, my darling little pooch, dead, gone, oh Syl I'm just a useless old hag."

"Right, bugger the kettle." Sylvia ran to the back of the shop and returned with a bottle of whiskey, poured two glasses and handed one to Gwyn. "Come on, sit down and drink it, steady your nerve." Gwyn bolted it in one and took a deep breath. "I didn't mean it!"

"Of course you didn't," said Sylvia, rubbing Gwyn's back "I know you loved that little dog."

"I choked him," said Gwyn, grabbing Sylvia's drink and knocking it back. "I didn't mean to, oh God! That pig of a man drove me to such a frenzy I didn't know what I was doing, I fell asleep and...He was dead, his little tongue hanging out...Oh how I hate myself!"

Sylvia topped Gwyn's drink to the brim. "Tell me Gwyn! Why do you stay?"

"What?"

"With Norm...Your husband!"

"I've been with him nearly forty years," Gwyn says, startled by the question. "You don't just leave, it's just not done. I mean, I've stuck it all these years, what's the point of leaving now?"

"The point is, Gwyn, you are not happy and haven't been for a long time, in fact as long as I've known you he's made your life a bloody misery!"

Gwyn shook her head. "Oh no, no, I'd look ridiculous, and anyway he'd never cope without me, he'd starve for a start."

"Well I'm leaving Morris tomorrow, and if the bastard starves then all the bloody better!"

"Tomorrow? But Syl love, where will you go?"

"You know where Gwyn; the same place you and Sally are welcome, and if that wasn't available then bloody anywhere he isn't!"

Gwyn gulps "What, with Fitz? Oh Syl, you'll be the talk of the town!"

"Oh I intend on being far more than that, they'll choke on the gossip by the time I've finished, old Tom will think all his funerals have come at once." Both laughed, Gwyn put down her drink and sighed. "God, I wish I had your courage!"

"But you have Gwyn. You've got more fire in your belly than an inferno."

"Fat, Syl; that's what I've got in my belly, fat! I'm an overweight old lady, whose flame has long been quenched by the dull drudge of life. I mean, look at you and look at me! You're slim, beautiful and worthy of a fresh start. And me, I'm a clapped out old rust bag overdue for the scrap yard."

Sylvia hugged Gwyn tightly. "Oh Gwyn, Gwyn, you are oh so much more than that!"

Gwyn stood and moved toward the counter. "No love! It's all too late, I took my pick off the shelf a long time ago, and it's too late now to put it back."

"Anyway, on a lighter note," Sylvia smiled. "Party! You and Sally are invited to my moving in party tomorrow night, and we'll drink and have fun without a single lousy man in sight, and to hell with the lot of them!"

The shop bell rang and the door opened and in slid Sally, as hunched and delicate as ever.

"Hello Sal!" Gwyn greeted her, as always, with a pitying tender smile. "You're not due in today?"

Sally trembled, her voice a quiver "Nor any day I've, uh… Come to give notice…It's Cuthbert!"

Sylvia sighed. "Now there's a bloody surprise!"

"Tell me what you smell," said Fitz, taking Sylvia by the hand.

Sylvia sniffed the air hard, gulping down the aromas. "Ah, magic is brewing!"

"Of course!" Said Fitz, dragging her playfully into the kitchen. Sylvia looked around the clutter of pots, pans and baskets of herbs that sat beside the teabags, sugar, condiments, and moved towards the stove and the steam of the brew, and again inhaled. "Right," she started. "Ah, wicked, yes wicked. It's deep! And wicked is forever deep, and there's a strength to it, not pungent, more a strength of the forge… Yes it has a will of iron, a fume to dominate, overbearing but irresistible."

Fitz clapped her hands. "Oh, very good; spoken like a true creature of the night…but there's more, so much more!"

Sylvia took another deep lungful. "Ah, heady, there's an illusion, a dizziness that draws you in…yes, definitely poison to an untrained nose."

"Fitz clapped again. "Oh well done, and your diagnosis?"

"Definitely Hellbore, and ah, yes Joe Pyeweed, and, and…"

"Go on girl," encouraged Fitz.

"Wait," said Sylvia, pacing the room; "of course, Toadflax… that's the illusion I can smell."

"And just one more." Fitz beamed with delight, in anticipation of a full house.

"I know it, I know it! It's cruel, and hides behind the others, a legend…of course I know, its Wolfsbane!"

Fitz threw her arms around her deserving apprentice, nearly toppling her with her delight. "Oh, Sylvia Bevan, what promise you are, what courage. Oh, truly you are worthy."

Sylvia beamed at the accolade "Have I passed then?"

"You don't pass dear. The Mother makes no judgement. No, what you do is bond, you bond with all the sisters long passed. Through your hopes, dreams and desires they breathe and ride the wind, for we are their heart, through our faith they live, and in return they will flood you with knowledge and keep you as a secret."

Sylvia kissed Fitz hard, with a passion. "Oh Fitz, you don't know how alive you make me feel, just the promise of you makes the world a wonder!"

Fitz poured the wine, a good heady red that held them in the mood, the fire crackled playfully and the snug little cottage cuddled them together "Ah, bliss!" Purred Sylvia, as they drowned together, entwined on the sofa, gazing at their dreams in the fire's glow.

Fitz ran her fingers through Sylvia's hair. "Not long now my dear, and you shall be unchained, lawless, and running riot, straight into chaos. Think you can bear it? I mean, Vicars wife runs off with the Devil's daughter, now there's scandal!"

Sylvia laughed and clapped in delight. "Oh don't worry, the scandal's already started!"

"Indeed. Oh, do tell." Fitz shrieked with delight.

"God yes! You've a very suspicious washing line, according to Old Tom Placard, adorned with the trappings of a whore."

"Oh, am I Indeed? Good, the more venom the better. I'll be the whore that bagged the Vicar's wife. You see Syl? The lower they place me, the greater will be his shame."

Sylvia, lost in thought took a sip of her drink. "He'll do everything in his power to ruin us, you know that Fitz!"

"Oh I'm looking forward to it, it's been to long since I sank my teeth into a good battle with the church and its damnation, and believe me Syl, when I bite I never let go, and I've a few scores to settle with Mr Morris Bevan!"

"Oh I love it when you talk bitch!" Both laughed.

"All set for tomorrow night?," said Fitz, topping up their glasses.

"Yes I'm all packed and him none the wiser."

"Are the girls on board?" Sylvia sighed. "Well…they're coming, but…"

"But what Syl?"

"Oh Fitz, it's Sally! There seems to be less of her every time I see her, little by little, that beast is squeezing the life out of her, and he's made her finish at the shop. The only semblance of a normal life and he's snatching it from her!"

"But she is coming?"

"Just about, Cuthbert is at some council or church business."

"And Gwyn?"

"Oh, I almost forgot; she killed her dog!"

Fitz nearly choked on her drink. "Why?"

"Accident I think, she thought she was strangling Norman, she's very upset."

"I bet! But you see, this could all be for the best, the more miserable they are with their lot, the more acceptable they'll be to change."

"Oh I don't know Fitz, they are a long time made, and undoing that is not going to be easy."

"Oh Syl, you worry too much. What I've got brewing could change a lamb into a lion. Why, one glass and they'll be ready to conquer the world, they'll spit out their husbands and the sorry life that comes with them!"

"Ooh, sounds potent! What does it do, this wonderful brew?"

"What it does, Syl, is waken the inner self." Fitz stood and raised her arms to the air. "It awakens the spirit of truth, the monster of our passions that dwells in us all, that smoulders like black coal in our belly, just waiting to explode and shatter whatever stands in its way.

An unstoppable force that fuels desire and rage and devours anything that denies it." Fitz slumped back down, kissed her lover and smiled. "So you see, my darling, you make sure they come and I'll change them all right!"

"Oh Fitz, it sounds wonderful…but a little dangerous?"

"Oh there's danger all right! A nice black cauldron full!"

THE BREW OF A FOUL WIND...

Councillor Boris Hardy sat in his over-sized office, in his over-sized chair in front of his over-sized portrait, pudgy fingers squeezed together on his over-sized desk, beads of sweat running down his pitted face.

"Damn this indigestion!" He cursed. The morning's meeting had been a disaster. The uncontrollable wind he suffered all through the night had shown no signs of abating. The committee members had giggled at first, as the rogue trumps rattled through the room. But the laughter soon turned to scowls of disgust as the smell became unbearable and with his backside showing no signs of surrender, and probably on health grounds too, the meeting was abandoned.

So, with a thousand apologies behind him, Councillor Hardy sat squeezing hard for control, his gut howling for relief. It seemed to him that his lot had gone from bad to worse ever since his encounter with that damned whore witch. Oh he'd ruin her, as he ruined everything else that defied him. But ruin took time, for now he would vent his anger and frustration on the junior clerk. "Peter, Peter!" He hollered and belched.

"Coming sir." Hurried a voice outside the door. The junior clerk entered the room as a huge explosion detonated out of the councillor's arse. Boris thumped the desk. "Blast this cursed wind!" Peter Bellroy was junior materiel, seven stone soaking wet, tattooed with acne, with a constant *'why me'* expression on his face. He bit hard on his lip, trying to control the rising chuckle that was screaming for release. "Ah...Yes Mister Hardy!"

"Wickle Cottage?" The councillor fidgeted for relief. "Who owns the property?"

"Ah, I've really no idea sir!"

"Well bloody well find out!" Screamed Boris, clutching his tender gut.

"Right away sir!" Said the clerk, heading straight for the door, desperate to leave and double up in peace.

Boris ripped open yet another indigestion tablet, poured a glass of water and swallowed. "Gads!" He gasped, even the water burned. He stood up and belched, trying any position for some sort of comfort. "Damn bloody wind..."A knock at his office door brought a groaning response "Yes, come in!"

Peter poked his head round the door. "It's the Vicar sir, says if you've got a minute, there's something he'd like to discuss."

"God are you mad boy, in my condition I'll..." The Vicar pushed past the clerk and entered the room, holding out his hand. "Boris my dear fellow." Boris took his hand. "Ah Vicar, what a pleasant surprise!" Boris clenched his gut for dear life, but the outcome was inevitable as yet another one rattled. "Oh dear me!" Said the Vicar, dropping the hand. "Spot of indigestion eh?"

"More than a spot I'm afraid, you will have to forgive me, Vicar, it is quite out of my control. But, please, please, take a seat!" Boris lowered himself cautiously back into his seat, his stomach growling with every flinch. Morris pulled up a chair, sat delicately down, folding one bean pole leg across the other, his crows nest neck holding the chiselled face proud. Boris smiled; well as near as damn it under the discomforting circumstances. "Well Vicar, what can I do for you?"

"Pest control?"

"But of course!" Boris belched and cringed in discomfort. "Umm, mice? Rats, insect infestation?" The Vicar shook his head. "Far more alarming I'm afraid, and definitely more troublesome...Catholics? Well, Catholic to be precise, and it would seem, a witch. Quite a disturbing mix, wouldn't you agree, loaded with imagery and superstition."

Boris leant forward, the movement triggering an involuntary duet from both ends. "Oh blast this bloody thing! Witch, you say, and by any chance does said person in question happen to reside at Wickle Cottage?"

"Why, indeed she does, councillor, and I have been told by a very reliable source that all sorts of mischief and devilry are taking place at said abode. I hope you understand, councillor, I have the well-being of my parish to consider. I can ill afford for my flock to be ensnared in the glitz of hocus pocus and papal bling!"

Boris snarled, his beady eyes darting, hands clenching "Oh, don't worry Vicar! I am all too aware of man's sloth of thought, faced with the smut of temptation. Oh yes, You've come to the right man, and whatever despicable notions you've got in mind, I would be only too happy to help with their fruition!"

"I take it you've met said person councillor?"

"Oh yes Vicar, we've met all right, and I am not likely to forget it any time soon. Bah, a bad-un, if ever I've seen one! And you know, Vicar, I'm not a superstitious man, but be damned; I've suffered this blasted flatulence ever since I left her company yesterday. Oh yes Vicar, she's trouble if ever I've seen it!"

"So I take it, councillor, that we are on the same page?"

"Oh, don't worry, the script has already been headed, and I'm sure two such worthy minds could come up with a satisfying ending."

"Well I was thinking, for the good of the parish of course, an eviction would suffice, nothing too messy, just a hitch with a contract. I'm sure a man of your influence knows the right strings to pull…Eh Boris?"

Boris sat back and smirked, his face distorting in the thoughts of malice. "Oh indeed I do. Peter! Peter!" The clerk soon hurtled into the room clutching a file of papers, he placed the file on the desk and grinned like a puppy expecting his bone. The Councillor just glared indifferently. "That's all Peter, off you go!" The clerk, quickly deflated, turned and left the room. Councillor Hardy's blood gout fingers hungrily tucked into the file. He pulled out the papers, read them and soon grinned from ear to ear. "Well I'll be!" He laughed, clapping his hands, letting off a volley of backside escapee's "Please excuse me Vicar, which I'm sure you will when I tell you who owns Wickle Cottage!"

The Vicar calmly smiled, containing any signs of discomfort caused by the recent omissions. "Prey do tell Councillor!"

"You Vicar, You own Wickle Cottage…Well, the church to be precise, but you, as its head, should smooth the way I've no doubt!"

"My, my, you must think me quite the fool! But you see, Councillor, the church has so many vested interests in the community it is hard to keep track of it all… as for smoothing the way, well one would have to tread carefully, I mean contracts and such things. But with backing from a worthy Councillor…"

"Oh you'll have backing Vicar, don't you worry about that!" Councillor Hardy stood, slamming a fist hard down on his desk. "I'll move mountains!" He hollered, his face flushing to purple. "To see that stinking whore out on the street, and I assure you I will leave no stone unturned, and I swear…Argh!" Councillor Hardy screamed in pain, doubling up, clutching his stomach, the exertion causing an atomic like chain reaction that howls out of his arse, farts overlapping and colliding in a desperate stampede for freedom, producing a grand fanfare of vibrating trumps. The Vicar fanned his nose and quickly made his excuses. "Ah, I'll leave it with you then Councillor… must dash, church business."

Councillor Hardy sat, deflated, in his chair, his hand clutching his still tender groin. He belched hard and deep, but still no lasting relief. "Blast her!" He bellowed, "I'll ruin every bone in her body! Turn me down? She'll be begging to lick my arse-hole by the time I'm through!" He leaned back and grinned, his thoughts awash in a tide of sweet revenge.

RUFFLED FEATHERS AT THE ROAST DUCK INN...

Gwyn soared and lightning thrilled through her body. What a party this was turning out to be. It seemed to her that up until this magical moment, her life had been in a deep freeze, and this was the thaw. Her senses seemed to melt into life, the numb of existence bursting into bustle, itching awake and teasing with tickles, every dormant nerve and sensation. She felt as bold as an adventure and younger than birth, as she awoke in this season of new found bloom.

"Oh my!" Gwyn cooed, and her knees buckled. She clutched a chair and ground her teeth, as a shock, crisp as ice, crackled down her spine, causing her whole body to thrash and twist in the motions of love and hate. She screamed, curled her toes trying to clutch on to the world for dear life as a bubble of bliss burst inside her, knocking her off her feet and sending her crashing to the floor. Gwyn sat up, clapped and cheered, legs kicking with delight "Oh God, oh God I feel like the World has climaxed inside me!"

Sally rolled in the mud, Sally rolled in ketchup, flour, and smeared her face in tooth paste. She thumped into doors, dived onto sofas, pulled feathers out of pillows and howled in delight at every whim of destruction. It seemed to her, that up until this magical moment, her life had been spun in a web, her emotions swallowed in silk, her dreams hung as untouchable titbits before her eyes, belonging always to the spider that weaved her life. The feeling surged her forward, giving balance where no balance should be. She hung, laughing, on the void of impossibilities, her face chaffed by a warm gust of freedom, her dreams cuddled snugly to her heart, belonging and breathing with her at last. She ran through a riot of colours, all smashed together in a mirrored reflection of angles that twisted out of sense, to splash together in a wonderful chaos of impossible art. Sally chattered wildly, her ears whistled and her eyes danced. She spun and spun and the world wrapped round her, folding her in promise and the gentle squeeze of hope. "Oh God I'm the wind!" she cried, dripping in honey.

Sylvia and Fitz smiled at the spectacle of bliss before their eyes, indeed all hearts were warm as the potion settled. "Hope is root?" Said Fitz, gazing deep inside her lover. Gwyn jumped up and whooped loudly. "I'm having an orgasm with angels…I need a man!"
Sylvia laughed out loud. "God, Gwyn! That's a bit of a come down from angels."
Gwyn shook with emotion. "Well my dear, one has to be realistic."
Sally ran, doors slammed and opened as the cottage and garden became her track of free will "Wee, wee, I'm the wind." She whistled by. Gwyn whooped and cheered as she soared past. "She's mad!" Gwyn gasped, as Sally showered the room in hundreds and thousands.
"Not at all," said Fitz joining in with the chaos. "She's herself at last, she's like a vintage champagne that's waited decades to be corked and now bubbles free. Go girl, go!" And relentlessly on she continued, boundless in energy.
"Wine, wine and music." Sylvia twirled, grabbing bottles and glasses and pumping up volume. They all drank and danced with greed. Sally burst through the door. "The moon, the moon!" She howled, with tears in her eyes. "Ah!" Fitz smiled. "He's calling us out to play, begging us to be wicked."
"What!" Startled Gwyn. "We can't go out like this, people will see us!"
"See what Love?" Fitz reached over and kissed Gwyn's lips. "Who we are?"
"Well?" Gwyn mused "I…"
"What's the point in just showing ourselves who we are, Gwyn? We need to show the world who we are. We need to go through that door and blast the town to pieces, to show all we are not made, but born! We are not taught by them, but are tutored by our nature, and we don't belong to them, for we

are daughters of the earth...And by all that! We now live, and to hell with the lot of them!"

Gwyn sucked in an ocean of air and screamed. "FUCK EM ALL!"

The Roast Duck Inn was instituted with men. This was the frothy world of slops and die-hards, where emotions were wrought on anvils. All conversation was hard boiled and duelled. Wit was acid dropped and gutting in damnation. Tender hearts and thoughts were flayed and hung, bloody, to dry. Indeed, this was no place for weak hearts to badger for shoulders, and any blubs or tears where answered by a bicep and a good thick ear.

The air in the Roast Duck was a pollutant of belched brown ale and lung filtered smoke. Musty glasses hung above the bar on rusting hooks, the bar itself screaming for a polish.

A few isolated drinkers dotted through the room, nooked in crannies, their only attention their bubbling pint and peace to consume.

Norman Stubs propped the bar, his weathered face Dai-capped, his bony hand raising his glass, not sipping but gulping his pint like a real man. The fellow next to him blathered in his ear. A scrawny individual, noted for being unappealing, and unkempt, with a very noticeable Adams Apple that seemed to punch his words home. Young Slug dragged his sleeve across his hooked, dripping nose. "Seems like everyone is having a go?"

"Go at what, Slug?" Norman sighed, lowering his pint. "You know, with that Irish slag at Wickle Cottage..." Slug thumped down his pint. "I mean, what's wrong with me!?"

"You're an ugly bastard, that's what's wrong." John Bishop hollered across the room. A thick set individual with a rock hard face that spat straight talk with no nonsense.

"Aye," joined in Norman. "Not even a whore is that desperate."

Jane the barmaid sponged swill off the bar and tapped Slug's shoulder. "Should get yourself a nice little wife, Slug?" Norman nearly choked on his pint. "Or a goat?" The whole bar exploded in laughter. John Bishop quickly chipped in. "Aye, even his hand rejected him last night, what chance a bloody wife?" The serious business of drinking resumed and all was hushed. Slug tilted his head in thought. "Eh Norm, have you been there like?"

Norm sprayed froth across the bar. "Fuck me Slug, what sort of question's that? Let me tell you son, I'm sixty five years old! Forty of them years I've been there and it's taught me one thing..."

"And what's that then?" Said Slug, eager for miracles.

Norm cleared his throat. "I'd rather be somewhere else!"

The barmaid stopped her cleaning, folded her arms and shook her head. "And who says she wants any of you?"

John Bishop piped up from his paper. "Of course she'd have us, have all of us no doubt, except Slug...woman's a whore. All sorts back and forth there, even that fat bastard Councillor Hardy!"

"Well, sorry to disappoint, lads," said the barmaid with a cocky smile, "she doesn't sell her body, she sells fortunes, been down for a reading myself...and if you took the time to notice, a lot of women visit, not just fat councillors."

"Don't talk to me about councillors!" Croaked Ron the Resurrection, stirring from one of his many catnaps; a bone thin old man with a long exhausted tombstone face.

"Huh," laughed John Bishop. "Look out, Ron has risen from the dead again!"

"Fourth time today I reckon." Norm raised his pint. "Good to have you back with us Ron!"

"Less of your bloody cheek, young Stubs!" Wheezed the old man. "Huh, councillors; snivelling little bastards all of them! That's all they do, stuff their faces, their pockets, and other men's wives." John Bishop nodded in agreement, but the Resurrection was just getting started. "I went up there once. I can wear a tie, I told them. Can I have a free bloody meal or a free bloody house? Could have broken my neck; no bloody lighting, dark streets!"

Norm shook his head. "What the bloody hell you rattling on about Ron, for God's sake give it a rest!"

"I'm eighty three boy, I'm bound to be deaf...And don't talk to me about God and that bloody church of his..."

"No one has Ron!" Gasped John Bishop, but the old man blathered on. "Baptised I was; my head shovelled into a bowl of iced water, now there's holy for you...Huh, good and right for me my Mother said, she was a bloody liar mind! I had polio, T.B. at twelve, bloody whooping cough, you name it I had it. Bastard, fat lazy Priest, never cleaned the bloody bowl... Blessed, be damned! The only thing our village was blessed with was bloody typhoid!"

Norm shook his head, disbelieving. "What the hell?"

"Get back in your bloody coffin Ron!" Chipped in John Bishop. "And give us some bloody peace!"

"Peace, peace?! I'll give you bloody peace, a peace of my bloody mind! And...And..." Ron the Resurrection yawned and soon snored himself back to the edge of death, his mind dancing muddles ready for the next outburst.

With the mayhem over, they all guzzled back cosy with their pints. "I still might go down there! I mean, worse that could happen is I'm just sat there gazing into a crystal ball?" Slug day-dreamed, gazing blank into the void of chances. Norm put an arm around Slugs shoulder "Look boy! There's no smoke without fire, maybe she's a whore or maybe not... but there's something not right there, I tell you! For people to blather so, there's something amiss...Anyway, women will be the ruin of you boy!"

"Well that's fine by me!" Slug slurs, the grog kicking in. "I've got nothing to ruin!"

Gliding in the arms of lullabies, the four pioneers left the cottage and braved the night.

The air outside the cottage was crisp as ripe apples, its breath sharp with life. The town nestled ghostly in moon tipped gold, the deep dark, choking in the sky prince's glory.

What sound there was seemed to dance in echoes, however close, it kept its distance, giving thought to a place of mysterious whispers. They reached the bustle of the square and Sally whirled through it, her delicate frame seeming to float as she spun and flirted with phantoms. Gwyn was titan in her stride, her steps sure, as her downtrodden life kicked back, now happy for the first time to please herself. Fitz and Sylvia beamed, proud, as their protégés shed their chains and hurtled into life. "God," gasped Sylvia. "I'm bursting with life!" Fitz drew Sylvia into her arms and kissed her, unashamed, for the world to witness, full in the face of scandal. Sylvia giggled as a schoolgirl, unbelieving, in the broad daylight act that would doubtless send shudders through the ranks of the Godly. "To Hell with em all!" Said Sylvia, fingers flicked to the Heavens. "I am who I want to be." She grabbed her lover and returned the favour in heightened passion, fondling her lover's backside, for full effect. The bustle of evening revellers jarred to a halt, conversation freezing on lips, as the obscenity before their eyes shocked the square to silence. Fitz let go of her lover and turned to face the crowd and its damnation. "Are we disturbing your misery? Or are we fucking turning you on?!" The crowd turned blue and gasped as one, fascinated and disgusted by the abomination before their eyes. Fitz just laughed through the tide of contempt and it was at that moment that Sylvia Knew. She knew, from henceforth, invitations would cease, and no longer would she have to attend, the *Green Fingered Ladies*, *Afternoon Tea Club*, or the *Quilters monthly Ballroom dance*, there would be no more baking classes at Polly Smalls and no more tea and sundries at Elizabeth Procter's. Sylvia smiled besides it all, for it was done now, her future forever changed and sealed with a kiss. Fitz continued tormenting the crowd as it shuffled off, shaking its head and tutting its displeasure. "Oh well," said Sylvia, "no guessing what tomorrow's headlines will be!"

Fitz shook her head. "Headlines! Oh my dear, the night is young, and who knows what will happen next? Well, my dear, this act might not even make the back page!"

The Roast Duck Inn now babbled and drooled with consumption. The easy flow of evening had guzzled down and awoken the indulgent fool. Talk was now cheap and easy, and things best left unsaid now galloped free. Norman Stubs and

Slug, tangled together at the bar, clutching the counter for dear life, squawking and slopping drink as the pub turned boat and tilted. "Aye, only one way to treat a woman..." Slug waited for Norm's hiccups to subside. Norm pointed a finger that floated on its own accord, failing to pinpoint its target.

"Badly!" Norm thumped the bar, laughing and laying more hiccups. "I tell you boy...um, where was I? Oh yeah how ever good they are, you make 'em feel it's never good enough...the more you get out of 'em see? The sweeter your life will be!"

Slugs head hung in misery. "Fuck! A right bitch would do me...fuck the housework, ironing, I'd be happy do all that for just one bloody good shag!"

Norm slammed down his pint. "Toughen up boy, hear me! Bloody ironing, what's the matter with you? You start that malarkey and the buggers will have you giving birth next!"

But Slug had switched off to the ear bashing as soon as the bar door crashed open. He peered through his self-made haze. "Hey Norm!" He furiously tapped the old boy's shoulder, but Norm was in full rant and knocked the hand away. "Let me tell you!" Norm fumed.

Slug stood numb, as Norm's wife approached and perched herself behind her husband, his warning lost as he now ogled the string of babes who floated into the bar. Fitz gave Slug a teasing wink that brought a quivering smile to his face. Sylvia blew a kiss and Sally twirled her gown, gently brushing his face.

"Oi, you dopey fucker!" Said Norm, shoving Slug's shoulder. "Never mind them, bloody bimbos! I'm trying to learn you boy, how to put the bitches in their place, how to bend the bastards to your will, and all you do is plead like a bloody puppy! You've no bloody balls you're..." Norm's attention is grabbed by a firm punch to the square of his back. "What the..." His eyes bulged, as the last person he expected to see smiled back. Norm got over the shock and instantly puffed himself up with threat. Gwyn smiled back into the features of intended menace. "Like to put bitches in their place, eh Norm? Well why not try this one?" Norm took a good grip of the bar and bellowed. "GET THE BLOODY HELL OUT OF HERE! You hear me woman? And I'll deal with you…"

The punch was worthy of any backstreet brawl; it shot jet stream with just the slightest twist before impact, and hit the target with anvil force, square and on the button. The detonation was instant, as the bridge caved and taught skin flapped, letting out a face fart of snot and crimson that showered the bar. Norm folded like a deckchair and slumped like a burst balloon.

"Fuck!" Said John Bishop.

"Oh dear!" Choked Slug, as the rest of the bar gawped silent.

"Right girls!" Said Gwyn, dusting her hands free of blood and snot. "What we drinking?"

Shock soon simmered and eased into laughter, after all it's not very often you see a King get knocked off his castle. The girls sat, sipping French brandy, fortified with a stiff Port. Ron the Resurrection had risen again, and now stared beady eyed about the room, ready to scold the bastards who had trespassed on his sleep. Sally twirled before him humming a mindless tune, ripping up beer mats and sprinkling crisps like savoury confetti.

"Am I dead?" Gasped the Resurrection, his bony finger pointing towards Sally.

"No, unfortunately!" Butted in John Bishop, walking towards the bar to check on his K'od chum "But bloody Norm might be!" He bent down and slapped his mate's face. Norm bubbled some words and began to snore. John Bishop walked towards Gwyn, his ruddy, bare knuckled face scowling. "What the bloody hell! What sort of company you keeping woman, have you no respect? That's your husband!" He swung his attention towards Sylvia. "And you! You're the Vicar's wife, for Christ's sake! And what you doing bothering with that whore!" He growled towards Fitz. "Now get the lot of you home before there's trouble!"

Sylvia smiled and cat walked towards him giving off signals of a million dollars. She gently tapped his pickled bulb nose.

"Was dear…,I was the Vicar's wife. You'll see, it will be front page gossip by morning."

"And I was the Devil's!" Said Fitz, getting in his face. "And if I can bloody handle him, I'm sure I can handle you!" The bar, once again, was loaded with tension as eager punters jostled for a viewing. John Bishop was a man of few words who could talk to any man in knuckles, but women? He nervously looked to the bar. "O! love!" He hollered at the barmaid. "You going to carry on serving these slags, after what they done to Norm?"

The barmaid shrugged her shoulders. "Won't be the first fight in here, eh John?"

John Bishop shoved fresh air out of his way as he stamped to the door. "I'm not staying in this fucking zoo!" And off he went, cussing and swearing no return. The door slammed and the pub again settled and the booze flowed and the night began to dance.

The booze flowed hard and fast and Gwyn became a sex goddess of magnificent proportions, she heaved herself up to display her charms table top high. The table creaked and cried under the weight and Ron the Resurrection feared death once again, as the mighty sex bomb wobbled above him. "I need a man!" She screamed. "A red hot, boiling lump of beef cake!" She stuck out her backside and shook it with invite. Slug stood transfixed, jaw dropped, gawping at Gwyn who throbbed and pulsated before him. He looked to the floor, at his mate who lay at his feet, still out for the count. Slug's moral scales lifted and fell. He eyed the room, hedging his bets, no takers it would seem. Indeed, what competition there was either roared with laughter or sat indifferent; that certainly improved his chances. Slug picked up his pint, swallowed a gut full of Dutch and advanced. The tap on Gwyn's leg was a nervous kitten whisker stroke. She peered down into the disaster of Slug's face, his ebony and ivory teeth set in a gormless grin. "I'm a man!" He slurred, his bloody eyes popping, his protruding Adam's apple rising and falling in rapid gulps.

"Why, so you are." Purred Gwyn, jumping from the table and crashing to the floor. "Well honey, why don't you show me what a man can do?" And without further ado Gwyn grabbed Slug's arm and dragged him, flaying and crashing through the bar, giving no time for second thoughts. She smashed through the toilet doors, shoving her hapless victim in, and the door slammed, private.

"My God," gasped the barmaid. "You're all fucking bonkers!"

Slug's loss of virginity sounded like a blood curdling affair, howls of mercy thumped through the toilet walls, transfixing every punter's attention. Sylvia turned to Fitz, hand held to mouth in shock. "My God, Fitz! Was that potion a bit too potent?"

Fitz laughed. "Well there's also the drink to consider... there'll be no shying back to servitude now, we will be the dirt of the town's shoes, pariahs, shunned by the very people we want to ignore...perfect!" Fitz again roared with laughter, but all Sylvia could manage was a nervous smile.

Norman Stubs groaned awake, holding his thumping head. And as he came to his senses, the entire bar took a sharp intake of breath. He slumped to the bar, with every eye in the place magnifying his every move "My bloody head!" He groaned. The racket from the toilet seemed to be reaching a climax and the bar gritted its teeth, wishing for its deflated conclusion.

"You want to stop that?" Said Norman, pointing towards the toilet door. Bloody kids, no shame!"

The barmaid gave Norm a tender pat on his hand. "I think you've had enough Norm. Time for bed eh?"

Norm shot a blurred eye around the room. "Aye, maybe I have an al.I" And off he shuffled, cradling his tender bonce.

A very disorientated Slug wheezed out of the toilet door, and it seemed to all that the former virgin had learnt the hard way. He stooped through the sniggers of the bar, looking more in agony than ecstasy, his bug eyes darting nervously, his body tense as if fearing further attack. He made gingerly for the door and shoved through into the night, and for once without a word.

Gwyn, on the other hand, entered the room triumphant, her nose good and powdered, with not a care for the obvious attention. Sally greeted her friend with a kiss and a shower of pork scratchings "I bless you!" She whispered in her ear and twirled away.

Fitz and Sylvia cheered and hailed her conquest with a round of drinks, while the rest of the bar, their humour spent, mumbled smut and damnation. Gwyn sat with her friends and beamed. "Hmm I needed that!" And she rubbed her hands raw with glee.

"God, girl!" Said Sylvia patting her back "I bet that shook off some cobwebs?" Gwyn smiled, smacking her hands in joy. "Twenty bloody years worth...And you know? I could do it again....And again, and again!" She shook, her body buzzing with excitement.

"Right then girls!" Said Fitz, standing. "Now for the highlight of the night. Raise your glasses and let's drink to the Devil... For tonight we settle scores, tonight we put fire to iron and kneel no more. For tonight ladies, we take battle to the Lord!"

Morris Bevan was afloat in hymns, he stood proud in his polished oak dining room, conducting the strings of the Lord. Sylvia was inconveniently late, and that meant cold supper, but he'd deal with that later. For now the wine flowed and heaven's orchestra surfed through his soul, filling him with a giddy sense of pride. The knock at the door was unusual and certainly not asked for. He placed down his wine, sighed deep and made for the door, grooming himself along the way. He opened the door and stood guardian in posture. "Hello... funny!" He quizzed, peering outside and seeing no-one. "Hello, hello!" He puzzled, his craned neck protruded, as he scanned the garden for the source of the knock. "Now!" A voice hurried out of the dark. Morris turned towards the sound, then a knock and a shuffle and blackness. He felt arms holding and pulling, and the muffled sound of women's whispers and laughter. The sack was tied tightly over his head and, struggle as he might, there seemed no escape. He was jostled roughly through the home. He heard again his music, as his arms were wrestled out and he felt a sharp stab of knots as his hands were bound. The sack was roughly dragged over his head. Morris blinked as light again joined him. "What in God's name!" He howled, trying to rise and getting yanked back, his hands bound tightly to a radiator, the heat of it adding to his discomfort. Bent double, he twisted, trying to get a view of his assailants. His wife stooped into his face. "Hello Morris," she smiled. "I thought we'd play a new game tonight."

"What the bloody hell… have you gone insane?" He growled, desperately yanking at his bonds. Sylvia laughed. "What? Is there something wrong, but I thought you liked a bit of bondage? So much so, I've brought along a few friends… more the merrier, eh?"

Fitz next appeared, tensing a whip in front of his face. "Hello Vicar, I hope you don't mind, but I so enjoy a bit of S and M, and Sylvia said there's plenty of room on your arse for us all to have a go." She brushed the whip teasingly across his face. Morris tugged for all his life was worth "You Fucking Whore! I'll bloody kill you for this!"

Fitz clicked her fingers. "Gwyn, down with the pastor's pants, if you please."

Gwyn rubbed her hands with relish. "Oh yes, for I do believe he's been a very naughty boy! Putting his willy where it's not wanted!"

Morris thrashed and screamed as Gwyn unbuckled his belt and roughly yanked down his trousers and underwear, revealing a very sickly, white spotted arse.

Fitz handed the whip to Sylvia. "I believe the first stroke should go to the lady of the house."

Sylvia kissed Fitz and the whip cracked. And Morris howled as the whip welted his raw behind. In turns, the three thrashed till the white of his buttocks flushed, and on they continued, the whip cracking to the beat of 'How Great Thou Art'.

Sally, on the other hand, was busy with mess, and as her three friends laboured on, she assaulted the kitchen in a rage against order. The contents of cupboards were sent crashing to the floor, jars smashed and jams and pickles smudged and rolled, she laughed tears as the crockery flew, shattering and sending shrapnel that clattered through the air in a glorious flight of chaos. "Oh God, I love the mess!" Sally howled as she bulldozed into the next room. She entered the room to the sound of the Vicar's yelps, hymns and her three friends beautiful laughter. "Oh, yes, yes!" She cried. "Porcelain? A vulnerability of delight." And quickly she set to it. "Free, free," she sang as icons and fair ladies crashed off shelves. "No! Screamed the Vicar, as irreplaceable treasures smashed, worthless, to the floor.

"Oh my!" laughed Fitz. "Is nothing sacred?" And the sacrilege soared as the house of God became an asylum. "Blood!" Panted Fitz. "I think he's learnt his lesson!" Morris Bevan was crumpled on the floor, as shattered as his best bone China, his face a twisted, mangle of hate and pain. "You...You...think you'll get away with this!" Sylvia grabbed a tuft of greying hair and forced her Husband's head sharply back and she peered deep into the dark of his soul, the mean chiselled face stared back and bared teeth. "You'll rue this bloody day woman. You hear me?"

"No changes there!" Sylvia patted his cheek. "I've rued every miserable fucking day of my life with you, you sick little monkey. Now you do your worst...but remember, no more will I bend over and take it!"

The girls hugged and cheered and toasted the conquest with the Vicar's best red. The deeds of the day executed to the letter, making a fine diary of scandal and retribution.

Fitz gave the Vicar's backside a last playful slap. "Goodnight Vicar, perhaps I'll see you in church some day?"

"Church!" Spluttered Morris. "You Devil whore bitch, such as you will find no welcome in the house of the Lord!"

Fitz laughed. "Well he gave you the keys, so he can't be that choosy. Night Vicar, don't do anything I'd like to do, God wouldn't like it!"

"Wait!" Morris screamed. "Untie me! You fucking whores! Untie me, untie me...wait! Un-fucking tie me!"

The girls giggled and made for the door, leaving the carnage and howls behind them.

"Pray to your God." Fitz shouted back. "For salvation and a penknife, Vicar!" And the door and mercy slammed behind them.

WILDFIRE...

The night sulked into day and dawn ignited over the gentle vale of Sickle. People sparked back into life as the sun's bloom rose over the earth. Eyes cranked open, mouths stretched, breaking the webs of slumber, and bones, old and young, heaved to attention ready for the grind of the day. The mind next, gently yawned into function as it slotted into place the order of being.

In number sixty two The Avenue, brains were fast pumping back to life and recognition.

Gillian Huws slipper-shuffled to the kettle, her thoughts full of kids and breakfast, and another bloody day. She poured herself a cuppa, lit a fag, and prepared to bully the house awake. She sighed deeply as the steam and smoke stirred her senses, gently lifting her back to the land of the living. "That's better," she smiled, and with the blindfolded morning's duties done, she allowed herself reflection. She remembered the rare rib-eye at Renaldo's, smothered in honey and mustard sauce; she remembered giggles and wine, music and dance, and the bone of her husband. "Ooh!" She purred, aroused in thought. "Like teenagers again," she said to her unresponsive mug, and laughed out loud "Necking on the square, whatever..." A Flash high-jacked the memory and paralysed all other thoughts. Gillian was stuck, mid-track, in a jaw dropping moment, struggling hard to believe her mind. She whooped with the certainty and ran for the stairs, eager to share the realisation. "John, John!" She hollered, and waited for the groaning response "Oh God, do you remember? The Vicar's wife's a lesbo!"

Rumour smouldered in The Crescent at first light, and like any good blaze it needed time and heat to kindle. Doors opened, revealing half dressed neighbours, all eager to bellow the flames. Heads popped up, peering over walls and fences, revealing hunters who had risen early, desperate to catch any ear, and the fires rampage began, over garden fence and hedge.

"SLUG!" Gasped Mabel Greenway.

"In the toilet of all places," Choked Mary Robinson "I never liked that Gwyneth Stubs…Fat and common!"

"She always had the makings of a whore," said Mabel, catching her breath and quickly using it. "You could see it in her mouth, the dirty bitch!"

"Well I've heard she's had a couple of unsavoury objects in her mouth, and Slug's was not the first" Said Martha Ash, appearing suddenly, desperate to cast a stone.

"Ah, that poor man," sighed Mary Haggard "Old Norm's done well by her!"

"And Slug of all people!" Said Mabel, shaking her head in mourning. "I mean…If you'll go with that…"

"Perish the thought," gasped Martha, shaking the vision out of her head. "I bet she's swimming in viral."

Mary shuddered. "Ooh, the scratchy bitch!"

The Grove provided a more refined level of gossip which was definitely invite only. This well heeled district held special favour with the Lord and took all church business deadly serious, with a stern sense of gospel, for God and the word belonged to them.

Tea and damnation prepared itself on the garden patio residence of Elizabeth Procter. Her two invited V.I.P's sipped their tea and looked bitter.

"It's a sin, of course!" Began Elizabeth.

"The woman always had a bit of gutter about her." Margaret Mugford slithered in.

Helen Nolan patted dry her lips and croaked. "I do believe the Vicar must have picked her up on the bottom of his shoe!"

"Liberal!" Spat Elizabeth. "Liberal values, she stunk of it! Huh, help the needy, that's all she harped on about. *Never mind the needy,* I used to say to her… What about the *church roof and the good folk who use it?!*"

"She always had that way." Helen mused "Making light, with that annoying happiness… a skip to her step, instead of using a respectable gait."

"I like the past tense," quipped Margaret "For believe me, past is where she now is! Yes, and for the best I say! She always thought she was something, parading about like a dog's dinner. Huh, at her age!"

"There'll be a meeting of course!" Said Elizabeth, pouring more tea. "I mean, the Vicar must explain himself…He must have known about his wife's sordid taint…I mean a fool could see the woman was far from decent."

Helen snivelled. "It's brought shame to us all…Damn her! The whole Vale will view us, second class and filthy. Oh, I can hardly bare it! Reputations washed down the drain because of that abomination. We should have known! She never looked the part."

"Oh, don't you worry! Said Elizabeth, standing and pointing a stern finger. "We've got wrath and the Lord on our side; and I, for one, have never taken filth sitting down. No ladies, out she must go, her and that Irish whore! There will be no place for the ungodly to weave their modern corruption in our sweet parish; not while I've got a bible by my bed!"

The vendor's baits of sticky sweets failed that morning, as mothers quickly booted their kids to school. All of them eager to dispose, and thanking the Lord for the relief of education. With their broods safely caged and mastered, the hens nested and prepared to lay their mischief.

"One at a time in an orderly queue…that's what I heard!" Said Olive Brooks, casting the first stone. The squabble of voices rose for attention, a cluck of mad hatters, all bullying for an audience.

"That's the last time that trollop Sylvia Bevan looks down her nose at me!" Said Alice Barlow, folding her arms high under her chin in an act of resolution.

"Makes you wonder just what she was looking at, the dirty mare!" Chipped in Susan Jenkins.

"My husband was there," said Martha Higgins, with an air of authority. "Said he never saw or heard the like; grunting and panting...In public mind, bold as brass!"

"Oh, and with that Slug... I mean, when was the last time he cleaned his teeth?" Said Anne Evans, with a shudder.

"Mark my words," interrupted Doreen Pew. "It will be the death of poor Norman Stubs, living with the shame!"

"Oh I know," butted in Helen Thomas, "and he's always been a lovely provider."

"But ladies, you're missing the point!" Said Tina Sullivan, leaving the sentence hanging to build up the climax. "How can we look to a man for spiritual guidance...knowing, mind, that he shares his bed with a woman who bats for the other team? It's about as unnatural as God ever intended!"

"Ooh, if we all behaved like that there'd be...There'd be none of us here to behave at all!" Said Janet Smith, struggling as always to find the right words.

And so the inferno spread, blazing through every terrace, grove and avenue, a firestorm that swept through retail, stalling shoppers in every aisle. Jams of people blathered; regardless of traffic, or rights of way, eager not to miss a word and, more to the point, to add to the telling. And the inferno raged, now regardless of the truth as the night's events gained legend.

By the time night again crept in, there had been at least three attempted murders. An orgy at Wickle Cottage every other Friday. An epidemic of syphilis and the condom market crashed. Sylvia Bevan had tried it on with a Headmistress, a lollipop lady, a factory cleaner and the undertaker's wife, and Gwyneth Stubs had shagged the entire bowls team, the bugle player of the local salvation army and did a striptease every other Thursday at the O.A.P.'s Forever Young Society Dance. Indeed, the wildfire engulfed the town, never in memory had there been such a glorious smoulder of scandal, and folk intended to spread it like ash.

A BLOOM OF WORRY AND BOILS.

Cuthbert Combs twitched, violent tics hammered his face and crawled under his skin. His eyes pinged in their sockets, bulging with tension. Furious boils erupted into pools of rashes; all vying for space on his hard boiled head. His round rimmed spectacles steamed with sulphurous discharge, his shoulders jigged to the rhythm of madness and his nose bubbled.

"For God's sake!" Fumed Morris Bevan, "will you bloody well keep still?" What the hell is wrong with you?"

"Me, me?" Stuttered Cuthbert. "What's wrong with *me*? Have you by any chance noticed the state of your home…?! Have you no shame!?"

"I'd say it's your wife who has no shame…CUTHBERT!" The Vicar tried once again to sit, and again jumped up and yelped in pain. "Oh me, bloody arse!"

"My wife?" choked Cuthbert. "What on earth has Sally got to do with this? This disaster of home keeping!"

The Vicar stooped carefully towards Cuthbert, pointing a bony finger. "She did not come home last night…did she? That's why you're here, covered in your worry boils and rashes."

"As a matter of fact, she did not! And I can't help but notice that your wife seems to be somewhat absent."

"Oh, believe me Cuthbert, there's no somewhat about it, they've both fucked off with that Irish whore, witch, tinker whatever she is, the three of them, with some fat old tart in tow."

"Oh, this will be your wife's doing, Vicar! Education in a woman never sits well. To own comes with a certain responsibility; something, it seems, that you have sadly neglected!"

"Oh Cuthbert, how little you know me! I'll do a damn sight more than neglect. I won't be happy till I've fucking crucified the bloody lot of them!"

"Ah, we're back to training. If you, Vicar, had bothered to spend the hours that I have in the pursuit of domestic perfection and obedience, you would not be so flippant to throw it away. I mean, if you train a dog to sniff out gold, you don't do away with it, if on one occasion it happens to shit on the carpet! No, what you do is rub its nose in it and carry on. So, Vicar, it all comes down to what the hell is to be done..."

A stern pounding vibrated through the room, a most urgent hammering that demanded on the door. "Who the fuck is that?" Cursed the Vicar, just finding an appropriate padded spot on his chair. "Ah, if you wouldn't mind Cuthbert, I've just this moment found ease."

"Certainly. Ah, ease from what?"

"Oh, blasted piles have dropped, you know how it is!"

"Indeed I do not!" Said Cuthbert, turning up his nose and making for the door.

Councillor Hardy bulged into the room, and like any room he entered he gave off an air of owning the immediate surroundings. "Good God!" Bellowed the Councillor, and roared with laughter, his mirth shaking his belly like a jelly. "Been having one of your famous orgies, eh Vicar? Funny, I can't remember getting an invite!"

Morris Bevan winced, a sharp twinge rushing up his backside. "I can assure you Councillor, there was no orgy... And I do not find my predicament even mildly amusing."

"A bit of a domestic." Chipped in Cuthbert.

"Domestic!" The Councillor again chuckled. "You and him both, eh twitchy!"

Cuthbert's face rippled with annoyance, his eyelids fluttering at an alarming rate. "And just what do you mean by that?"

Councillor Hardy invited himself into a seat. "Best you sit an' all, twitchy! I'm afraid you and the Vicar's domestics have become very public property."

Cuthbert and Morris sat at the table, sullen, waiting for the Councillor to spill his beans and tidings. The Councillor folded his podgy hands and began. "Well gentlemen, laws have been broken and that's for sure. Where to start, that's the problem!

"Just bloody well start at the beginning!" Fumed Morris. "And cut the bloody dramatics!"

"As you like it! Seems your wives, gentlemen, have turned somewhat... Feral! We have witness accounts of vandalism, public indecency, unnatural coupling, group sex, witchcraft, the soliciting of riots, and it would appear Vicar that your wife has more than just a friendly interest in this Fitzpatrick. Do you want me to continue, or do you get the picture?"

Cuthbert scowled. "I can assure you, Councillor, that any untoward behaviour concerning my wife was, without doubt, orchestrated by alien forces! You see, I am of a very old school, a school where behaviour and conduct was never left to chance and, with that in mind, I can assure you that my wife was conducted, by myself, to the highest pedigree. And that I had long ago defeated the destructive elements of free will. My wife, in short, Councillor, is bereft of thought and quite useless without the reins of guidance."

The Vicar banged the table. "Whereas mine, Councillor, Is just a gay whore bitch! Now then, what are we going to do about it?"

Councillor Hardy quipped. "Well it's that Irish witch of course. She's the one who has sent this town and its sanctity of wedded harmony plummeting into the depths of the Devil's anus!"

"I want the damned whore out!" Morris raged, fists clenched with pulverising force in front of the Councillor's eyes. "You have the necessary paper work Boris?"

"Indeed I do Vicar. And don't think for one minute that I have been idle in their processing, but I feel that last night's antics have somewhat upped the ante, and a simple eviction, to me, seems to be a rather mild form of retribution. As they say, gentlemen, there is more than one way to burn a witch!"

"Oh I agree!" Said Morris, rubbing his hands. "And her lovers!"

"Oh they'll burn alright!" Said Councillor Hardy, his face plump with smiles "Rumour is already toasting hot, a couple of sparks in the right place and...BOOM!"

"Boom?" Quizzed Cuthbert. "If you don't mind, I would prefer my wife back in one piece, un-burnt and able bodied, so she can once again service my needs to my impeccable standards. Bits of her, gentlemen, are no good to me."

Councillor Hardy laughed. "Oh, don't worry twitchy, take her home, lock her in and slave her to death for all I care, and the fat one, she can go and fuck every man, dog or bull in the vale! But the other two love-bird's? Well, they are a blight to our God fearing community; and by the time I've finished the community will do all the burning for us."

Cuthbert stood. "Well gentlemen, you continue with your little games, I've a Wife to retrieve." And without further ado, Cuthbert made for the door.

Morris, for the first time that, day smiled. "So I take it, Councillor, you have a plan?"

"Oh that I do Vicar. You see, revenge is one thing, and profit another; I believe I have found a way to have our cake and eat it. After all, you own the stage, I pull the strings, so all we have to do is get rid of the puppets."

"Hmm!" Purred Morris. "Interesting, please do tell!"

"What!" Protested the Councillor. "With a dry throat?"

Morris raised his throbbing backside. "All right, Boris, there must be a bottle here somewhere, intact?"

Bad news seems always to be delivered by a best friend, after all, why should a stranger get all the fun. To have any chance of ruining somebody's day, in the town of Sickle, one had to be up early. Very early indeed to have any hope of being the original bearer of ill tidings. Knowing this, John Bishop woke at the crack of dawn, eager, it would seem, to jump out of bed and push his good friend over the edge. For his own good, of course, he convinced himself.

John Bishop rushed to Norman Stubs' door, with the excited steps of a child's first Christmas morning. Norman Stubs woke, not knowing whether someone was knocking the door or his head. He prised his head slowly out of its slumber, inching it slowly, to limit the shock. The first attempt proved to be a total failure as his neck cranked, groaning in protest at the weight of his anvil thick head. His head crashed back down, and the shock of impact joined the jostle of hammers already pounding Norman's brain as the expected pillow revealed itself as cold, hard, stone. "Ooh, me fucking head!" Norman whined, eyes pealing open, taking in the kitchen base camp, proof of his failed bedroom summit. The hammering door was now accompanied by intense hollering. "All right, all right! Give me a bloody minute!" Norman unlocked himself, groaning with the effort and, slow as a funeral procession, made for the door. He gently sprung the latch, bracing himself for the painful charge of sunlight that always seemed to delight in the night time reveller's discomfort. With the door just ajar, John Bishop barged through, eager not to miss his chance.

"What the bloody hell, John!" Yelped Norm, turning his back and heading for the living room, with John in hot pursuit.

"Do you remember last night?" Said John, cutting straight to the chase, and knowing full well that unconscious men usually remember very little. But for all that, it is a text book move delivered in a way that builds up the climax, giving the victim's mind thought to a multitude of horrors. But Norman Stubs was made, it seems, of sterner stuff and just shrugged his shoulders. "Remember what?"

"Bloody hell man, your wife of course!" Said John, confident that the proclamation would get him a bite. Norman scowled as the hook dug in deep. "What about my wife?"

John Bishop smiled inwardly, knowing full well he'd broken through Norm's defences. "Well, not for me to say really."

"Fucking right it ain't!" Barked Norm. "I'll give her a shout and cut out the middle man."

Norm made for the stairs. "Gwyn, Gwyn…What the, Gwyn!" Norman thumped up the stairs. John Bishop took off his Dai Cap and squeezed it hard, bracing himself for the killer blow. He didn't wait long for the thumps to descend, and for Norm to enter the room with the visitor's desired result engraved on his face. "Where the bloody hell is my wife, John?"

"This is what I've been trying to tell you Norm! Look, best we sit down."

John played the game to perfection, and he huddled close to the cup of Norm's ear making sure his good friend didn't miss a drop.

"FUCKING SLUG!" Choked Norm.

"Certainly seems that way" Said John, lowering his voice to grave concern.

"But, but…Where the fuck was I?"

"Well, that's the other thing I've been getting to, I'm afraid Gwyn knocked you out; one punch, mind, hell of a hook. I mean, just look at your shiner!"

"My Gwyn you're on about? No, can't be!"

"No doubt I'm afraid, I seen it, and so did the rest of the bar," said John Bishop, sitting back in the style of a good job done. Norman's Stubs' jaw went in to total free-fall as the facts and consequences digested, and his thoughts and guts turned to acid. His motion of speech seemed to freeze on his face, then just as quickly thawed with a surge of boiling rage. "That fat, useless, free-loading warthog… after all I've done for her! Well, I tell you this John; she won't get the house, I'll fucking well see to that!"

"And who could blame you Norm, let her wallow with them other bloody slags!"

"Aye, and wait till the kids find out…She'll be sorry, my side they'll take!"

"Well, stands to reason Norm; I mean what's right is right!"

Norm slumped with his head in his hands. "My bloody life I've given to that woman John, my bloody life! And all she ever done was bloody moan! Anyway, she'll be sorry, she'll bloody miss me before I miss her!"

"Course she will Norm, be back here on her bended knees, begging!"

"I could have left her years ago, but for the kids! God, when I think of all those birds! And what did I do? Stayed with that fat old bag, bloody woman's an embarrassment! I was ashamed to walk down the street with it on my arm, John; but for the good of the kids, I did."

"Aye, they're all the bloody same Norm. Take my Mavis, God rest her soul. Hour glass she was when I met her." John mimed her shape with his hands. "Damn aye, put a bloody ring on her finger, couple of months later and you couldn't park her arse in the garage."

Norman shot out of his chair, his wrinkled brow knotting, he grabbed tufts of his greying mop and tugged at it in a frenzy. "Fuck me! Slug, Slug, of all the fucking people! I mean, what the hell does that say about me!?" Norman kicked the chair, instantly regretting the barefoot strike. "Oh me fucking toe!"

"Now calm down Norm, things might not be as bad as they seem." John waited for his hopping friend to settle. "Now, why don't you get yourself sorted, get some clean clothes on and we'll pop out for a pint? Grab the bull by the balls, as it were. Show them no shame, and if we see that Slug you can put a fist right down his ugly gob. Do it now! Right boy? Because, believe me, in a couple of weeks you'll be shaking his bloody hand! Now go and get some clean clothes and let's get ourselves a gut full of beer, they ain't yet found anything better to put the world to rights."

Norm calmed down as the drinkers logic, again, comes up trumps, the old art of never doing today what you can put off till tomorrow. Norm shook his dust filled head, took a deep breath. "Right you are boy!" And made for the stairs.

John Bishop, alone in the room, smugly smiled, eager to get to the pub and show off his trophy. He leant back and thought of all the *well done* pats, and solid as a rock comments.

"OH FUCK!" The scream brought back John from his daydream. He ran to the foot of the stairs. "Christ, you all right Norm?"

"No I'm fucking not! Fucking fat lazy bitch left before she done the ironing! Eh John, what you like at ironing shirts?"

John Bishop laughed. "Chuck it here boy, and I'll show you how it's done."

When you spend your whole life waiting for death you have plenty of time to observe the living, and Tom the Placard certainly made life a spectator sport. He knew every boundary, and when it was crossed. He had a red card instinct for fouls, and a sixth sense for turbulent tactics that disrupted the harmony of the town's fair play. But most of all Old Tom held the Lord's whistle and he was all too eager to blow it, and the debauchery of the night's events would never be lost to the town's greatest linesman. The serve was out, and old Tom was about to inform the greatest umpire of them all.

He knelt in his deliberately sparse bedsit, bible clutched for dear life, his old yellowed eyes wet with emotion, fixed upon painted idols of his saviour, his only adorned cheer, and Tom readied himself to talk to his best and only friend. "Oh Lord, I see it now! Oh yes, why that witch was allowed to dwell among us. Like Jesus laid the bait for Judas! This Fitzpatrick, *herald of the false Papal faith* and *dabbler in the black arts* and forbidden lust, I now see as vital; a vital to your great plan! For already, the scum of our community are flocking to her banner, creeping out of corners where even I, Lord, your most diligent bloodhound, failed to sniff them out. I see now, Lord, that the beast nestles close to the cross in order to butcher the virgin at the heart of our faith! But Lord, the beast is dumb and has been somewhat premature with his hand, giving me time to counter the strike. For I shall rouse the faithful onward to battle, and I feel sure that this will now be the war that ends them all!"

Old Tom got to his feet, his rusting joints creaking with the effort. His stern, weathered face, showed just a glint of a smile, so slight to be undetectable to the untrained eye. He walked over to his prized placards, to make his choice. Tom laughed. Today's choice stood begging before him. *'And the Riders of the Apocalypse Shall Ride Doom Amongst Us.'* Old Tom rubbed his hands. "Perfect. Now we'll see!"

WHAT YOU WISH FOR...

My fine and perfect wife,

I struggle to know the reason why. What could I have done to wound you to the point of danger? Oh, my dear, how I fear for you, astray in the wilds of the world.

Could it be me and my eternal struggle of insuring your safety and well being that has wounded you so? If so, may I forever wander this earth with the knowledge and pain of this broken heart. I sincerely hope you are still following your hygiene procedure, for I could not bear to see such living purity exposed to the deadly microbes that stalk our breath in a constant campaign of annihilation. God, how I ache to protect you, to shield you behind the might of Milton. Oh how I miss you, you see I'd sterilise the very ground you walk on. I'd bleach the world so it was pure for your touch.

Well, my dear, I'm afraid the time is now late, at least late for me, for I find in these lonely days my strength failing, to the point where I left a cup, a spoon and a plate unwashed for a whole night; can you imagine? I hope you don't think any less of me for sharing this pitiful episode, but I'm afraid my health has quite abandoned me, even now while I write my head pounds with protest and my vision fails. But enough about me, as long as you are well, then all is well my dearest love.

Oh just one more thing before my sight again fails me; I find myself, of late, desperately short of breath, it seems my asthma chokes me in grief, quite relentlessly. So, my darling, if one morning I fail to wake, know now that I will always love you.

Yours forever, Cuthbert.

Sally placed down the letter and sobbed. Gwyn leant across the table and placed a reassuring hand on Sally's shoulder. "Now, Sal, don't cry!"

Fitz came in from the kitchen and glared at Gwyn. "I told you to throw the bloody thing on the fire!"

"But!" Protested Gwyn. "It's her letter, it should be her decision to read or burn it, I, mean if it was me, I'd want to read it!"

"Read bloody what?" Said Fitz, grabbing hold of the letter. "I bet this scrawled bullshit is loaded with self-pity and bloody misery!"

"He, he, can't breathe!" bawled Sally, blowing her nose and wiping her tears. "He loves me! He sounds so lost."

Fitz sat and clutched Sally's hands. "Of course he's lost, he's lost you! Tell me, Sally, what have you lost, eh? A life of servitude, a life that was not your own…A master and a bully! Or is there something we're missing? Was he caring? Do you miss that, his attention and devotion? Or is it his wit? Does he make you laugh? Because, if he does, God girl, you're good at hiding it!"

"I don't know what it is?" Protested Sally.

"Oh I know! Snapped Fitz, dropping Sally's hands and clicking her fingers "He's a wonderful lover, it must be that, for there's nothing else."

"What?" Said Sally shaking out of a daydream. "No…No! Cuthbert doesn't touch anything unless absolutely necessary, far too much moisture and leaks! Oh no, that sort of thing is a breeding ground for cross-contamination, every kiss is a mini plague. Cuthbert knows about these things, he takes it very seriously."

"What Cuthbert takes seriously, Sally, is control, and by all that's damned! He's done a fucking good job on you!" Fitz stormed back into the kitchen and Sally huddled and sobbed. She looked to Gwyn and whispered. "I never asked for any of this, I came for the night, not two weeks!"

"I know Sal, neither did I ." Gwyn reassured. "You leave it to me. Gwyn stood and made for the kitchen. Fitz kneaded down hard on the dough she was preparing, her technique more boxing than baking.

Gwyn coughed for attention. "May I say something?"

"What!" Barked Fitz, not bothering to turn.

"She's a delicate heart, you know!"

Fitz slammed down the dough and turned to face Gwyn. "You think I don't know that!? You think I don't know what she is? What he's made her; you think I do all this for myself? All that I did, Gwyn, was awaken what was burning inside you… And do you even wonder what that feeling was, that burning? Do you know what that force was Gwyn, that searing heat that erupted deep inside?"

"I…I…"

"Of course you don't know! You've both been chained and denied so long you don't even recognise yourselves! You stand there and think you deny me; when the only thing you are denying is who you were born to be!"

"I've been married for over forty years, I can't switch it off just like that!"

"Oh, but I wish you could Gwyn, you and Sally, for God knows since I met the pair of you, I've lived your bloody misery!"

"Well there's no need."

"Oh believe me, Gwyn, there's every bloody need! You weep, scream, and drown in your pitiful lives, and when someone throws you a lifeline, you kick it away and sink straight back down to the bottom!"

"Well, if staying afloat means shagging strange men in toilets, perhaps I'm better off drowning!"

"Oh, you just don't see it, do, you? What, who, or where you fucked does not bloody matter, what matters is you were both alive, not just existing, not plodding through your damned routine to keep your masters happy! You were pleasing your God damn selves, and looking at the pair of you now! Being free and yourselves has scared you both to death."

Gwyn shook with anger. "Free! Free, I've been too ashamed to leave this house, for the past two weeks!"

"Well believe me, Gwyn, I am not your husband and you are free to leave at any time, shame or not!"

Sylvia walked in to the kitchen. "What the hell's going on? You woke me up... And poor Sally is alone in there, breaking her heart!"

Gwyn rubbed a tear from her eye and took a deep breath. "I'll see to her." And she stormed out of the kitchen.

Fitz glared into nothing, with her arms folded strangle tight. Sylvia knew the look all too well; it was the smouldering start of an eruption.

Sylvia put an arm around her lover and gently combed her fingers through her hair. "They're our friends Fitz, I mean, God knows we've made enough enemies, let's not fight each other!"

"Fight?" Sneered Fitz. "They don't know the meaning of the word, they've been far too long cowered. Tell me Syl... What is it with women and beatings? Why do they just lay back and take it, as if it was their birth right?"

"I don't know Fitz, but it took it me long enough."

Fitz took Sylvia's head in her hands and stared deep into her lover's eyes. "Oh no. You, my dear, took it, as long as was needed, and always fought back! You had a price and you knew one day he'd pay it, whereas our friends in there come cheap, by the dozen!"

Gwyn held Sally in her arms and the tears flowed. "I must go to him Gwyn, I mean, what if he dies? I'd never forgive myself!"

"I'm sure it won't come to that. Oh dear, sorry Sal. How can I reassure you when I can't reassure myself? But you do what you must you're lucky, at least you have the option. After my performance, I think mine are limited to say the least, I don't think Norm would ever have me back!"

A gentle tap at the door stalled the conversation. Gwyn and Sally looked nervously at each other. "Ah, I'll get it," said Gwyn, "probably just a reading for Fitz, nothing to worry about."

Gwyn headed for the door, gently edged it open and stood rigid with shock. "Oh my God, Norm!"

For the first two days Norman Stubs drank to his freedom, toasting the single life and damning the scourge of women. The lads patted his back and stood him pints, and hailed the hero who battered the Slug, regained his pride and put mirth to rest. Norm and John Bishop became the lads again; picking fights, playing pranks and drinking far too much.

The kids parachuted in the moment the S.O.S was received, and the three spent a glorious evening pulling can rings and dragging mother and wife through every single crumb of dirt. Sandra had always been a gobby bitch, whose mouth usually drove Norm to despair. But now he found he revelled in the slaughter that weaved out of the needle sharp tongue. Norm digested every word as if it were the newly discovered meaning of life as Sandra called her mother all the bad words under the sun. Dave, his son, was made of few words and seldom disagreed. But he nodded furiously with every damnation, adding *bitch* or *slag*, which was a lot for him, and pleased Norm even more. With the night ending in a successful bonding, oaths were sworn at the door. Sandra promised every other, to clean the house, do the laundry and prepare hot meals. Norm offered a couple of bob that she first refused, but in hindsight, she thought, might come in handy. Dave agreed to juggle his busy life of signing on and playing sick to take Norm shopping every Wednesday, but quickly laid down his price to save confusion.

The arrangement worked well for the first fifty quid. Sandra arrived, ironed a shirt washed a cup and boiled an egg; held her hand out, took the cash, and thereafter made a thousand excuses.

Dave, on the other hand, did not show at all, but wondered if the cash was still on offer. Times were hard, he explained, and he feared the grand kids would suffer. Oh to be a well man he whined, as his palm was crossed with silver.

The second week sobered and old Norm discovered that youth was a one way ride, and his ticket was a long time clipped. His kidneys groaned through excess, begging him to act his age. His bowels lost their clutch as an ocean of booze turned his motion to jelly. His face lost itself in a neglect of stubble and, for the first time in his life, he out smelled his favourite blue cheese.

The home was now a graveyard of burnt toast, shirts and failed attempts. The leftovers of daily life cluttered the home, forming their own waste and dirty laundry mountains. Takeaway meals vied for odour supremacy and their unwashed remains furred in triumph.

Norm sat diseased and broken, following the tick of the clock for no apparent reason. A can of brown ale was warm and choking and had somehow lost its eternal appeal. Nothing had taste and nothing mattered.

Gwyn and Norm shared a couple of gob-smacked moments, looking at each other like they'd both just risen from the dead. Norm took off his cap and Gwyn broke the silence. "Norm!" Was as much as the shock would allow her to muster.

"Gwyn!" Shuffled Norm.

Gwyn yanked her collar to release the flush. "Yes!" She said with a rising blush.

"Hmm." Began Norm, fidgeting for control. "Time to come home, it's where you belong."

Gwyn was flabbergasted, a whole unasked for sentence. "But I shagged Slug!" She blurted, unable to think of anything else to say.

"Well! Reckon you did! But I also reckon you were not of sound mind. Everyone says the same!" He lied.

"Do they?" Beamed Gwyn, with a flash of hope.

"Aye, company you're keeping, they also say…"

"Yes," said Gwyn. "Yes, yes…Wait here."

Gwyn re-entered the cottage, looking at her three friends. Sally sat, still damp with tears. Sylvia clutched a cup of tea, with a look of concern. Fitz stood, dusted with flour from the morning's baking, her long gold hair tied back, revealing the hard of her mood that scowled toward Gwyn.

"Fallen for it, eh Gwyn?" Said Fitz, before Gwyn had the chance to say a word.

Gwyn took a deep breath. "I'm going home."

"But of course you are!" Fitz quipped. "What else would an obedient old maid do?"

Sylvia moved towards her old friend. "But Gwyn, nothing will change, you know that. And do you really think he'll forget and forgive?"

Fitz laughed. "Oh he'll forgive her all right, long enough for her to do the dishes, clean the house and readjust to her place in the world... which is somewhere under his feet."

"I'm not you!" Gwyn snapped. "I'm not some mystery that has arrived on the wind! I'm a mother, and yes, an old maid! And yes, I moan about my bloody lot, but it's too late! Whatever dreams I had are just haunted hopes that long ago died."

"And out there!" Said Fitz, pointing to the door. "Stands the person who killed you. He is the one who pulled the trigger... And what do you do? Go back to die again!"

"I'm sorry! I know I've let you down..."

"No Gwyn!" Fitz shook her head. "You've let your dreams down, your hopes, your courage. But don't worry, I mean, all said and done, you're just doing what you're told."

"Maybe... Right!" Gwyn said with a heavy sigh, and turned for the door.

"Wait!" Sally stood up, clutching tight her hankie. "I'm coming too."

"Oh no Sal! Not back to him!" Pleaded Sylvia. "He's a monster! You can't!"

"I'm sorry Syl, but all I can see is his poor dead face. I'd never forgive myself."

"Just Go!" Screamed Fitz. "The bloody pair of you, go back and get what you deserve, your fucking chains look lost without you. Go on! Go scrub and nurse their every little whim!"

"Fitz, don't!" Gasped Sylvia.

"You plead if you want to Syl, but I, unlike them, beg no one!" And Fitz stormed out of the room.

"She'll calm down," said Sylvia. She threw her arms around them both. "Now you both take care; and Sal, if he hurts you?"

"Oh he'd never hurt me!" Sally said, with solid certainty.

"But he does, Sal, and if things don't work out, you're always welcome, any time."

The three hugged again, then Sally and Gwyn headed through the door.

ON THE SIDE AND UNDER THE TABLE...

Morris had always had his bit on the side, his appetite would always demand more than just one lover. Pauline Huws was the church cleaner and she had been scrubbing the church, and the Vicar's cock, for years. Derek Huws, Pauline's husband and the church organist, chose, for the sake of peace, not to know; a mild mannered man with the sort of face that encouraged abuse and betrayal, which proved to be ideal for Morris to conduct his sport, safe from rumour and damnation.

With the church doors bolted and shut for worship, Morris was free to let the devil in him soar. Pauline Huws was cuffed to the alter, just below the marbled icon depicting the mercy of Christ. Spread-eagled, backside bare, she squirmed in anticipation, bracing herself for the crack of leather. Morris charged, throwing his full weight into the first strike, the lash launched; the arse welts leaving a trail of raw, red protest.

"Say it!" Barked Morris, flexing the belt and preparing for the second strike.

"Ooh, more tea Vicar...And not quite so hard this time!" Groaned Pauline in feigned pleasure.

Morris, regardless of mercy, delivered his next strike with further furore; the lash bit deep and the bonded slave howled.

"Ouch, that bloody well hurt!"

"Say it!" Morris screamed above the pity.

"Ah Mm……..More tea………V….Vicar!"

And again Morris charged, howling with fever. Pauline now screamed and offered no tea, as the pain dug ever deeper, and again and again, until finally exhaustion tamed the beast.

Morris now sated, calmly un-cuffed his victim. Pauline turned and vented her fury, her face as red as her backside. "Have you gone insane? That bloody well hurt!"

Morris just smiled at the crumpled mess that huddled pitifully beneath him. "Pathetic!" He snarled. "Now go, I've a sermon to prepare!"

"Bastard!" Snapped Pauline, pulling up her knickers and down her dress and storming out of the door.

Morris smiled at the icon of Jesus. "Mercy," he laughed. "Dear me, no, you won't find any of that here!"

The Blodger Brothers scrapyard lay at the edge of town. Their land contained rags, bones and rogues. Weather hardy and weasel sly, hair and faces as dark as the deals they dealt in. The three brothers lived to pump iron and profit. Not even the sun was too hot to handle and any deed, however dirty, could be bargained for a price.

Councillor Hardy's bulk looked somewhat unemployed amongst all the graft of the yard. He wobbled and puffed up to the Blodger boys H.Q., a building that seemed more clapped out than the car wrecks that littered the grounds. Rory, the oldest and meanest of the three, chewed straw, leaned against the shack and watched the Councillor approach.

It was a warm day and Boris sweated profoundly. "Morning!" He panted, moping his sopping brow.

"Aye!" Replied Rory, looking the Councillor over from head to toe.

"How's business?" Said Boris, levering for conversation.

"None of yours! Drawled Rory. "That's how business is."

"What if I was to say I could put a lot of scrap your way, would it be any of my business
then?

"Depends,," said Rory, lighting a fag and blowing the smoke in the Councillor's face. "You see, Councillor, me and my brothers aint used to getting help from the civic centre. Quite the reverse in fact…You and your cronies usually end up costing us money, blocking trade and hampering our free market."

Councillor Hardy laughed. "Now come on Rory, we both know the market you talk of, can be a little bit… Let's just say, too free? So shall we just cut to the chase and talk, what you can do for me, and what's in it for you?"

Rory smiled. "Feel free Councillor! I'd do a deal with the Devil for the right price!"

"Oh I know that!" Said Councillor Hardy, offering his hand. "That's why I came."

The Vicar announced to the town his recovery from illness, which most of the town did not believe, and the bells again rang, announcing the dawn of the Sabbath, and on this particular Sunday it was not just the faithful who dragged on their Sunday best. The streets had a festival feel as folk muttered their way to church, all jostling forward in haste for the best pew. The gossip was still red hot, these many days past the scandalous events, and on this particular Sabbath the Vicar had promised the good people of the town an explanation, of the debauchery that had swept through his precious parish.

Morris Bevan stood on his altered roost, hawk-eyed, looking down, on prey and predator, as they swarmed into his service. Morris held his bean-pole frame proud, his face grave as a killer, steadying his nerve with a will of iron. The Vicar waited, patient for the whispers and titters to subside, cleared his throat and prepared once again to lie.

"Judas! Did Jesus Know? Did he know it was he who would take the Silver? And if so, why hold him so long to his bosom, why bother to love, when that love would be betrayed?

In short, is loving the wrong person a crime? If so, then I am indeed guilty and must live the sentence of a broken heart. But forgiveness I ask from no man! The Lord and the Lord only, shall be my judge, and like Adam I shall not waiver in the face of vipers."

Morris paused and surveyed the room, judging the mood of his congregation, as he readied himself for the buglers charge.

"Life is but a test, with love, I believe, being the greatest test of all. Have I failed? Or has love failed me?" Morris again scanned his audience, hoping to see his vie for pity showing in their eyes. "But I am a man, a man well schooled in the ways of the world and with my faith to comfort me, I will again prosper, and God willing, I may once again cherish that greatest of gifts..........Love!" Morris took a deep breath and held his head high, his face changing from the misery of jelly to a stern of stone. "BUT WHAT IS UNNATURAL TO GOD, should therefore, be unnatural to his Children. AND THE CORRUPTION OF THE GIFT OF LOVE IS ABOUT AS UNNATURAL AS IT GETS!"

The congregation, now excited, chattered and giggled, this indeed is what they came to witness. Morris drank in the mood and attacked. "MAKE NO MISTAKE! We bear the burden of God's scripture; and it is us! He entrusts to enforce his teachings...For, oh yes, Satan has a ferocious appetite, fuelled by an eternal urge to corrupt the teachings of the Gospels. He shall never waiver, oh no! Every waking day, he strives to warp and distort our feelings and desires, turning God's gifts of beauty into sordid wishes and acts of filth!"

Morris smiled to himself, as his words invoked his desired reactions, and the hard core of his congregation stood and gave homage, to himself and the Lord. Morris could sense the fight his well placed words had stirred, and judged the moment right to deliver his war cry. He signalled for silence and readied for the kill. "Hocus pocus, the dark arts; call it what you will. A bit of fun to some, I've no doubt, some here have had a little dabble, a harmless, reading of palms or cards, a glimpse of the future, or a word with the dead...OR A PACT WITH THE DEVIL!"

Morris paused, lancing the eyes of his congregation. "I would consider my wife, or indeed, the person I knew, as my wife, to be an intelligent and moral creature. Indeed, in the twenty or so years we have had the pleasure to serve among you, I would not hesitate to say, she has been, by my side, part of the moral compass of this fair town, and so I say to you; what power, what corruption does this viper that has nestled among us possess? And if she bears the might, to bend so easily the mind of a scholar! Then what hope for them, weaker of mind? What hope for the innocent?" Morris let the question hang, letting his assault slowly digest. "Innocence is the lamb that nestles safe in the arms of the Lord...And the lamb represents our children, and we are the shepherds of that precious flock. And I ask you, does the good shepherd allow the wolf to roam free amid its flock? Morris glared accusingly at his now captivated audience. "NO, NO, NO! What the good shepherd does is load his catapult, and run the beast from his sacred flock and lands. I tell you all, we have such a beast among us, a beast all too ready to ravish and corrupt our virgin flock. Now is the time for this community to take arms and rid this town of the monster who sees fit to corrupt the teachings of the Lord. IN GOD WE TRUST!" The congregation roared to its feet and Morris gloated with triumph, ready to deliver the killer blow on his despised foes. "So with me…"

"THERE IS NO TIME!" Morris turned, snarling towards the interloper. Tom the Placard walked on to the dais, arms raised to the heavens. "Fuck!" Cursed Morris under his breath, Old Tom was more efficient than a fire bell at emptying a room, Morris tried to smile, and put a brave face on the situation, but already he could see the congregation was becoming unsettled. "Worry not!" Continued Tom, unaware, or unconcerned at the daggers aimed his way. "For it is the end, for sure, the Lord has sent a sign, and that sign is the very beast that stirs among us! Charge your souls, I say, for weapons will be rendered useless, and…"

"Yes thank you very much Tom!" Said Morris, grabbing the old man by the shoulders and trying to guide him off his stage. But it was too late, the church was emptying quicker than a diarrhoea sufferers backside. Silence. Morris glared at Tom in his now empty church. "Oh well done Tom!"

Tom smiled, missing the sarcasm. "Why, thank you Vicar! I think, between us, the gravity of our message has finally hit home."

"Indeed Tom. And I have a little message of my own just for you."

Old Tom stood to attention, eager for instruction. "Fire away Vicar, my mind is always open to the council of the Lord!"

"Indeed!" Spat Morris. "Well, open your mind to this, fuck off and die!" Morris then calmly folded his hands behind his back, and strolled out of his church, leaving Old Tom to ponder on the statement. Could it be the Vicar knew something he didn't? And was the time for judgement arriving sooner than old Tom expected, or did the Vicar, indeed just tell him to fuck off? He concluded that it really made no difference, for these were indeed trying times.

THE MARCH OF OMENS...

And it was at this time that a nasty head cold plagued the town, causing violent coughing, running noses and puddles of phlegm.

And it was also at this time that a storm deluged the ageing sewer system, sending a flash flood through the town that engulfed shoes and soaked socks. The storm raged on, lightning forked and electric and radio, and for the better off, televisions, failed in the prime of their peak audiences.

The next morning woke to sunshine and sour moods, spirits dampened by head colds and a loss of entertainment.

And it was at this time that Mrs Smith noticed a spot on young Winnie's cheek. A spot that was quickly followed by another, and another. The child's back, in rapid time, was smothered in a pus-oozing pox. With haste, she knocked the neighbours' doors, comparing backs with other broods. Parents stormed their stairs, dragging bewildered children out of beds and stripping them on the spot. The bells of panic soon hit the town as the pox of chickens raged.

No tea in the morning is bound to set a bitter mood, kettles and lights become useless without their sacred sauce, and with the kids now in quarantine and under feet with no radio or television, the mood of the town hungered for blame and the gossip roared into a blaze of fire-storms.

Tom the Placard revelled on the edge of darkness, in total bliss, as things got worse. Biblical was the storm, of that Tom had no doubt. He had spent the night bare to the glory of God's wrath, hammered by hail-storms, arms stretched out to the heavens, begging the bolts of the Lord to flash through his bones and smite him to paradise.

Alas, he woke once again fully intact, but for once, this did not totally dampen his spirits. He looked through the poke of his window and quickly sensed the mood, he quickly judged he was still alive, but the day had a definite feel of being numbered. The square was filling, even at this early hour, and tongues were already hot from wagging. Tom could sense the jangle of nerves, could smell the sweat that bleached through collars and he felt the motions of unease. Indeed this must be his moment. The moment laughing lost its sense of humour, steps lost their skip and folk jabbered with doubt. Tom walked amid the gossip, proud. His placard for the day; *Kneel now, and sink no lower*.

Superstition, they say, is only an accident away and with the Vicar's grave omens of decadence, the balance of normality tipped, the mystery of supposed stuff and nonsense soon took grip and myth quickly galloped into fact.

Megan Small had spent her youth travelling with fairs and knew her onions and demanded through experience that people now marked her words. "Oh yes!" She nodded with certainty. "I've seen it all before! We had this witch, you see; very similar to that Fitzpatrick, actually. Any one day they told her to pack up her cards and leave; I can't remember why, but she was a nasty piece of work. Anyway, the next day strange things started to occur, the tumbler broke his leg, and I mean he'd tumbled for years with never a scratch. The juggler misjudged and fractured his skull. Ooh, all sorts were happening, then finally the Ferris wheel burst into flames."

"Well I never!" Gasped Janet Smith. "Only the other day our Freddy broke his leg, and he's been walking for years."

Phyllis White growled into her speech. A particular nasty individual who was always ready to dig a grave. "And don't tell me that storm was normal?" She screwed her face and snarled. "The Lord won't have it! This filth that festers among us; harbouring devils, that's what we're doing. The Vicar's right, and if they can penetrate to the heart of the church... Well, what chance the rest of us?"

Hillary Thomson, a twitchy individual who stroked for attention, felt her way to the heart of the action. "Beware the children, that's what the Vicar said! The Devil feeds on the weak!"

"Oh God!" Howled Nora Becket. "My Timmy woke this morning with an eruption of boils and rashes, scratching like hell-fire! It's not normal, he's got such lovely skin."

"The Bridgewater's boy's the same." Chipped in Martha Watson.

"And the Benet's little girl, poor lamb, is smothered from head to foot. It's pitiful to see,"

choked Mary Robinson.

And the list of supernatural mischief grew, leaving not a single soul unaffected. Old Tom stood patient, sensing his moment. He allowed the crowd to reach its frenzy and pounced.

"Now is the day, a day when time will stop and mean no more. The Good Lord will sit back no longer, he shall vent his fury and punish those who have shunned the cross!"

"Well why doesn't the Good Lord just vent his fury on them who deserve it and leave the rest of us in peace?" Spat Phyllis White.

"Yes!" Barged Hillary Thomson. "We don't all want to die just because of a couple of bad apples."

"I knew it was a filthy thing, the moment I clapped an eye, strutting her free-will about the town, bound to lead to trouble!" Hissed Mabel Greenway.

"Things have gone from bad to rotten since she arrived!" Hissed Doreen More. "Ooh she's as sour as a crab-apple……..And as far as I can tell the Church and God have done nothing!"

Phyllis White again barged her view forward. "Oh, they done something all right! Jumped in bloody bed with her! Don't tell me Saint bloody Morris Bevan didn't know!?"

Old Tom could do nothing but watch as the Ladies' tongues ran rampage.

"Probably watched!" Quipped Hillary Thomson. And the squabble of hags gargled and croaked with laughter.

"Ladies, Ladies!" Hollered Tom, now perched on the town bench for maximum attention.

"We must stand together and defy the will of the Beast..."

"Ah, piss off! Snapped Mary Robinson. "I'd rather stand in a high tide than stand by you!"

And on that parting note, the clutch dispersed, leaving Old Tom once again to preach to the wind. Tom, as always, carried on regardless, as the rampage of women set out to plunder and dissuade any good intentions.

THE NIGHT OF THE WEASELS...

The bell clanged and youth hurtled free from the grinding jaws of education, all swimming for their lives to reach the golden shores of ignorant mischief. Away from the Masters' rule they slapped and kicked each other in a frenzy of freedom. The day's humdrum of knowledge pissed out of their brains, and they gloried in the bliss of feral idiocy.

Morris Bevan stood starched, stiff, his height always providing the perfect perch to look down on others. The bombardment of playground genocide, braked sharp as the enemy of authority loomed before them, their backsides immediately twitched, warning them of the cost of bad behaviour.

"Good Afternoon children," said Morris; half smile, half threat.

The brave troop all jostled for a quick getaway, answering their *good afternoons* in unison and running for the hills.

Timothy Walton was a good boy, which was why he was ideal. He was a boy who whistled for company and kept close to his shadow. First into school and last to leave, he trailed behind the pack, close enough to see them and far enough to flee.

Morris stepped out of the church grounds and blocked the lad's path. "Ah, young Master Walton," said the Vicar, using his best cheesy. "Just the lad?"

Timothy, as always, feared the worst; in his experience nothing good came out of human contact. "Hello Mister Bevan." He stammered in nervousness, looking over his shoulder and praying another Master Walton was walking behind him.

"Have you a minute?" Said Morris, putting a heavy hand on his shoulder.

"Well, mam expects me straight home after school, otherwise she says she worries."

"Oh, what a fine considerate lad you are...But I'm sure your Mother, would understand you spending a few spare moments with me, especially when you tell her that you will be doing your first ever solo at the coming Easter service."

The little lad's eyes lit up. "What, me?"

"Why indeed! Can't think of anyone more deserving, why not you?"

Timothy eagerly nodded. "Mother will be proud."

"Of course she will!" Laughed Morris. "Let's go inside, and plan your big day."

Fitz buried her head in the complex pages of alchemy, letting its mystery distract her from the mood of her lover. She flicked through the pages with intent, determined not to be distracted. Sylvia waited and waited for attention, until finally she could wait no longer. "I'm worried about them!" Fitz remained silent in study.

"Oh, woman!" Said Sylvia, shoving her lover's shoulder. "I'm talking to you!"

Fitz slowly closed the book, took off her glasses and smiled. "Yes, you are talking, but you're not actually saying anything I haven't heard a thousand times since they left."

"But they've gone…Back to them, and all that entails." Protested Sylvia.

Fitz stood, walked to the kitchen, then returned with a bottle and two glasses. "And the World goes on. Drink?"

"Oh, how can you be so flippant, so, so…cold!?"

"Sit!" Commanded Fitz. She poured two glasses. "Did you really think, Syl, that it would be that easy? Did you think that I could just brew a potion, weave a spell and change the World? The strongest magic, Syl, is here" Fitz pointed to her heart. "And if another puts claim to the heart then that spell is the Devil to break! I opened them, I dug deep to bring them back; alas… there was no one there!"

"But Sally? Gwyn, I know, has fight, but Sally…He's a monster, Fitz; subtle, but a beast all the same, he controls every breath of hers."

"Look, I can't change minds and I can't control their lives or decisions. Freedom means choice, for right or wrong, and in that I have no claim or part."

Sylvia knew her argument was pointless, Fitz just could not fathom dependency on others or the thought of blind devotion. To her, the human will, was sacred and prized above all other aspects of a person's calling and duty, a duty that should be served to themselves. Sylvia knew, she was not without pity, far from it, but she strongly believed in free thought and self-preservation. Sylvia took a sip of her drink and looked at her lover, she would not give up; just because you couldn't bend iron it should not stop you trying. "Well I shan't give up on them, sooner or later they'll need our help and I intend to be there for them."

Fitz smiled. "Very commendable dear!" She closed her book and picked up her glass. "Just be prepared for a long wait. Now, there's a garden to tend…You coming?"

"But he's never late, never, never!" Said Patricia Walton, as she desperately paced her living room. Her husband Derek looked up from his paper and huffed. "For God's sake woman, one hour, that's all it's been!"

Patricia snatched the paper and threw it across the room. "It's Timothy you're talking about, you know, our son! The boy who still sleeps with the light on and cuddles his teddy in bed."

Derek shrugged his shoulders. "Well perhaps he's finally grown up and he's out with the other lads playing football or the like?"

Patricia Walton shrieked in horror. "PLAY!? With his asthma? Oh you really don't know our boy at all, do you! Timothy doesn't play with ruffians, he's terrified of them. No, he studies and reads so he can be better than them, and, and he's never, ever, ever, late! Why, sometimes he's so early, it seems he's home before he leaves!"

"All right woman, for God's sake calm down. I'll give it another hour and I'll start looking."

"Another hour!" Patricia picked up the crumpled paper and threw it again at her indifferent husband. "Oh why don't you start looking in two hours and give the bloody murderer plenty of time to dispose of the body!?"

Derek brushed away the paper and stood. "Now get a bloody grip woman, you're hysterical."

"Of course I'm fucking hysterical! Our boy is missing you fucking imbecile! Now, while I phone the police, you get out there and bloody well start looking!"

"Police!" Gasped Derek. "Don't you think…"

"I can't bloody well think about anything! Anything except our missing son! So get out of that fucking chair and FUCKING DO SOMETHING!"

Sergeant Brinmore Hardy was of a button popping weight. He and his dear brother, Councillor Boris Hardy, had been in an eating competition since birth, with still no obvious winner. Mean-eyed, with the personality of a rattle snake, Sergeant Hardy viewed the whole world as a criminal. With a total disregard for community relations, Sergeant Hardy bullied his way through his investigations, viewing all suspects, without exception, as guilty, unless of course they were able to fill his ravenous backhand. The phone rang on his cluttered desk and the Sergeant instantly viewed it with suspicion. He picked up the phone. *'Sergeant Hardy'*, is the only information he's prepared to give. "I see," he continued with a mouthful of biscuit. "We'll send someone straight round." He placed down the receiver, waited a couple of seconds, picked it back up and dialled. "The lad's been reported missing…Goodbye."

He dusted the crumbs off his tray top belly, popped out of his chair, squeezed his helmet onto his mirror smooth head, strapped it under his chins and headed for the door.

With the nerve of the town already teetering on a cliff top, it took no time at all to plant a forest full of ill seeds and stir the town into action. The search party gathered at the square, pitch-forked hungry, eager, more for blood and excitement, than deliverance, and also eager for someone to pay for these days of routine upsetting uncertainties. Constable Nigel Hastings, a particularly good and honest, unassuming individual, stood under the statue of the town's brave bugler, and tried in vain to assemble order with no success. "Make way, make way!" A voice bellowed. The throng parted quicker than the Red Sea as The Hardy brothers stormed into the crowd, their bulk bouncing aside the onlookers who stood in their path.

"I'll take charge here," said the Councillor, shoving the hapless constable aside. His brother heaved the Councillor on to the bench and stood military like below him. Two pairs of piggy eyes stared ice cold into the crowd. "You all know me," began the Councillor, "and my brother." Sergeant Hardy tugged at his collar in a show of authority. "Now you can search the fields, dredge the river if you like, but we all know deep inside you'd be wasting your time. Strange things have been occurring in this town of late and we all know which way the foul wind has been blowing. I'd like to consider this community to be open and welcoming to all... alas, that charitable spirit can sometimes leave us wide open to them who feed off kindness and goodwill. Ladies, gentlemen; I believe we have allowed a Viper to slither among us. A creature of unnatural pleasure, a proven destroyer of faith and the sanctity of marriage, qualities that I know, are jealously guarded in this town." Councillor Hardy paused, letting the crowd stew in his obvious conclusions.

"Wickle Cottage is where I'd cast my net, where I believe this despicable business will start and end. Most of you here are God fearing and heard the Vicar's words of wisdom spoke just this Sabbath past. Beware the corruption of our children; words, I can assure you, as a father I took full heed of! Now we can stand about and hope for the best or, for the sake of our children, we can damn well take the bull by the horns. Bloody wake up and do something about it!"

A hand rose amid the crush, seemingly unmoved by the Councillor's call for action. "What if the lad is just stuck up a tree?"

"What if he's bloody tied to one?" A man snapped in response.

"I know the lad!" quipped a voice of authority. "He's more likely to be stuck in a dolls house than, be stuck up a tree!

Lad's a mammie's boy, I'm surprised he escaped out of the folds of his mother's apron!"

A very ruffled, dodgy looking individual chipped in. "Well, my boy disappears for hours on end and no search party goes looking for him!"

"That's because he's a little bastard!" Growled Sergeant Hardy. "And while we're about it…"

"All right, that's enough!" Shouted the Councillor. "I too know the lad, and it is, as Mister Marshal says; he is more likely to be stuck in a doll's house than up a tree, which makes this all the more sinister. He's a good boy, a choir boy to boot, with not a whiff of trouble about him, easily lead into who knows what. Now, what could a witch do with that? Oh yes, you heard me right, a witch! Make no mistake, the woman openly admits it, and our good Vicar is proof of her devilry. Now some might shrug that off as a load of old mumbo jumbo, but there's a child's life at stake, and I don't know about you, but I think it puts a sinister twist to the supposed harmless use of a crystal ball. So, are you with me?" There are a few mumbles as folk chew over the Councillor's call to arms, slowly but surely the mumbles gather momentum as the fever of mob rule bites. Councillor Hardy bellows his war cry, stoking the crowd's ague. "ARE YOU WITH ME?" The words punch home, the jury is out and the mob is on the march, roaring for its hung court justice.

The mob bounds and growls past the Roast Duck, just as Slug decides to wobble home. He eyes the gathering and quickly concludes there's a party on offer. He hops down the pub steps, and waves for attention. "Wait for me, wait for me!"

The sun was just slipping into slumber and darkness was gently rolling over the hills. Fitz and Sylvia had just put the finishing touches to a good day's weeding and pruning, when the march of boots thumped towards them. "Fitz?" Said Sylvia, pointing towards the dust of the throng. Fitz turned and looked towards the disturbance. "Get inside!" Fitz commanded.

"But what do they want?" Puzzled Sylvia.

"I don't know Syl; but I don't think they're popping round for a cup of tea. Quick, in!"

Fitz bolted the door just as the mob engulfed the cottage. Sylvia bolted and shuttered the windows. Fitz next grabbed her old twelve bore and loaded it.

"Oh my God!" Gasped Sylvia. "What on earth is that for?"

"Protection, Syl. Believe me, there aint nothing uglier than a mob, and I should bloody know, I've been subject to a few."

"I'll go and talk to them; they know me, I can calm them down, there must be some mistake?" Says Sylvia, making for the door.

"NO!" Yelled Fitz, gripping Sylvia's arm tight. "Oh they know you all right, but just what do they know? Do you think your darling husband has just taken what has happened on the chin, Syl? Believe me, whatever this is about, he's played a part in its brewing!"

"Come out and show yourselves!" The call was echoed by a savage roar. Fitz unbolted a shutter and peered out. "Uh, it's that fat Councillor, oh he's enjoying this...I'm going out!"

Sylvia grabbed Fitz by the arm. "God, no love, you said yourself, it's not safe!"

"And you think it's safe in here?" Fitz shook off Sylvia's hand and made for the door. As she opened it the mob, as one, surged forward, and as one they backed off when they noticed the gun.

Fitz aimed the gun directly at the Councillor. "What the fuck do you want?"

Boris Hardy just smiled. "Now, now really! You are not going to use that thing...with an officer of the law present? That would be very misguided."

"Oh no, Councillor. What *would* be very misguided, would be you underestimating my resolve. But if you come any closer, I'll show you how resolute I can be!"

Sergeant Hardy pushed his brother aside. "I'll handle this!" He grunted. "I, Madam, am an officer of the law..."

"And a fat, lying, cheating, disgusting pig, just like your brother," said Fitz, now aiming the gun at the Sergeant.

Sergeant Hardy growled; his piggy, mean fisted eyes stabbing at Fitz. "You will, Madam, step aside and permit us entry, then when our search is completed, it's down to the station for a couple of questions."

"And just why would I do that, Sergeant?" Fitz gently put her hand on the trigger.

"There's a lad missing, and we strongly believe that you know something of the child's whereabouts."

Fitz shook her head and laughed. "And if I was to say I know nothing about it, would you all just fuck off?"

"Oh no!" Said the Sergeant, shaking his head. "You see, you seem to have made a couple of waves since you've resided in our, once tranquil community!"

"You mean I stole the Vicar's wife, and kneed your slob of a brother in the balls when he tried to get his hands inside my knickers!" The revelation caused some muttering and tittering among the throng that immediately stirred Councillor Hardy into action. "You will allow us entry!"

"Over my dead body!"

"FIRE, FIRE!" The scream came from the crowd and was echoed by several other warnings. The throng pointed to the cottage, all gawping in shock. Fitz turned, just as Sylvia's screams were heard from inside the cottage. "YOU BASTARDS!" Screamed Fitz, dropping the gun and hurtling towards her burning home. She pulled open the cottage door and the smoke bellowed out, but regardless of the danger, she plunged into the gathering inferno, yelling for her lover.

Nobody noticed the three weasels that crept up from the river bank. The mean, twisted creatures blended in well with the tight, sharp claws of thorn and bracken. The Blodger brothers were masters of incognito. And nobody but the moon noticed the sneak of their souls stalking black through the dead, dark night, with their mean hands clutching intentions of destruction and profit. And nobody noticed the canny eyes and fingers that peered and fumbled with the can of petrol. The petrol that was poured over thatch and wood with care and duty and deadly intent, and until that blood curdling scream nobody noticed the flames and smoke that engulfed the cottage.

The raging mob, at first, howled with bonfire fever, but as Fitz plunged heedless into flames, the festive mood of the mob faded, and folk sobered in the wake of mortality and the rising furnace. Sergeant Hardy blew his whistle. "Right! Home, the lot of you, home! We'll deal with this!" The mob shuffled uneasily as the structure of the cottage began to crack and cave in but, as the flames and danger increased, they quickly shelved any ideas of heroics, dispersed and scampered home. The Sergeant then radioed for assistance, probably a lifetime too late. "On their way!" He grinned.

Councillor Hardy glowed with flame and triumph. "Oh dear! He quipped. "I hope they get here in time." The Brothers then moved back to a safe distance and laughed.

The growling head of the mob cowered on its return, as folk sulked back home with not a thought of poor, lost Timothy Walton, and who could blame them, after all they had done their best.

The Blodger brothers dusted themselves down and made for the pub to get alibis and a pint. Of course, the Councillor's well laid plan did suggest burning the cottage after the occupants were carted away to the station, but suggestions always came with a nod and a wink. And besides, what were rules for If not to be broken? The round, of course, and many more, was stood by Councillor Hardy. This night's work would keep eyes blinkered from their dodgy deals for years to come, not to mention, the leg up on trade, and the pick of the best scrap. The three weasels raised their glasses, smiled and toasted the foul night and its glorious gains.

Timothy Walton ran, he was desperately late for tea and was sure he would get an enormous row, even though the Vicar had reassured him everything would be all right, he couldn't help but worry. But surely the glorious news he had to tell, would earn him a special treat and all would be forgiven. He decided to deliver the good tidings as soon as he entered the home, thus vetoing the scolding. He opened the front door hollering. "Mam, Mam, guess what the Vicar wants me to do?" With no reply he ran upstairs; perhaps his mam was lying down again with one of her notorious headaches. But no, not a sign. Down the stairs he went and into the kitchen, his belly growling, reminding him he was late for tea. He headed for the larder and grabbed a pot of home-made plum jam, spread it thick on a chunk of bread, went into the living room and turned on the television. "Must have Gone Shopping!" He shrugged and gnawed at his door stopper, without a care in the world.

Whether the hanging tree ever hung anyone remains to be seen, but folk reckoned if it hadn't then it certainly should have. It stood atop Bell's Barrow Hill, an imposing, wicked, gnarled, lump of timber, with its bows twisted and withered. It seemed to be desperate to clutch at a life and choke it to death. Folklore did not have a good word to say about it, and in its long, long years it had throttled princes, betrayed heroes and held harbour, and execution for witches, warlocks and hunch backed kings. In the modern age, Bell's Barrow Hill was often scaled by young lovers, and proved to be a prime spot for a lad to scare his darling into his arms, play the knight and get what he was hoping for. But on this particular night the two figures that stood beneath its moonlight scattered limbs had anything but love on their minds. Indeed, if anyone had noticed the two silhouetted shapes; the one gnarled, lean, tall and scythe hooked, the other stumped short and hog bellied with glutton, they would probably have believed that the executioners of old had come again to purge the town of witchcraft, with ducking stool and gallows.
    Morris Bevan had demanded this moment, this moment of total, mind-blowing revenge, and where in the world better to view one's triumph than the vista of Bell's Barrow Hill. Boris Hardy, on the other hand, thought nothing was worth the effort, except for money of course.
    The smoke of ruin still rose up from Wickle Cottage, the choke of its destruction, losing its mass and drifting in

harmless wisps to the heavens, as if there, butter would not melt.

Morris looked down upon the devastation, and took a good lung full of air. He smiled. "You know, Councillor, I can almost taste death on the wind. What a glorious night...You're sure they didn't get out?"

"Sorry Vicar, but I can't see how they could have! I mean, plan was to oust them before fire started. Bloody Blodger boys, always too keen with mischief!"

The Vicar laughed and clapped his hands. "Oh my dear Boris, there is no need to apologise, as far as I can see the outcome has been quite splendid."

"You think so?" Puzzled Boris.

"But of course, my dear chap."

"But your wife!"

Morris gave the Councillor's shoulder a pat. "Why, my dear fellow, the bitch had it coming...And this way is so much neater, don't you think? Nobody to contest or brew trouble. In short, Boris, we have eliminated all opposition, and nobody will be any the wiser. Beats eviction every time, don't you think?"

"Hmm," groaned Boris. "There'll be an inquiry, mind, bound to be!"

"An inquiry? I'm sure that you and your worthy brother can more than handle the inconvenience of an inquiry. I mean, what else are you paid for, if not to cover things up, turn the other, and make a profit? And believe me, Boris, there will be plenty of profit with all that land to develop, land that we now know, through your diligent book-keeping, belongs to the church...my church!"

Boris smiled and rubbed his hands warm with the thought of money. "Oh indeed. I reckon six or seven good plots on that land, and that adds up to quite a tidy sum and, you know, half the town was there tonight. I'm sure I could find one hapless idiot to shoulder the blame!"

Morris laughed. "Now that's the low down snake I've come to know and love!"

Tom the placard knelt by the smouldering remains, arms flung high to the heavens, his joy drowning him in tears. The week had proved to be revelation after revelation, a thunderstorm of omens had pounded the town, making, he was sure, even the most sceptical, cower for forgiveness. Tom sang to the heavens, his voice ragged raw from smoke and praise. "And the temple shall fall!" He repeated endlessly into the night.

Timothy Walton now lay smothered in kisses and tucks, snug and safe in his bed. His Mother had howled at first, but a flutter of puppy eyes soon put anger to rest. And with the news of the Easter service and his crowing roll, in no time, he was her darling little boy again, promised a treat come morning, all was forgotten and all was forgiven.

THE CHAINS OF FORGIVENESS...

Gwyn separated whites and woollens, bed sheets and towels on the kitchen floor, and still she sobbed. She must have cried an ocean since the happy reunion. Forgiveness, it seemed, was mostly silent, and reply to her conversation was delivered with nods and grunts. Norm had a constant *shit on his shoe* look on his face, every time he looked at her, and the magic moment of hands held on her return had soon turned to a cold shoulder.

Woollens and whites first, dust before you vacuum. Open the windows, however cold, and air the room. Chop the vegetables, trim the braising steak, put on the boil and simmer for at least four hours, and then tackle the stairs, right into the bedrooms and, of course, bathroom and toilet last. Nothing had changed except the fight of equality had settled to become a duty of repentance. Indeed, Norm's coronation was now total, and he ruled his realm free of usurpers, sitting smug in his crown.

Gwyn sat and sighed and sipped her cup of tea. She was determined to be content, never mind how miserable she felt, life had to go on, and the dust, she felt sure, would eventually settle. The night of depravity still haunted, and she avoided exposure as much as possible. Shopping trips were conducted cloaked, scarf and collar pulled tight to shield face and shame, but still she felt the penetration of those who knew and scorned.

Busy was the answer, it kept the guilt and shame at bay for, alone with her thoughts, her mind tore her to pieces and plagued her with rewinds of toilets and filth and the heady swill of indulgence. "Oh it's all right for you!" Gwyn seethed accusingly at her mug. "Fitz the free bloody spirit! Oh God, what was I thinking? Freedom is for those who have nothing else," she concluded, and ploughed back into her chores.

"Look at Dad, look at him!" Sandra spat the words in her mother's face, the grease of her gob spraying and lubricating the seemingly endless tirade. The air turned blue as soon as Gwyn's darling daughter entered the room, her lack of vocabulary leading to an all out assault of F's and C's and, as ever, poetically delivered with the slang and bile of the gutter.

Gwyn sat hunched and shaken in shame, soaked in sobs and speechless, taking every punch of the vocal assault that she now believed she fully deserved. Sandra paused, looked at her mother making sure her words were causing sufficient misery and soldiered on. "With fucking Slug! Of all people, in a fucking pub toilet! Tell me, how do you think your grandchildren are going to cope? Knowing their Gran's a whore!"

Gwyn had been through this a thousand times, it seemed, since her tail between her legs return. Sandra would scream and demand and Dave would tut and sigh and hold his hand out for yet another tenner.

Gwyn wiped her eyes and attempted a smile towards John and Jack, her darling grand children who, if affected, certainly didn't show it as they scrammed and gouged each other over ownership of a water pistol. "You two! Fucking cut it out!" Screamed Sandra, walking towards them with a raised hand. The two angels quickly scarpered to resume their war out of sight, blowing raspberries at their oppressors.

"I, I…Don't know what came over me," said Gwyn, her voice weak and racked with sobs.

"Bloody Slug!" Snapped Sandra. "That's what came over you!"

"Sandra please?" Gasped Norm. "The memory is still raw." These were his first words of the visit and they were pampered with self-pity. Sandra ran over and smothered her father in kisses and apologies. "God, Mam…You really don't know how lucky you are having Dad, do you?"

Gwyn took a deep breath and blew her nose. "I know I done wrong by him…"

"Huh!" Sandra lit a cigarette. "Done wrong! God, that's putting it mildly! All Dad's done for you, and you do that to him! And I tell you now, Mam, most men wouldn't have had you back. And if Dad hadn't, nobody, including me, would have blamed him! Ooh, you've bloody shamed us all, I can barely bloody look at you! And at your age, it's fucking disgusting!"

Gwyn just sat, her head hanging in shame, as the two pairs of eyes scolded right through her.

"Right!" Said Sandra grabbing her coat, "I'm off. I've run it by Dad, my washer's broke again, so if it's not too much trouble I've brought a couple of bags and I was wondering if you could wash them for me?"

Gwyn smiled, feeling wanted at last. "Of course I will San! I'd love to."

"Well if it makes you that happy you can iron em an all. That's if you haven't got any other plans, of course."

"No, no, of course I will Love."

"Right, that's that sorted. Come on Dad, you look like you could do with some cheering up, you can buy me a drink down the Duck."

"Ooh, yes!" Said Gwyn, standing-up. "I can watch the boys."

"Thanks, but no thanks, Mother! They can play in the park."

FRESH IS VIRGIN, VIRGIN IS PURE AND PURE IS GOD. STALE IS THE DEVIL THE DEVIL IS FILTH AND FILTH IS DISEASE.

And so was written in the home of Cuthbert Combs, set in stone and never questioned. To him the words stood divine, to his wife the words stood as law. Unsoiled was victory and every waking day needed to be a triumph.

The cleaning rota had increased tenfold since Sally had made her heartfelt return. Totally necessary, as Cuthbert had explained; hard work was healthy for both the mind and home and Sally grafted from dawn till dusk to scrub the abode, and in doing so purged herself, through the godliness of labour, the taint of her soul.

Cuthbert had made a remarkable recovery as soon has his grief stricken wife had walked through the door and was, in no time, fit enough to show and display the new order of business, leaving no detail, however small, free from scrutiny.

ORDER IS PEACE, PEACE IS HARMONY AND HARMONY IS FAITH. CHAOS IS HELL, HELL IS RUIN AND RUIN IS DECAY.

The blackboard was neatly drilled and plugged to the kitchen wall, a coherent form of order through communication and, as Cuthbert had explained, no longer would there be an excuse for misinterpreted commands. The board was explicit and bold in letters, never ending and relentless, and was always to be studied before breakfast, thus ensuring order was always first course.

DUTY IS SALVATION, SALVATION IS HOPE AND HOPE IS BELIEF. SLOTH IS DAMNATION, DAMNATION IS DOOM AND DOOM IS FAILURE. All law according to the gospel of Cuthbert Combs.

Evening and Morning check lists neatly typed and filed; entries to be made daily. As Cuthbert explained, not only would it keep an invaluable record of duties performed, it would also ensure any unforeseen problems were dealt with swiftly and efficiently, thus quickly eliminating any threat to home or wellbeing. I mean, he added, his Wife's reckless behaviour had nearly killed him once.
Too ensure his personal safety, and for his wife's own good, Cuthbert had designated himself master of keys, meaning lock down was total. Gone was the shop, and Sally's pleasure in charity and her contentment in the act of goodwill. Shopping trips were seldom, with Cuthbert making good use of his lunch breaks to purchase the essentials, thus leaving Sally undisturbed in her daily grind. Sally's only relief became Sunday Service, a day when she could filter the bleach and

detergents out of her lungs with the good Lord's fresh tasting air. She missed her friends.

Sally wept, it had happened again. She sat at the kitchen table surrounded by ripped packets and spilled contents. This unexplained behaviour was making a difficult life even more troublesome and Sally was at a loss to explain to herself why on earth she had done it, and with every packet, tin and carton itemised there was no hiding the wanton destruction from Cuthbert's intense scrutiny. He'd caught her in the act, the first time the fit of destruction struck, and Sally swore he would have hit her if it was not for the risk of spilling blood. But instead of violence Cuthbert contrived a punishment that would at least be beneficial to the home, and Sally had scrubbed and scoured right through the night and had to forfeit her chocolate treats until the books once again tallied.

Cuthbert was due home at any moment and Sally trembled, if she had been permitted a key she would have run for her life, but escape was impossible, so she just waited for the inevitable turn of the lock and the entrance of constructed fury.

Spot on the ball of five thirty the clink of keys slammed positive into the lock; the door, and doom, creaked open. Sally's delicate frame shuddered and twitched with fright as Cuthbert entered the living room, he looked towards the wreck of his sobbing wife and guessed the rest. In times of dissatisfaction Cuthbert always raised and aimed his spectacles like the sights along the barrel of a gun. His body would erupt in spasms, and his eye lids would violently flutter.

"You've done it again, haven't you?" The words slithered out of his mouth, his tongue forked with displeasure.

"I don't know what's wrong with me," said Sally, choked with emotion. "I just go blank…"

"Nonsense!" Snapped Cuthbert. "Of course you know, this is defiance, plain and simple. The filth you chose as company has corrupted deep into your bones and lashes out of you, in a trail of destruction. You and your fellow conspirators won't be happy till you see me dead."

"It's only some biscuits and…"

"Only some biscuits! Oh it's only? Those two little words are the catalyst of every man made disaster, a flippant phrase to sweep aside duty and wallow in the arms of sloth. And remember this! One small germ is a host for a multitude, and just one sloppy oversight opens the flood gates to filth. Don't you ever, woman! It's only! Me again!"

Sally retrieved every packet, carton and jar from the waste bin. Cuthbert observed, pen and clipboard in hand, making notes on the afternoon's fit of devastation. "I'm considering chains," said Cuthbert, peering over his clipboard.
"Chains for what dear?" Puzzled Sally, rising from the floor.
"Why, for you of course!" Cuthbert replied matter of factly.
Sally paled, for this was indeed a new level. "Chain me! But why?"
"Why, to stop you destroying our home, not to mention our health. It's just a matter of time with such behaviour, for our safety to reach a critical level; and critical, Sally, is a situation I could never allow."
"You can't!" gasped Sally.
"Oh I think you'll find I can! But at the moment it is just an option. Now then, let's tally the damage."

Sally sat in darkness, letting the whispers of the night tease her mind with the hope of a place far away. The shadows formed the faces of her friends, they frowned and were dark with sorrow. The shadows beckoned her to join them, and how she wished she could. She shook her head and sobbed, and in despair the vision changed to anger snarled and turned to pitch. Of course there was nothing, she was alone and trapped through her own choosing, and that choosing was now, no choice at all.

OUT OF THE ASHES...

The cellar door opened to a world of ash, dust and slim remains. Four walls stood buckled and charred and opened to the heavens. The dew of morning had made a paste of soot that smothered and spoiled all that survived the flame. Fitz rose into ruin and heartbreak, a life time of love and labour gone in a flash. Little things that meant nothing to anyone, but everything to her, wrenched from her heart and trampled into pulp with the care and grace of a slayer. This was not the first time Fitz had faced ruin, but every time she faced it she hoped it would be the last, and each time, that hope was dashed.

She knew all too well the freedom that the common man craved was shackled with rules and *do nots*, and anything outside their perception of a free World was quickly stoned and run out of town. Nothing for them had changed, not since the days of the workhouse, only now the peasants were tossed peanuts and given a key. They all still sweated blood for their masters to keep their heads high, all the time believing it was done with their own free will.

She let the cellar door crash to the floor to spoil and buckle with all the rest, and stood in the mid of carnage. Sylvia followed and like Fitz, was soiled with the fire's destruction. Sylvia edged towards her lover and gently took her hand. They both stood in silence, giving thoughts time to digest and gently simmer to conclusions.

"Time is never the same," Fitz said, breaking the stone of silence. "It fools you into believing that where, and who you are, is forever the same. Years creep by and nothing changes, and you are lulled into believing that this is who you are, and who you will always be. Yet in a few fleeting moments a lifetime passes, and once again we are chasing and racing against it; hoping we have enough time left to start again."

Sylvia squeezed Fitz's hand. "We will start again," she reassured defiantly.

"Oh I know," said Fitz, taking Sylvia in her arms. "But before you start, you must finish, and this place, and me, are far from finished!"

The wind blows and dead memories take to the air and soar, forever lost. Sylvia clutched tight to her lover. "Where shall we go?"

Fitz smiled. "Oh I know where, believe me Syl, there's always somewhere, and there's a certain place and a certain someone that I've put off visiting for quite some time. Old Ma Mugs they call her, and they say she's the best Syl, the very best!"

"Ma Mugs?" puzzled Sylvia. "What an odd name!"

Fitz smiled, a smile that was hard and determined. "Indeed! But there is nothing odd about her power, Syl. She is a legend in the ways of lore and craft and one of nature's greatest students, and I intend to learn Syl; to learn enough from her to return and repay this town in kind."

Tom the Placard had doomed himself asleep, fatigue had nailed him to the spot, and he now woke, dew soaked, and back locked into the cold cast dawn. Every morsel of his body ached with the chill of saturation, from the freeze of the night that had bitten deep into his bones.

He looked like the death he yearned for as he unpicked himself from his bed of thorns. He slowly eased his joints into motion, and shuffled to view again the burnt remains of judgement. He peered hard through the half light of dawn and the fire's smouldering swansong. "Devils!" He gasped, catching sight of the charred beings that stood entwined in a seemingly gothic stone embrace. Old Tom had no doubt these creatures before him had risen from Hell and, fearless, he stormed towards the fiends of darkness with the pride and courage of all the holy saints.

"Come devils, come to the light and feel the fury of the Lord!" Tom howled his warning, his hand raised as a weapon of God.

Fitz broke from her lover's embrace and stepped, cat cunning, towards her accuser, her eyes seeming to hold the flame of the night's inferno, her appearance as dark as the bringer of death. She faced Tom, and even with God himself on his side he shuddered.

"Oh I'm worse than the devil!" Said Fitz, grabbing the old man by the collar. "You see! He's down there, and I'm up here, and while he plays little games to tempt and trick you I go straight for the throat! So you run back and tell those maggots that burrow deep into their peers arse-holes, that they've awoken far more than their miserable little gobs could ever chew!"

Tom tugged himself free of the Devil's clutch. "You'll not win!" Said Tom, backing away.

Fitz laughed. "Oh but I don't want to win, winning is the dream of losers. I, old man, am out to ruin! For ruin is the ultimate rout, far more pleasing than a silly little goal, don't you think?"

Tom backed away, keeping his eyes firmly fixed on the demonic apparition. "The Lord is my shepherd ..."

"Then run off little lamb," mocked Fitz, "run away before the big bad wolf blows you and your God down!"

"My God shall not be blown aside by you, or your false idol, for his judgement is soon to be total!"

"Oh you think so?" Fitz threw her arms high to the heavens, arched back and rose, snarling as a wolf. Old Tom screamed as the air around him turned solid as a fist and knocked him off his feet.

Tom looked to Fitzpatrick, eyes a bulge with disbelief. "You summon the aid of as many fowl fiends of hell as you can, demon. They shall not cower me, not while the Lord is my shepherd!"

Fitz growled down at the old man. "Go! Go on! Go back to the righteous and tell them hell is coming!" Old Tom struggled to his feet, pointing a warning finger. "Your days are numbered, beast. You hear me?"

"GO!" Snarled Fitz. Old Tom ran as fast as his old legs would carry him, gibbering gospel and looking skyward for back up. "The end! The end! He howled into the horizon, never looking back.

Sylvia walked towards Fitz. "That should keep him ranting for a decade or two. God, girl, you're a fierce and wonderful beast. Old Tom will be preaching your damnation from the roof tops!"

"It's perfect!" Said Fitz. "The town will wake this morning, squeamish, a ticking time- bomb of doubt, all their bravado crushed by self-preservation, and they'll be pointing fingers at anything that moves, and Old Tom ranting and raving of Devils and spectres should start a nice little tide of unease."

"He won't scare Morris, or that fat Councillor, Fitz, with tales of the dead."

"Oh I know, it's the living they worry about; and two in particular. For, if they meant to kill us Syl, well round one to us wouldn't you say? Come on, we have things to do and the rest can wait until we are ready."

THE TURN OF BLAME AND GAIN...

Slug was obvious and all too easy; a hopeless drunk with the memory span of a goldfish. He had no one, so it stood to reason no one would care.

Sergeant Hardy pounded on the hovel door. The wooden door creaked and paint peeled and crumbled like dandruff. "Open up! It's the police!" Said Sergeant Hardy, puffing out his chest with walrus pride. His sidekick and lackey, Constable Jeremy Wiggins; a bright, bug eyed little squirt with a shiny complexion and a haste and flap attitude that was always clumsy to please, buffed the grim plastered window with his once spotless sleeve and peered in with a stern dedication. "He's sleeping on the sofa Sarge," said Jeremy in his, as always, medal eager tone.

"Right, that's resisting arrest in my book," growled Sergeant Hardy. "Break down the door, Constable!"

Immediate was always Jeremy's response to an order. "Right away Sarge!" And without further ado he halted traffic, made his run, and launched himself with a reckless regard for safety, straight into Slug's front door. The weather-worn plywood partition exploded on impact, sending shards of splintered carpentry on to the street, and the lack of shoulder resistance sent Constable Wiggins tumbling head first into Slug's cluttered hallway.

Sergeant Hardy, eager to arrest, manoeuvred his bulk over the spread-eagled Constable. "Good shoulder, lad."

Constable Wiggins was ecstatic with the minor praise, as he always was. He shot up from his prone position, immediately producing a salute of such stern ferocity it near damn knocked his head off. "Yes Sir! Thank you Sir!"

The two officers entered the slum of Slug's life. The living quarters reeked of sour churned alcohol fermented into vomit, intertwined with the mash of well crusted socks and soiled week old underwear, tainted with the curse of stewed cabbage.

"Jesus!" Gasped Sergeant Hardy, desperately clipping his pugged piggy nose.

Constable Wiggins' peach complexion had turned milk bottle white as his nostrils involuntarily filtered and separated the offending odours. "Smelly bastard, sarge! We could have him for this!"

"Oh, don't worry Constable." Choked Sergeant Hardy. "We are going to have him for a lot more than being a dirty smelly bastard!"

Slug still remained wrecked in slumber, unaware of his uninvited guests. He laid beached on his buckled and stuffing bared sofa, trousers round his ankles in a failed attempt at undress, his face dribble glued to the well encrusted pillow, surrounded by an ocean of chip wrappers, empty flagons, cigarette ash and stale laundry.

Sergeant Hardy puffed his belly out to full importance, with Constable Wiggins Quickly following suit. The Sergeant produced note book and pen and prepared himself for his lifetime's greatest pleasure. "Terry, Arthur, Bowen. I arrest you on suspicion of arson. Anything you say will be ..."

"He's not responding, sarge!"

And indeed Slug spluttered and snored, totally unaware.

"Well then, Constable, we'll have to make him respond... truncheons!"

Constable Wiggins quickly unclipped and held his baton forward with a steely determination.

"Hit him Constable!"

"For the Queen and God Sarge!" Said Constable Wiggins, launching himself at Slug and whacking him full force on his bare boned shin.

Slug shot out of slumber with a blood curdling scream. "Ah! Me fucking leg!" He jumped up, the dribble glued pillow still attached to his cheek, he hopped, tumbled and crashed through flagons and waste. "What the fuck!?" Gasped Slug, noticing the officers for the first time.

"I tell you what's fucked!" Scoffed Sergeant Hardy. "You! Terry Arthur Bowen, I arrest you on suspicion of arson with intent to endanger life. That is, of course, if they are not already dead, which will then of course make you not just fucked, but also, well and truly!"

"I haven't done nothing!" Protested Slug, still wincing in pain and clutching his throbbing leg.

"That's for the courts to decide," sneered Constable Wiggins, still holding his baton above his head, threatening and advancing.

"Where exactly were you last night?" Said Sergeant Hardy, pen and note book at the ready.

"Umm," began Slug, scratching his head. In the Duck… Yeah, I'm always there."

Sergeant Hardy scribbled and looked up. "All night?"

"No, wait a second!" Said Slug, a dawning of realisation showing on his face. "I followed the crowd…Party, yeah, loads of people must have seen me…Wickle Cottage. Everyone was there, all angry and shouting about some young kid…"

"Right, stop there," commanded Sergeant Hardy, writing furiously. "In your words." Sergeant Hardy continued, peering through his notes. "Followed the crowd. Is that correct so far?"

"Yeah, yeah," Slug nodded in agreement.

"People were shouting about some missing child." The Sergeant again looked at Slug for verification, and again Slug nodded. "Got angry." Pressed on the Sergeant. "Decided to…

"No wait!" Protested Slug. "I didn't say I was angry, I…"

"Your words" Interrupted the Sergeant, with a point of his pen. "Got angry and decided to start a fire, to teach the child grabbing bastards a lesson."

"No! No!" Screamed Slug, trying to rise and wincing in pain. Quick as a flash the Constable threw himself between the Sergeant and the rising, soon to be convicted, felon. "Stand back Sergeant, the man's obviously a killer!" And for the second time the constable discharged his truncheon and caught Slug another stinger on his one remaining good shin. Slug howled in agony. "YOU FUCKING BASTARDS!" Next the Constable put Slug in a headlock. "Prisoner secure, sarge!"

"Splendid Constable, what a credit you are to the force."

Slug was yanked through his home, head locked and whimpering from the pain in his raw, buckled legs.

"Where's my fucking door?" Slug mumbled through the choke hold.

"Don't worry lad!" Sniggered Sergeant Hardy. "There'll be plenty of doors where you're going, and a damn sight more secure than that cardboard cutout."

Councillor Hardy was at his desk, doing sums, lovely money sums, his grin growing as the figures multiplied. Beautiful noughts were zipping across the page as his calculations were drawing to their tremendous climax. Without a word, and in keeping with the secret codes of greed, he slipped the piece of paper across the table. Morris Bevan picked up the piece of paper and his eyebrows gently rose in surprise. "Hmm, that much!" Purred the Vicar, looking to the Councillor's door.

"Don't worry about privacy, Vicar, no one enters here without my permission."

The Vicar looks over the figures again. "And you're sure the figures tally Boris?"

"Oh if there's one thing I'm sure of, Vicar, it's the counting of coin, I've had the knack since childhood and I never miss a penny."

The Vicar nodded his head. "Quite a considerable sum."

Boris clapped his hands with relish. "Oh, believe me, Vicar, land is gold and with the right friends in the right places that gold shouldn't be long in the digging!"

"Hmm, five plots in all…Surprising!"

"Think of it, Vicar, as us doing our bit for the community. Five lovely, spanking new homes to replace one crumbling old cottage, and…"

The Councillor was interrupted by a thump, thump on the office door. The Vicar slipped the precious piece of paper into his top pocket.

"Who is it?" Barked Boris.

"You're brother." Came the gruff reply.

"Ah, excellent," said Boris, instantly rising to unlock the door. Brinmore entered the room.

"Is it done?" Questioned Boris, before his portly brother had time to settle.

"Of course!" quipped the Sergeant. "Safely locked up in the station without a leg to stand on."

Boris laughed. "No good drunk anyhow. Yet another favour we've bestowed on our precious little town, eh Vicar!"

"Boris, your charity and goodwill astounds me!" Said the Vicar with a smile. "And has he confessed and signed his life away Sergeant?"

"Not yet Vicar, but he's already screaming for a pint. Another hour, and the promise of a bottle of scotch and he'd be willing to sign my fucking arse-hole! Anyway, never mind the trivia, have you worked out my cut?"

Boris sniggered. "Oh please do forgive my brother, Vicar, and his battering ram charm. All in good time, Brinmore. The flames have not yet been doused, and you are sweating for your pot."

"Oh but I know you all too well, brother! And I'm guessing them plots were bartered and sold before the match hit kindle, and remember this; while you two sit behind the scenes summoning and dishing out your devilry, my neck is out there on the line, in the thick of it, so you'd better make sure that pot is full to bursting, brother!"

Boris tapped the table top firmly with his pen. "You'll get your fair share, brother!"

"Well that will be a first!" Snarled Brinmore, leaning on the desk and in to his brother's face.

"Gentlemen! Gentlemen!" Said Morris, standing and placing a reassuring hand on both brothers' shoulders. "There's no need to fight; why, this should be the hour to rejoice! Not only have we rid the town of two very disruptive and dangerous souls, we've also made a tidy little profit for our troubles, well deserved I'd say, for ridding the Lord's garden of serpents!"

The two hog heads remained, piggy eyes locked, grunting, snout to snout.

"Come on boys?" Pleaded the Vicar "There's really no..." Boris and Brinmore roared with laughter, pulling ears and slapping cheeks in rough guy play. Councillor Hardy flopped back into his seat. "Don't mind us, Vicar," said Boris, hanky mopping his sweaty brow. "Me and darling Brother here have always been the same! He likes to have the lot and so do I, been like it since we were kids, character building our Father used to say."

"That's right!" Nodded Brinmore "Odd numbers, that was his trick."

"Odd numbers?" Puzzled Morris.

"Oh yes!" Chipped in Boris. "Three sausages."

"One bike." Added Brinmore.

Boris Grinned, "And seven pennies, and we'd fight like fuck to claim the odd, and Father would sit back and laugh his fucking bollocks off."

"Oh very interesting," sighed Morris. "And a fucking Partridge in a fucking pear tree…Now, Gentlemen, can we get back to business, and…"

For the second time a thump at the door disrupted the plotters. Boris thumped the desk in anger. "Who the fuck is it! I said, do not disturb!"

"Sorry sir." Came the muffled voice of Peter Bellroy the hapless clerk "But…"

"Oh come in boy!" Fumed Boris. "I can't talk to a fucking door!"

The timid frame of Peter Bellroy squeaked into the room. "I'm really sorry Councillor! But I don't know what to do?"

With the door open the three plotters become aware of the problem. "The Devil has risen!" Wailed a voice outside the chamber.

"I'll deal with this," said the Sergeant, stomping to the door and reaching for his truncheon.

"No, wait, wait, Sergeant. Its only old Tom" Sighed Morris, with his head in his hands.

"That's what I, came to tell you Councillor," said Peter still, clutching the door in case a speedy exit was needed. "He's been ranting for ages, demanding to see you and the Vicar… Mister Hardy, he's scaring the clients."

"He's having it!" Boomed the Sergeant, grabbing the door and pushing the clerk roughly out of the way.

"No! No, Sergeant!" Said Morris, standing and running to the door to calm the situation. "If you hit him, you'll only encourage him. Let's just see what he wants, and then we can simply send him on his way."

"The Vicar's right," scoffed Boris, spitting bits of chewed up boiled egg all over the desk. "The man can rant like that for days." He swallowed the last of his egg and mops away the crumbs. "Better to lend him an ear and then tell him to fuck off and, if you like, perhaps a little tap wouldn't hurt."

The words of wisdom seemed to do the trick with the baton happy Sergeant, and slowly he lowered his truncheon, walked back to the desk and plonked himself down. The Vicar instructed the clerk to permit the raving old man.

The unkempt, ragged form of Tom the Placard soon hurtled into the room, and he did look a sight. His jacket soil stained and torn, bits of bramble and twigs clinging to the dust of his mopped grey hair, his eyes raw red and bulging with shock, his lips all a bubble with a rabid white foam.

"Good God!" Gasped the Vicar. "What the Hell has happened to you!?"

Old Tom panted, his breath trying to clutch on to his words. "The Devil, that's what's happened…Water please, water!"

"Here!" Said the Vicar, dragging a chair to the desk. "For God's sake sit! And I'll get you a glass."

Old Tom took a seat and quivered like a jelly, spilling more water than he was drinking. "I saw it! The Devil himself, and oh, Vicar, I don't know how to tell you this, a demon was with the damned weaver of lies and…It has possessed your wife Mister Bevan!"

"So, the bitches are alive!" Scowled Boris.

"It would seem so," said the Vicar, standing, and pacing the room in thought.

Sergeant Hardy slammed his fist hard on the desk. "Not a problem! We arrest them for faking their own deaths and wasting police time."

Tom jumped out of his seat. "You fools! You can't just apprehend Old Nick, he won't have it! God is our only hope… Tell them Vicar!"

"Ah, now Tom?" Said Morris, placing a hand on the old man's shoulder. "These have been a very troubled couple of days, and emotions have been running high…"

"I KNOW WHAT I SAW!" Tom belted out the words, shaking with emotion. "Tell me Vicar, have you ever seen a man or woman, rise from flame and summon the wind to smite their enemies? It's the end, I tell you, the end! You need to gather the faithful, Vicar! And give them the shelter of the church before the fiend has time to cast his net!"

Sergeant Hardy stormed over and grabbed Tom by the scruff of the neck. "You'll see what I fucking well tell you to see, you shambling old wreck. Now get out! And let us be about our business and blabber your balderdash to someone who gives a fuck!"

For the second time in one day Old Tom stood, gobsmacked, his bottom lip all a quiver. "Vicar! Well, I never..."

Morris Bevan smiled at the old man. "Well as I said, Tom, nerves in the town are a bit frayed at the moment, what with missing children, and the fire of course. Perhaps a lay down and a good sleep?"

"I know what I saw Vicar! But I can also see that my warnings are falling on deaf ears. Well, I'll bid you... gentlemen... a good day, and God help us all!"

And without further ado Old Tom made for the door and resumed his ranting.

Morris walked to the door and peered into the hallway. Satisfied of privacy, he gently closed the door and walked back to join his fellow conspirators. "Well, gentlemen, it would seem our troublesome whores are still alive."

"Huh! Councillor Hardy dismissed the information with a wave of his hand. "So what, we never intended to kill them. No change as far as I can see, either way we're well rid."

Morris stroked his well-polished chin, milking his thoughts. "Hmm, quite so! But I must say, I was quite warming to the idea. I mean, death is the ultimate knot to bind loose ends, and that Fitzpatrick does not strike me as a shrinking violet, and as for my Wife, well let's just say she has far too much ambition for a Woman!"

"Well they better not show their faces round here!" Bellowed the Sergeant, caressing his baton. "I don't discriminate! I can crack a feminine skull as easily as a male one!"

"Exactly!" Roared Councillor Hardy, his bulge bursting out of his seat as he made for the drinks cabinet, grabbing a bottle of a good stiff Double Malt. He set three glasses on his desk and poured. "You are honoured, gentlemen, guests." He laughed. "For even with family, I usually serve the cheap shit. But the thought of such vast profits must have released a hidden generosity deep inside of me." He poured the golden spirit into three glasses. "Enjoy, gentlemen, and let's all drink to destruction and rebirth. Ha,ha ash to cash gentlemen, ash to cash. Cheers."

THOUGHTS OF SMOKE...

Misunderstandings are always brought about by others, who these people are nobody knows. They float like mist into conversation and, unnoticed, knit the patterns of mischief and hearsay. These creepy individuals slick over reason, their tight clutch of glib, choking common sense and turning communities of respectability into blood thirsty inquisitions. With their poison laid and the bait digested they mysteriously vanish, a whisper on the wind that leaves nothing, not a face, or even a name.

Hilary Thomson didn't believe a word, and was quick to point the fact out. "Oh I knew! I said all along his mother uses so much cotton wool I'm surprised the lad can breathe."
"The lad's a prisoner of mollycoddles," said Olive Brooks. "I mean, two hours, that's all he was gone for, and she was phoning the bloody police. And all for nothing."
Tina Sullivan wagged her finger. "And with the Vicar all along! I mean, how safe is that?"
Doreen Pew nodded determinedly in agreement. "Yes! And poor Sylvia Bevan. I mean... I always liked her!"
"Anyone can make a mistake," said Mabel Greenway, her face tugged in pity.
"And that no good Slug," spat Phillis White, instantly turning pity to hate. "Always been drunk and shameless. Ooh, hanging's too good for his like!"
"Burn him they want to!" Said Mary Robinson, lighting a fag. "And see how he bloody likes it."
"Ooh the poor Vicar!" Blubbered Janet Smith. "He said if his Wife had a good wash and repented he would have taken her back. Ooh, the mercy of faith! The poor Woman won't be able to wash now will she?" And Janet burst into tears, leaving her listeners, as always, baffled.
"Well, one good thing," said Tina Sullivan, providing a shoulder for the sobbing Janet Smith. "Norman Stubs and Gwyn are back together."

"Huh!" quipped Phillis White, grinding back to her usual snarl. "But for how bloody long, I mean, the drunk she shagged is now a murderer! Ooh, if I was Norman Stubs I'd pack her case and point her to the gutter, let her wallow in the filth she so desperately craves. That's of course if the rats will have her. The fat slut!"

"Well that Patricia Walton better not put her face in front of mine." Quipped Susan Jenkins. "She's the catalyst for all this."

"Blood on her hands" Growled Hillary Thomson.

"It's not right, her boy doesn't even play football! Squeaked Megan Small, aghast at the thought.

Doreen Pew tutted and shook her head. "All this trouble for a bloody mammie's boy!"

Elizabeth Procter poured tea from her divine teapot into her equally divine bone china cups. Margaret Mugford and Helen Nolan picked up the brew, pinkies pointed skyward, and sipped with perfection, not dribbling a drop. The sun was once again favourable, so the posh gossip was once again patio served. "Well ladies, in my wildest dreams I would never?" Began Elizabeth, dishing out the wedges of Victoria Sponge. "I mean, these sorts of things belong to slum dwellers and delinquents, mobs and arsonists, mind! In our Godly town, ooh the taint of it."

Helen Nolan gobbled down a gob full of sponge and bouldered into the conversation. "Ooh, the Vicar must be beside himself with shame, losing a wife twice in as many weeks, and to such unnatural behaviours."

"Oh I don't know!" Said Margaret Mugford. "He's probably relieved, I mean, who knows what other scandal she could bring to his name and station? I mean, she proved herself to be anything but what we thought she was. Makes you think what other tricks and blasphemies she had up her sleeve."

"Here, here," said Elizabeth, tapping the table with her spoon in approval. "Better death than shame, let God be her judge and leave the living for those who know how to conduct it, and who follow the script of the good book."

"Ooh, that's slightly harsh, Elizabeth!" Gasped Helen Nolan. "I mean, we all make mistakes."

Elizabeth slammed down her cup. "My dear, you can't mistake yourself into someone's bed, and you cannot mistake a woman for a man!"

"Quite so," said Margaret, quickly joining forces with the attacking party. "You cannot live as an example to the church and faith and display the horns and debauchery of the devil."

"Exactly!" Applauded Elizabeth. "It confuses the lower classes and, as we all can now see, that only leads to trouble."

"Ooh, I see!" Mused Helen. "I never looked at it that way."

Elizabeth quipped. "That's because, my dear, when you look at a picture you only ever see the frame."

OLD AS THE HILLS, MA MUGS...

"I'm old as the hills," and indeed, looking at the hag before her eyes, Sylvia would not doubt it. For, as witches were fabled to be, Ma Mugs was the full biscuit. Her head was as weathered as a rock face, tanned as leather and gnarled as old oak. Her body was sharp edged and spindled, her hands bleached and knotted through use, her fingers transparent, skin revealing talons of bone. She constantly cackled, bare gummed, and was, without a doubt, as scary as fuck. The cottage, too, was classic in form and location. Rooted deep in an old dark wood that weaved in defiance, a canopy to deny the sun. The Hag's lair was gingerbread thatched, its walls blistered and crawling with creepers that seemed desperate to choke and smother all life and stone. A view from a window was futile as the boil and dust of centuries blacked the world out and cloaked the shady deeds that brewed within.

The interior was proof that the forest did indeed provide, and timber was chiselled and hewed for every need. The log fire burned, licking hungry at the pot of cast iron that belched out its mysteries in a devil of colours that stung with danger and poison. The wooden rafters bulged with the dried herbs of glade gardens, that hung in promise, waiting for the stew of the pot and release of magic. *What else but a witch,* thought Sylvia, what else indeed!

For two days Sylvia and Fitz had tramped through fields and hills, scrumping in hunger and bedding in foliage, off the road and out of sight. Sylvia was worn through it all, but Fitz seemed to fuel on her anger and pushed a pace of fury, and by the time they reached their haven, Sylvia was spent and blistered. Sylvia's poor feet were being re-born in water as hot as she could stand it, while in her hand she cupped a brew that tasted and smelled of earth and moss, disgusting, but good, she was assured. And as the brew steamed through her, she had to admit that it seemed to be doing the trick.

Ma Mugs rocked in her chair, puffing rings of thought from an old clay pipe, caressing purrs from her charcoal black cat, her deep stained eyes observing every move, as Fitz and Sylvia gorged on a piping hot stew, their first decent meal in days. Sylvia had longed for these comforts, a log fire and hearty meal, in the days trekking the wilds, but now she had them, they brought little comfort. Even Fitz seemed to be tense in the old hag's company, and her lover seldom wavered.

Ma Mugs bellowed a huge puff of smoke that choked the air and pointed her pipe at her two uninvited guests. "Oh yes! Old as the hills...But tell me my dears, how can that be? How can a soul match granite in time?"

Sylvia looked nervously at Fitz as the question pierced, after all this was her territory. She, like the Crone, was a daughter of the night. Fitz placed down her bowl and, for a few moments, juggled the question. "Wisdom!" Said Fitz. "Wisdom passed and left by others, for knowledge passed shall be eternal."

"Huh," croaked the Hag. "Half an answer from half a witch. It is not passed, it belongs. For they who wield it are part of me, all our sisters gone before dwell and share my soul. Tell me, Fitzpatrick of the Emerald Isle, what do you share, besides a couple of cheap tricks? The turn of a card or the line of a palm, all for some grubby pennies off them who will mock and scold you, and damn you to hell!"

Fitz took a deep breath. "That's why I'm here, to learn. That is if you think I am worthy of teaching."

Ma mugs laughed, shooed off the cat and crippled to the fire to poke its flame. "Well," said the Crone, turning to face Fitz. "You don't give a very good impression on your first day at school, appearing here, with this pretty little filly of the Lord. Oh yes, I can see the scripture stamped through her bone! Tell me, Fitz, what do you intend to do with it!"

Sylvia shot up from her chair. "Fitz! I don't like this, not one little bit...And if you don't mind, I'd rather leave!"

"Oh I don't mind at all!" Snapped Ma Mugs.

"She too has suffered by the hands of the church," pleaded Fitz. " She too seeks wisdom, and is a worthy student."

"Huh!" Spat Ma Mugs. "What do you know of the cross and its spite, its vengeance? What do you know of its murder and hate, and its eternal crusade of persuasion and persecution?"

Sylvia pointed a finger towards the old woman. "I married the church, and lay with its lies and denials for most of my life, I have drunk and eaten of its poison, and I do not have to justify my suffering to an old twisted hag!"

"Syl!" Gasped Fitz. "I think that's enough."

Ma Mugs just sat back and puffed, there was no roll of thunder, no blast of lightning, no retort to the insult, no casting of spells or curses, just a roar of laughter. "There's a spare room, top of stairs, you can use that...I take it you lie down together?"

"That will be fine," said Fitz, taking Sylvia's hand and heading for the stairs. "My, she certainly rattled your cage!"

"Well if she feigns to be full of wisdom, you would have thought she'd be wise enough to learn some manners!" Huffed Sylvia.

The spare room was damp, cluttered and adorned with the hues of moss in varied stages of growth. Sylvia looked to the well soiled and crusted bed. "Oh God, Fitz! I bet that bed's crawling! Ooh, and with who knows what?"

"Well," said Fitz with a shrug. "It beats a hedge!" And, cautiously, they both crawled in.

Sylvia woke into extraordinary comfort, her body that had shivered into the horrors of the bed clothes, now nestled under a mountain of snow white down, warm but light as a cloud. Beneath her, the mattress cuddled her body, soaking her up into the caress of a giant marshmallow. She lifted her head in wonder, the pillow that supported her instantly puffing back to full life. "My God!" She gasped, as the scent of the room filled her senses. Wild flowers burst from their urns in a display only rivalled by nature, the room was spring coloured and as bright as joy. The windows slightly ajar, permitting a gentle breeze to flutter the fine laced curtains that danced in the dawn of sunlight.

Sylvia shook Fitz to rouse her from slumber, too shocked to utter a word. Fitz slowly yawned back to life, and sat up. She rubbed her eyes back to life and her jaw dropped.

"Oh fuck! Oh no, no, no! I should have known..." She gasped, and buried her head in her hands.

The knock on the door was gentle, as was the voice; "Breakfast awaits." Both rose from the luxury of their bed, Fitz mumbling and shaking her head in frustration. What was wrong, Sylvia could only guess, as Fitz grumbled damnations and made for the door.

The whole cottage, it would seem, had gone through an astounding transformation, either that or the two had been spirited away in the dead of the night. Gone was the cobwebbed, smoke choked room, gone was the belching cauldron and its fumes of sulphur, like the bedroom, decay and neglect had turned to a bursting array of health and beauty entwined in the art and fragrance of nature.

They both sat expectant at the table, minding their manners in the way of scolded children.

"Won't be a sec ladies...Please make yourselves at home." Came a voice from the kitchen. A voice that did not wheeze or croak, or grate the nerves. No, this voice spoke in a melody, crisp and lucid. And the look of the Lady who entered the room was the next startling surprise of the day, more headmistress than witch. She walked straight backed holding firm the tray that held the cosied tea pot and racked toast. Robust and toned fit, with a stern but honest face, she wore the silver of her hair bundled tight at the nape.

She laid down the tray and sat. "Shall I pour, ladies?"

Sylvia smiled. "Oh, please. I must say it all looks...Very nice."

The tea was poured and an awkward silence settled. Fitz, Sylvia noticed, was chewing thoughts through her bottom lip, gnawing away till she picked her moment.

"You must think me a fool?" Said Fitz, finally releasing her lip and taking the plunge.

The mysterious host placed down her cup and smiled, looking Fitz steady in the eye. "I'm afraid, my dear, I do! You trusted to sight over wisdom, you put myth before knowledge and plunged right into a fairytale of goblins and old crones, and the dreadful lair of Old Ma Mugs…Of your friend I would expect it. But you, my dear, were blinded by your vision and really should have known better! Ooh, and by the way, the name's Martel, far more civil, don't you think, than old and scary Ma Mugs? Though I must say she does have her uses."

Fitz sighed deep. "Look! I was tired and angry, when I arrived. I know it's a lame excuse, but what I heard…"

"What you heard, dear," said Martel, topping up the tea, "was a child's bedtime story, a boogie creation weaved by men for their own ends. Perhaps an image comical, to some…But, as we both know, an image conjured with deadly consequences! Ah, what was it Cromwell said? Warts and all! A fine declaration indeed, for men. For men have always had the liberty to be what they will, for good or ill. But for us, the fairer of the sexes, why, we must always hide something, lest we are found out and accused! Oh yes my dears, it is a man's world and he knows just how to ruin it."

"They ruined us!" Fitz growled, her fire returning. "Tried to burn us alive…"

"And you need vengeance!"

"Yes!" Said Fitz, her fist clenching hard with the thought. "But I need to be more…To get it!"

Martel smiled. "Magic, my dear, is being torn by its roots from the earth, where as we harvest and tend what the Mother gives us, man in his eternal hunger, loots and lays waste to what he needs, and turns the magic to science, with no thought to the Mother and her gifts of creation. And I'm afraid, my dear, you are getting pulled along with all the rest in the wizardry of electricity and the motion of automaton. In short, my dear, you've gone soft."

Martel cleared the table, with offers of help refused. Fitz and Sylvia sat sullen, Fitz for obvious reasons and Sylvia silent, probably to show her lover support.

Martel left the room, then returned buttoning her coat. "I must pop out for a while, but you're welcome to stay, for as long as needs be. I shan't be gone long and don't worry, I'll leave the broom, there's a perfectly good bus service in the area." Martel laughed, Fitz forced a smile that fooled no one, and Martel made for the door.

"Ooh," said Martel, turning as she was about to leave. "If you want to make a start on your re-bonding with nature, then the garden could do with a bit of a turning, a bit of encouragement to carrots and the like. If you feel like it, of course, you'll find tools and suitable attire in the garden shed. See you later."

A bit of graft did indeed channel frustrations, Sylvia had a thousand questions on her mind concerning the strange events of their first evening with the even stranger Martel. But for now, she deemed it wiser just to let sleeping dogs lie. Fitz and Sylvia ploughed into the task of digging and weeding till the fall of evening. Finally spent, they hosed off the grime of the day's graft. "We don't have to stay, Fitz. We are free, we can go anywhere, and start again!"

Fitz shook her head. "And just what will start again, Syl? The whispers, the pointing fingers of blame and shame; the shun of another community for just being in love and being who we are. Do you really want to go through that again and again? For wherever we go there will always be a Councillor Hardy and a Morris bloody Bevan." Fitz threw down the hose. "No, I have run enough, I refuse to be bullied out of another narrow minded town."

Sylvia embraced tenderly her lover. "If you say so. Come on, let's have a cuppa."

"Education is not a weapon my dear." Martel finished pouring the tea, and took her seat at the table. "I mean, the hunger for knowledge should not be driven by the goal of knocking someone's head off!"

Sylvia could already see problems, even at this early stage of the relationship. Fitz's eagerness to press Martel for her secrets drove her to pounce on Martel as soon as she entered the room. Sylvia looked at Fitz as she bit down hard on the scolding, and Sylvia could feel her struggle for control. "Then tell me, just what does the Councillor, the Constable, the Vicar, Priest; our so called betters do with their education and power, if not wield them as a weapon to gain victory for their own ends? For I have known many but yet have not met one that doesn't play the game to achieve his own goals, regardless of the lowly vanquished he tramples beneath him."

Martel sipped her tea, seemingly unmoved by the tirade. "Then they answer to their own Gods!"

Fitz punched the table. "But I don't want the fuckers to pay when they're dead! They deserve to pay now!"

Sylvia placed a hand to stay her lover as she started to rise. "Fitz! We came to Martel, I think she deserves courtesy."

Fitz sat back down. "I'm sorry, it's just…"

"Oh I understand," said Martel. "It's just the fact, that you have had enough of the injustice of this World."

"YES!" Snapped Fitz.

"And you think that you are alone with these thoughts? And say I did have the knowledge to put destruction at your fingertips? A spell or a curse to vanquish all enemies, so that no one could slight or harm you again? Could I be sure that you wouldn't use such knowledge for your own personal power and gain, hmm?" Martel looked questioningly at Fitz.

"But…That is not my way!" Fitz protested.

"Okay, but what about the other poor down-trodden souls? Should they too, have this deathly power to wield their revenge? Are we to start a war between oppressed and oppressor, and just what shall the end result be, eh? Probably all that will be achieved is the oppressed will become the oppressors."

Fitz sprang out of her chair and the chair tumbled. "I thought, as kindred spirits of the Mother we would be on the same page; that you like me, would be tired of the injustice we go through, just because we are judged weaker, stranger or just disobedient to their will."

Martel just shook her head and sighed. "My dear child, we are indeed on the same page; and if I did not recognise a kindred spirit...Believe me, you would not be sitting at my table. And I am indeed prepared to help a fellow sister who is in keeping with the mother. The problem lies in just what you expect that help to be!"

Fitz calmed. "I need knowledge, for I have tasted your wisdom, but I need so much more!"

"And that I can offer my dear. But whether you are wise enough to take that wisdom, I'm afraid only time will tell."

Fitz lay awake long after Sylvia slept, her thoughts consumed by the faces of all the foes who had hounded and beat her, all along the journey of her life. As a child the hatred had cowed and scared her, leaving her bare to the wounds of sorrow. But the skin of a wound toughens, shielding the victim against further blows. Fitz's self-pity had been a long time swallowed, and no more would she crumble, lay down and play dead. The thoughts stirred a fever, she needed to feel the chill and wonder of the night. She walked to the window, threw open the shutters wide, and felt the ice glory of the wind sharpening her resolve, and shocking her mind back to the fight. She looked to the heavens, the moon swung at its crescent, and she swore on the glow of its beauty, by the time it hung full she would fill its night with blood.

FOR THEIR SINS...

Tom the Placard stood naked before his mirror. The wrinkled and tarnished old man glared back. "This is how I came into the world, this is what the good Lord gave me and it is how I shall leave it. Let them see me, and see then if they can ignore the naked truth!"

Tom's cross was for special occasions and Tom believed the moment was special indeed. Never in his lifetime had he been so convinced of the end. Signs and omens were bursting to life at an alarming rate and Tom believed it was just a matter of time before the riders of God's judgement appeared over the horizon, racing across the world and drawing its final curtain. "I shall die for their sins." He pledged to his image. "I shall walk the world as bare as the Lord made me, void of man's sinful trappings, at peace with my maker, ready to greet his judgement and happy to leave this life for a far better place."

Old Tom picked up his cross and made for the door. His hand froze on the latch as he sucked and held his breath and prepared himself to plunge naked into the town. Tom knew the sight of his aged and worn body was sure to get attention but, he reasoned, wasn't attention his aim in life, his duty to the Lord to prepare his subjects for the great reckoning? Tom turned the latch, placed the cross on his shoulder, and stepped bare as a new-born into the day.

It was a warm and glorious day and the square was a bustle of weekend shoppers and loungers, all enjoying the sunshine and company. The little lad was enjoying his ice cold dollop of ice cream as Old Tom approached. His tongue froze on the treat at the sight of the naked old man. The lad yanked hard on his mother's sleeve to get her attention. "Mummy, mummy." He hollered. "Is that Jesus? I can see his bum!"

"My God!" Gasped his mother. "Have you no shame? You dirty old man!"

"For your sin's madam!" Tom replied, regardless of shame or modesty. "For your sins, for all your sins!"

If it was indeed attention Tom was seeking, then the stunt proved to be a startling success. The sight of the crinkled pensioner, private parts free and swinging, drew eyes like magnets, and in no time he was the town's main focus. Folk laughed or jeered or hurled abuse and growled with insults. But Tom just marched on regardless dragging his cross through the square. "For your sins." Tom repeated over and over, as individuals cluttered together, quickly forming yet another mob that yelled, laughed and raised fists in hot pursuit.

Tom marched out of town with the mob hot on his tail, passed the burnt remains of Wickle Cottage, through the meadow and to the foot of Bell's Barrow hill. There he laid down his cross, spread his arms to the heavens and began his sermon, regardless of the hecklers. "For your sins I stand naked before you and ready for judgement. But are you ready for your judgement?"

"I'll bloody judge you!" Bellowed a voice from the crowed. "I judge you to be off your fucking rocker, you crazy old git!" And the crowd roared with laughter.

Tom again raised his arms to beckon the jeers to silence, and waited for the laughter to abate. "I know what I saw! Devils rising from the ashes, and I warn you all! Hell knows what's coming and it will not sit idle. The devil will barter for every soul he can, in his final push of defiance."

A young, muscle bound lad snorting testosterone, shoved to the front of the throng. "Someone should give you the bloody push you frothing geriatric. Get home and get yourself decent before I come up there and beat some decency into that sagging arse of yours!"

"I've faced Hell itself." Bellowed Tom. "And I ain't cowering before any mortal. God protected me then, and I've no doubt he will again. Can't you see a telling when it slaps you in the face? Can you not see that I have been chosen to pull your souls from the abyss of no return? I am your only voice and your only choice; believe in me and the good Lord will lead you to salvation!"

"Move aside, move aside!" Said Sergeant Hardy, his gut like a wrecking ball splitting the crowd, his truncheon raised and swinging with threat, and as always his trusty lap dog, Constable Wiggins, hot on his tail, puffed up with pomp and eager as always to impress his master and earn another pat and bone. "What in God's name are you up to you fucking old fool?" Roared Sergeant Hardy.

"Exactly!" Snapped Tom, pointing at the Sergeant. "In God's name is all that I do! I warned you Sergeant and your brother! And you shall not still the Lord, and you shall not still me!"

"Oh, you think so?" Said the Sergeant, unbuttoning his tunic and handing it to the Constable. The Sergeant carefully heaved himself to the foot of the hill, panting hard from the meagre elevation. "I'm the…Huh…Bloody…Huh…Law around…Huh…Here…And I arrest you for gross indecency…Huh…And inciting riots"

Old Tom stood his ground as the Sergeant loomed before him, red faced and sweating gallons. "No man is above the law of the Lord! Madness has burrowed deep into our community and the devil rides the mob, inciting abduction, arson, there are murderers and demons amongst us, we are ripe for damnation!"

"Why you meddling old bastard!" Snarled Sergeant Hardy. "I'll give you murder!" And with that the Sergeant raised and slammed down his baton on the hapless old man's head, instantly releasing a deluge of the old man's sacred claret that coursed down Toms aged skin, forming channels in the wrinkled folds. The crowd in unison gasped in horror as the old man slumped to the ground, but the Sergeant was far from finished, his malice pumping his frenzy in an attack of savage blindness. Down again came the truncheon, and again, the dull thud of bone and wood crunching home its message of pain.

A hand grabbed the Sergeant's arm, defying his next delivery, Morris Bevan then wrapped an arm around the

Sergeant's throat and yanked hard to drag the hunter off its helpless prey.

"What in God's name?" Screamed the Vicar. "Have you lost your mind?"

The Sergeant exhaled deep, calming his beast and preparing for stand down, his face blotched red through fury, his cheeks bulged and ballooning for breath.

"He...He." The Sergeant rested hands to knees, clutching hard for breath. "Resisted arrest..."

"Well you're not going to be able to arrest him if he's fucking dead." The Vicar whispered in the Sergeant's ear. "Now for damage limitation, why don't you fuck off back to the station and leave this great dollop of shit you've dumped for me to take care of... Before we become engulfed by the mess your bowels?"

"I'll phone an ambulance," said the Sergeant, heading down the hill.

"The man's a fucking liability!" Fumed Morris into the face of Councillor Hardy.

"I'll have a word with him," said the Councillor, who seemed more concerned with quaffing the Vicars best claret and smashing his face full of cheese and crackers.

"Have a word?" Gasped Morris. "A fucking straight jacket would be more suitable, the man's a homicidal lunatic!"

"How we was brought up, see!" Said Boris, wiping crumbs of his jacket. "Farther always taught us; if in doubt lash out!"

"Yes, yes I know odd numbers and all the rest of it. I must say, your father must have been a delightful individual."

"He was firm..."

"Oh, don't tell me, but fair!"

"God no! He was firm and a right bastard to boot, but it didn't do us any harm. I mean just look at us; both pillars of the community, top of our game. You don't get anywhere by being fair, Vicar, you of all people should know that!"

"And also, Boris, you don't get anywhere being fairly fucked! People are not as stupid as they may seem. Well, not all, and attention gathers rumour and those idiots who can't think for themselves will eagerly rally round the thoughts of them that can, and the last thing we need is questions."

"Questions!" quipped Boris. "What questions? You underestimate apathy my dear friend, people don't meddle in the affairs of elected officials, we simply complicate the process making it too taxing for them to bother! Why, have you ever seen official documentation from the civic centre? Uh! Dear Sir or Madam is about as lucid as it gets, and if there are any smart Alec's out there, we make damn sure our backs are covered in small print!"

"And what about the church, eh Boris? They too are pretty well covered in small print, and the last thing we need is their eyes focused on this parish. I mean, we can already boast of two near riots, an old man nearly beaten to death by an officer of supposed law, not to mention, of course, two suspicious deaths which now seem most unlikely, unless of course you believe old Tom's version of devils rising from flame. And then, of course, the burning of parish property, and the subsequent redevelopment of said grounds, and I can assure you of this; The church regards its income as being most sacred, and they might not have noticed the loss of revenue from Wickle Cottage yet, but any focus upon us now could soon draw eyes to ledgers."

"Huh!" Boris shook with laughter. "You don't think we passed the rental on! My dear fellow, that income has been filling the council coffers for years! Why, the only reason you know about it is because of vested interest. Oh, my dear Vicar, you worry too much! I've been an accomplished bastard for as long as I can remember, and I can assure you of this I am bloody good at it!"

"All right Boris, I know the depth of your depravity is without limits. But we still don't know the fates of my darling wife and that whore she's bonded with, they could return and stoke trouble. As a matter of fact, knowing my wife, I quite expect it. So please, get your damned bloodthirsty brother in line!"

Boris slugged back yet another claret, then wiped his chops. "I'll have a word!" He belched and topped up his glass.

Old Tom woke to the clatter of church bells ringing in his ears, and a blaze of pure heavenly white. The air tasted new born and fresh as spring. "Ah!" Croaked Tom. "At last!" A hand that could only belong to an angel gently moped his brow.

"Come on!" Snapped a voice, breaking Tom's paradise. "Bloody sit up, I haven't got all day to fuss over you, I've other patients to see too."

Tom looked up and noticed the bull bodied nurse that towered above him. She next roughly yanked up his sleeve, squeezed his wrist and timed his pulse.

"Is this heaven?" Mumbled Tom.

"Blimey!" Cackled the nurse. "I've heard the General called a lot of things, but heaven ain't one of them. Now sit up, I've got a bandage to change, and we best be getting you to the toilet, before you have an accident, and if that happens you'll be seeing Heaven sooner than you think!"

"Oh no, no." Old Tom sobbed. "I can't stick it a moment longer! When Lord? When will you claim us?"

"Oh and that's another thing?" Said the nurse, pulling a fresh bandage from her trolley; "There's a lot of people here closer to God than they'd like to be! So if you could please refrain from singing the Old Rugged Cross in your sleep, it would be much appreciated. Or of course I could always wheel you into the store cupboard where you can sing your dirge till you're blue in the face."

"Oh shut up!" Groaned Tom, falling back into slumber.

HAPPY NEVER AFTER...

Gwyn didn't know where the slap came from, but Norman did. It came from the banter that had resurfaced at the Roast Duck Inn ever since the time of Slug's arrest. *The Bonnie and Clyde of Sickle* was the line that tickled ribs, and no prizes for guessing who was Bonnie and who was Clyde.

Her husband, Gwyn knew, had been a lot of things in his time, but wife beater was never one of them. Gwyn could still feel the ice sharp twinge on her cheek, hours after the delivered strike. Norman, of course, had blamed her for ruining his trouble free life, and stirring the beast of buried violence, that was part of the make-up of every hot blooded male. The sobs Gwyn sang poured straight from the heart, and wailed of misery, shock and a soul in desolation. Norman, of course, could not stand the sight of a woman in tears, so he quickly left for the pub, for another round of booze, biffs and banter.

Sandra put it to her Mother that it was bound to happen, and more to the point, what the bloody hell did she expect?! Get over it, she spat; dropped off her washing, borrowed a tenner and made for the door.

Dave was a tad more sympathetic, in Dave's strange way. "He should not have done it!" He said, fingers fidgeting in his empty pockets. However, he added, "Dad has got a lot on his plate, and it's different for men, take me," he continued, "as broke as a peasant's back, but too proud to admit it." Gwyn offered a fiver, but was quickly informed it would not cover the bus fare. She was then, just as quickly, reminded of her grand kids and promptly emptied her purse.

And so here she sat, as lonely as no one, nothing to hold on to except her shattered nerves; no hope, no reason, devoid of purpose, just an old woman expecting nothing more than death.

She thought about her friends; dead or missing, she suspected the latter as no bodies had been found, and she was sure she would feel something, if they were indeed dead.

The thought of them was about the only company she had. Oh how she missed conversation, especially the conversation that came with a smile, a joke and a caring word. Gwyn smiled at the memories, the carefree days spent stacking shelves, making a brew, gossiping with all sorts about all sorts of things. But the smiles of yesterday would never last, a grim shadow would come and swallow the cherished past, and Gwyn's mind would be engulfed by the image of a soiled splattered toilet and the decayed gob thrusting its tongue and licking her face. She could still hear now, the pants and grunts and the punter's laughter, clapping and goading as her fat arse played the rhythm of fornication on the soiled bog door.

"I'm disgusting, disgusting!" She screamed at the ever present nightmare. "The kids are right! Of course I deserve it, that and a lot more, I'm just a stupid, dirty, old woman," and with tears again in her eyes, Gwyn picked up her daughter's washing, made for the kitchen and again sweated and grafted for her sins.

Sleep was a prize welcomed, but it seldom arrived. Every night was a wrestle for the spot that would tempt sleep and still the pain, but the more she fought for the treasured release the more it denied her. Each night, it now seemed, the chance of sleep was lost in a heap of tangled sheets and boiling frustration. She was at war, she had long ago concluded, and a steady march of madness was routing her sanity, the heavy Jack Boots of bedlam crushing under foot all reason, leaving just a pulp of humanity.

Gwyn heard the front door open, as she did every night, never mind the hour. Norman was now drinking more than he breathed, but she dare not question it. After all, just how many times can you take the blame? Within seconds of entry, the first crash vibrated through the home, followed by the all too familiar yells and curses. Next the puffs and pants as his jacket and boots defied him and stayed lodged on back and foot. But he'd get there in the end, after a couple more grunts and fucks. Thump, thump, four pawed for balance, her husband was finally on his ascent of the stairs. The next scene could go one of two ways, either Norman would grumble obscenities outside her door and make for the spare room, which was hardly spare any longer, or if he had the legs he could open her door and insult her to her face.

Gwyn watched the door handle drop and knew then which option her husband had chosen. Norman slurred into Gwyn's room in a smog of belched liquor, bone fermented to jelly, he staggered and reeled towards her, pointing a mean finger. "You...you... fucking ruined me!" He said, the effort of speech slumping him to the wall.

Gwyn threw back the bed sheets and rose. "Oh Norm, can't we just put it behind us and start..."

"And don't bloody...make... big thing, what happened today..."

"It's, forgotten love" Gwyn pleaded, sensing hope and reaching out for her man. "Can't we just start again? We were happy once."

"FU...Hic...Fucking happy? You've made...Hic...A bloody fool...That's me...Bloody laughing stock!"

Gwyn, in desperation, grabs Norman's arm. "Oh please love! We can't go on like this, it's not healthy."

"HEALTHY!?" Norman straightened up and took a huge gulp of a sobering breath. "I'll tell you what's not fucking healthy...Hic...Shagging in a grotty old bog with an even grottier fucking man, knickers round your fucking ankles, your arse splashing in piss...With that fucking degenerate slobbering all over you...God knows what you picked up!"

"STOP IT NORM...For God's sake...Just stop it!"

"Not a problem," said Norman, yanking his wife's hand off his arm, then opening the door and leaving the room without another word.

Gwyn's whole body tensed in frustration. She tore at her hair and screamed. "YOU WANTED ME BACK...YOU! And what for? What bloody for?"

Gwyn howled and crashed to the bed, the march of insanity turning to a stampede, as all logic and hope crushed in despair. She cried and wailed lonely into the night until, finally, exhaustion, at last, gave way to the sleep she so desired.

THE NON CONFORMISTS...

Martel had said that Sylvia had the mind and heart for nature, without doubt a herbalist in the making, which suited Sylvia just fine; better to have the peace of the garden to tend and sooth the soul, than be stuck in between the riot of two stubborn minds. Fitz was not a good student, nor was Martel the perfect tutor, but the difference being that Martel did not have to be anything, it was Fitz who had come knocking, seeking Martel's favour and Martel was not about to forget the fact. Martel was mockingly cutting with a wit as dry as tinder, and any scolding, which was frequent, was served in acid. Sylvia had lost count of the amount of times she'd heard the thunder rumble and seen the storm brewing in Fitz's eyes, the flush of red showing the strain of control as Fitz desperately applied the brakes to halt her charging temper. No, the garden was definitely the place to be, amid the tranquillity of bloom, nothing stirring but the whisper of a breeze.

Sylvia was pruning rose bushes when chaos came home, Fitz crashed through the garden gate, steam roaring through her nostrils, her mood steamed with frustration, the amber of her eyes seeking only murder and seeing nothing else. Sylvia would not approach, she had learnt her lover well, and knew she only simmered in solitude. Next through the gate was Martel, looking as well kept as ever with not a breath out of place. Martel, as always, held herself without a hint of emotion, and it was plain to see, whatever had bothered Fitz had not troubled Martel in the slightest. Martel gently strolled towards Sylvia, inspecting her as she advanced.

"My!" Martel said with a smile. "The garden has never looked finer! You are doing an absolutely splendid job...you are, my dear, a credit to nature."

"Thank you," said Sylvia, returning the smile. "Ah, she seems a bit upset again...is everything all right?"

"Right! Oh my dear, nothing is ever right, we just make the best of whatever's wrong. And, as for upset, well she's bound to be that! At the moment I am turning her world upside down, and what she thought was a long time finished, she now knows, has barely begun."

"I know she has a temper, but she has a good and kind heart."

"I don't doubt it for a second my dear. But it is not her heart that is causing the problem; that honour, my dear, goes to her head. It is so clouded with vengeance it is obscuring thought, and that my dear is a bit of a handicap when you are seeking knowledge."

"She's had enough!" Sylvia sighed. "Enough of being hounded out just for being who she is."

Martel laughed. "Oh my dear, if she wants popularity she's picked the wrong vocation! Why, it wasn't that long ago the only popularity we enjoyed was when we were being dunked on a stool, or burnt at the stake! Tell me, why do you think a so called witch is despised so much?"

Sylvia pondered the question. "Fear, fear of the unknown!"

"Oh it's fear all right! Man's fear, a fear of non-conformity; fear of the woman who shuns his law and thinks for herself, and it's as relevant today as it always has been, just without the stake and the ducking pond."

"I see!" Said Sylvia. "We can't win."

"Oh we never set out to win, a tie would suit us just fine, equality requires no triumph. But even equality poses a threat, for equality frees the slave...And then, my dear, who's left to do the ironing, the house work and bend to their desires? I mean, the two of you together have even denied them their lust, oh the bloodiest of slaps, how could you choose a woman over a hot blooded male? You two really are the Queens of pariahs! Now, enough speculation, you must be ravenous after all this graft!"

Fitz hated school, and it was fair to say that school hated Fitz. A conventional education was never going to suit someone who was anything but conventional. The village where she grew up was a pauper's spread; a coastal community with nothing to boast about but hard graft, dirt and rags. The wealthy of her community were those who ate twice daily, and Fitz's family, some days, did not eat at all. So those in the village who aspired to the dizzy heights of a daily roast, would mock the urchins that begged crusts below them, and indeed mocked she was. She was mocked for hunger and her skin that clung to bone. She was mocked for her clothes that looked like they'd been handed down more times than a baby's rattle. She was a constant target for bullies and potatoes, and a prime example for the classes, shame and the teacher's cane. So, early in life, fate made her choices and pushed her to the edge, and on the edge was where she made her home. Her school became the great university of nature, and her Deans, the travellers who held no sway to society and its discriminations. And so with moonlight to guide her and music to move the soul, her learning began, all a far cry from blackboards, canes, and the Master's oppression.

Fitz sat on the edge of the bed, thankfully alone. She knew it was her fault and that she should be grateful, but she hated slapped wrists and, God knows, her wrists had had their fair amount of slaps in the weeks she'd been here. Martel struck without emotion, and was impossible to fathom. She digested Fitz's rage, and just looked on bemused as a mother would its child, and of course that made matters far worse. But most troubling was the nagging thought that she was actually learning very little, if learning at all. It seemed to Fitz that she was back in the hated class room, being told once again how worthless she was.

She snapped out of it, pulled on her dress and took a deep breath, determined to reign in her mood and be a good girl, and not ruin another supper. She looked in the mirror, ruffled her hair and composed herself. "I will be good!" She promised her reflection.

Supper, like everything else in Martel's lair, was flawless, perfectly balanced, wholesome and nutritious, with not a vitamin or calorie overlooked. Fitz entered the room, sat as straight as good manners, without a hunch or posture of indifference. Sylvia, as always, beamed when she saw her, reached over and gently kissed her cheek, whispering sweet nothings. Martel was loading the table with her delectable fare and, as always, an art work of baking and roasting was laid to feast the eyes. Fitz thought to herself, *If I could pick up some cooking tips it would not make the visit totally pointless.* Martel sat and poured the wine, and with the glasses topped, the food was passed, with nods of gratitude, followed by the usual silence, which would never last.

"The trouble is..." said Martel, breaking the silence, "most Gypsy magic is a jumble of curses and constructed fortunes, wielded for personal gain and spite, and the spirit guidance you seek and need does not look favourably on magic for personal gain and malice."

Fitz laid down her fork and pondered the statement, determined to maintain control. This topic had been bitterly contested these past few weeks, with Fitz standing the ground and corner of the only folk who had showed her kindness and belonging. But this time Fitz was determined to stay composed and debate with reason, and stop this endless cycle. "They also gather herbs of healing, and apply the lore to any that need it."

"They also sell pegs, my dear, no doubt to bring good luck to wash days."

"Well..." Fitz paused and calmed, already a sharp edge cutting at her tongue. "They have to live, I mean did not the witches of old take a coin for their cures?"

"They did," said Martel, offering more wine. "But they also protected crops, warded against evil spirits and acted as midwives, guiding the new born souls of rich and poor alike. You see, payment was tribute and never demanded, their duty forever to the mother and the care of her gifts."

Sylvia took Fitz's hand. "But Fitz heals! I've seen it, and she never gets thanks, let alone money!"

"Very commendable, I'm sure" Martel paused and fidgeted with her glass. "You see, evil is, ultimately, a choice. But once that choice is made there is no return...and I know this! For it is the evil of men, or women, that summons the beast, the beast then feeds and grows within, and of course, if the host is clever enough, he cloaks and rules his monster...and it becomes a very powerful ally."

Fitz's spirits lifted at the words, sensing at last some constructive information. "So what you are saying is, evil is an entity, a separate being?"

"Well...not quite, let's say the host feeds the monster and through him the monster grows, but indeed, yes. it is a creature."

Sylvia shakes her head. "So everyone in this world that is bad, has a monster inside them?"

Martel laughed. "Oh no my dear, what a world that would be! No, bad is an option, sometimes an option regretted, that belongs to us all, but evil is a choice. It is a way of life, a career move, you might say, and the only life the wielder will probably know. And more than that, like any other life skills, it can be handed down the generations, so that old hatreds and prejudices are forever instilled in the beast. In theory, my dears, you could be facing the beasts of the witch hunters of old!"

"Fitz banged the table. "What must I do?"

"Well I'm afraid, without knowledge, not a lot! That is, of course, unless you throw caution to the wind, get a gun and blow their heads off!" Martel smiled. "But of course, if you had decided on that course of action, you would not be here."

"Anything! Fitz hammered the word home.

Martel poured more wine. "For evil to flourish it must fool all. And these men you speak of, men you say who have risen to the highest ranks of their society, obviously cloak their monsters well, and bluff all into believing they are worthy and trusted peers, and a benefit to the community. Am I right?"

"Hmm," started Sylvia, "Councillor Hardy is well known, mind, for his dodgy dealings."

"Ah!" Martel smiled. "But these so called dodgy deals, just make him a bit of a jack the lad I'm guessing? I mean, no one ever sees the monster until they cross him, or interfere with his interests. Ring any bells?"

Fitz perked with interest. "So what do we do?"

"You must expose the beast, take away their guard, and let their own monsters destroy them, in short, let the megalomania inside them take full hold."

"How?" Questioned Fitz.

Sylvia rose. "This sounds like a long and in depth conversation, I'll brew some tea!"

"Firstly, do not expect of me any spiritual weapons of mass destruction, I do not wield ruin in any shape or form, my gifts, as should yours be, revolve around the nurture and beauty of life. I do not, never will, weave in the webs of death, for life given or taken is for the mother to decide."

Fitz spread her arms and shook her head. "So what is there?"

Martel smiled. "Why, my dear, what there is, is the ultimate revenge…the perfect crime, as it were. What you do is evoke the monster to destroy its own host…"

"But how!?"

"Really!" Huffed Martel. "Your impatience is, without doubt, your most annoying trait. Now, if you will just sit and listen, your schooling in this most particular art may begin."

Sylvia came back into the room with a tray of tea and biscuits. Her smile and mood evident. No doubt well relieved at the peace between the two warring rivals. "Tea, ladies!"

Both smiled and accepted the hot beverage. Sylvia sat and sipped her tea. "Well, isn't this civil, not a hint of blue in the air and…"

"OH MY GOD!" Fitz exploded out of her seat, sending crockery and cutlery flying, her colour had drained to the white of death, her face a twist of terror. "OH MOTHER, NO! OH SALLY, SALLY! NO, NO…"

A CLEAN KILL...

That smell, Cuthbert stood stock still in his hallway, frozen by the odour that bombarded his delicate senses. Just lately, every home coming had been littered with the surprises of some disorder or other; nothing was running to his demanded perfection and it would simply not do. Oh how he despised those who had corrupted his wife, derailing his well programmed spouse and turning her into the erratic shambles that each night he had to come home to. The years spent, the endless hours employed, training a simple soul to reach the highest level of human pristine, hygienic, control and behaviour. In Cuthbert's eyes, life was a manual and therefore it should be lived to the letter, each day being a fresh page that should be studied and delivered without question.

Cuthbert straightened his tie, applied sufficient pressure to the door handle and slithered into the living room, as always his entry was made with a critical eye, inspection instant and total. It did not look good, indeed Sally seemed to have reached a new level of disarray, and a tangled mess of twitching squalidness sat before him. Sally's nerve control, it would appear, had fragmented to an alarming level. She sat shaking and gibbering, giggling, eyes darting, her fingernails tap dancing on teeth. A quiver started from Cuthbert's temple and slowly rolled through his body. The room was a scene of war, an affront to decency, a slum worthy of scum. He could have cried, but Cuthbert never did. He ignored his wife for the moment. "You'll keep," he hissed, and slowly he stalked through the carnage. Laundry that should, without question, be aired folded and stacked in appropriate piles was strewn over floor and furnishings, all crumpled and soiled. A vase of fresh spring flowers that Cuthbert supplied daily, lay up-turned, the vase shattered, flowers scattered, turning to death, their life source dripping on the carpeted floor, posing an imminent risk of mould. The chaos was overwhelming, papers torn and scattered like confetti, cushions gutted, their inners spilled with random abandon. Next Cuthbert edged into the kitchen, holding his breath. This department of the home held a multitude of potential hygienic disasters, and Cuthbert now feared the worst. The horror that greeted him was crushing; his sterile, beautiful domain had been turned into a paradise for microbes and Cuthbert could now imagine the stinking little creatures multiplying by the millions on the spilled food that was smudged and dolloped all over his immaculate, washable surfaces. Cuthbert feared for his life, as he death marched back into the living room. Sally still sat, totally consumed in her breakdown, shying and cowering from her husband's glare.

"Well this certainly is a new level!" Cuthbert paused. "That smell?" Cuthbert's nostrils sucked and vacuumed the air, twitching with indication, until the sensitive equipment finally homed in on the intrusive odour. "Upstairs!" Cuthbert pointed to the suspected crime scene. "What on earth have you done?"

But Sally remained totally unresponsive. She chittered and twitched and mumbled yards of jumbled nonsense. Cuthbert advanced towards the stairs and the source of the nostril intrusion, each footstep brining him closer to the source of ill. First he checked the bathroom, a good first choice, he thought in the search of alien odours. But no, the bathroom seemed undisturbed, though obviously not this day cleaned. Next the spare bedroom, seldom used, so was it possible that some foreign object could have escaped his meticulous scrutiny, but again he drew a blank. As he turned to face the master bedroom an almighty waft of filth hit his nostrils full throttle, the musk gulping deep inside causing a bubble of churning bile. Cuthbert wretched and held his nose, placing a shaking hand on the door knob. Slowly but surely he reigned his pluck and advanced into the now obvious war zone, his very being shaking with the thought of what the purity of his eyes might witness. He scanned corner to corner, gagging as he did so, as the level of stink soared. And then; Cuthbert knew such things existed, but he had avoided eye contact with one all his life, never peering down into the pan after the foul deed was done. And now, before him in, of all places, his bedroom, right in the middle of his sunflower duvet, Cuthbert had his first eye contact. The turd steamed in a slithering curl, bumping out its fetid smog. Cuthbert's mouth jarred, locked open. "NOOoooo!" The scream was as a drone, steadily rising in pitch. The drone grew and grew and funnelled through the home. Next, Cuthbert's legs buckled, his bone turning to pulp under the weight of the horror. Cuthbert slumped to the floor, his jellied limbs desperately trying to propel him out of the room and away from the accursed bog beast, that he believed was out to destroy him. Finally he heaved his reluctant legs out of the bedroom, slammed the door shut, and sat, gasping in relief, until the memory and the vision of hell returned un-beckoned. Cuthbert staggered to his feet, determined to make the toilet before the insides of his stomach added to the carnage. He made the bathroom by the grace of God, clutched the bowl for dear life and let the gross witness of his gut spew forth.

The reflection that greeted him was bone white, his heavy rimmed glasses magnifying burst vessels angry and red through strain. Cuthbert scrubbed, flossed and purified himself back to life. Next came the bleach, gallons of it soaking everything in sight, in a frenzy he battled his eternal enemy until he was convinced of its destruction. Cuthbert, then satisfied, composed, staring at his mirrored image "Something now must be done!" He hissed at his determined reflection.

Cuthbert sat as calm as a Sunday morning, oil-skinned from head to toe, hands gauntleted up to the elbows, an old gas mask now raised and sat perched on his forehead. All his troubles dissolved and flushed away. Funny, he thought, the turd had proved to be the most problematic part of the whole operation, but after a few technical errors he achieved a solution. The bed clothes were handled with pincers, duvet rolled with the avoidance of any bodily contact, and with haste bagged. Then along with sheets, pillows, bedspread, in fact near enough the entire bed furnishings, were flung to the flame of an all consuming and purifying bonfire. The very same flame proved also to be invaluable in the second part of Cuthbert's operation.

Sally remained totally unresponsive through the horrors that unfolded. She remained seated, an oblivious wreck of humanity, completely beyond the doctrines of control and civil instruction. Cuthbert quickly came to the conclusion that his wife was a 'right-off', and like a rabid dog, was beyond training, and had become a danger to herself, and more importantly, a danger to the delicate metabolism of Cuthbert Combs. The sight of his pathetic spouse rekindled memories of his mother's later years, as her mind slipped into the destructive corridor of dementia. A selfish ailment that posed great risk to others, greedy for its attention, all consuming and totally unhygienic. Cuthbert remembered the prized pills that debilitated and prevented his Mother's contamination. Cuthbert reached into the medicine cabinet which, untouched by his wife's rampage, remained in its alphabetical order. B for Barbiturate. Cuthbert returned to the living room, pills and a glass of water in hand. Sally did salivate as Cuthbert wedged the tablets into her mouth, but he was unconcerned, the gauntlets proved to be a priceless safeguard.

Sally eventually dribbled into unconsciousness. Cuthbert studied the silence of his wife, planning his next move. A fireman's lift was both practical for victim and safe for the fellow doing the lifting. Cuthbert had long been plagued by wicked contractions involving the lower spinal column and was always alert to the possibility of inflicting further damage, but sometimes in life, risks had to be taken, even for the meticulous Cuthbert Combs. Luckily, Sally was of little weight, quite manageable, even for Cuthbert's delicate frame. She sat petite, a hammock that slung well and settled without problem on the curve of Cuthbert's shoulder. The stairs demanded time and a steadfast attention, so with each step Cuthbert paused, adjusted the weight when necessary and advanced, step by cautious step.

Finally Cuthbert reached the giddy heights of the bathroom, gently he placed the moaning, still unconscious Sally down on the toilet seat. Next he plugged the bath and released its flow, tepid of course, a subtle heat that would not stir a reaction from his now totally unreceptive wife. With the tub filled, Cuthbert gently lowered Sally into the water, she floated for a while, and Cuthbert smiled, this is perfect, just how he would like to remember her, silent, still and well behaved. Next, Cuthbert gently applied an index finger to the centre of Sally's brow and with minimum effort pushed down. Sally's head submerged without any resistance, her rustic curls fanning out on the water's surface, her delicate, mousy features shimmering beneath the rippling liquid. Cuthbert bade a *bon voyage*. Then the bubbles came, burst into air, and Sally was gone.

Cuthbert removed the gas mask and the gauntlets. He stripped off the oil skins, folded them and sat back down, with not a thought out of place. He had made himself a good strong cup of herbal tea to steady the excitement. All in all, he thought, a very trying day had all worked out for the best. The bonfire was now calming to ember, with the scorch of flame consuming its fill, a fitting end, Cuthbert mused, to the enemies of purification. He would wait till morning, when the cinders cooled, and remove anything damning that denied the flame. He was confident in the task, for he knew he could be far more meticulous than any sloppy police forensics could ever be, and anyway, he was sure it would not come to that. After all, he had friends in high places, and all of them rotten to the core, all with more to hide than a bent accountant's ledger.

Cuthbert stood and prepared for bed, taking a good breath of trouble free, pure bleached air. "Spic and span." He chuffed to himself, as he stretched his yawning limbs. "A place for everything, and all of it back in its place." Of course, he would need time off work to get the equilibrium finely balanced, juggling both career and vital home hygienic duties. But he'd manage, and who better, perhaps this was all meant to be.

Cuthbert made for the stairs, the strain of exhaustion kicking in. A puff of a breeze stroked his face. Cuthbert turned. "Funny!" He mused, and quickly set about checking windows.

But, as he'd thought, all windows were secure, as he knew they would be for it was a duty of high priority, visitors were seldom welcomed at Cuthbert's abode, never mind intruders. Next sensation out of place was a gentle tingling that tickled Cuthbert's ear drum, followed by the slightest wisp of a giggle that echoed and fluttered by. Then a crash that made Cuthbert jump out of several skins. "Who's there?" His voice quivered in its intended authority. Then Cuthbert saw the shattered glass splintered across the floor. He bent and picked up the broken picture frame that contained the memory of a wedding day. Cuthbert looked at the photo and smiled, "You were so well behaved back then." As if in answer, a warm gust of air seemed to blow straight through him, the gust bellowed out the curtains, then all was still. "That you Sally." He smirked. And so what if it was, the spirit of his dead wife, he thought. She'd forgive him, she knew everything he'd done was for the best.

WHAT SALLY SAID...

"The first day back, I knew. His mood made the very air thick and hard to swallow, his face was constantly set in a hard line of grim determination and I believe, in that moment, I saw the man, my husband, for the very first time, and I knew he was not, and never was, the man that wrote that letter of love and devotion. The door closed, the creaking of hinges and the snap of the latch hitting home, spelling the end of my freedom. It was a sound I carried to my grave, that awful sound of loss, that final slam of crushed hope... I could see the punishment forming in his mind, the cruelty weaving in his eyes, plotting revenge on his well trained creature that had dared to defy him. There was no remorse or joy of reunion, not a word or gesture of love or caring, just a glare of ice cold triumph. I should have left then and there, I should have run for my life and never looked back. .But somehow I felt I deserved it, after all, had I not my chance? So I concluded, this was obviously who I was meant to be."

Fitz eyes and mind were closed to the world, her head swayed as she gripped on to Sally's thoughts. For a few moments Fitz was silent, and all that could be heard in Martel's cottage was the sound of Sylvia's sobs that echoed deep from the heart, as her dead friend's misery was spilled out to the world from beyond the grave. Martel reached her hand across the table and gripped Sylvia's tightly. Fitz's head rolled violently, her eyes again closed, she spoke, and Sally returned. "My life was again his to judge, and had I not broken every rule of his court, he would never forgive, and I believe, I always knew that. The breaking began before even a speck of dust could settle and I was chained to the will of Cuthbert Combs, a will that demanded the impossible every waking moment of the day...I could feel my mind tearing, every move I made, my nerves tensed and locked me in fear and drowned me in sweat. I walked a tightrope, with every step and breath I took. I was living in glass, and I knew soon my world was sure to shatter. So when I opened my eyes and my vision shimmered just under the surface, I was relieved, the water become my door to freedom. I felt no pain, for I believed I could suffer no more. Instead I embraced my drowning as my liberation. I remember death and I remember waking, I floated into a calm...And then..."

Fitz wailed, the wail turned into a scream as her eyes shot open, she jumped out of her seat. "It clawed at the water... It was chasing me through death...He was chasing me through death. I rose, and the town spread below me and claws and monsters rose with me; I could sense the chase as I soared, could feel their need to devour me. But, it would seem that fear died with me and I knew they could not take me. A glow of calm soothed into my soul, and I laughed, for then I knew, I was free of the world and him, a hush of beauty was calling me, an irresistible embrace that would hold me in peace for eternity. But I cannot rest, not yet, while he still lives. For I shall haunt him till his dying breath. And only when his last breath has passed shall I take that embrace."

Fitz halted, she held her head in her arms as she teetered, her legs unsteady, as reality returned. "He killed her!" She gasped.

Sylvia ran into Fitz's arms. "Oh God, Fitz she drown...He drowned her!"

The two embraced and emotion and tears flowed. Fitz took a deep breath. "Come on Syl, let's sit, we've a lot to talk about. He won't get away with this!"

"I think a good stiff drink is called for!" Said Martel, rising and making for the kitchen.

"I need sleep, Fitz...I can't think, let alone talk." Sylvia trembled, she broke from her lover and headed for the stairs.

"Syl!"

Sylvia turned. "What?"

"I'm sorry, you were right, I should have tried harder to stop her!"

Sylvia smiled. "Oh, I don't blame you...Sally would not see any creature suffer, not even him, it was her nature...And he knew that, that's the trap he laid. But you promise me Fitz, whatever it takes, whatever it is you and Martel can do, you promise me it's enough to kill Cuthbert Combs!"

Martel tilted the bottle and poured a generous measure of brandy, which Fitz drained, instantly holding out the glass for another. Martel again topped the glass. "How much of it do you recall?"

Fitz took another sharp shot. "Most of it I think, though it's all slightly hazy."

"It always is; the monsters she spoke of, the ones that appeared after death, you know about these?"

Fitz's shook her head. "I…"

"Well they are indeed monsters; the monsters of men, spirits of evil, shadows that find kin in the hearts of wicked men or women. And as I told you, they lie cloaked deep within, hidden, an unseen ally that partners the greed and megalomania of many a devil that dwells amongst us."

Martel stood and left the room, moments later she returned and placed on the table a stone urn, again she sat. "You asked what you could do to reveal the monsters you are up against!" She pushed the urn towards Fitz.

Fitz picked up the urn and looked to Martel. "What is it?"

"This contains the Ashes of innocence. It contains the blood of martyrs, the flesh of the persecuted and the bones of the betrayed." Martel paused, she looked to Fitz for a reaction.

"And what good is it to me?" Fitz shrugged. "Will it kill Cuthbert Combs?"

"It represents the souls of all who have suffered through the will and force of evil. It is greatly cherished, and I am its guardian."

Fitz could hold rein on her patience no longer. "But how can it help me?"

Martel smiled. "Well that will depend, my dear, on the purity of your soul."

"Then when do we begin? For I have no issues in regards to the purity of my soul!"

Martel again smiled. "It is late, such business requires the peak of concentration and strength, for if you do indulge, then believe me, you shall certainly need both. So I suggest a good night's sleep, then tomorrow…well, tomorrow we shall see!"

Fitz quietly slipped into bed, she lay, closed her eyes, but found no sleep as her mind filled with thoughts of revenge, the faces of her foes appearing as distorted, snarling animals, that gnawed at the corners of her mind.
"Fitz?"
Fitz turned and embraced her lover. "I thought you slept!"
"No. You know, up until tonight, I thought this would all pass, time would indeed heal, you would finally run out of patience with your tutor, and we would simply start afresh, find a new place to live far from Sickle, my husband, and all the damned rest of them!"
"I've done that Syl, so many times. Yet look where I am!"
Sylvia kissed Fitz hard, holding her with all her strength. "Then no more, no more will we be cowed, and whatever it takes, whatever danger, whatever must be done, we shall do, we shall do it for Sally, Fitz, and for ourselves."

THE LOCK HORNS...

The two goat heads locked horns in the centre of the council chamber that stood as the Stags Hall, and pushed with the force of all their might, their breath heaving as they struggled to hold ground and shove their rival into the zone of defeat. The spectators included, Bull, Stag, Ram and Antelope, all growling and baying, like the beasts they represented, for their particular choice of champion. Boris Hardy's wit had always given him the edge over his fury minded brother, and he never entered any contest without a plan of foul play. Boris slipped his hand off his brother's shoulder, grabbed the waistband of his trousers and yanked down hard. The trousers slopped down around Brinmore's ankles, Brinmore loosened his grip and howled in protest, giving Boris the opportunity of an unguarded assault. He rammed into his brother with all his might, sending him tumbling in a knot of trouser legs, beyond the red taped boarder and out of the competition.

Boris removed his goat horned helmet and snarled his triumph, punching the air in victory. His furious brother panted and puffed to his feet in a red boiled fury. "Foul play I say, foul play, I demand a re-match, brother!"

Boris laughed. "Why, my dear brother, one would have thought, you would have perfected the art of losing by now, for God knows you have had enough practice."

Brinmore threw down his horns and head-longed into his brother, his hands hooked as claws, trying desperately to gouge out his sibling's eyes. Boris, anticipating the move, stepped aside and Brinmore smashed into a Ram, growling in frustration.

Bill Marshal, the lead Bull, stepped in to the makeshift ring and grabbed the arm of Councillor Hardy, raising it in the air. "Fellow beasts." He paused, letting the room settle, and allowing Brinmore Hardy to calm. "I give you this year's Goat Major and head beast of our annual festival...Councillor Boris

Hardy, who has locked horns and proved his worth. Please show your favour with the bay of the beast. And the horned Devils, howl with fur roar."

The gong was sounded and dinner was served, the brotherhood of Lock Horns prepared to feast, dickie-bowed and tuxedoed up to the nines. The circle of tables they sat at made all members feel as splendid as knighthood. They all sat puffed of chest, quaffing the best red and swishing their Napoleon brandy in the style of indulgence.

Peter Bellroy, the hapless cleric, was the lamb of this rabid pack, the up and coming Lock Horn who was denied the indulgence. Trouble was for Peter Bellroy, he had been up and coming now for several years and still carried the shame of the fluffy white sheep cap that mocked his worth in the society of beasts. Bill Marshal, the lead Bull, was an ox of a man, muscle-bound and a savage bully and was particularly relentless in the badgering of the twigged framed, spotty young clerk. So, demands and threats echoed through the chamber as Bill Marshal heckled and beasted the young man.

"Peter, Peter!" Screamed the Bull, banging hard his goblet on the fine white clothed table. Peter Bellroy shot out of his seat and scampered to his tormentors call. "Ah, yes Bill?"

"I feel my shoe lace has untied, probably due to your sloppy knot tying in the first place!"

"I do believe the little runt would like to see you with a broken neck Bill?" Sneered Sergeant Hardy.

"Well, best I break his first," said Bill, grabbing Peter's neck and thrusting it under the table. Peter quickly set about the demeaning task.

Boris Hardy sneered. "Hey Bill, you sure that's all he's doing under that table? You know what they say about a spring lamb, they can suckle your eyeballs out of your cock!" The chamber erupted in laughter. Bill reached down and hoisted Peter up, flinging him across the room. "Get out of there, you dirty little scrag!" And again, roars of laughter as Peter scurried out of harm's way. Brinmore rose as Peter passed, placing a boot up his backside to help him on his way. "Aye!" He quipped. And that's the only horn he'll ever get!"

A gong sounded for a second time and a roar rose to the dome of the chamber, as the blood roast beef was brought, carved and served with a pulse to the plate, seasonal vegetables and a rich stock gravy completed the culinary delight. All loosened buttons and gorge, all, that is, except for one. Cuthbert Combs hated the gathering, and refused to be horned. But to not attend was never an option. After all, one had to keep in with the pillars of the community, and every pillar he knew was a Lock Horn. Of course, he brought his own food, carefully prepared with his own meticulous hands. He nibbled at his safe celery as all around scoffed their deathly raw rumps of contamination. Never mind, he thought, once the feast was finished and the speeches made he could quietly slip away. He took a sip of his tonic water that he had first checked for a secure seal, and watched his fellow beasts digest, with a look of disgust etched on his face. It slopped, out of nowhere, down the front of his shirt, a slick of grease, stewed gravy that slithered a brown, damning trail that dolloped on to his lap. Cuthbert froze in horror as the enormity of the stain dawned, he looked to his lap were the pot stewed filth had settled, knowing full well that to move it, he must first touch it. Cuthbert turned to regard his neighbour, a certain Cecil Bowen, a farmer of all things, and all the proof Cuthbert needed. "Did you do this?" Cuthbert barked at the oblivious Cecil Bowen.

"What the bloody hell you on about?" Growled Farmer Bowen.

"This, this scandal…you did, didn't you, admit it man!"

Now, farmer Bowen was of the order of the Ram, he was headstrong and forthright, and like most Farmers he did not look kindly on bankers. He stood up, towering over the limp frame of Cuthbert Combs. "Seems to me you've made some kind of mistake, and an apology, I feel, is in order!"

The room fell silent as the farmer growled down on Cuthbert Combs.

"Why, you farmers your all filthy beasts!" Yapped Cuthbert. "Shit spreading yobbos who deny the bath tub and contaminate everything you touch, and…"

Before Cuthbert could say another word, out of thin air, a full boat of gravy launched, hitting him true in the face, its muck splattering his glasses, even dripping in his unguarded mouth and straight in to his precious digestive system. Cuthbert was aghast and in a panic of quarantine, as the room erupted in laughter. In a rage of possible contamination, he stood and threw a blind punch which, sightless, was going nowhere. Farmer Bowen took his time, gripped the thrashing idiot's head, and delivered a sharp and snapping knockout blow.

Cuthbert could feel the ice sharp sting of water as his senses once again got a grip on life, his eyes blinked back to light.

"Their coming!" A voice hissed as he awoke. Cuthbert shook his head. "What…Sally!" He could see her through the haze of waking, his dead wife, right before his eyes as plain as she was in life. Cuthbert jumped up, howling in alarm. "Who's coming? Sally, Sally!"

Councillor Hardy grabbed Cuthbert's arm. "What you on about, you bloody idiot? Your wife is not here, that's for sure!"

Cuthbert squealed in panic, just what did the Councillor know? "What, what do you mean my wife's not here? Just what are you suggesting?"

"What am I suggesting? You're with the Lock Horns, boy. Bloody hell, has that punch taken all your senses? You'll find no bloody women in here, now for God's sake get a grip!"

"She was here I tell you, right here! And get your bloody, grubby, fat hand off me!"

Before the Councillor could utter a word, Cuthbert broke from his grip and hurtled towards the door and out of the room, with jeers and heckles on his tail. Morris Bevan took a sip of his wine and slowly digested the erratic behaviour of his friend. Something was amiss, and Morris did not like missing pieces, they had a habit of being found at the most unfortunate times.

"Hmm!" Boris quickly dusted off the incident. "Perhaps our reluctant treasurer should adopt a pair of rabbit ears?" The lock Horns, at that remark, tittered back to ease.

With the feast devoured and the disturbance over, plates were cleared and fine wines were served. This was the time when glasses were charged and toasts came abundant, as the Lock Horns bragged and boasted their worth, full bellied and proud as punch. Councillor Hardy stood, placed down his gob stopper cigar and belled his glass for order, and slowly but surely the pack responded to the Goat Major's command and the room fell silent. "Fellow Lock Horns," began the Councillor. "It is a great honour for me to stand before you once again as your Goat Major…"

"Only by default." Interrupted his sour faced brother.

Boris just smiled at the slight. "As you can see, my fellow Lock Horns, my dear brother does not take losing lightly, even after all these years of coming second best to me, he still can't quite get the hang of it." This met with laughter and jibes from the gathering. The Councillor waited for the silence to resume and continued. "So once again Horns Day is almost upon us, the grand festival of the beast, a day when our noble society indulges the little people of our blessed community to a day of festivity and fun, all provided by the generosity of this fine brotherhood."

The self-praise resulted in a standing ovation, with pot-bellied, cigar puffing men quaffing out hear hears and jolly goods, all plumply pleased with themselves.

Councillor Hardy cleared his throat and unfolded a piece of paper out of his top pocket. "Special thanks this year goes to our dear butcher and friend Matthew Thomas, for the donation of two hundred delicious meat and potato pies for Sickle's world famous pie eating competition, which I shall of course enter. And perhaps my dear brother will learn his lesson and avoid another thrashing by abstaining from the duel…"

Sergeant Hardy shot out of his seat, fists wagging in threat. "I'll eat your bloody liver, brother, for no man can out gorge me! I'll eat every pie, chop, heart, lung, the butcher can provide! Why, I'll fucking eat the butchers wife, as fat as she is!"

"Well you're the only man here with the guts to do it!" Countered Boris. The room once again became an explosion of revelry. Councillor Hardy beckoned for silence. "And next on my list is thanks to Farmer Bowen for knocking out idiots. But more importantly providing vats of his famous gut rot scrumpy."

This met with rapturous applause, from the now well sotted Lock Horns, who bellowed and roared and bayed like hounds. Councillor Hardy again summoned order with spoon and flute. "And now, fellow beasts, I would like to call upon our righteous brother, Morris Bevan, to take the chair and remind us of this year's charity donations."

Morris slowly stood, every movement carefully constructed with grace. He cleared his throat, smiled and began his speech with perfected glib. "My dear brethren, I am once again proud to stand before this most noble institution, to announce this year's recipients of our annual charity bonanza." Morris picked up one of several envelopes placed before him. He drew out a paper knife and carefully spliced the paper container, he smiled, pausing to build up the tension. "And the first worthy cause to receive the magnificent sum of two hundred pounds, goes to an institution close to my heart and I believe close to the hearts of all Lock Horns…The Sickle Boy Scout Brigade." The gathering hammered the table in approval. "And to accept the award I'd like to give a big hand to the Scout leader, our very own Sergeant Brinmore Hardy"

Brinmore stood and bounded with pride towards the Vicar, hand extended, Morris held out his hand to receive the shake, only for it to be brushed aside and the envelope, without further offer, snatched out of his hand. "Hard cash I deal in, Vicar, not sweaty palms," said Brinmore with a snarl. Morris reddened and tittered politely. Sergeant Hardy Puffed out his chest. "I believe in boys, I believe in the big boy who shoves himself forward to become a man, the boy that kicks the sand in the eyes, so he can get what he wants. I've no time for the little squirts of this world, who whimper their way to adulthood, telling tales because they can't win a fight and soaking their mother's aprons in tears. No, gentlemen, all the cubs in my troop turn into wolves, I can assure you of that. And with that in mind, this money so generously donated will go for much needed equipment to the Sickle Boy Scout Boxing Club. Hit em hard and keep em down, that's what they learn on my watch." Brinmore finished off, rabbit punching the air and grunting back to his seat to the roars and bellows of the Lock Horns.

Next up for the gift of two hundred pounds was the Sickle Anglers Society, the cheque received by none other than Councillor Hardy himself. Quickly followed by the Eighteen Holers, received by Desmond Small, the best par the town could offer, to cheers of fore, fore! Minor donations followed, the Bog End Orphanage received the grand total of twenty pounds, St Helens Help for the Needy, seemed to need very little help at all, and was awarded eight pounds fifty, and even that small sum was handed over with heckles and calls to bloody well help themselves. But the biggest donation, of four hundred pounds, Morris awarded to his own blessed church; 'to go towards the disaster of the roof', which had collected a small fortune over the years, but still sadly leaked.

With the donations over, Morris ascended to the chamber's main focus of pomp and ceremony. The thick red velvet drapes had stood centre stage, covering the immense framed monolith for the duration of the festivities. Immense in size, just waiting for its grand unveiling. To most, what lay behind the velvet shroud was not a secret at all, but they all played the game to add to the climax.

Morris Bevan stood, hand poised on the drop cord. He summoned the Hardy brothers to join him, which aroused a hero's ovation. The two sumo warriors stood on the dais waiting, fingers pinched behind their backs, chins held high. Morris waited for silence, then began. "My dear friends and Lock Horns it was a hundred years ago that this bold brotherhood was brought in to being. Its heart and spirit will always reside with one man. One man, who constructed this bold brotherhood in his image, and his blood and soul run through this society, keeping solid its character and steadfast will. Of course, I am talking of no other than, the only man who will ever carry the title of The Grand Bronze Bull. Gentlemen, may I unveil for you, our once leader but forever mentor, the Grand Father of the two noblest pillars of our dear vale. The legend that is...Amos Dunstable Hardy!" The Vicar tugged on the cord and the curtain parted and the air was sucked dry out of the room. The revellers erupted in outrage at the spectacle before their eyes. Indeed, the Grand Bronze Bull had a full beef head that scowled down on the viewer with menace, the horns of his helmet protruding high in splendour. But what spoiled the effect of domination and self-importance was the roughly scribbled spectacles, moustache and beard that adorned the masterpiece. Councillor Hardy gripped the Vicars throat, again pipping his brother to the post. The Councillor roared in the vicar's face. "Who defiled my Grand Father, Vicar?"

Morris tugged himself free of the grip. "Never mind the comic spectacles, have you read what's written?"

Councillor Hardy gaped close at the portrait and mouthed the words written bold in scarring black ink. "Fire starters... What the...?"

Cuthbert Combs marched straight-backed through the council chambers on to the street, his senses on full alert, eyes darting as he puffed along in panic. He came to his front door and sighed with relief, as he put key to lock, but before he even opened the living room door he could sense disorder. "Whatever next?" He moped. Slowly, and with prayer, he gently edged the door open and discovered that his instincts once again did not let him down. The room was trashed beyond recognition, not a single item overlooked for destruction. It looked like a stampede of stallions had rampaged through his beloved fine polished dwelling. Priceless articles of pure perfection lay shattered or torn into irreparable ruin. Cuthbert's rage was at a loss, with no wife to vent its lash, it over boiled into a tantrum and the masterpiece of perfection that was Cuthbert Combs, finally lost control and imploded in on itself, in a fit of froth and mind chewing bedlam. He tried to break that which was already broken, howling like the delinquents he so despised. "You failed me, you failed me!" He ranted at shadows, as he pounded his head with his fists as tears, always denied, finally tumbled down his face. The letters took shape before his gob smacked, dampened eyes, red and dripping they scarred the wall. M, U, R, D, E, R, E, R. Cuthbert screamed from the blood raw back of his throat, a howl that issued from the devil of his soul, a tormentor finally tormented and staring straight in to the hell that he himself wrought. "Sally…….STOP!"

Only the Vicar and the Councillor remained, the Sergeant had quickly set about grabbing throats and hurling accusations at all and sundry, determined to beat out a confession to this most appalling of crimes. But with a thousand throats squeezed and all to no avail, he finally left the chamber, straight for the station to start an investigation, and he assured all, no stone or bone would be left unbroken or unturned.

"But who would have done such a sacrilegious thing?" Said the Councillor, thumping the table and taking a good stiff shot of brandy.

The Vicar quipped. "You know who! Or do you believe Tom's version of demons rising from the ashes?"

"No, no it's not them, my brother's on high alert, and believe me Vicar, my brother is as diligent as any dragon when it comes to guarding his gold! What about the fat one, you know the dirty bitch who dogged Slug in the toilets!"

"Oh, have you seen her of late?" The Vicar sneered. "Gwyn, I believe her name is; oh she's pathetic, scampers at her husband's feet, while he mopes and drowns himself in brown ale and whiskey, only coming home to give her a well deserved clout, by the look of her eyes."

"Well that just leaves dear old Cuthbert's wife!"

The vicar took a sip of his brandy. "Are you serious Cuthbert? Ever since that night, he has her firmly under lock and key, and believe me, he is not a man who takes defiance lightly."

The Vicar paused for a moment then shook his head. "No, no, believe me Councillor, there are only two players in this game! Two players who have the wit and resolve to brew up trouble, and my guess is they have only just begun."

Boris shook his head. "They're dead, I tell you! Don't doubt the amount of enemies me and my dear brother have gathered over the years, and our father before us, not to mention the man hanging on the wall, with the scribbled moustache and glasses! This is all part of the game, and my brother will no doubt break a couple of heads, but the way I see it, if that's their worst, I've nothing to worry about." Boris stood and topped up both glasses. "No, worry not Vicar. Why, we should be celebrating!"

Morris took a sip of Brandy and shook his head. "No, no, I tell you, something is not right. I mean, was your Grandfather a renowned arsonist?"

"Certainly not!" Boomed Boris. "He was a renowned bastard, a man not to cross. A lot like my brother, my father reckoned, and I can assure you, if he had a gripe, he'd sort it with fists not matches. Now, for God's sake, vicar! Get a grip and relish our triumph."

Morris prized instinct above all other senses, and instinct had served him well in his cloaked world of ruthless ambition; and at this moment, his instinct was screaming for attention, nibbling away at his nerves, and alerting every sense to imminent danger. Besides the obvious threat posed by his ex and her partner, Morris had to deal with two very volatile bed partners. Boris had some understanding of tact and discretion, required in the World of underhand dealings, but the brother, Brinmore, was simply a thug in a uniform, with the tact and discretion of a serial killer. But what really made the man a liability, was his sense of invincibility, and that, Morris knew, was the gravest threat of all.

A PARTING VISIT...

At last Cuthbert could rest. His home, though bereft of certain destroyed items, was now back to his matriculate standard. He sat sipping a much needed cup of herbal tea, and viewed the silent, empty room with suspicion. His mind had juggled with a thousand probabilities but not one seemed probable. He surmised that if he was indeed being haunted by his deceased wife, he still had a chance to appeal to her better nature and justify, to what he believed was, his necessary course of action. But for now, all Cuthbert could do was sit and suffer his loss of control.

The spirit of Sally soared high above the town, relishing the freedom of death. She giggled and danced with the glow of moonlight, enjoying the mischief she was denied in life. She passed her beloved shop, the only treasured moments of her wasted life. She floated above the Vale seeing its beauty for the first time, and she realised in death, that earth could be heaven without the demons of men to scar it. She now wandered free in the prison that was her home. Cuthbert sat hunched in fear, her lifelong jailer looked bereft of power without his captive to cage. Sally ever so gently released a shimmer of ripples, a wave to softly disturb the room, a slight glimmer of motion, just enough to question reason. Cuthbert's senses, blood hounded into action, his nerve reaction, snapping into life. "Sally!" Cuthbert stood and scanned the room for phantoms. "You must believe, it was not you, that I killed, no, no, no! It was that witch! She, I believe, possessed you, I only ever loved you, and..." The crash of a door and Cuthbert cowered and screamed. "NO, NO, PLEASE..." Sally blew like a whirlwind through the home, undoing Cuthbert's precious order, his pain evident as his text book life was torn to pieces before his very eyes. Cuthbert stood and, with a futile gesture, spread his arms and tried in vain to net the airborne objects that now littered his air space. The room rippled with giggles as Sally played, delighting at the absurdity before her eyes as her master and murderer finally arrived at the dock of wits end.

Cuthbert fell to the floor, covering his ears and wailing. Sally looked down and smiled as the darkness of his actions surrounded him and gobbled up all hope, leaving him blind and lost with what he deserved.

Gwyn sat alone in darkness and Sally could sense the misery of her thoughts. She was thinner than Sally remembered, and she looked older and spent of joy, the iron will she always had seemed to have, smelted with her troubles. Sally approached, gently kissing her brow, Gwyn stirred for a moment, aware of something that was nothing, and returned to her search in the depths of oblivion. The spirit of the home, to Sally, stank of misery, there was no love here, just the tick of a clock, steadily marching aimlessly through time. Sally wanted to tell her that she deserved to be happy, and that her life was hers to live, and was not for others to harness. She wanted to tell her that Fitz was right all along and that people from all walks of life and cultures, even housewives had the right to happiness and free will. But most of all Sally wanted to tell her that there were people who loved her, for that was probably all Gwyn needed.

She blew a kiss and bade farewell, they would meet again soon enough, she was sure.

Sally felt ice, the sweet tune of the air grew steady to a droned dirge, a heavy sense that told of doom, a flash of darkness noticeable only to the dead.

The shadow of Norman Stubs crept silent into the room, as still as only death can be. He looked to Sally, puzzled. "Who are you?"

"I was a friend to her," Sally smiled and pointed to Gwyn.

Norman looked to his hands. "I feel thin...Nothing!"

"You are nothing, nothing but a memory, now!"

"I dream" Norman looked to her, a fear glowing through him. "Am I...Am I dead? I feel cold, please say I dream?"

Sally shook her head. "Your life has now become a dream...You failed her...Look!" Sally pointed to the crumpled misery of his wife.

"I do love her, I tried...I know I dream, tomorrow I'll tell her."

"Sally again shook her head. "Your time for telling has passed. What regrets you hold, you will now take to your grave."

"No, no I'll wake and tell her I love her!"

Sally smiled. "That's all she wanted, just that one small word that proved a mountain for you to move. So I guess you gave up!"

"I, I will tell..." Sally watched as Norman Stubs slowly faded into memory, his spirit claimed and wrenched from the earth. She looked back for a final time at her dear friend. "Be strong, Gwyn, for what little time is left, can now be yours."

Gwyn immediately felt the emptiness, and screamed. She had not discovered the lifeless body of her husband till mid-morning, when she entered the spare room to rouse him for lunch. The thought of his corpse being alone all that time racked her with guilt. In a daze, she finally left his side, came down the stairs, took a deep breath, picked up the phone and spilled the heartache to his beloved children. Sandra arrived first and pushed her mother aside, denying her the comfort of any embrace. "Where is he?" She barked prodding her finger deep in Gwyn's ribs.

Gwyn pointed with a shaking finger to the stairs. "The spare room," she managed between sobs. Sandra stormed the stairs, using her haste as a symbol of devotion.

Dave appeared next, but did not have the stomach to view the corpse.

The undertaker proved to be efficient with both measurements and controlled pity, details were taken and the body removed. Sandra hugged the coffin all the way out to the hearse, swearing devotion and cursing revenge on the cause of her father's demise.

And so the remains of a family gathered. Gwyn's grandchildren, who understood nothing of death, took the experience as a huge adventure and acted out death with pop guns, taking full advantage of the solemn misery and causing more havoc than usual.

Gwyn sat rocking and ringing the misery out of her hankie. Sandra puffed furiously on her cigarette, and Gwyn could see the storm of her brewing. Dave sat silent as usual, his mood and features, as always, devoid of emotion. Finally, Sandra's dam burst. The tirade started with a pointed finger directed at her mother. "You caused this, dad died of shame!"

"The drink didn't help mind!" Offered Dave, slugging back his fourth can of bitter.

Sandra quickly turned on her sibling. "And why do you think he fucking drank so much, Dave?"

Dave squirmed uncomfortable on his seat, as he always did when facing confrontation. "I'm just saying, that's all."

"Then fucking well don't say Dave, talking doesn't suit you!"

"Oh please don't argue, both of you." Pleaded Gwyn. "We need to be strong for each other."

Sandra's venom was immediate and she pounced on her mother's words. "Oh, strong like you were for dad is it mam? There!" Sandra spat the word like a curse. "Dave, she is the reason dad drunk so much, our own darling mother!"

"Oh please don't San," sobbed Gwyn

"Oh but it's true, mam! Dad always enjoyed a pint, but he never drowned himself in the stuff, till you whored yourself with another man." Sandra burst into tears of rage, Gwyn rose to comfort her, but her daughter quickly upped her guard. "Don't touch me!" Gwyn quickly sat back down, out of reach of her daughter's fury and thoughts once again sank into silence. Dave pulled the ring of another can and Sandra paced the room, building up to her moment. "Right mam, there are things I know dad would want me to have, and I'm having them. The car, for a start, and…"

Dave's apathy was immediately shelved at the mention of the car. "Eh, I fancied having that!"

"Oh I think you'll find, Dave!" Sandra spat at her brother. "That I was the one who was there for dad when he needed someone and anyway, you have a car."

"It's a wreck, and you know it! Hasn't run for years, and I can't afford to fix it."

Sandra shook her head. "As I just said, Dave, I'm having it, it's what dad would have wanted, because I was there in his time of need."

"Only because he brought you free drinks at the Roast Duck! Tell her, mam, I need the car!"

Before Gwyn had a chance to respond Sandra hurled a beer can at her brother's head, screaming as she did so. "And what would you use the car for Dave? For driving down the dole every Thursday? I'm the worker and I'm having the fucking car!"

Dave pouted. "Well I'm having dad's tools, especially the power ones, and…"

"Tools?" Gasped Sandra. "And what would a lazy fucker like you need tools for?"

Dave stood to meet the challenge. "There's lots of things need doing in my house and they'd come in handy."

Sandra moved straight into her brother's face. "Oh they'll come in handy all right! Handy when you porn them up the Ex-servicemen's Club! God, I bet your little brain is calculating their value already! And you'll sell theem at a snip for a couple of drinks."

"Mam, tell this bitch…"

Gwyn's nerves are finally frayed to the bone. "STOP IT, STOP IT! The pair of you! I can't take much more, please just leave me, I can't think."

Sandra just smirked at her mother's torn emotions, holding out her hand. "I'm not leaving till I have the keys for that car!"

"All right, all right," said Gwyn, going to the sideboard and getting the car keys which she slapped into Sandra's hands. "Here! Now please, both of you, just go. I really want to be alone."

Sandra sneered. "Well you've certainly got your wish now mother… For, alone you are!"

Sandra and Dave quickly rounded up the grand kids and headed for the door, bickering about who needs, and who's having. Gwyn slumped into her armchair in a fatigue of grief.

The door finally slammed and the bickering became a distant echo. Gwyn heard her husband's car rev and speed away and now, in her solitude, the tears and longing could really begin.

Gwyn sat alone in darkness and smiled, the shock of her loss digging deep into the past, finding the treasure of her happy days and memories. Gwyn remembered the young man who came calling, spruced to the nines and holding nothing but a bag of nerves. She remembered her father on that first date, coming to the door and looking at her suitor from head to toe. She remembered how cute young Norman looked as her father gave him the third degree, fiddling with his tie and looking at his shoes. She remembered the beam of his lovely smile as permission was granted and, hand in hand, they made for the dance, and of course the first kiss... awkward, but amazing. Norm was a stickler for tradition, and on a bended knee he made his proposal and whisked Gwyn away to her dreamed of fairytale existence. Next, vivid reflections of her wedding day came to mind in startling detail. She could see, plain as day, the posies, the ribbons, the fabulous tiered cake, the nerves at the altar and that binding kiss that sealed vows and love.

Sandra was their first born and Gwyn remembered Norm all fingers and thumbs waiting for the midwife and cursing every second until she finally arrived, and the happy moment when Norm was called into the front room and Gwyn passed their new born to her husband's proud but shaking hands. She remembered his fear at holding something so precious and fragile, and his smile as he tenderly kissed their daughter's brow, and proclaimed his undying love.

Grief would permit no distraction from this forever lost fairytale existence, and Gwyn howled at her loss, and plunged straight into the pit of blame. As hard as she tried, as furiously as she shook her head, she could not dislodge the soiled pub toilet, as, un-beckoned, it took centre stage in her mind, taunting her with what ifs. Sandra was right, she concluded, she might not have pulled a trigger or dished out poison, but the venom of her actions had killed her husband all the same. She clutched the wedding photo deep to her heart, fell to her knees and prayed for forgiveness, for destroying the perfect life she now believed she'd had.

A DRINK OF BLOOD AND BONE...

Sylvia could feel the air of ritual as soon as she woke, and quickly decided she wanted no part of it. Breakfast was taken mainly in silence with Sylvia concluding whatever secrets the two sorceresses were keeping tight under lip, did not involve her. So, quite relieved not to be included, she cleared the table, made the excuse of needing a brisk walk, and with no objections she left the room.

Martel placed the drink down in front of Fitz. Fitz peered through the steam of the beverage, and sniffed at the pungent brew that bubbled inside the goblet with a fierce life force. "Shit!" Said Fitz, turning away from the brew. "That smells so bad. What is it?
"Blood and bone dear; a test, a bonding."
Fitz gulped hard, held her nerve and placed her hand on the goblet. "And no doubt part of the test will involve me drinking this disgusting smelling brew?"
Martel nodded and smiled. "This, Fitzpatrick, will be your judgement. You see, this before you can harness the force of innocence but you must first prove yourself worthy of this force of purity."
Fitz held herself firm, gathering her resolve. "And just what will happen when I drink it?"
Martel shrugged her shoulders. "I have no idea, I have never before drunk from the ashes of the dead."
"God!" Gasped Fitz, you make it sound so appealing." Martel just smiled. Fitz looked hard at the cold stone urn that was placed before her, its beauty somehow now seeming quite deadly. "It won't prove fatal if I fail...Will it?
Martel looked deep into Fitz's eyes, holding the stare. "We are not having cold feet are we?"
"No, no! Protested Fitz. "It's just, Sylvia, I..."
"Have no fear, what you drink, after all, is the spirit and blood of innocence. It has no will to harm, but it will judge you. It will judge, whether your heart and soul are worthy of the aid

of purity. In short, my dear, it will show you yourself, and where the test lies is whether or not the participant can face who they really are. And I must tell you, many have failed, and truth of their being has exerted a heavy price. For, you see my dear, nobody really likes to face who, deep down inside, they really are!"

Fitz nodded and without another word, picked up the goblet and in one hit, bolted down the menacing looking brew.

For moments there was nothing except the potent tinge of the brew, a mix of metal and earth that slugged its way through Fitz's system. Fitz gulped as the mixture settled like lead in the pit of her gut. Then the revolt, a tide of nausea rose up from her stomach, Fitz swayed, breathing deep to hold the alien substance that her body strived to reject. The effort sent a rush of tingling pin pricks through her blood, her temperature soared and Fitz floated as her mind started to swim through illusion. Fitz giggled, she had never sat in a raspberry jelly before, or indeed had she ever spoken to a person who was made of the wobbling desert. Martel wobbled so bad that Fitz concluded she must have surely come out of the mould too soon. Fitz doubled up in laughter. She pointed at Martel and tried to warn her that she was in danger of collapsing all together, but her words came out in a tangle of echoes, a monologue of mumbo-jumbo, that intensified the laughter to the madness of hysterics. Fitz rolled off her chair and, in a state of slow motion, closed her eyes, thrust forward her arms to protect herself from a landing that seemed to take a lifetime. When the landing came it was into a deep carpeted pile of marshmallows. She opened her eyes, and the mirth, along with the jelly, was gone and the cartoon fruit illusion was replaced by a cold grey stone world, a world that Fitz knew all too well. The vision was a shudder, a deadly thrust and stab of the past. Fitz's lungs desperately clawed the air for a grip of breath as her childhood, choked in misery, came back into play.

Fitz knew she was behind the closed door, huddled on the foot of the stairs, as her father paced into view, his face as grim and bare as the cottage they dwelt in. "She's your father's brother about her, and that's what attracts the devil!" Her father always pointed his words, every syllable and sentence a curse or threat. His life was poverty and misery, every action and word reflecting his anger and despair. "No wonder we are cursed!"

Fitz's Mother's only joy in life was to mock her Husband's misery and she never missed an opportunity. "She is what you bring, she is your baggage. Just look at the failure that surrounds you. Huh, the great provider could not even muster a son to be proud of! Oh no, your loins are as barren as your life, and what little they did provide, has proved to be as hopeless as everything else you touch! Our daughter, dear, is down to your failings, like everything else in our miserable existence!"

Her father's point advanced into her mother's face. "She's the curse I say, born of you. Why, there's Gypsy in her, I swear it!"

"And just what are you saying?"

"You know what I'm saying!"

Fitz knew what was coming, there was only so much hate that words could carry before the discussion was once again finished with fists. Fitz covered her ears as the familiar tone and beat of violence bruised into life, as her parents once again battered the frustration out of their worthless lives.

Tears of anger, they were the only tears Fitz ever possessed, for the world she was born into did not pamper to pity. So she ran from the words, cursing her life and the people who controlled it.

She ran deep into the woods, the trees shielded her from the world and all the mean creatures that meant her harm and ill fortune. The old oak stood ancient and proud, central and king of her forbidden, cloaked world. She knelt by the foot of the great tree, breathing hard to still her tears of anger, then she began to dig, her hands furiously clawing earth from the foot of the tree.

"And why would a pretty young thing like you be delving into the foot of the old oak?"

Fitz could still feel the shock of surprise and shame as the old woman rumbled her intentions.

Ingrith, she was called, and she was as ancient and weathered as the oak that stood before her.

"They hate me and wish me dead!" Snapped Fitz.

The old woman shook her head. "So your answer to the problem is the Worm of Magrot, quite a nasty response don't you think, to people who only actually wish you dead? What a revenge its service would bring, digesting any life it touched with its plague of rot and maggots;ooh, a truly gruesome demise! And one so young to summon such evil."

"They're horrid, they blame me for everything! They wish I'd never been born!"

Ingrith laughed. "Yet, despite their wishes, born and alive you are!"

Fitz realised through the vision, that the words the old woman spoke that day had stayed deep in her heart.

"Don't you see they destroy themselves? And tell me, what can they blame, when your journey begins and they are no longer your ward who will they wish dead then, each other? For they have long ago denied themselves any chance of hope, whereas you… You, my dear, have all the hope the long road of life can offer. So you see, by destroying them you destroy a bit of yourself, and hope may keep its distance. So why bother to taint your soul and destroy that which is already destroyed?" The old woman laughed and the woods spanned, roads forked like lightning, showing an intensity of destiny, a thousand reasons and ways that blurred together in a kaleidoscope of memory. Fitz saw through the vision that every action held a choice, every destiny stood on the crest of a forked road, a cross way of decisions and every choice tested the soul, every action held a reflection of touched lives. Fitz bit down hard to stay the roller coaster of illusions that tumbled her through the corridors of her life. She was desperate for an end but lacked control, as without mercy the visions smashed through her mind. In a horror show of helplessness, she became aware of a weave of wickedness that laughed and mocked her journey. Instantly she knew the shadow, for it was part of birth, part of life, a tail that never left, but bided time endlessly, in the hope to fulfil its greed and corrupt destiny. For the shadow was the wrong road, the great game changer that struck through the blindness of anger. It was, in essence, the fatal mistake that would bind her with it for the rest of her days, and Fitz knew, it was only through the strength of will that such was denied.

The shadow filled the illusion, its form becoming the only vision allowed, its hunger for dominance consuming its target and demanding attention. The strangeness of the phantom was almost at once familiar, and Fitz understood the being as well as she understood herself, and she knew, she held the key that could open the lock to its existence. For just one step through the door of its temptation and that choice and the road were taken. Fitz ran and spiralled through the twisting chambers of her mind, the black void of her pursuer an ever present danger. She ran and ran denying both it, and herself until finally, the free fall dragged her and helpless she tumbled. The crash to reality was a tidal wave that rose and surged, dropping its traveller down hard on the welcome shores of sanity, where the tempest of the mind receded and slowly Fitz rippled back to where she belonged.

The thirst was intense and Fitz took hold of the second glass that was offered and again downed it in one. Martel joined Fitz at the table, this time offering a drink with a stiffer substance. "So you have seen your shadow?"

Fitz gasped, taking hold of a deep breath before she made her reply. "That and more."

"What was it the old woman said to you? Why partake in the destruction of people who will inevitably destroy themselves…"

"But how did you know?"

"My dear, I was with you every step; how else could I judge you? I now know your every hope and fear, and more importantly, I know you have a good and true heart. Here's the aid you desire, congratulations, you have what was needed to pass."

Martel placed a small leather pouch on the table in front of Fitz. Fitz picked up the pouch, opened it and inspected the contents. "And just how will a pouch full of ashes aid me?"

"We all, my dear, are stalked by shadows, but only when the shadow is accepted does it become a monster. You remember our conversation concerning the monsters of your foes?"

Fitz nodded. "Yes, but…"

"The ashes, my dear, represent purity in its hallowed glory, and is a blight to all evil. Just the taste and smell of it will infuriate the beast, to the extent that the host will, for a time, lose control of its underlying devil. In short, my dear, the mask will slip and hell shall spew forth in a surge of self-destruction."

"But how do I get near my enemies? I mean, they are not going to invite me in for a cup of tea!"

Martel Smiled. "Really, Fitzpatrick, do you have no faith in magic? All you'll require is a good gust of wind. I take it you could manage that?"

Fitz just smiled at the sarcasm.

"And a spell or two, then let the show begin. But know this, Fitz, there maybe more monsters in the town than you know of, so be on your guard, the safety of the innocents will be in your hands. You could be a very busy girl!"

By the time Sylvia returned almost a full bottle of brandy had been consumed, and the two schemers sat deep in conversation, and to Sylvia's relief both were intact and the mood felt pleasant, even a little jovial. Sylvia took off and hung up her coat. "You two look somewhat pleased with yourselves" Fitz ran over and embraced her lover, kissing her hard. "Oh, I am very pleased my dear, for tomorrow we go home."

It was just before dawn when Fitz rose, the house was still silent in sleep, when she quietly opened the front door and slipped out. She wandered deep into the wood, her steps hurried with purpose. One memory the illusions had invoked had remained fixed in Fitz's conscious, the Worm of Margrot, all through the evening it had gnawed away, steadily chewing her thoughts till a plan had slowly nibbled to life, and she would not this time shy from its aid.

She found an ancient oak, knelt before it and spread her arms in homage. "Oh mother, give me decay, give me the heart of corruption that feeds on the poison and disease of this world, so it will devour the ill and turn it back to blood and soil." Fitz took a deep breath, then using her hands, clawed and dug at the earth at the foot of the tree. She shovelled out earth, rummaging and searching as she did so. She dug deep, until finally, she found something. She tugged with all her might, she heaved till the earth gave up what she sought. The fungus was a deep oil black that filled both of Fitz's hands, it slithered to the touch, trying to slick its way loose of her grip. Fitz set it down as the smell of decay near overwhelmed, the orb lay and pulsed with life. Fitz opened the sack, picked up the orb and placed it inside. She looked down on her prize and drew the strings.

She smiled to herself. "Well, Martel, I never said I was perfect; and you'll see, not all gypsy magic is fruitless."

COMETH THE GREAT DAY...

IT'S BIGGER THAN CHRISTMAS. Proclaimed the bold banner, spanning the breadth of the square.

Old Tom the Placard hobbled beneath the town's proud heading, his face still puffed and bruised. The sign announced Sickle's big day, Horn's Day, the Festival of Beasts. The festival that Tom believed was pagan and an affront to the Good Lord. The festivity was exclusive to his home town, and Old Tom had campaigned for years to get the heathen society and its blasphemous rituals banned, but to no avail. The Brotherhood of Lock Horns had more pillars than a Roman temple. It was, in Tom's eyes, an orgy of indulgence for the cream of Sickle's society. Never mind how much they harped on about their wonderful charity donations, Tom knew the society was well rooted in the art of personal gain.

The square was a bustle of preparation; carpenters hammered and sawed through their tasks and stalls and platforms took shape. Tom new every construction and its purpose and had protested in front of everyone. The boxing ring took centre stage, a place where young men would prove their worth on the battered face of a fellow human being, their hands raised to the air in triumph and blood, and then the winner would no doubt boast his worth in cider and carry off the damsel. The village green would be home to numerous sports of power and pain, with not a grain of the Lord's mercy given. The banner strung across the sacred house of the Lord would read First Aid Station. Tom had stood battle with many a Vicar over the years, concerning the church's participation, only to be countered with the age old excuse of generous donations, and leaking church roofs.

But it was the opening ceremony that revealed the devil and his play. The stampede was as barbaric as it was pagan. It was when the Lock Horns and their eager sycophants would don their grotesque horns of Satan and charge through the streets grunting and howling like the hordes of hell. He could picture the children with a manic fever in their eyes, lusting like Imps, and pelting the passing beasts with ripe tomatoes or even riper stones. Oh yes indeed, the church was busy every Horn's Day.

Tom was looking at the inn keeper of the Roast Duck setting up his braziers ready for the hog roasts that sold like hot cakes, when a tap on his shoulder brought him out of his thoughts. He looked up, straight in to the beady eyes of Sergeant Hardy.

"Hello Tom," said the Sergeant, with his ever present snarl. Tom cowered and immediately raised his arm in defence.

"Now, now, Tom, there's no need to be afraid!" Sergeant Hardy sniggered. "Because I know from henceforth, you are going to be a good boy and there will be none of these petty protests that nobody gives a shit about."

"It's my right," began Tom, with a quiver in his voice.

Sergeant Hardy grabbed Tom by the collar. "It is your right, old man, to follow the word of law, and guess who, enforces those laws? Now I know, you can be a cantankerous old bastard, and when I was a constable I had to put up with it. But, as you can see, I have gathered a few more strips since then and on my watch trouble making little fuckers like yourself will not be tolerated, especially as my brother, this year, is the Goat Major! Now, this is his show, and I love my brother dearly, Tom, and if anything should upset his apple cart, I leave you in no doubt, it will upset me! So, if I see just a hint of a placard with a Jesus saves, or some such bollocks… Well, you better hope he means it, because believe me, Tom, he'll have a devil of a job saving you from me! Get my meaning, old man?" Sergeant Hardy gave Tom a tight squeeze on his shoulder and plodded away to continue his beat.

Night masked the homecoming, and while the town slept, the town's biggest scandal in a generation silently slipped back in.

Sylvia and Fitz reached their goal and sighed with relief, and thanked their luck that the old shop had remained closed since their departure. Sylvia reached into her pocket and pulled out the shop keys. She took a deep breath and prayed the church hadn't changed the locks. She turned the key and, with the sound of a click, they were in.

Fitz turned on the lights. The shop seemed untouched from its last day of business. Sylvia picked up items of clothing from the shelves. "It looks the same as the day we left it, yet so much has changed!"

Fitz smiled. "Change, I believe, Syl, Is a constant. For nothing ever remains, so it is pointless to mourn its coming. No, far better we hold its reins and ride it into being, let others grieve for times passed, and let's make tomorrow ours!"

The flat above the shop was dusty, cold, and smelt of damp and neglect, so the first line of duty was for the two avengers to feather their nest. They set about the task with vigour, eager once again to have a place that resembled a home. Well into the night they toiled, giving every bit of grease and elbow they could muster, until finally they agreed, for now it was as good as it could be. From the flat's small terrace, the two ladies had a clear view of the square beneath them, but remained safely hidden from prying eyes below. They huddled together, looking down at the preparations that still continued well into the night. Fitz wrapped Sylvia in her arms as the chill of evening bit. "Look at em all Syl, scurrying about, getting the big day right for their masters."

Sylvia turned and looked intently at her lover. "You planned this, didn't you? It had to be now!"

Fitz shrugged her shoulders and smiled. "I don't know what you mean…"

"Of course you do! That would explain the tantrums and impatience with her. You wanted the spectacle."

Fitz laughed. "Okay, I did. And why shouldn't we have an audience? They did!"

A PLACE FOR FLIES...

Cuthbert Combs was a gibbering shadow of his once well constructed self; order and control were gushing through his fingers, causing nerve spasms that at first sprinkled him in spots, turning quickly into erupting puss bulging boils. His inhaler was almost constantly in his mouth as the panic of disorder crushed down on his lungs, squeezing him blue with suffocation. Work was now out of the question, with the initial clean up taking a gruelling two days and nights. Oh how he slept that night when his graft had taken back control, even missing the crucial six o'clock alarm call. But when Cuthbert Combs again rose, a shocking two hours late for life's duties, he again stood witness to chaos and destruction, and he screamed the scream of the tormented, trapped in a bubble of nightmares, and he sobbed and started again, and again, and again.

Cuthbert lay on his bed, wasted in sweat, compelled once again, to sort and clean the endless circle of repair and destruction. With each attack, Cuthbert's health and strength sapped. But his nature would compel him to strive for perfection until the bitter end. There was no logic to the thought, but then again there was no logic to his situation, but he knew it was his deceased wife who was the cause of his pitiful situation. Cuthbert scowled at the thought, all he had done for her; providing her with a clean and safe environment, working all God's hours to see she wanted for nothing. Cuthbert's thoughts turned to her devil born friends; could not Sally see that they were the cause of all this? It was they who ruined what he had strived to create, why does she not torment them? After all, didn't he have the good grace to take her back, and attempt to save her? Finally Cuthbert could feel the sleep descending that his worn tensed body craved. He closed his eyes, knowing full well that, come the morning, he would be back on the wheel.

Silent is death and the one who wields it, and silent was Fitzpatrick as she stalked towards her quarry. The sack on Fitz's shoulder now writhed and bubbled with life, and Fitz was nearly overcome with the stench of decay as her prize sensed its moment and prepared to gorge itself on life.

The open window creaked in the breeze, but the home remained still and silent. Fitz could feel Sally and knew the window was her doing. She could hear the gentle, whispered encouragement of her friend as she carefully pulled herself up to the sill and quietly dropped down, into the home of Cuthbert Combs.

She could hear from the stairs the gentle rattle of Cuthbert's breathing, and she smiled at the thought of that wheezing, mean sound being forever silenced. The content of the sack had started to ooze its corruption, hungry to burst and devour. She could feel on her shoulder the wriggle of the lava, restless, sensing their purpose. She slowly lowered the strap off her shoulder, placed the bag gently on the floor of the living room, and carefully untied and pulled the bag open. The ball of black, oozing fungus slithered on to the floor, seemingly pulsing with anticipation. Almost instantly a black, blue veined slick seeped across the floor, the smell of its decay overwhelming to the senses. Next, maggots the size of mice bared their sick white heads, mouths agape, showing miniature razor sharp teeth. Fitz smiled. "Try cleaning this, Cuthbert Combs!" She smiled, leaving the room as the corruption rapidly spread in her wake.

Cuthbert's eyes triggered open, he looked immediately to his watch, six o'clock, dead on. Punctual, a good start, he thought. Then the smell. A lightning bolt of foul odours smashed into his senses, producing almost instant bile. Cuthbert struggled to get his head over the side of the bed as froth and spittle wrenched up from his gut. He was powerless to halt the contents of his gall bladder, as acid tore through his throat, his eyes bulging blood red with the pressure of revolution, his gut a strain of cramps and spasms. He heaved himself empty, but still he heaved as the lining of his stomach came under attack, bits of it departing his gut in flecks of spewed blood. Cuthbert stood, hands quaking on his knees, the convulsions halting as his system finally emptied. It was the final straw. He had to get out and leave this home, Sally and her devils could have it. The idea settled and tickled Cuthbert's fancy and he was surprised he hadn't thought of it before. He still had his savings, a tidy sum in fact, more than enough for a brand new one bedroomed flat, ideal for him in the present situation, easy to keep clean, near his work perhaps, totally practical. Cuthbert stood up straight and tried as best he could to brace himself. It would take all the courage he could muster to open that door and face whatever horror was causing the foulness that assaulted him. He took a deep breath and instantly gagged, regretting the action. He quickly reached for his hankie and placed it over his mouth. He closed his eyes and prayed, reached for the door knob and edged the door open.

All the nightmares of the insane could have not prepared Cuthbert for the abomination that assaulted his eyes. "My God, my god!" Cuthbert's body locked in horror, his senses struggling to comprehend the reality of the impossibility that loomed before him. The stairs, the walls, even the ceiling was covered in a forest of fungi, of all colours. Grey with black under bellies fanned out the size of large cats, enormous domed red fungi, white spotted fungi that grew tiered towering above him. Slug textured veins dangled like snot from ceiling down to the floor. Cuthbert swayed, a nausea of light headedness threatening to tumble him at any moment. He teetered forward, his feet plunging into a slush of decay. "ARGHH!" He screamed, diving headlong back into the security of the bedroom. He slammed the door, pushing against it to make sure of its protection. "Oh my God, what am I...?" Cuthbert's eyes popped at the sight before him, in the moments of the doors opening the corruption had spread. The spring flowered wallpaper had soiled black with damp, little heads of fungi popping instantly into life, their foul blooms spreading the deathly odour. Cuthbert thrashed and howled in despair and jibbered. "Oh God, Oh God! This cannot be happening?!" He paced the room, his mind a scramble of desperation. "I must get out, I must be brave. Just this once I must, I must!" And with no other option, he opened the door and plunged into his unimaginable hell. His feet struggled to make ground as they were sucked down by a carpet of rot. He pushed on through tendrils of gunk and a forest of fungus. He slipped several times, as the fusion of rot sucked him to the floor. Cuthbert gagged and sobbed as the ooze smothered him in its ghastly corruption. Finally he crawled to the foot of the stairs, heaved himself up and teetered precariously on the edge of an abyss. The stairs acted as a weir for a cascade of gunk and decay that flowed down, pooling on the ground floor below him. The internal sewer belched its fetid odour of rot right through Cuthbert's senses, he turned a deathly pale as his stomach rioted in protest. Cuthbert's body convulsed, thrashing wildly and he quickly lost his footing and slipped and slid down the torrent of rot, screaming as he did so. He landed with a squelch and scrambled to his feet with the intent of making a dash for the door and freedom.

And before him was hope forsaken; it towered as a giant, a toadstool, tree trunk thick; its head cracking through the ceiling, barring any exit through the front door and the way to sanctuary. Cuthbert's thoughts flapped, his mind a scurry of bedlam and fear as every option was thwarted by the madness of his situation. "Back door, back door, oh please, please, the back door!"

Cuthbert had to shove hard on the living room door, breaking it free from the veins of corruption that plastered it. He entered the dark of his living quarters. Every wall, even the windows were smothered in black; the floor was veined with sluggish blue tentacles, and at the room's centre lay a black seeping mound of slime, the hub of decay pulsed with life. Cuthbert stood transfixed, his eyes unable to peel from the horror, and then he saw them, the foul white heads protruding, jaws open snapping hungry at the air. With no other option, he gingerly stepped into the horror of the room and as he did, so the black of the room moved, just a flutter at first that rippled along the walls. But when Cuthbert took another step they launched. Flies as black as night and as big as hornets took to the air with a buzz that was deafening. "ARGHHH!" Cuthbert screamed, desperately flaying his arms, but to no avail. In seconds he was engulfed in a tide of bluebottles, he fell through the force of the onslaught, his body blanked out by a shroud of flies, his screams muffled by the devils that clogged his mouth and throat. Then as quickly as they came, they departed, to settle back to their screen of darkness. Cuthbert gagged, spitting limbs and wings of insects out of his mouth. He could see the back door, and it seemed to be free of obstructions. He calculated that if he was quick enough, one last dash could see him free, before they had time, to swarm again. Ever so slowly he started to rise, and then he felt it; an internal itch on his forearm, that slowly built to a deep burning. Then the tear; Cuthbert screamed in pain as the blood jetted out of his arm and the first maggot head appeared, its mouth digesting his flesh. Again he screamed, the primal scream of the doomed. He crashed to the floor as the sound of tearing flesh issued from all over his body, as a score of maggot heads appeared, all devouring his flesh. Cuthbert lay, his body thrashing in mindless horror. Then the giants left the hub, sucking their way across the floor, straight onto his bloating body. Cuthbert was paralysed with pain and fear, helpless, as the creatures mounted his face, his body now clutched tight in the locked jaws of unspeakable nightmares. In the early stages of death, he heard the crunch and felt the digestion of his eyes. "Sssss, Sally?" Sally hovered in, close to her departing spouse, just before his sight was totally devoured. He struggled hard for one last word. "I, I..." Sally smiled into the face of his misery. "Bye, bye, Cuthbert Combs! Now I can rest."

The ambulance and fire service clanged their bells through the streets of Sickle. Sylvia peered through the closed curtains. "Something's happened?" She called back to Fitz.
Fitz enters the room, drying her hair. "Cuthbert Combs is dead Syl, that's what's happened."

"My God!" Said Sylvia, with genuine surprise. After all, it was not that long ago she was a vicar's wife, knowing as little excitement as the roll required. "But how can you be sure?"

"Sally told me, she said it was a fitting end. And she's gone now, Syl, to that better place, wherever that may be. She is at peace."

A tear came to Sylvia's eye, but she took a deep breath and smiled. "Good!" She snapped the word. "The end you spoke of he fully deserved. One down, and onward we go!"

The residents of Primrose Crescent had never seen anything like it, and most agreed that probably the entire world had never seen anything like it. Huge toadstools covered the walls of Cuthbert Combs' home, growing ever larger in front of the human eye. Sections of the wall had already started to crumble and fall, windows shattered and crashed to the floor as the fungi claimed its domain. Albert Jenkins pointed his pipe at the dwelling. "Always been a strange one, that Cuthbert Combs. I'm not at all surprised something like this has happened."

Nora Smith nodded her head. "Forty years I've lived in this street, and not a good morning did you get out of him! A very, very strange man."

Old Dickie Frances waved his stick at the building in threat. "He had that mad scientist look about him. You mark my words, this will be some hair-brained experiment that has gone disastrously wrong."

"I wonder if he's inside!" Gasped Nelly Bridges, as a huge crack was heard and parts of the chimney crashed through the home, sending a cloud of dust and debris over the street.

"Well if he is," croaked Dickie Frances, moving back to a safe distance. "He's bloody dead now, for sure!"

"He had a wife!" Coughed out Agnes Sharp. "Petite, quiet little thing, quite charming really."

"Good God!" Exclaimed Nora Smith. "So he did, Sally her name was. I haven't seen her in a long, long while."

"Well," said Albert Jenkins, "she either left him, or if not, I'd say she's dead too."

The clang of bells sounded and a fire engine came screeching into the street, just as a huge rumble issued and the entire building collapsed. The fire engine screeched to a halt, the Fire Chief swinging out of the door ready for action. He looked to the enthralled spectators, too engrossed to move out of harm's way, all bent-kneed, covered in mortar and coughing dust through their nostrils, then looked to the totally flattened home. "What the fuck?" He gasped.

Dickie Frances pointed his stick towards the Fire Chief. "Earth to earth I'd say, and all to dust."

THE EVE OF REVELATIONS...

"Are you listening to a fucking word I'm saying to you, Councillor?" Morris raged and paced Boris Hardy's office. Boris Hardy just reclined into his leather padded chair, puffing his cigar and sipping his port, quite unconcerned with all the huff and puff the Vicar was blowing.

"First," barked the vicar, determined to break the councillor's apathy. "Norman Stubs, out of the blue, drops dead. You know, the fat one of the coven's husband. I had the occasional pint with Norman Stubs, and I can tell you for a man of his age he was fit as a fiddle. Then he drops!" The Vicar clicked his fingers. "Just like that!"

Boris Hardy took a huge puff of his cigar as he swivelled in his chair. "Now look, Morris, he drank himself to death, with the shame of his wife's whoring. Nothing strange there."

Morris flew into a rage. "And what about Cuthbert Combs and his home getting swallowed by a fucking huge mushroom?! DON'T YOU THINK THAT'S A BIT FUCKING STRANGE!?"

But Boris just quipped at the Vicar's tirade. "Huh, bad hygiene."

The Vicar was aghast, and tightened his fists in frustration, he slumped in a chair fighting for control. "Tell me, Boris, are we talking about a different Cuthbert Combs? Not the Cuthbert Combs who was my church secretary, the Cuthbert Combs who would violently convulse if he so much as caught a whiff of a day old fart? For God's sake the man used to put on rubber gloves to wipe his arse, a man who would dust and polish his home, twenty to thirty fucking times a day. And you sit there and tell me he died from poor hygiene!"

Boris stood up and slammed his hands down on his desk. "So just what the fuck are you applying then Vicar?"

"Witchcraft Boris, witchcraft!"

Boris looked firmly at the Vicar, then burst into laughter. "Are you losing your fucking mind, Morris, witchcraft? You had better watch what you're saying, or they'll truss you up in a white sack and throw away the key."

Morris shook his head in frustration. "Don't you think, there have been a couple of strange happenings since the night of the fire, Boris? Old Tom seeing two figures rising from the ashes, it could only have been them. Nobody should have survived that inferno...And then on a personal issue, to you and your darling brother, the defacing of your grandfather's portrait, with the word's fire starters; who else knew about the fire Boris? And if not them, you tell me who in this town would have the gall to sneak into the council chambers and vandalise one of your family members, eh?"

"Don't kid yourself, Vicar, you don't rise to the dizzy heights of society like me and my brother without gathering a few enemies along the way."

"Enemies still value their necks and teeth, Boris, hell of a risk for just a splash of paint! And then of course there's today's incident, there are scores of people who saw it and will bear witness, and they say that Cuthbert Combs' home was engulfed and destroyed by a mass of giant fungi!"

"And you believe, Vicar, that it is down to the black arts?"

"Did Fitzpatrick ever deny she was a witch, Boris?"

"Yes, but she proved to be just a tinker and a whore."

"Well that tinkering whore, Boris, managed to bewitch my wife and her so called friends, into a frenzy of madness, and believe me, Boris, I've the scars on my arse to prove it."

"So just say, you are right, though I very much doubt it, what exactly can we do about it?"

"We stay vigilant, on our guard, and if we see them, we deal with them as our ancestors dealt with all old crones"

"And just how was that, Vicar?"

"We kill them, by whatever means."

Boris stretched and yawned. "Right, Vicar ,if that is all, we have a very important day tomorrow, and I think this year's Goat Major needs his beauty sleep."

"Fine, Boris, but you just remember, be alert!"

Morris did not sleep easy, a thousand possibilities, of murder and revenge, nagged preventing slumber. The fat councillor had always been blinkered by self-importance. Like the kings of old, he believed he was ordained by God and was therefore indestructible. He was, Morris concluded, a sloppy and dangerous bed partner, slow of wit and clumsy to the important details of corruption. And then of course, the brother, Sergeant Brinmore Hardy; a walking, one man genocide, who despises anything he could not fit in his pocket. His warnings fell on deaf ears, but Morris knew his wife, she was certainly nobody's fool, and intelligence in a woman was impossible for the brothers to comprehend. And then the bitch, Fitzpatrick, a troublemaking, upstart, and the brew, Morris knew of all this. Morris mistrusted her, way before she abducted his wife and claimed her for her lover; a free mind, Morris knew, was the devil to control, holding a banquet of mischief that it craved to dish out on eager ears.

Horns Day; the Vicar now felt sure was a day the assassins would again strike and Morris would need to be alert and stay on his guard. And again he tried for sleep, not thinking for one moment the only one he'd have to guard against would be himself.

The moon was glorious and full, shining gold its light as a guide to magic and its wielders.

Fitzpatrick towered, unseen, above the town, perched high on her terraced wall, arms spread to the heavens, the wild of her hair blowing. Indeed, she would need no aid of magic on this night, Mother Nature providing all the wind she needed. The folk below bustled through the evening, the party starting early in anticipation of the morrow's festivities. Fitz and Sylvia could hear the grunt of boars and the bleat of goats that echoed up from the street below, as opposing tribes of Lock Horns drank their fill and roared their challenge, all hungry for the morrow's bedlam. Sylvia spat over the terrace wall. "Fucking animals, I hate them! You know, Fitz, if it was not for you, I'd be there tomorrow, as I was every damned year, smiling politely by his side. With him handing out trophies and rosettes to every bloodthirsty bully boy in town.",

Fitz smiled down at Sylvia. "Don't worry, because after tomorrow the beast shall roar no more. It is time, Syl." Fitz turned away from her lover and again spread her arms to the heavens. She took a deep breath of the bracing night air and began. "Though through change, Mother, the hearts of men remain the same cold and black of blood. Evil is a root that grows deep and eternal, gripping the will and minds of the weak; readily they accept the seed and plough their greed, over goodness, peace and nature. With blood and bone I call the beast forth so all shall know its name, its play, its game, its demon." Fitzpatrick stood majestic, her arms swaying as she conducted the gale. The orchestra of nature roared and the town banged and clattered with its song. Fitz opened the leather pouch, grasped her will hard, determined in the moment, as in a rush of triumph she scattered the ashes to the wind.

Fitz and Sylvia gazed skyward, as the ashes rose into the heavens, and just for a moment the light of the moon shimmered red through the dust of blood and bone.

The butcher, the baker, the candle stick maker, whatever vocation in the town of Sickle, that evil disguised, would be incensed by purity this night. The very smell of it, an addiction to the lust of monsters that smouldered hidden, deep in the dark chambers of their hosts. The smell of virgin, untouched by sin, was as ravishing to the beast's senses as morning bacon, proved bread and heady summer wine. To understand the monster's urge to rise and riot, one would have to understand the craving for murder, blood lust and wanton destruction. One would have to understand the hate of sanctity, the corruption of goodwill, that could spread like wild fire through the world of men, engulfing the words of peace and harmony, till only ashes, and darkness remained. So for the sake of all that's evil, the beast must rise and devour this night.

Nightmares rampaged through dreams as thoughts were swamped in torture, their wishes soaked in blood. Wives and lovers made for spare rooms as their partners twisted into gargoyles, ranting and raving and gibbering murder.

Fitz and Sylvia remained huddled together, staring out at the night and the mischief they'd weaved. Fitz could feel the force of the magic, a force that throbbed gently through her senses. On the wind she could hear the whisper and wail of the dead as they teased their past tormentors. She laughed, oh how long she had waited for this one chance, to rise and bend no more. "Come on," said Fitz, pulling her lover close. "I feel tomorrow will be a busy day!"

HORNS DAY...

    Ethel Sledgewhick, was a mean hearted, twisted old bitch who hated kids, which was unfortunate in her chosen career, as Sickle's lollipop lady. For thirty long, fucked up years, she had bitten her lip, ground her teeth and lead the disgusting little bastards across the road. Her greatest desire was to be witness to a pile up on a zebra crossing; she could imagine the carnage now, little limbs and golden locks all entwined together in a fusion of twisted metal. She'd delay calling the emergency services, of course, and glory in the spectacle. Alas, thirty years and not even a bump. Besides hating kids, Ethel also had no time for men, which was probably just as well as she harboured the looks that most men would not want to spend any time with. She had masked her feelings of hate well over the years, smiling and patting their disgusting lice riddled heads, carrying the deception so well, that she even received presents off the little worms at break of term, which she of course quickly discarded in the river Bow, just in case, she should catch some horrid midget pox. But this morning she had awoken with a deep and severe loathing, and a rage she felt she could no longer deny. She had decided to forsake shaving on this morning of action, she looked in the mirror and quipped. "Let the little bastards see me in all my feral beauty." It was Saturday and, of course, Horns day, but still Ethel donned her uniform, for today she had a plan, a plan that was going to release the steam that had been years in the boiling. "Revenge is a head-on collision," she said, cackling at her reflection. She placed her cap military like, adjusting the peak, so that it held a shadow of menace upon her brow. Next she took hold of her lollipop, feeling its weight. She had always viewed this symbol of safety and goodwill as a potential lethal weapon, it certainly had the weight to inflict damage and the circumference of its head meant one good sweep could topple many a brat, especially the grubby little heads of her intended prey. So, with her imagination frothing her desires into a frenzy, Ethel Sledgewhick tightened the strap of her bonnet, opened the door and marched off to war.

Harold Turbot, better known in the community as Chuckles the Clown, was a miserable, obese, heartless bastard, who never brought his work home. In twenty years of marriage his wife Norma had never seen his funny side. For his two young children, Mabel and Mark, the clown's face held nothing but fear and pain, a mask of rage and pure horror that snarled when it used its belt. Never, for them, the clown's rubber hammer that only split sides and attacked with jokes. Harold was changing into Chuckles, and the living room sat silent as he applied his paint. This was never a good time in the home as Harold tried to adjust into a creature of jollity. But this morning, the transformation seemed to be sending him into a frenzy, and without warning Harold hoisted the mirror over his head and crashed it down to the floor, showering the room in splinters of glass. The following verbal assault on his family was immediate and expected. "Did one of you bastards just laugh then? Eh, eh?"

The family cringed in fear, the children trying to lose themselves under the table, his wife trying with all her skills to shield the kids and quell his rage. "No dear, never, Mable has a bit of a cough, that's all."

Chuckles the clown lobbed a plate across the room, his rage inflating faster than his comic balloons. "Why, you lying two faced cunt! Don't you think I hear enough laughter in work, people fucking pointing? Ooh, look at the funny man, the big fat bastard, look at his silly nose and trousers…AND NOW I GET IT AT HOME!"

Chuckles hurtled across the room, grabbing his son by the scruff. "Look at me boy, do you think I'm fucking funny, do you think your father's just a big fat joke here to amuse you?"

The lad cowered in fear. "No dad, no!" The lad pleaded. "You're not funny at all."

Chuckles raged, spittle spraying the child's face. "Hear that mother? This cheeky, gobby little bastard reckons I'm no good at my job. Why you ungrateful little git, I suppose I'm funny enough to bloody buy you shoes and keep a fucking roof over your head! That funny enough for you?"

Chuckles raised his hand to belt the lad, and Norma grabbed the arm mid-air. "Oh please, Harold, don't black his eye, not today, it's Horns Day and the kids have been so looking forward to…"

With his free hand Chuckles span round, catching his wife a belter on her disobedient gob, she staggered back howling in pain. Chuckles calmly removed his bright yellow and red jacket from the back of a chair, ignoring the sobs that now filled the room. He turned a pointing finger towards his wife. "You're all grounded, you hear me, Horns day or not, fucking grounded!" And with his law laid down, Chuckles made for the door, mumbling under his breath. "Just let some other fucker laugh at me today!"

Peter Bellroy was the lamb amongst the wolves. The hapless clerk was bullied and badgered from dawn till dusk, be it in his place of work, the council chambers, or here today standing at the top of West Brook Road, waiting for the legend that was the stampede, to start. He stood ridiculous, as he did every year, hating every moment of the town's most prestigious event. Unlike his peers, there was no grand horned helmet or snarling mask that covered half the face, turning the proud owner into a raging beast. No, Peter Bellroy was a sheep head, a young lamb, and the only one. This position of shame was given to the new lads, the up and coming Lock Horn. Trouble was, Peter Bellroy had been up and coming now for five torturous, humiliating years, seeing new members achieve their horns, lads younger than himself, adding to his shame. What made matters worse was that Peter had no ambition to be a Lock Horn in the first place, and the only reason he put up with the charade was through obedience, for not to do so would be a definite insult to his boss, Councillor Hardy. So, just like most other things in his hen-pecked, badgered life, poor Peter had to bite down hard on his bottom lip and get on with it.

And so here he stood, just one nail-biting hour before the stampede began. Peter stood, six stones of him, soaking wet, his helmet a mass of fluffy cotton wool with floppy ears, an elastic band wrapped around his head securing a black button nose. He sulked. Outside The Fox and Hounds things were heating up as Lock Horns galloped down tankards of beer, all ranting and roaring with laughter. Peter was at the beck and call of the Ten Lead Bulls; these muscle bound bully boys, would lead the charge of a hundred Lock Horns and another good hundred hangers on, right through the town, and on to the square where they would break, fill up with more beer at the Roast Duck Inn, before continuing on to the rampages, finally, at Devil's Plunge Gorge. But of course, before that treasured end, which for Peter could not come soon enough, there were the big and little bastards who lined the gauntlet, hungry for violence, eager to pelt them with rotten fruit, or even ripe stones, with Peter always getting more than his fair share. And then of course the fights that would break out amidst the ranks, as Horns of different orders tried to break through the ranks of the Ten Leading Bulls. Peter had lost count of how many times he'd been thumped, bitten or near trampled to death, and for some reason the mood to Peter, seemed more aggressive than usual on this Horns Day morning. It was a glorious day for the festivities but the mood seemed very overcast indeed, several fights had already broken out, with the Lead Bulls sparking at the smallest sign of banter. Peter tried to keep a distance, but it was never going to work, not with him being at the beck and call of the parched Bulls.

"PETER, PETER! Get your lazy cock plugged arse over here, you snivelling little bog rat!"

Peter looked nervously toward the roar that demanded his service, and gulped. Big Bill Marshal's beef boiled head scanned the crowd with murder in his eyes, seeking the sacrificial lamb. "Coming!" Bleated Peter, scurrying quickly towards the lion's mouth. Peter looked up into the furnace of Bill the Bull Marshal's eyes, clutching tight at his shit. Bill looked down on the thing he was about to step on, shoving his tankard in Peter's face. "What the fuck is this?" The Bull bellowed.

What the fuck do you think it is, ran through Peter's mind, but he didn't have the death wish to say it, so as always he took the safe option of idiocy. "Ah, it's a tankard, Bill."

The slap hit as hard as any punch, and tolled bells in Peter's ear. Next Bill screwed his scruff and with ease yanked him off his feet, and Peter reached the lion's mouth in full face of its roar. "You're taking the fucking piss!"

Peter gulped so hard his throat near reached his toes. "No Bill, never, I…"

"Look, you fucking imbecile!" Bill Marshal up ended the tankard over Peter's head. "See? You are as dry as my fucking throat!"

"Ah, sorry Bill." Peter stammered, fighting for words. Bill the Bull dropped him, rammed the tankard into his hand and Peter quickly dashed for the bar with bleats and baa's ringing in his ear from the mocking throng.

"Hey Bill," said Mark Watson, a lesser Stag head, pointing to Peter as he scurried to the bar. "Where's the little lamb's fucking tail?" Bill was just about to respond, with some no doubt cutting remark, but he was interrupted by a fellow Bull, Arnold Lock. "Perhaps Bill wore the fucker out."

The throng outside the pub roared with laughter, all bleating and mocking Bill, who looked none too pleased about it. He turned on the joker. "Well it was a damn sight harder, Arnold, wearing out your wife's fucking fanny, bloody thing could fuck all day and still weep for more!"

Arnold Lock turned a blood red, steam bellowing out of his nostrils. "What did you fucking say?" He fumed, placing down his tankard.

"You fucking heard," scoffed Bill. "I believe the thing between your wife's legs is fucking indestructible mate. I mean, it would need to be, with the amount of cocks she shoves inside it!"

"GRRR!" Was the only response Arnold made as, horns down, he crashed into Bill, the thud of giants vibrating through the crowd, who all revelled in the carnage, quickly joining the bedlam, throwing their own boots and punches.

Peter emerged from the bar into a theatre of madness as the rout of Bulls turned into a free for all. His instinct for survival kicked in, and he ducked down to an invisibility level, edging and praying his way through the carnage. Finally, with just minor scrapes, he emerged out of the ruck, found a doorstep, sat, and took a huge gulp of Bill Marshal's pint. "Oh my God!" He whined at the tankard. "I want to go home."

It was Chuckles the Clown's job to entertain the masses as they waited patiently for the stampede to begin. Hemlock Green was a mass of stalls and attractions, it contained everything a festivity could need, everything from hot dogs to faith healers. Chuckles moaned and whined through the process of setting up his stage, till finally the task was completed, and before him stood the miserable lot of his livelihood. Chuckles scowled, looking at his bright red and yellow back drop with a huge image of Chuckles himself in full forced hilarity. The balloons were inflated, his comic props laid out and ready for his performance. Chuckles stood back and took a huge slug out of a bottle of whiskey, preparing himself for yet another mammoth day of humiliation. A growl rumbled inside him at the thought of the fat, silly, man heckles that were a definite feature of every show, and more so on Horns Day. Chuckles gnashed his teeth, looked at his watch, ten minutes to go before a swarm of cheeky little bastards and their whore mothers and blagging fathers arrived. Chuckles turned as he heard the tell-tale sound of approaching laughter, and then they came, a mass of lollipop sucking kids all pulling at their mother's sleeves and pointing towards him, the silly man. Chuckles grumbled under his breath. "Just laugh at me today, you little cunts."

Chuckles plodded and sighed onto the stage as the mob positioned, ready for the show. His burning instinct was to start by asking the crowd what the fuck they were all looking at, but he fought hard to still the burning desire. So instead, he opened up the show with a more standard "Here's a balloon."

He picked up the sausage shaped balloon, twisted it a couple of times. "A dog!" He snapped, and tossed it into the crowd. He then picked up another balloon and twisted it. "A sword." And again tossed it into the crowd, he was about to twist his third balloon when a little boy yelled out. "Make us laugh, mister"

The catalyst; Chuckles growled. "What do you think I am, you little bastard, a fucking clown?"

The crowd gasped at the offensive retort from the supposed to be funny man, and the first heckle of the day was delivered. "Yes." Bellowed a man in the crowd. "And not a very good one." This got the first laugh at of the day. Chuckles seethed. "And what are you good at mate… fucking your mother?"

"You cheeky fat bastard!" Raged the heckler, trying his best to wade through the crowd to get at the fat clown. The little lad burst into tears as his mother thundered on to the stage, and proceeded to pound her fists on Chuckles' arm. "You horrible, horrible man," she howled. "You've no right being a child entertainer."

"You want entertainment?" Snapped Chuckles. "Ever seen a bitch fly, kids?" And with that Chuckles booted the woman, sending her flying off the stage and crashing into the crowd, and her son howled all the louder.

"Anybody else what a fucking good laugh at me? I'll marmalise the whole fucking lot of you!"

"Try marmalising me, fatty," said the heckler, who had finally reached the stage. Chuckles reached for the first weapon he could get his hands on, which unfortunately for him happened to be his giant balloon hammer which he struck with almost no effect on his all too eager attacker's head. The attacker slapped the balloon weapon out of Chuckles' hand and smashed his fist through the clown's rubber nose, connecting with the real thing and cracking bone. The crowd whooped with joy as blood sprayed out of Chuckles' nose, all now totally engrossed and enjoying the clown's hilarious performance. "KILL THE CLOWN, KILL THE CLOWN!" The crowd roared in unison as the show intensified. Chuckles stood, dazed from the clout, put his hand to his nose and, on seeing the blood, snarled in anger, picked up a custard pie and hurled it straight in the face of his attacker, then with his opponent temporary blinded, Chuckles charged. The crowd went wild as his rival desperately tried to shovel the gunk out of his eyes. The vast bulk of chuckles smashed into his target, sending both crashing on top of the clown's box of tricks, gadgets whiz, squeak and whistle, with streamers and jester heads on springs, zipping into the air. The man choked for breath under chuckles' weight, Chuckles smashed his fists again and again into his crushed opponent's defenceless face, until, exhausted, he could punch no more.

Chuckles wobbled to his feet, totally exhausted. He turned to the crowd, panting and sweating, the white of his face paint taking on a tinge of pale blue. "See...UH...See...Uh...Who's laughing now...Who's..." Chuckles' face locked in agony, which brought fits of laughter to the crowd. He clutched his chest. "Call an ambulance, I think I'm having a..." And without another word the fat clown's heart exploded and he crashed to the floor, stone dead, to a standing ovation, and howls of laughter, giving, in death, the funniest performance of his life.

The little lad turned to his mother, now fully recovered after her dramatic stage exit. "Oh Mother, I think this is going to be the best Horns Day ever!"

A deep bellowing blast echoed through the field and a huge cheer erupted from the crowd as the horn was sounded, announcing to all the start of the stampede. Vendors closed their stalls, children and adults alike checked their bags for rotten fruit and veg which they would convert into missiles, and charge through the green to get the best road side position. And within minutes, the field stood empty, empty that is except for one blue and very dead clown.

Tom the Placard was the first to receive a pelting as he was every year. He stood on the road outside the safety of the spectators barricade, with the placard he reserved for every Horns Day. *Beware False Idols*. Tom screamed to be heard over the jeering mob. "This is a pagan day, driven by the greed of bankers and town officials. It is a savage, satanic ritual and an affront to the Good Lord. It is an open sacrifice to Christian values and you should all leave now before you become as corrupted as the participants."

As always, Tom's words fell on deaf ears and the first missiles of the day were launched, quickly followed by a tirade of abuse aimed at the hapless preacher. Tom kept on protesting, regardless of the physical and verbal abuse, until two constables approached. One placed a hand on Tom's shoulder. "Come on now, Tom, you know what the Sergeant will do if he sees you, now you don't want any more of that treatment I shouldn't think."

"Yes!" Joined in the second constable. "And old Sarge is in a savage mood this morning."

Tom shook his head. "I've the right to my opinion, the same as these devil worshipping vagabonds."

The two constables, without another word, dragged the protesting Tom away, which resulted in a roar of cheers from the crowd.

It was only the sounding of the horn that staid the violence. The now bloody and torn Lock Horns dropped their fists and formed in ranks, waiting for the second blast that would begin the charge. Peter Bellroy's rank, as always, was a lonely place, isolated well to the back of the rabid mob, the isolation and his woollen head guaranteeing that he would receive more than his fair share of missiles and rotten fruit. The second blast of the horn sounded and the Locks Horns bellowed and roared with delight. The stampede began, and the thump of the legion stormed into life. The first stage of the stampede was usually the most docile, with no advantage to be gained, Beasts just kept their heads down and prepared for the pelting. But on this particular Horns Day, shoves and knocks were already manifesting as the different orders of Horns jockeyed for position. The Bulls still held the line, and probably would until the Rush, the final stage from the square to Devil's Plunge Gorge, where all hell, for certain, would break loose. The stampede reached the bottom of West brook

Hill, before them loomed the steep climb of the High Grove Way, then once the rise was crested they would reach Hemlock Green and the pelting would begin. Peter shuddered at the very thought, remembering the bicycle that clocked him last year, and near enough knocked him out. The horde panted its way up the steep embankment. Peter bit his bottom lip, not long now before hell broke loose.

Ethel Sledgewhick lay in wait behind the bushes, by her loathed zebra crossing. Oh how she hated this place; standing, smiling, for hour upon hour in all kinds of weather, helping little bastards across the road. It took all of her resolve, some days, not to push the grovelling little shits under a car. She gripped tight on her lollipop stick, the symbol of a child's safety, now held with a darker intent. Laughter, giggling, could this be what she was waiting for? Ethel peered up the street and, sure enough, there they were a group of eight to ten children, unsupervised; perfect. Ethel waited for the giggling little wastrels to near, picked her moment and stood imposing before them, lollipop pushed forward in threat.

"Hello Miss Sledgewhick," said Alice Humphries, giving the lollipop lady a beaming smile. "There's no school today, were all going to the pelting, want to come?"

Ethel rubbed her whiskers and snarled. "Now, why would I want to go anywhere with you disgusting little sewer rats?"

"Eh, that's not very nice," piped up Barry Bridges.

"Well guess what?" Said Ethel, raising the lollipop above her head. "I'm not very nice." And with a scream she charged. The children instantly screamed and scattered. Ethel swung her lollipop wildly, catching a few heads and limbs, the children howled in pain and fright and scarpered with the demonic lollipop lady hot on their heels. She screamed after them. "Come back you little bastards, let's see if you can fly across the fucking road!"

The howling children turned a corner and plunged straight into Hemlock Green and the charging Lock Horns. The children howled in panic, being stuck between the devil and the deep. Ethel screamed behind them "Come back you little bastards, I'll flatten the fucking lot of you!" Folk quickly became aware of the little mites' plight and grabbed and hoisted them over the safety of the barricade. But no such assistance was offered to the now totally enraged Ethel, whose screams of anger turned to horror as awareness of her peril loomed. The stampede reached a frenzy as the pelting began, and the air filled with missiles. The Lead Bulls were not about to stop for anyone or anything, as missiles found and hit their targets. Ethel's scream was blood curdling and short, cut off by the hammer blow of impact. Quickly she went down under a hundred hob-nailed boots, her body crushed and pulverised under the galloping rage.

The pelting hit a frenzy as the lower classes vented their rage and envy on the cream of their community. Bankers, Judges, Landlords the Police and elected officials, in short the backbone of the Lock Horns were splattered with the town's frustrations. But one eager participant, it seemed, cradled a conscience. David Berry was the one who checked his missiles for ripeness, making sure the fruit was not too hard to harm his intended target, and it was he who juggled missing the start of the pelting to zip off to the nearest phone box to call for medical assistance for the mortally stricken clown. it was a hard decision, even for a Christian soul like David, for there could be no doubt the jester was a twat, and probably a dead twat at that, but David could not live with himself if he thought the man had the slightest chance of life and redemption. With the ambulance on its way David dashed back to rejoin the pelting, eager not to miss all the fun. David quickly grabbed an over-ripe tomato and struck the Lock Horns Lamb straight in the kisser. It was one of many for Peter Bellroy, as he had expected, he soon became the prize coconut, the, lamb to slaughter that always drew the greatest attention. Children mocked him and bleated like sheep as he approached and they hammered him with missiles. He was pelted with rotten tomatoes, and over-ripe fruit, either item being more desirable than the green, rock hard potatoes, or the bicycle that hit him last year. He judged to being just about half way through the ordeal, and his lungs already burnt through effort, his eyes stung through the puss of rotten fruits, his head was bruised and swelling with a score of angry lumps and still the heavens were awash with missiles. Then without warning, Peter's foot hit something solid, and it sent him crashing to the floor. His knees broke the fall and tore through the friction and Peter howled in pain. The crowd roared with delight as the stampede advanced without him, leaving him totally exposed, and the pelting reached fever pitch. Peter struggled to his feet as a storm of missiles smashed into him, he briefly glanced at the object that caused his predicament and downfall. Ethel groaned and slowly raised her head, which was quickly pelted with tomatoes. Peter's usual instinct would have been to assist the hapless, trampled soul, but an even greater instinct kicked in first, that of life preservation, and he hobbled as quick as he could to rejoin the pack.

Ethel Sledgewhick groaned to her feet and snarled at the heckling mob, full of horrid little brats. She raised her lollipop in fury and screamed so loud that she didn't hear the warning from the bellowing onlookers. Indeed, the last thing Ethel heard was the clanging of bells. She turned her head just as the ambulance screeched, applying its brakes all too late for Ethel. The impact sent a shudder of cracked bones through the air, Ethel's bulk was sucked and torn and dragged under the wagon of mercy. The spectators fell silent as the ambulance finally halted, revealing the lollipop lady who, without a doubt, has popped her clogs. Ethel lay torn and broken in a bloody heap, her lollipop twisted around her body, reading, *Road Safety First.*

Fitz and Sylvia had a grand view of the square from the shop's loft window, and they could feel the tension and simmering violence from the arena bellow. The junior bouts were the first of the day and the ring that stood centre stage on the square was a scrum of disgruntled, bickering parents, all prepared to fight to the death for the honour of their violent little angels. Indeed, the fights outside the ring seemed more entertaining than the official bouts. Fitz shook her head. "Not a poet to be among them!"

Sylvia laughed. "What, in Sickle? I should think not, that vocation is sure to get you a beating! Even the church encourages what they call the noble art of…"

"There!" Fitz points to the edge of the crowd. Sylvia peers through the crowd. "Ah yes, if it isn't our fat Sergeant! Ooh, he does not seem in a very good mood."

Sergeant Hardy steamrollered through the square and, indeed, his mood scorched all around him as his temper blazed.

Fitz smirked. "He's the devil all right."

Sergeant Hardy was dragging his portly lad by the ear to the ringside, jostling and shoving all in his path, and even from Sylvia and Fitz's perch, high above the square, they could well hear his curses and obscenities. "Oh dear," said Fitz, shaking her head. "He does seem in a bit of a mood!" Both Ladies laughed, knowing the clock was ticking.

The Lock Horns poured into the square to howls of triumph. Barmaids and barmen greeted them with trays of ice cold, frothing ale, which were greedily grabbed and quipped. Peter Bellroy picked a lonely spot in a shop doorway and collapsed to the floor, every nerve in his body screaming for rest and mercy. Just one hour, now, to compose before the rush would begin, hence the bloodiest part of the day, and Peter was worried that he did not have much blood left to lose. He sat and sobbed at his hopeless situation, he was damned, his life devoid of decisions and free will. There seemed no end to his misery. His Father would damn him to hell if he ever had the nerve to speak his mind and say he didn't like rough sports or being a Lock Horn, or that what he'd really like to do is read and cycle through the countryside and live a life of peace without being in the employment of the dreadful bully, Councillor fucking Hardy. Peter covered his head and tried his best to disappear. In his pitiful state, he failed to notice the shop door edging open behind him. He jumped as he felt a tap on his shoulder, quickly composing before he was disgraced yet again by his tears. But there was no raging bull or goat glaring down at him, just a kindly smile. "Peter, isn't it?" Said Sylvia, bending down and offering him her hanky. Peter struggled to his feet. "Oh, Missus Bevan! I thought..."

"I know what you thought," said Sylvia looking the lad over, "my God, look at the state of you!"

Peter gave a long sigh. "The stampede, you know how it is, makes a man of you!"

"Makes a fool, more like," said Fitz, emerging through the shop door.

"Oh my God they're looking for you! They suspect you're not dead, Old Tom..."

"I don't really care what they think, they know!" Snapped Fitz.

"Steady Fitz," said Sylvia. "Peter's a nice lad, still working for that horrid Councillor?"

Peter shook his head. "I hate him, I hate all of this, it's the last thing I want to be doing."

Sylvia stroked the lad's brow. "Well who knows, perhaps you won't have to do it for much longer?"

"PETER, PETER!" The all too familiar voice bellowed across the square.

"Oh dear," sighed Peter, "that will be Bill Marshal, I'd best be gone."

"And why is that?" Questioned Fitz. "It's plain to see you don't won't to go!"

Peter shook his head. "It's my duty, as the Lamb, to wait on the Lead Bull, I've got no choice!"

Fitz grabbed hold of Peter's arm as he made to leave. "Now you listen to me, young man, today is going to be a day of choices, today is the breaking of chains, a chance for all to charge free and make their own decisions. And that, my lad, will show far more courage than holding your tongue and following the commands of this bunch of rabble."

Peter hesitated for the briefest of moments, until Bill Marshal hollered his name once again.

"Off you go," said Fitz, shooing him with her hand. "But you remember this; if you see a chance today, an opportunity to change you're miserable lot, you make sure you grab it with both hands. For today, I promise you, will give forth a bounty of opportunities."

"Okay," said the bemused lad, and he quickly hobbled to his master's call.

Fitz and Sylvia edged through the crowd, heads scarfed and eyes down. Sylvia shook with nerves. After all, talking about being bold was far easier than being it, and she would never possess the bare faced courage of her lover. The square felt like it was being held at a knife point, the throng on the brink of madness, being staid by just the finest tightrope of reason. Sylvia looked at the faces and the eyes that stared right through you into the void of bedlam. Laughter that rose for no reason and brows that creased in strain, struggling to contain a smouldering rage. Fitz turned to face her lover. "I know, let's go to church!"

"What!" Sylvia gasped. "Oh I don't…"

"Missus Bevan?" Sylvia turned in alarm as Tom the Placard placed a hand on her shoulder. "I saw you dead!"

Fitz knocked the hand off Sylvia's shoulder. "What, jealous are you Tom? Jealous that we achieved your life-long ambition, and are yet here to tell the tale? Perhaps it's us that your Good Lord favours? My, my, all that endless devotion for fuck all!"

"This is no resurrection!" Barked Tom. "This is the eruption of damnation, a plague of devils has crept through this town, and feeds like mould on the good people of Sickle, and it is you!"

The explosion halted time, a shuddering thump to the senses that derailed all from their tracks. Folk covered their ears and looked to the heavens, a huge plume of black smoke pumped into the air from the outskirts of town. People quickly composed when they realised they were still intact and pointed to the heavens as the black plume climbed ever higher. The grateful survivors began to cheer and clap, taking the combustion as part of the show, a grand firework with a tail for destruction.

Fitz laughed. "There's hell for you, Tom, and they all love it!"

A blast of a horn is the next sound to thud through the square, announcing the final stage of the stampede. The rush was about to begin and the crowd went wild.

HORNS DAY - THE BLODGER BROTHERS...

Rory, Zac and Archie, the three Blodger brothers, slept in their shack amid their sacred scrap, and on this night, the eve of Horns Day, the brothers' sleep soon turned into a nightmare of troubles, and they lay twisted in their soiled sheets wrestling with their dreams. The night became a vision of unspeakable horrors as simmering doubts manifested into probabilities. The brothers groaned and snarled in their slumber, as betrayal weaved its illusion, knitting worries into fact and dismissing all doubt.

Rory, the eldest and sharpest, was the first to rise. He had something on his mind. He dressed quickly, ignored the kettle and made for the yard. He passed row upon row of piled high scrapped cars and metals and headed with purpose to a particular piece of twisted carnage. He crawled through a tunnel of mangled metal until he came to a rusted old car boot. He brought out a key, turned the lock and reached in, retrieving a strong box wrapped in old sacking. With the second key he opened the lock and smiled lovingly at the wad that sat inside. Rory justified his little stash as a privilege of the eldest brother, after all his father, though leaving the yard equally to all three, entrusted Rory to maintain the status quo and to have a plan in place for any troublesome rainy days. Rory again smiled to himself, thinking it would have to be a monsoon before his brothers caught wind of his little secret. He placed the box back in its hideaway, locked it, double checked that the stash was safely secured and crawled back out of his glory hole. The first thing Rory saw as he emerged from his hideaway was the old Elm tree that stood centre of the yard; a grand old tree surrounded by a sea of ruin. "Hum," he grunted. "Young Zac loves climbing that old tree." Rory was about to walk back for a cuppa when a thought hit him; *just why does Zac like climbing that old tree?* His scrumping days were long gone and there were no apples to be had anyway. Could it be young Zac was hiding something? With the cat and his curiosity already killed, Rory started scaling the Old Elm, ever so slowly, for it had been a long time since Rory had scrumped apples. Midway up Rory came upon an old Woodpecker's nest, he reached inside and sure enough his suspicions were confirmed. He pulled out the securely tied, swathed bundle, untied it and tutted. "Why, the sneaky little bastard! Oh well, here's to rainy days."

With his brother's stash now safely secured under his lock and key, Rory again headed for the shack and his first cup of tea. He passed the barn wherein lay the rusting old Mustang that Archie had spent near a life time restoring, with still no noticeable improvement. Rory was just about to walk by, when a thought hit him; *why did Archie spend so much time in that wreck with no obvious result?* Rory walked into the barn, opened the car door and looked under the seats, behind the dashboard, in the glove compartment; nothing. He was just about to try the boot, when his sharp money grabbing eye spied the slightest bulge protruding from the car's underlay. He ripped the carpet back and there, sure enough, lay an oil rag wrapped bundle. "Fuck me!" Gasped Rory "I'm surrounded by thieves!" Once again he crawled into his glory hole and laid another egg in his nest.

Archie and Zac rose together, the weasel like siblings sniffed nervously at each other without saying a word. The door swung open and in walked Rory.

"Where the fuck have you been?" Snapped Zac.

"Fucking earning coin, while you two lazy fuckers waste it, lying on your fucking backs!" Said Rory, grabbing the kettle and filling it. "Tea?"

"Not like you to rise and not wake us?" Questioned Archie.

Rory swung round to face his brother, kettle pointing in threat. "Fuck me, don't you think I see enough of you bloody ugly little bastards? Or do you want me to take you for a shit next?"

Archie and Zac both grunted in reply and quickly put on their clothes, refused tea and quickly headed out to the yard, both with a nagging feeling that something was amiss.

Zac leapt off the tree and stormed across the yard, meeting Archie as he bounded out of the barn. Both brothers snarled at each other and together they mouthed, "The thieving, fucking bastard!"

Rory walked into the yard, cup of tea in hand. "Something wrong, boys?"

Archie turned towards his brother, his face racked with rage. "You know what's fucking wrong!"

"Yeah, you know!" Added Zac.

Rory just smiled in the face of his brothers' rage. "Well I aint gonna know jack shit, lest you tell me."

"You've taken something!" Said Archie, pointing threat in his brother's face.

Rory placed down his tea. "Taken what, Archie?"

"MY FUCKING STASH!" fumed Archie.

"Yeah and fucking mine!" joined in Zac. "I had it up that tree…What you gonna tell me, a fucking squirrel took it?"

Rory rolled up his sleeves. "Now then, maybe a squirrel did take it, and if he did it would serve you right keeping money back from our joint enterprise, and…"

"Oh, and I suppose said squirrel opened a car door and took off with mine?" Growled Archie.

Rory shook his head. "Well, well our old Dad will be turning in his grave, seeing the disrespect you show me, the eldest, and now head of the family."

Archie's laugh was grating and laced with scorn. "Respect? Dad always told us not to trust you, said you had the snake of Mother's Father about you."

Rory didn't say a word, he just chewed furiously the insult over and launched, smashing into Archie, fists flying. Archie quickly went down under the force of his brother's fury, coming under a storm of blows.

Zac was always one to use a weapon, preferring the security of something more solid than his fists. He held the shovel firmly in both hands, testing its weight and judging the best spot on Rory's head to deliver a knock-out blow. There could be no room for error, for his elder brother had the fight and fire of a lion when roused. The shovel hit its target with a sickening thud and, much to Zac's relief, Rory dropped like a sack of shit. Archie pushed off the dead weight of his brother and got to his feet, bloody and bruised. "That'll teach the bastard," said Archie, spitting out a loose tooth.

"Yeah," panted Zac, keeping an eye on Rory, lest he should rise and vent his fury.

Archie put his hands on his knees, taking in much needed air. "So Zac, this stash of yours?"

Zac's hands tightened on the shovel once again at the mention of his stash. "What about it?"

"Well it's the first I've heard about it."

"You'll get the fucking same as Rory, Archie, if you fucking start on me!"

"I aint gonna start! Just wish you could have trusted me, that's all."

"Aye, like you trusted me!"

Archie straightened up. "Anyway, best we get back what's ours before that old bastard comes round. Any ideas?"

Zac considered for a moment. "Well he's always potching about down bottom yard. I reckon we should start there."

"Good as anywhere, I suppose," said Archie. "But it ain't going to be easy, the crafty old bastard is as shifty as a rattle snake when it comes to money."

It was a good hour before the brothers found the well hidden and carefully constructed burrow between the tangle of scrap and old bangers. It then took another good hour of ripping through rusted hinges and metal before they prized open the boot and found the strong box. Archie grabbed hold of the box and quickly crawled out of the tunnel with his brother worming inches behind, they emerged, into the light, Archie clutching jealously tight the strong box. Zac, sensing mischief, grabbed the shovel off the floor.

"Good idea," said Archie. I'll put it on the floor and you break the lock with that shovel."

"And then?" Questioned Zac.

"And then, fifty, fifty Zac, what else?"

Zac raised the shovel over his head. "Fifty, fifty brother, what else?" Zac swivelled the weapon at the last minute, aiming it at his brother's head just as the bullet exploded through his neck, sending blood spraying over Archie. Zac gurgled as blood bubbled out of his mouth, his eyes slowly losing sight of life. He crumpled to the floor, dead and forever out of pocket.

Archie looked up at the demon of his approaching elder, wiser brother, his rifle aimed between his eyes. "PUT DOWN MY FUCKING BOX!" Barked Rory, staring steady along the barrel.

Archie slowly placed the strong box on the ground and rose slowly, keeping a close eye on his deadly brother. "I was keeping it safe for you, brother, making sure that thieving little bastard didn't take it."

Rory laughed. "Sure you were brother." And without another word he pulled the trigger home. Archie's dive averted death by inches, but still the bullet caught flesh, and Archie howled as blood poured from his shoulder. He darted into the jungle of scrap, bullets howling overhead.

Archie slumped down, exhausted, his blood and energy draining fast.

"Not long now, thief," shouted Rory. Archie held his breath; his brother was far too close for a tell-tale sound to be made. "Yeah, an hour tops, I reckon." Gloated Rory. "Before every last drop of blood oozes out of your thieving fucking hide… best we talk, Eh? Sort this mess out before it's too late."

Not for the briefest second did Archie consider his brother's kind offer, he knew his brother well, and you'd fare better fucking his wife than his pocket. Archie judged the direction of his brother's voice, picked a route and started scaling the pyramid of cars, bounding over them in the opposite direction to his brother's voice. The clatter of metal and groans of pain, immediately alerted Rory. He looked up and spied his desperate brother leaping and bounding for safety. Rory smiled and cocked his gun. He had a fair idea were his sibling was heading, so steadily he advanced towards the showdown.

Archie hit the ground running, but the giggle and the click of a loading gun told him his efforts had been in vain. Rory's smile was black, toothless and devoid of mercy. "Bye, bye brother!" He spat, and without another word he squeezed the trigger home. The realisation of doom came on a reel of slow motion for Rory, for as the trigger sparked with life, and his brother's dive for survival froze mid-flight; Rory, all too late, noticed the ticking time bomb. "OH SHIT!" was Rory's last will and testament, as the bullet struck the storage tank of boot-legged fuel.

The firestorm instantly wiped the slate clean, as every speck of Blodger was smote from the face of the earth, a furnace of justice that bellowed its judgement with a tower of smoke over the town of Sickle. Earth to earth, rag to bone.

HORNS DAY - THE HARDY BROTHERS...

Brinmore was fucking angry, and so was his wife, Wilma, and their son Thomas. In fact, even the cat and the goldfish looked bloody livid, the whole family woke seething and boiling with blood lust. The home of turbulent squalor looked even more upset and disorganised, as the family prepared for Horns day. Brinmore's darling wife stared lovingly at her breakfast, making her biggest decision of the day; which sausage to eat first. It would not take her long to prepare herself for the festive event, she'd just shovel on a dress, ladder her tights over the enormity of her arse, raid the fridge for snacks and make for the door. Brinmore looked down at his son as he battled with his top button, press-ganging his neck against its will. "You make fucking sure you beat your fucking cousin's head in, in that ring today," said Brinmore, waving a fat finger in threat. Thomas and Harold, the Hardy brothers' boys, were in their early teens. Both boys were greedy, fat and mean like their fathers had intended. They were bred to battle and hate each other the Hardy way. The boy didn't even look up from his breakfast, he just mumbled with a fully stuffed gob. "I'll fucking kill him!"

"Yeah," screeched his mother, in between big fat helpings of fried mash and swede. "Show you're fucking father how to do it!"

Sergeant Hardy smashed his fist into the table. "I beat my brother constantly."

His darling wife laughed. "Course you do, that's why he's wearing the Horns of the Goat Major this year and you ain't. That's why he pulls the strings from his plush office, with his plush salary and you dance a jig every time he gives you a tug."

"HE CHEATED!" Roared Brinmore, snorting gallons of snot in anger.

"So!" Retorted his wife. "He still fucking well won!"

Brinmore raged. "Why don't you shut your big fat greedy gob, you disgusting fat bitch!"

"Hit her, Dad!" Chipped in his son.

The Mother quickly vented her anger at her boy. "SHUT YOUR MOUTH YOU LITTLE CUNT!"

"Enough!" Brinmore turned a deep, bloody scarlet. "I warn you both, I've a fever to kill this day, just one opportunity I need and I swear I'll wring some fuckers neck! And you, woman, if you want to bring some victory to this family, enter the pie eating competition, for God knows there can't be a bigger gob or gut in the whole wide fucking world!" Sergeant Hardy ducked as a fried egg hurtled across the room. "And clean that fucking up, you bitch, I'm off! And Thomas, you spar till it fucking well hurts, because if you lose today I'm going to show you what pain is all about." And with that, Brinmore placed the stag's horns on his head and made for the door with the screams of his brood behind him.

Boris Hardy's wife, Agatha, sat at her fine teak table with a polished expression on her face. The woman was delicate and bone china thin. Her rapier pointed nose jutted out accusingly at everything in its aim. She was a distasteful creature who spat venom with never a good word, her manner always served with a twist of poison. But it suited Boris just fine, the home was well kept, his boy, though not loved by her, was nevertheless well turned out and Boris was left to do as he pleased. But this morning, Boris had woken on a knife edge, his whole body ached with the strain of staying his fists. His son, sensing the turbulence in his father's scowl, kept his head down. Boris stood in front of the dinning room's grand, gold framed mirror, suited in official black of office, all that remained was to place the Goat Horns upon his head and he was ready to conquer the world. With the helmet firmly placed, Boris twirled to face his audience, peacock pride smudged on his face. "Well?" He questioned.

Harold, his son, got to his feet clapping and cheering as he did so. "You look great Dad...And one day I shall wear those horns and do you proud."

"Course you will, son. Well, woman?" He spat at his unresponsive wife.

Ever so slowly, Agatha's crane knotted neck, cranked and locked into focus. She looked her husband from head to toe, with a slight curl of mirth on her lips, and a deep loathing in her eyes. "Huh! You look ridiculous!" She rasped. "But then, you always do."

Within seconds Boris had shattered his wife's face, finding her wafer thin bone structure easy to crack. Her pin boned hook of a nose snapped like a dry twig under the force of his hammer. Then he ragged her like a dog tearing at a toy doll, smashing the lithe frame around the four corners of the room. Agatha lay crumpled and wrecked, her blood soiling her pristinely kept home, groaning and chocking in a daze of agony.

Boris, a blood boiled red, panted in a deep growl of fury. He looked to his son who stood tucked and quaking in a corner. "Here's your chance boy, how many lads of your age dream of kicking the fuck out of their domineering bitch mothers?" The boy looked to his father, unsure. "But, Dad…"

"KICK THE FUCKING WHORE!"

Harold, with the mixed emotions of fear and excitement, set about the task with vigour, his boot crashing down on his mother's chest. He grinned in delight at the sound of splintering ribs and the wheeze of breath that rattled from his mother's battered lungs, thoughts of her constant scolding driving him on. Next he football kicked into his mother's gut. Boris roared with delight as a volley of boots rammed in to his loathed spouse. Harold finished with a winning strike to the head, and father and son stood side by side, looking with pride at a good job done. Boris ruffled his son's hair. "That's my boy! If anything stands in your way you knock the fucking thing down, you hear me? Anything, anyone, don't give the fuckers a single inch or they'll take you for a fucking mile."

Harold shook his head. "Yeah Dad, knock the fuckers down."

"Now then," said Boris, as he headed for the door. "You damn well make sure you do that to your cousin this afternoon, or I'll….be doing it to you! Now get that bitch off the floor and clean this place up, I'll catch you ringside later."

And without another word, Boris bullied out of the door and marched off to chaos.

The Lock Horns roared as their leader, The Goat Major, Councillor Hardy, stood staged before them, arms raised to the heavens. Only one lone Stag stood unimpressed, not sharing his comrades enthusiasm, and while the throng bellowed their appraisal, Sergeant Hardy remained at the alfresco buffet gorging himself, spitting out crumbs and obscenities.

"Quite a firework, eh?" Said Boris, pointing to the black smoke that belched above the town into the heavens. "I hope the fuckers had a long fuse, or by the look of that smoke they'll be walking about with short fucking arms." The jest brought a howl of laughter from the blood thirsty pack. Stags, Bulls, Rams and Antelopes rutted the ground and clashed their horns. Boris waved his arms for silence. "But this is what it is all about, our glorious day, a day when we can shelve the hum-drum, and be the beasts we were born to be. For, to be a man you must savour the wild and embrace its savage heart." The crowd surged forward, different factions shoving and jostling with their rivals. Boris held himself proud as a King, looking down on his subjects, with a grin, scorned with satisfaction. "For I tell all, the bleeding hearts who look down upon us, stay the fuck out of our way, for we shall trample underfoot the runts of this town, the spongers and loafers who cry and whine at their pitiful lot. And I'll tell you now, they'll get no mercy here, for our God is the might of success, our temple the mint of coins, for like the beast that we are born, survival is beheld of the fittest, and all the rest will claim the dirt they so deserve."

The manic of the crowd erupted, packs exploding into their tribal chants. Boris raised his hands into the air. "My fellow Lock Horns, a century ago my grandfather set our noble association into being, calling on real men to take the challenge and live and rule by the rod. For make no mistake the challenges met on our noble stampede are the challenges of life, and the men who stand proud at the Devil's Gorge are the men who will flourish in life, their heads held high with the might of power pressed into their fists! So without further ado, for I can sense your hunger, your yearning to crush all that stands in your way, gentlemen, let the rush begin and may the boldest beast claim its prize. Onward to blood! Onward to glory! And let the beast of men charge forth!"

The roars and cheers were deafening. Tankards and trays of food crashed to the floor as the Lock Horns grappled for position. The Bulls, once again, held the line, waiting for the final horn to sound. Peter Bellroy was now positioned central to the pack, the rush being the stage of the stampede, where the Lamb can prove himself and rise through the ranks. All he had to do was get past ten violently insane Bulls, all built like brick shit houses, with a lust to kill anything that breathed so Peter could not foresee promotion any time soon. The horn sounded, the madness reared its insanity and galloped into bedlam, with every tongue except for Peter's, savouring the glory of blood and victory.

The square abated to a simmer as the rush headed out of town. Revellers refilled at the bars, and punters gathered ringside, waiting for the afternoon bouts to begin. Spectators took their turn at the buffet, feeding on the scraps that the Lock Horns had discarded. Councillor Hardy approached the buffet where his brother still gorged. "Nice horns, brother."

Brinmore, without looking up from his food, snarled. "Why don't you fuck off brother?"

"Now, now." Boris laughed. "That's no way to greet the Goat Major!"

Brinmore spun round to face his smug sibling, his mouth and chin a mash of grub and grease. "My boy will wipe that fucking smile off your face when he caves that lady boy of yours fucking face in!"

Boris went right into his brother's face. "What, like he did last year brother? If my boy is as you say, a bit of a pansy, then what the fuck does that make yours?"

Brinmore growled and lunged at his brother's throat. Boris grabbed his brother's hands and both stood locked, glaring fury in each other's eyes. "I tell you what," snarled Boris, "after my lad has swept your boy off the canvas, why don't me and you do a couple of rounds?"

"Deal!" Growled Brinmore, and they unlocked and headed to the ring.

The rush actually began with a canter, with everyone conserving energy before they arrived at Thatcher's Lane. Thatcher's Lane was the gauntlet; a narrow country road, high hedged, a perfect vacuum for compressed violence. It was where the Bulls would link arms, creating a bottle-neck for opposing Horns to fight it out before the final rush to the finishing line at Devil's Plunge Gorge. Peter gulped, knowing full well that this pleasant canter would not last long. For just ahead he could see the open mouth of hell in the form of Thatcher's lane. Peter could hear blood boiling all around him, he could smell the fever, its scent swarming the senses with the rank taste of riot, as the opening loomed, ready to plunge his world into the deadly crush of mindless agro. "LINK ARMS!" Howled Bill Marshal, as the lead Bulls hammered into the lane. Peter prayed to all and every God he could think of and was, alas, answered by none, as he was swept along by a tide of rabid drool into Thatcher's Lane and the clutches of madness.

Fitz could see the smouldering hell of Boris Hardy as he belched out his war charge. The fever of his rage was all consuming, sapping his great bulk of moisture, his skin blotched and cracked, parched and arid as a desert, the corners of his lips curled and frothed rabid, his eyes bulging with the strain and fury of his heartbeat. Fitz and Sylvia did not hide, they walked uncloaked through their home town. This, after all, was judgement day and Fitz had no intention of shying from her mischief. All around Fitz could sense and see her handy work. She could see the strain on faces as the monsters struggled with their inner demons, the bleeding, cracked lips, the blood orange eyes, the on edge reactions and the jittering nerves. Fights broke out for minor provocations, a simple nudge in the tightly packed crowd could, in seconds, result in the bloodiest of confrontations. The whole bizarre was wired, charged with madness, you either held the raving insanity or by God you felt it. The whole square had the feel of eruption, a powder keg of trigger happy anger. Fitz nudged Sylvia for attention. "Oh look dear, here comes our two fat friends, heading for the ring by the looks of it. Fancy taking in a couple of bouts, dear?"

Sylvia smiled and took her lover's arm as they jostled through the crowd.

The Hardy brothers shouldered and bullied their way through the crowd, ready to take, as always, their hog's share of the limelight. They grunted threats and insults as they barged their way through the crowd, aware as always, of the fear they commanded. Both brothers heaved themselves into the ring, raising their arms into the air and bathing in the sycophantic accolade their position demanded. Two young podgy lads entered the ring, both piggy eyed, their features like their fathers, tensely viced in loathing. The brothers raised the hands of their protégés, bragging their boys before the crowd.

The Hardy brothers stepped out of the ring, screaming commands at their sons, who wait tensed and poised, waiting for the bell to sound and their battle to begin. The referee for the fight, a slither of a man who was the unfortunate owner of a short straw, trembled into the ring, his mind awash with thoughts of elsewhere. "Ladies and Gentlemen." Began Horace Phillips, his eyes a twitch of nerves and his bald pate a gloss of sweat. "I want a fair fight."

"Well you better keep an eye on that cheating little bastard!" Screamed Brinmore, pointing at Harold. Horace looked nervously at both men, fearing the worst, and without another word he darted for the corner and the bell rang.

The two boys prowled into the centre of the ring, to a deluge of cheers and heckles as they tested the water, circling and flexing jab and cut. Both fathers screamed for blood, eager for the crack of bone and the knock-out blow. Thomas was first to take the plunge, with a flurry of jabs that found their mark. Brinmore howled with delight and Boris seethed, howling obscenities at his son. Harold, egged on by his father's wrath, countered, diving head first into his cousin. He rammed forward, the crown of his head connecting with Thomas's nose. Thomas howled in protest as his father dived into the ring. "Foul, foul!" Yelled Brinmore, as the bell sounded. Brinmore grabbed the hapless referee by the scruff. "Are you fucking blind or paid off?"

"Sour grapes, brother" Laughed Boris. "First blood to us."

Brinmore dropped the ref and growled, marching his son into his corner. Both fathers howled commands and instructions at their sons. The bell again sounded and the two boys entered the ring with the weight of their fathers on their shoulders. Thomas wasted no time and again lead into the attack, catching his cousin well, with a combination of hooks and jabs. Harold countered with a flurry of careless swings that his cousin easily fended off, immediately countering with another volley of well placed shots that sent Harold sprawling to the canvas.

"Get the fuck up!" Howled Boris at his dazed son. "Or be damned I'll put you down and you'll never rise again!"

Harold rose to his feet, straight into his cousin's gloating face and the count was stopped. Harold then took the advantage as his cousin dropped his guard and charged, grabbing Thomas around his neck and ramming his free hand with lightning force into Thomas's groin. The boy howled in pain and crumpled to the floor, clutching his throbbing balls, the surge of nausea turning his face an instant sickly green.

Brinmore's reaction to the blatant low shot was an instant storm of violence. The Stag Head bounded over the ropes, his actions fuelled by a scorching rage. He thrust himself forward, grabbed the bewildered Harold, raised him with ease above his head and tossed him out of the ring and into the crowd. Young Thomas, knowing what was good for him, quickly scarpered before his Uncle Boris could reach him and dish out some more of the same. A blood curdling scream belled from the opposition's corner and within seconds the Goat Head was also in the ring. The two beasts steamed with venom, their beady eyes locked in the gaze of intended murder. "So, it's come to this, brother!" Snorted Boris.

Brinmore growled deeply. "What else could it come to, brother? Your undoing has been a long time waiting."

The two beasts circled and the crowd went wild, all eager to see the two loathed brothers tear themselves to pieces. Fitz grabbed Sylvia by the arm. "Come on, let's get to the front!" Sylvia pulled back. "No Fitz, they might see us…"

"Oh Syl, I'm going to make sure they see us!" And without further ado Fitz dragged her lover through the crowd to get a ringside view.

Peter Bellroy felt like a freshly squeezed orange with the juice of his life force being crushed out of his backside. Thatcher's Lane felt a thousand miles long as the surge moved a step forward and ten steps back. The fighting was fierce and bloody, more savage, than any year Peter could remember, and the end seemed like a dream, that belonged to anyone but himself. The Bulls held firm, inching forward then locking down causing, havoc as Goats, Stags and Antelopes battered each other black and blue to gain position. When the release came the feeling was that of a drop on a big dipper, Peter took a huge drag of air as the vice of the throng released its grip and lunged forward, sweeping him along in its wake, as the Rush surged for its climax. Peter went in to free fall, emerging on his knees from the hell of Thatcher's Lane. The Bulls had already reached the finish line at the foot of Devil's Plunge Gorge and were roaring in triumph, and that should have been the end of the madness. However, the roar of triumph from the Bulls was to be short lived as the surge of Lock Horns continued forward, their rage far from abated. The Bulls braced themselves, fists at the ready, and the clash of blistering frustration thudded into life with splintering force. Peter had to get away from the madness before he was killed, he looked for an exit, going back was out of the question, the brawling was fierce right up to Thatcher's lane. Then a thought from his past gave him a glimmer of hope.

Peter ducked and weaved through the melee, ignoring the stray punch or kick that connected as he scrambled, desperate to reach his haven. The tree grew sheer from the side of the Gorge, Peter knew the spot well, it had afforded him triumph in the game of hide and seek a thousand times. He had to be careful on the descent, but Peter judged it safer than the company of rabid beasts. He firmly grabbed the bough of the tree, edged out slowly, reached midway and dropped. The ledge that broke his fall was a good four feet into the cliff face, with an overhang that shielded him from view. Peter slid down on to the sill and sighed deeply with relief. The ease of tension and peace of mind instantly brought out the thump of deep bruising, but Peter cared not and smiled. "Safe." He closed his eyes, relishing the rest and solace of his bolt hole.

He woke to silence, not a curse or a thud or a howl of agony could he hear. His plan had worked, the pack had departed and he could return home and not worry about another cursed Horns Day for a full glorious year. Slowly, and with care, Peter took hold of the bough and heaved himself out of the gorge and to the safety of the cliff top. He dusted off his hands and screamed to the heavens. "Ha, ha, I done it, no more fucking bulls and kicks and…"

"WHO'S THERE? HELP, HELP, DOWN HERE!" Peter jumped, instantly looking round for danger, but he could see no one, and again he heard the call. "Help please, please, down here!" The voice was below him, coming from the Gorge. Peter ran to the location of the voice. "Hold on just a moment." He peered down over the huge drop. Bill Marshal's beetroot red face stared up, his teeth clenched hard as he teetered on the verge of oblivion, his hands clutching root for dear life, his foothold a mere shadow of a sill. "Oh dear!" Gasped Peter.

"Never mind oh dear!" Fumed Bill, his tone a growl, and a quiver of desperation. "Fucking do something Bellroy!"

"Ah, of course…Let me think!"

"Well don't think too fucking long." Peter bent down and started to lower his hand.

"Come on now, Bellroy, you get me out of here and I'll make you a Lock Horn, lad, no more fluffy ears eh!"

Peter touched the woollen hat, he'd almost forgotten it was there. He yanked the emblem of shame from his head and flung it to the floor.

Bill grinned back, his teeth clenched in effort. "Now, for fuck's sake, hurry up and get me out of here!" Peter withdrew his hand and stood up. "What the fuck are you doing?" Roared Bill.

Peter gazed down and memories of the man and the torment he'd inflicted flooded into Peter's mind, the beatings, the endless humiliation, the teasing, the fetching and carrying with the only thanks a sock in the mouth.

"Do you know?" Peter smiled. "The last thing in this world I would care to be...Is a fucking low down, stinking, Lock Horn."

"Why you!" Bill wobbled and screamed in alarm. "Bellroy... Stop bloody dithering boy! I'm warning you!"

"I don't think you're in any position to warn me Bill!"

Bill, boiled purple with strain, gritted his teeth and hissed through his clenched teeth. "I'll see you dead for this, Bellroy...Dead! NOW FUCKING PULL ME UP!"

Peter just smiled, recalling what Sylvia Bevan's friend had said to him. "Oh I don't think so Bill, you see today is a day of opportunity, and if it comes your way, you must grab it with both hands."

"What the fuck you on about? You wimp faced, spotty little bastard!"

"Hmm," mused Peter, "I wonder if you can take opportunity with both feet?"

"WHAT THE FUCK!" Peter looked down into the eyes of his despised tormentor, raised his foot and stamped down hard on the knuckles of Bill Marshal. His hands instantly popped open and Bill Marshal plummeted. "ARRGHHHHHHHHH!"

Peter grinned, watching his tormentor tumble to certain death, for the first time ever feeling responsible for his actions.

He heard far below the distant thud of impact, and clapped his hands with joy. "Now there's opportunity for you."

The scene resembled Greek mythology; a canvas painted in the time of chaos, two gigantic grunting beasts, one half goat and the other half stag, shoved into an arena amid a sea of baying hounds, all panting for the sight of blood. The mob surged forward, all eager to witness the suffering of the worshipped but loathed contestants. The brothers circled, tensing biceps and snarling in threat, their faces turned gargoyle with rage. "You're too fat and old for this game, brother." Mocked Brinmore, as he feigned a lunge forward.
Boris laughed. "I've beaten you, brother, in every contest life has to offer, and I cannot see this bit of a skirmish being any different!"
Brinmore now laughed. "Oh but brother, I intend on dishing out far more than a bit of a skirmish!"
And with that Brinmore growled and crashed into his brother, the shudder of the clashing titans thudding through the audience, causing a roar of excitement. The brothers locked and heaved back and forth in a see-saw of stalemate. Heads crashed and Brinmore saw an opening and locked tight his teeth on his brother's ear, shaking and tearing like a hound with a hare. Boris howled in agony and thrashed wild, to release his brother's vice like grip, and the blood poured. In desperation, Boris plunged a thumb into his brother's eye, and now, Brinmore howled, releasing his brother from the savage chewing. The brothers parted and licked their wounds, both winded and panting for breath, and this time Boris was the first to advance. Taking advantage of his brother's blind side, he hammered his fist straight into his nose. Brinmore toppled back from the impact, sprawling on the ropes, and Boris was on him again, smashing down fist after fist on his brother's face. Brinmore crumpled under the force, but as he went down he grabbed for his brother's shirt, yanked down hard and both crashed to the canvas with an earth shuddering belly flop of flab. And the crowd again went wild as the two fat boys rolled and grappled on the deck, and for the second time that

day the chant of *kill* echoed through the streets of Sickle. The brothers again parted and struggled to their feet, Brinmore being the first to rise, as he readied his shaking fists. Boris needed the help of the ropes to winch up his bulk as he stopped, panting for breath on the ropes.

Fitz picked her moment well; she pulled herself up to the ring and whispered into Boris's blood soaked ear. "Remember me, fat boy, I'm the whore who's going to fuck you up!" Fitz dropped back into the crowd. Boris, puzzled, shook it off and turned to face his brother, then the realisation hit him. Boris turned his head. "Oi, you're that damned witch, I'll…" And, distracted, he heard his brother's roar all too late. As he turned to face his brother he saw the raging stag, head down charging towards him. The antlers of Brinmore cracked through ribs with ease and pierced straight into the cushion of the Councillor's heart. Brinmore yanked free of his antlered helm. Boris teetered before him, mouth agape in the horror and realisation of the conclusion in fatality. His mouth bubbled blood and his eyes bled tears at the inevitable loss of life. Brinmore smiled. "Who's laughing now, brother?"

Boris pointed a shaking, damning finger towards his brother. "You, you, ARGHHHH!" And with his last act in the role of his violent, mean, twisted life, Boris plunged forward, and with all his dead weight rammed the horn of the Goat Major straight through his brother's eye, smashing through the socket into the sponge of his brain.

The macabre spectacle pivoted and locked, as the two brothers embraced in death. The cry for blood now choked the crowd, and a shock of silence blanketed the square. Folk stood, eyes bulged in horror, as finally their wishes were fulfilled and death stood before them. A crash brought a gasp from the throng as the brothers fell, stone dead, all the way down to meet the Devil of their maker. No one but Fitz could see the black mist that clawed out of the brothers, an ugly taint that hit the air like poison. Nor could they hear the howl of the damned as hell spread its arms and claimed them.

HORNS DAY - THE BEAST OF MORRIS BEVAN...

Morris Bevan; this was the slick taint of Hell that cherished all to suffer. This was the same tormentor that had struck the flame, strung the gallows and ducked the stool, the same beast that rode the plague winds through the ages of mankind, bringing with its' tempest the seeds of envy, lust and loathing. The Demon that stood at the foot of Morris's soul, was the face of genocide and hunger, and as always, it nestled in the bosom of man's faith and sanctity, twisting the righteous to purge with the cross and kill for the good of Heaven and Earth. This was the scolding flame of hate, an ice cold soul, bereft of pity. Morris did not sleep well on this fateful night.

The world woke grey. Morris was never the blind sword that thrust in rage, he was the word behind the strike, the command behind foul deeds and the keeper of the ill gotten gains. He was the mastermind amid the mindless thuggery, the King of ploy and the cloaked betrayer, and until this day, deemed himself far too important for death or madness.

The ache was all consuming, an unstoppable pulse that was beating Morris into a blinding rage. He sat; fists clenched, jaw locked, trying to cork the dark webs of thought that were weaving through his mind. His well cloaked pleasures, he felt, were tearing to the surface, going way beyond the tasters he allowed. He imagined his wife, racked, screaming for mercy, as he defiled and brutalised her to the brink of death, allowing life, only so he could take more. The thoughts lanced through the tips of his fingers and they hooked and dragged through the leather of his chair, clamping down hard until the tips bled. "AGHHHHH!" The scream burst the chains, and his rage and desire ran riot. He exploded, the urge demanding destruction, as he launched himself into a feast of mindless carnage. Every object of his once fine, polished, antique dwelling that would crack or shatter, fell to his wrath. Morris ceased only through exhaustion, his knuckles bruised with aggro, his sanity as ruined as his home. He stared into the face of his saviour, the man he feigned to serve. The teak framed icon of Christ looked down, hands spread in mercy. Morris laughed. "What the fuck are you looking at? You of all people must know me!"

Pauline Huws knew he was there, hiding, probably some new game he had in mind. She smiled, feeling the flush of expectant pleasure. The façade of her squeaky clean veneer allowed itself a dip into her dirty, sordid, cloaked, desires and she tingled at the thought of forbidden penetration. She carried on cleaning the church, going along with the Vicar's little game, she felt sure it would not be long before he'd pounce and bind and ravish her.

The hot breath on her neck and the low rumble of a growl, was somehow alarming, but Pauline steadied and purred. "Feeling somewhat hot this morning, are we Vicar? Must be all the talk of horns in the town! " The tug of her hair cracked her neck painfully back, jarring with the force. Pauline howled. "Oh, easy! You nearly ripped my head off!"

"Who's to say I didn't try!" Said Morris, spinning the church cleaner round to face him. Pauline's smile cracked at the sight of Morris Bevan, his thick grey mop mounted, stiff as board, spiked and twisted. His complex was a sickly green that seemed to glow in an aura around him. His eyes were a pulsed deep red, glassed and vacant; he towered over the cleaner, looking down. Pauline gasped. "Why, Vicar, are you feeling yourself? You don't look well at all!"

Morris Bevan laughed. "Oh, believe me Pauline, I'm as sick as it gets!" And with lightning speed he ripped the dress off the cleaner's back. Pauline giggled with excitement.

"What, you think it's funny?" Barked Morris. "I must be losing my touch." The punch discounted any thoughts of foreplay, it was a full forced belt that sent Pauline sprawling.

Pauline woke in the heavens, her vision clustered with stars, her mind as light as a cloud. She moved her head, and it thumped, the pain an earthly reminder. A sweep of nausea coursed through her, she tried to raise her hand to prevent the imminent flow of vomit, but the movement was denied, the hand bound, so the vomit shot and spilled down the front of her naked body.

"Oh bravo!" Pauline turned her head to locate the Vicar. "What have you done to me?" Pauline whistled the words, for the first time aware of the swelling of her jaw, her tongue flitted over her gums, locating the missing teeth. Again she tried to move, but she was bound vertical, and she looked up and could see she was strung on the holy cross. Morris slowly edged into her vision.

"You've fucking gone too far!" Sobbed Pauline. "Now fucking let me down, you bastard!"

Morris just smiled and strolled to stand beneath her. "Funny you should say that... *You've gone too far*... For you see, my problem has always been that I was never permitted to go far enough. It's the job, you know! It won't do, you know, a Vicar doing disgusting things to a married woman. Especially as her husband plays the church organ! Huh, funny that he plays with his organ, while I play with his wife! Ha, ha, that should send the saints crashing. But I'm sure I'll be forgiven, after all, if history has taught us one thing, the whore always gets the blame, and..."

"Let me fucking down you monster!"

"Tut, tut Pauline, language, please, do you know where we are?" Morris bent down, picked up a cane and thrashed its worth through the air. Pauline screamed.

"You know I never cared for or fancied you...I just cared and fancied what you permitted me to do...You dirty little scrubber! So, this progression in my desires, I believe, has been fuelled by the weakness of your will. As I said, the whore always gets the blame." Morris charged, smashing the cane into the front of Pauline's thighs. She howled in agony and Morris roared in ecstasy. "Oh how I love the sound of pain, a true tune that rings deep from the soul, a sound that cannot be feigned. There is an undeniable honesty in its plea. And you, my dear, will find you can play the tune very well indeed."

Morris again charged and struck, again and again. Pauline hung, her mind convulsing screams, her body weeping in agony. Morris ceased, sat, head bowed. "Oh God, how good it feels! You shall not deny me again, for I no longer need your glory. For glory lies in the hand of the tormentor...THAT!" He pointed to the cross. "Is power, there bleeds the free will of man, and if we were not made so, then we would not do so."

Morris stood, slipped a knife out of his pocket and walked towards Pauline. She now whimpered, the screams long ago like the dust of a carpet, beaten out. Morris cut his victim's bonds and Pauline crumpled to the floor. He hovered over the ruin he had created. Pauline slowly raised her head, and looked pleadingly at her attacker. "Please, please, Morris! Enough, let me go."

Morris smiled and shook his head. "Oh my dear, here we have before us, the dilemma of the naughty boy? Just who can you trust not to tell?" And he raised the knife.

Now, Morris understood the word frenzy, and for the first time he had permitted himself to get lost in its fever. His arms ached through the motion of the slash, his body buzzed with the high. This was his saviour, this was his gospel, how long had he wasted and denied who he was? This was the realm of another world, this was his paradise. He stooped over the corpse and reached inside the severed gut. He stripped off his top, cupped the blood in his hands and poured the gore over his head, spreading it over his face and body. "AHHHH," he purred. "The gravest taboo, the most sacred of perversions, the ravishing of life, to the climax of death, the ultimate intrusion."

"Please sir, does the Lady need a plaster?" The voice shattered Morris's reflections, he shot around to seek the source of the disturbance. The young lad stood at the church doors, holding the plaster high in the air. Morris roared with laughter. "AHHHH, but of course the gallant young scouts of the First Aid division, here to care for the wounded participants of our beloved festival. Well, young lad you can certainly try. Though I feel, the said sticker maybe a tad small.

I don't suppose you've got anything bigger, say a body bag for example?"

Tom the Placard was in a frenzy, Hell was obviously bursting through the town, and the Devil's victims were piling high. He ran from the square as quick as his old legs would carry him, eager to relate the gruesome demise of the Hardy brothers to the town's spiritual leader. Surly, he now surmised, the Vicar would have to act, and halt this pagan blasphemy. The streets he passed on the way to the Church were littered with brawls and battered losers. Tom got to the church doors and shoved them open. The young lad's sobs echoed through the temple, deep trembling sobs of horror. Tom entered the asylum of Morris Bevan, and hope for the world sucked out of his soul. Morris Bevan was bent low talking to the sobbing young lad. On hearing Tom's approach he raised his head. "Why, my dear Tom, the very fellow. I was just telling this delightful young lad about the sacrifices one must make for the Good Lord."

Tom walked steadily towards Morris, for the moment lost for words, as the full horror of his surroundings sunk in. Even in death the corpse of Pauline Huws seems to plead for mercy. Tom halted just before Morris. "What in God's name have you done?" He stammered the words, pointing a trembling finger at the mutilated corpse.

"Me?" Morris laughed. "Oh, you mean the cleaner! Oh, she always was a clumsy old slag. I don't suppose you would believe me if I said she slipped peeling an apple?" Again Morris laughed. Young Stanley Jenkins tried to run towards Tom, but Morris yanked him back. The boy howled in terror. Tom pointed a warning finger towards Morris Bevan. "Damn you Morris, you let the young lad be!"

Morris glared at Tom and snarled. "Fuck you Tom! Fuck you and your stinking faith and your stinking God and your stinking temple! You all kneel, here on this fucking floor, pity in your eyes, hoping for better. Oh how I despise the weakness of the lot of you!"

The words of sacrilege hit Tom like a blow from a hammer, his eyes filled with tears of betrayal. "I, I…"

"AND YOU!" Screamed Morris, tugging harder on the scruff of the young scout, who sobbed and thrashed in panic. "You are the saddest fucker of them all… What a waste of life you are…..ARGHHH!" Morris screamed as young Stanley used some scout initiative and sunk his teeth deep into the Vicar's hand. Morris released his grip and the boy bolted. Tom, seeing his chance, steamrollered into Morris knocking him off his feet. Tom near followed the Vicar to the floor, but he steadied himself and turned towards the lad. "YOU RUN BOY, RUN, GET HELP, TELL THEM THE VICAR HAS LOST HIS MIND!" Tom caught sight of the Vicar from the corner of his eye as he started to rise; quickly he legged it. The slick of blood proved catastrophic to Old Tom's escape plan; his feet hit the slick and he hurtled head over heels, landing with a sickening crack. Tom groaned, opening his eyes just in time to see the fist of Morris Bevan, seconds before the crunch of impact.

Tom opened his eyes and the world swam around him, and awareness placed him back in the asylum of Morris Bevan, Tom choked, spitting out blood. He tried to move, but quickly realised he was bound, tied to a pew, and helpless. Morris stood in a haze before him, the grin on his face as spiteful as a devil. Tom straightened himself and took a deep breath. "What have you done, Morris? What in Hell's name is the matter with you?"

"Good question Tom. Let's just say, I got out on the wrong side of bed this morning… You know? You would not believe the fucking mood I'm in!"

"Wrong side of bed! You've, you've killed her. Mutilated her!"

"I suppose I'm having a bit of a bad day, but fuck me it feels good! You see, Tom, there are those who say and those who do, there are those who dream and those who live. And I've dreamed of ripping her fucking guts out for years! I would not worry about it too much, if I was you, she was sure to be rejected on judgement day." Morris laughed. "God she was a filthy creature, up to all sorts, I'd go into detail but...Well, maybe not.

"But I suppose, Tom, that all depends on just who the judge is?"

"There can be only one judge, Morris!"

Morris smiles at Tom bends down and pats his cheek. "Oh my dear Tom your faith has always, truly astounded me..........Yes it really has, you see you have proved to me how pointless a life of chaste, devotion is! I mean you may as well have cut to the chase and died at birth......I mean what's the point in living! If you can't go around fucking every-one, and plundering the orgy of temptations that surround us!"

"I'll reap my harvest in the company and greatness of the Lord, Morris, with him and him only lies paradise."

"Oh, well said Tom, spoken with the soul and passion of a cucumber..........But do you know what is really upsetting about this day Tom?"

"Where do you want me to start Morris?"

"Oh very droll Tom, almost funny. No, what is really upsetting is, on my big day, a day when I have so, so much to do...YOU DECIDE TO POP OUT OF YOUR FUCKING HALO, AND PLAY THE FUCKING ACTION HERO!" Morris struck Tom sharp and hard on the side of his head and Tom reeled from the blow. "And now, Tom, I find myself short of time with still with some killing to get through. Tell me Tom, before the hordes arrive. Have you by any chance seen my lovely wife? Come on, I know she's in the town somewhere, I can smell the bitch, I could always trail her scent."

Tom raised his head looked Morris firmly in the eye. "I would sooner die, than give aid to devils!"

"Oh tut, tut!" Morris smiled and shook his head. "Then, old man, consider me your express delivery service. All aboard, keep tight your soul, and onward, straight to the gates of paradise, one way fare only!"

Death brought with it the still shock of silence, the instant crush of mortality that strikes hard with a sickening punch of fear, and the bruising of the town showed. People who howled for blood now hung heads in shame, and shied from the macabre spectacle of the brothers, who lay lanced together in death, their faces forever locked in a growl of hate. Fitz did not shy from the carnage, she looked down on the ruin and smiled, finding the slaughter a poetic and fitting end for her despised foes. She turned to Sylvia. "Now my dear, it's time to address the problem of your husband."

"HELP, HELP MURDER, MURDER, HELP?" Fitz's senses were sprung and on high alert, and she turned to the sound of distress. The Lady carried a young boy in her arms as she charged into the square, taking all attention from the grizzly spectacle at the ring. "THE VICAR'S GONE INSANE! NEARLY KILLED MY BOY, THERE'S A LADY DEAD MY BOY RECKONS, AND HE'S BATTERED OLD TOM!"

Morris dragged the battered and bound Tom up the twisting stone stairs of the bell tower. The old man groaned and writhed in pain as his old bones crashed and bumped against the rock solid stairwell. Morris reached the top and barged through the turret door, hoisting Tom to his feet. Morris's grin was a mix of malice and madness as he glared ice at the old man. "Here we go Tom," said Morris as he marched Tom to the turrets edge, forcing the old man's head to peer down to the drop below. "See, down there old man? There is your Jesus, there's eternity!" Morris placed a noose around Tom's neck and ran to the bells. "Now don't you go running off mind, God's expecting you!" Morris looped the other end of the rope around the bells, securing it tight. He pulled hard to test its worth, and roaring in glee returned to the old man. Morris grabbed Tom's hair and yanked his head back. "You must be fucking ecstatic…All your fucking life you've waited to breathe your last and now the great moment is here! Hmm, nothing to say, not even a thank you? Ooh, and I nearly forgot!" Morris took out a folded piece of cardboard with string looped through it. He placed it over Tom's head. "Ha ha your final placard!"

Tom looked the madman firm, in his damned eyes. "I have no fear in meeting my maker, Morris, for mine shall be the kingdom of heaven, and yours shall be the realm of flame, you are doomed for eternity Morris, you…"

"Oh fucking blah, blah fucking blah. Tell me, Tom, have you ever considered the fact that your invisible friend might not exist?"

Tom took a deep breath. "Oh he exists all right Morris. His light shines in the good hearts and deeds of men, and I have felt his glory and presence every waking day of my life!"

Morris laughed and shook his head. "Oh the grind of faith, I mean, what you put yourself through…The misery of it all, just too…" Morris tilted Tom over the edge, let him dangle for seconds then yanked him back. "Reach paradise, but what if paradise is just a dirty black hole full of worms that will suck you down to the bone, eh Tom, ever consider that? And bastards like me, who have spent a lifetime fucking whores and fucking people over, get away scot free, no judgement, not even for murder! Ooh, won't you look a fool, a fucking lifetime of devotion and misery for Jack's fucking shit and a hole full of worms!"

Tom held his head high to the heavens, closed his eyes shutting out the gloating snarl of Morris Bevan and he beseeched his maker. "The Lord is my shepherd I shall not want, he…"

"Ah!" Morris laughed. "That prayer rings a bell!" And with a shove, old Tom plunged into the infinity of his desired destiny. "GO ON BELL US A FUCKING SONG TOM!" Roared Morris Bevan, waving a fist at God and his heaven. "SWING TO THE CHIMES OF HEAVEN!"

At the same time as Tom's neck snapped, the church bells rang over the town of Sickle, the peal giving a toll of doom to the Ladies' words. The deep pitched boom echoed through the square, lending a dark depth to the day's events.

Fitz turned to Sylvia. "Oh God Syl, we should have known, we haven't seen him all day, we should have checked him first!"

Sylvia shook her head. "Oh Fitz, what have we done. I knew what he was capable of."

Fitz clutched Sylvia's shoulders. "Look at me!" She ordered. "We have done nothing...You hear me Syl? Never mind what has been done, this is who these monsters were, and are. And this town knew it, but chose not to know it. Now let's find Morris Bevan and see the world rid of him!" Sylvia brushed away the tears and took a deep, steadying breath. "Okay, let's go, oh God Fitz!"

As Fitz and Sylvia ran towards the church, the air of Sickle clattered in a bedlam of bells as the emergency services and the holy trinity vied for attention. The square quickly emptied as the citizens of Sickle, hurtled towards their new gladiatorial arena, a sea of zombies all curious as ghouls are to behold the foul nature of mankind. For this day of blood-letting was certainly not to be missed, and was sure to etch itself, deep in the conscious and history of the town, and not a soul was prepared to miss it.

The pendulum motion of the old man stilled and with it the peal of the bells, and the onlookers got what they came for. Old Tom hung lifeless from the church turret, his face choked to a cold death blue. Fitz and Sylvia edged through the peeping Tom crowd, who stood transfixed by the macabre curiosity.

Fitz moved closer towards the tower; the sign was crudely done, but the implication was obvious. The cut of cardboard was splashed with red paint, or perhaps blood. Fitz peered hard to read old Tom's last placard. *BE CAREFUL WHAT YOU WISH FOR.* Fitz spat on the floor. "Damn you, Morris Bevan...I swear I'll see you dead!"

Next the bells were replaced by the shrill of whistles as the incompetence of Sickle's Constabulary burst through the church gates. Fitz looked in disgust as the cronies of the late Sergeant Hardy puffed out their chests and bullied through the crowd, barking orders, and feigning superiority of being. Fitz tried to enter the church but was roughly pushed back by a young Constable, as the force of the law quickly linked arms, sealing off the crime and its business.

Fitz cursed. "Fucking damn them!"

Sylvia clutched tight to Fitz's arm. "Fitz, if he's in there they'll get him, they have too!"

"You sure about that Syl? Because I wouldn't bet my life on it, and anyway, do you think Morris is dumb enough to wait for them?"

Fitz and Sylvia waited patiently among the jostle and chatter of the crowd, the first sign of movement was a sound of friction and old Tom, without ceremony, was dragged up the wall.

"Move aside! Move aside!" A line of Bobbies drew batons and scattered the crowd. The Superintendent straightened himself to full pomp and barked out his orders. "Home, all of you, this is a crime scene and Police business only. Now off you fuckers go, or I'll do the whole bloody lot of you for obstruction!" The crowd groaned, hanging their heads like children denied a treat, but dispersed all the same and quickly re-gathered outside the church grounds. Sylvia turned to leave with all the rest, but was staid by Fitz's hand. "No Syl, I am not leaving until I find out if they have your husband, and who lies dead in that church." As the crowd limped away from the scene, Fitz stomped forward towards the Superintendent, who snarled at her approach. He raised his baton, and pointed it in threat, but Fitz stormed on. "Were the fuck is Morris Bevan, officer, and who else has he killed?"

"None of your damn business, Madam, now will you kindly…"

"I'll kindly fuck all! Till you tell me if you have him."

"We are dealing, Madam, with a double homicide, I have no time…"

"You lot couldn't deal with double line parking! Tell me, have you found Morris Bevan?"

"NONE OF YOUR GOD DAMN BUSINESS MADAM! Constable, escort these…"

"YOU KNOW HER!" Screamed Fitz, pointing at Sylvia. "Don't ignore the fact! Don't you think she's a little at risk, being that her ex-husband is the local mass murderer?"

"Madam, it is too early in our inquiries, to speculate on who the culprit maybe."

"OF COURSE IT'S FUCKING HIM!"

"CONSTABLE, REMOVE THESE WOMEN!"

Fitz and Sylvia were jostled and shoved by the Constabulary right out of the church grounds, with Fitz still spitting hell fire and kicking and punching any uniform in reach. Eventually the Officers managed to get the seething Fitz out of the church grounds, all nursing bruises for their efforts. Fitz stood outside the now bolted gates and hurled every curse her heart and soul could muster. Sylvia waited patiently for the furnace to simmer. "Come on Fitz, let's go. We need to look after ourselves, like we always do."

Fitz nodded and took one last look at the church as the first body bag was brought out. She pointed at the Superintendent. "If you imbeciles don't up your game, you'll be carrying a whole lot more of them before this business is through. You hear me?"

Fitz and Sylvia walked back through the town, and quickly bustled through the ever increasing crowds. The air was thick with gossip and assumptions, as folk competed to relate their versions of the day's horrors. Fitz walked in silence, with Martel's warning drumming at her senses. Was this flaw to her plan punishment for the use of the Magrot? Had she upset the balance of innocence? Fitz looked to Sylvia and knew; until Morris was found, she could not let her out of her sight.

THE ETERNAL HANGMAN...

Morris growled and pulled hard, Fitz screamed as a furnace of pain lanced through her body. "Yes!" Morris snarled, one hand punching the air in triumph, his other hand twisted in Fitz's intestines. Fitz tried again to scream, but the horror was overwhelming and the cry for help was choked in fear. Morris unwound her inners from his hand and slopped them to the floor. He grinned and turned. "If you think that's sick," he spat, "just wait till I start on her." Fitz followed his gaze as he advanced forward. Sylvia lay bound and gagged, her eyes strained and torn through the horror and hope lost for mercy. Morris stood above her, knife raised. "Fuck, I'm enjoying this!" He grinned, squeezing his cock hard. He drew the knife across Sylvia's bare breast and glared back at Fitz. "I'll teach you not to play games with me, you dumb whore, you really have no idea what you've woken... DO YOU?"

Fitz shot up from bed, her screams seeming an eternal sound that seeks haven through every dark tunnel that burrows through the realm of nightmares. She clutched her stomach tight and panted for air. Sylvia immediately woke at the sound of her lover's distress. "What is it love, bad dream?"

"He's in my fucking head Syl, I swear, he's laughing at us. He's a hot knife digging in me, tormenting me. He's more than the rest, Syl. Whatever drives him now hunts us, I feel it! It is deep, twisted and cunning Syl ...A monster!"

"It's still Morris, Fitz, and the man's a coward, he won't face this. He'll run!"

Fitz's shook her head. "No Syl, no, he isn't going anywhere while we still live. I need some air!"

Fitz stood on the terrace of the flat, looking down on the town as dawn broke. She was thankful for the chill of the breeze that refreshed her senses and steadied her pulse. She gazed around the still of the town below her, all was now calm. A blanket of mist sheets over Sickle, covering the scars and carnage of the festival's madness. The town appeared almost as if butter wouldn't melt in the hazy gold of dawn. The town, she knew, would wake soon enough and Fitz had no doubt that the busy-bodies would wake early, all eager to report. The shops and streets would soon fill with the clatter and wags of a thousand rabid tongues, as wives and mothers laid down the law and told it as it was, the bars would fill with squads of detectives all taking down clues while they gulped down their pints, putting the town and the world to rights. Oh Fitz knew they'd find no help here in this idyllic little vale, this middle land of decency, were folk held their noses high above the stench of the world, and she knew the good godly folk of the parish would soon sweep the whole embarrassing mess, neatly under the carpets, of suitable lowly culprits. Fitz hugged her shoulders. "Where in hell are you?"

The desk Sergeant had only managed his second cup of tea, when Fitz and Sylvia burst into the station. "Into thin air," said the desk Sergeant, holding his hands to the heavens, to emphasis his point. "How can you search thin air?"

Fitz slammed hard on the station counter, and the portly Sergeant jumped, near spilling his tea, but he was not to be shamed or moved. "How fucking long did you search?" Demanded Fitz.

The Sergeant then, in great detail, explained the force of the chill factor on a person's resolve, and operational functions, that and the lack of vision due to the descending blackness of night, had proved too much for the highly resilient and dedicated Bobbies to bear, and the search had been called off at midnight.

Fitz again slammed down hard on the station counter, her face burning redder with every strike. "THEN WHAT FUCKING TIME WILL THE SEARCH RESUME?"

The desk Sergeant scowled back at Fitz, showing total disdain for her lack of manners, but nevertheless, in perfect teacher to pupil form, he explained the complex process involved in the formation of a search party, right up to the complexity of paperwork and right down to the mundane, but timely task of cutting sandwiches and filling flasks of tea, vital, he explained, to keep the wheels and morale of the dedicated team rolling. And so it was, with Fitz's slamming, moving from the desk to the desk Sergeant's head, that Fitzpatrick was, once again, grappled by Sickle's Constabulary and dumped on the street, with the only clue a search of thin air.

Morris Bevan had not gone far, the town of Sickle, he knew, was a clutch full of idiots, and the only difference between the Police Force and the civilian delinquents, was a uniform. The catacombs that snaked their way through Sickle's under-belly spidered out of the church, and through the town and proved to be a fine labyrinth for monsters to burrow in. Morris sat slumped in the deep bowels of the town, his mind twisting and drooling in the delights of torture, he wanted more and he fully intended to have it. The beast was now complete, and there was now no flicker of a past life or the feigning of normality. Morris's humanity was now as stoned as a gargoyle, he did not crave food or rest, for his only hunger was a staple of hate, a hate that broiled through his bones turning his body and soul into a cast of cold iron. He gibbered and raved in the complete darkness, keeping company in his madness, as his thoughts schemed to eliminate the constructors of his demise. Morris could hear life above him and he laughed, no hurry, for he now had no time, so therefore, had all the time in the world.

Every corner held the possibility of an ambush, every doorway was cloaked in potential danger, and every face was a possible enemy. Fitzpatrick stormed through the streets of Sickle, Sylvia scurrying behind her, struggling to up keep with the march of frenzy. The world, to Fitz, had now shrunk down to a narrow corridor of paranoia, a tight claustrophobic weight that pressed down hard squeezing tension through every nerve of her body. Without a sound except the gasp for air, they stormed up Captain's Hill towards Sylvia's old home. The Vicarage lay hidden behind a jungle of neglect, Sylvia's prized garden, now choked in a stranglehold of nettles and weeds.

Sylvia paused to take in the ruin. "He never cared for anything, not life, beauty, nature, none of the wonderful things he claimed his Lord had gifted us. You'd think people would see that? I mean, he never really hid what he cared about, namely himself and power and donated coin."

"They knew who he was, Syl, his congregation, his cronies in different societies and institutions, all his middle class friends, who all believe the doors of paradise open for a respectable bank balance. They knew who he was, for they worshipped in the same temple of greed. And like him, love, they don't give a fuck for people, for they just care about their person!"

The Vicarage door was splintered and open, giving a glimpse to the chaos that lay inside. Fitz and Sylvia took a deep breath and entered the lunatic's playground. Fitz pulled the dagger from the inside of her jacket, and in silence the pair crept through the ruin of the home in search of a madman. Sylvia gaped in horror at the destruction, horrified by the consuming effort of rage needed to produce such carnage, for nothing in the home remained untouched by madness. But most disturbing was the blasphemy's that slashed across the walls, slogans proclaiming the twisted desires of the artist and his deathly intentions. Sylvia shook her head in disbelief at the vandalised icons and the defacing of the Lord, which Sylvia still held dear. Never in her life did she believe her husband was capable of such sacrilege. With great care and caution, they searched the home from top to bottom, once, twice and once again. "Fitz, enough!" Sylvia left the lounge of the home and slumped down on the patio step, holding her head in her hands. Moments later Fitz sat beside her. "We have to find him Syl, before he finds us."

"He could be anywhere Fitz! Anywhere! I say we go home."

"No! I'll be no sitting duck, I know he's coming for us Syl, I know it!"

"Well, you carry on, because I've had enough!"

"You can't be alone!"

"Oh I know that Fitz, I know it's me you fear for, so therefore if I go home, you will have to follow!"

"You!" Fitz struggled to find an argument, but there was none. So reluctantly she nodded and put an arm around Sylvia's shoulder. "Come on, home!"

"Pit a pat, pit a pat...They come home to nibble, all the little mouses, but carefully they peer for the big bad cat...And their whiskers tweak for a sound, lest they nibble their last." Morris's senses had tuned to the ways of the dark, the slightest shudder of a web, struck his sightless intuition and he could instantly pinpoint with sonar precision to its location. He crept, tiptoe silent through the cellar, his ears cupped to the air for the slightest sound and give away from above. Finally, the unmistakable sound of a latch dropping, and Morris near wet himself in a glorious rage of joy. Quickly he rammed his fist in his mouth to cork the elation that threatened to growl with lust for all the world to hear. "Not long now!" He whispered to the void, while wringing an invisible neck.

"Fitz, sit down. Drink some tea, you've checked the windows and doors, God, it must be a hundred times now!"
Fitz gave the entrance door to the upstairs flat a final stiff yank, sat and took the hot tea.
Sylvia ran her fingers through her lover's hair and kissed her. "Look, you need to unwind, he's the one who's running, not us!"
"Then tell me, Syl, why do I feel like his prisoner? Why do I feel like we are the hunted?"
"Think about it Fitz, the whole town knows Morris! Do you think, after what he has done, he could simply walk through the town unchallenged?"
"He's cunning Syl, and you saw the rage the ashes awoke in the Hardy brothers. And he's now desperate, he's got nothing to lose Syl. And I'm sorry, I do not think your dear ex-husband is one to simply walk away."
"Well he's going to have one hell of a job getting through your defences. Come on, I'm exhausted, it's been a tiring couple of days."

Fitz and Sylvia made for the bedroom, Sylvia turned out the lights, while Fitz picked up the hammer, crowbar and carving knife. Fitz winked. "You can never be too careful, after all my dear, there's a lunatic about!"

Up and out of the deep black earth and into darkness, slithered the worm of Morris Bevan. Slowly and carefully he placed down the trap door. Morris almost laughed out loud, and had to quickly stifle his erupting joy as he stepped into his enemies' lair. Silently, he sidled across the room, lifting the hatch of the counter. He paused, then at full stretch his fingers tip-toed along the charity shop's top shelf, feeling their way for a particular prize. The charity shop had proved to be ideal for Morris's hidden perversions, and it was for his own personal gratification that said flat was never let. For its upstairs was a perfect location to hustle in ladies of the night. After all, he had deduced long ago, they looked no different to the rabble that used the shop for everyday business. "Ah, ha!" Morris thumped the air as his fingers tickled over the top flat keys, who else but he was tall enough, or clever enough to know of their location. Morris smiled, totally in awe of himself once again.

Sylvia floated in a happy tide of pleasure, her senses smothered in love and all it hoped for. Fitz was all around, a part of her as vital as the beat of her own heart, the joy was a deep dream that was allowed to flourish as she slept, safe in her lover's arms. It was at first just a ripple of breath, but slowly the breath rose, there was a taste, a pang of unease as the breath gathered heat, vibrating through the calm. Then the surge as the gentle ripple of her dream swelled to the storm of a nightmare. "WAKE UP YOU FUCKING TWAT LICKING BITCH!" Sylvia knew right then, she opened her eyes and screamed. "FITZ!"

Fitz instantly shot up and Morris Bevan slammed the club down, the blow hit home, a sickening thud to Fitz's head. She slumped on impact, her last perceived sound the roaring laughter of Morris Bevan.

Morris Bevan's smell did not resemble life, he smelt of sweat, sulphur, earth and decay, and as he bruised and tumbled Sylvia down the stairs, she could feel the exploding rage of his heart.

Sylvia hit the shop floor with a crash. She tried to rise, dazed from the fall, but instantly Morris was on her. She tried to scream, but his fist smashed into her face, knocking her silent. Sylvia lay stunned and helpless, as Morris wrapped the twine around her arms and legs. Morris propped her upright against the wall and gloated right into her face. "This rope! Does it remind you of the last time we were together, hmm? Of course it does, you and your friends playing their silly games...ON MY FUCKING BACKSIDE!" Morris slapped her hard across the face. "Oh, you modern day women eh? With, with your fucking upstart ideas! But I don't mind you if you revert back to helpless little girl mode and plead for mercy, you never know your luck, I might fuck you, before I kill you!"

Sylvia stared hatred at her tormentor. "If I die, I die, and my only regret will be you! For since you, I have lived and loved!"

Morris clapped his hands and laughed. "But for the briefest of moments; pity I'm going to fuck it all up for you. What's your lovers name again? Ah, I remember, Fitzpatrick. What a fucking stupid name, no wonder she thinks she's a man!" Sylvia tried not to, but the mention of Fitz, and the tears rolled. She hung her head. Morris yanked her chin up. "Women, eh? Must be hard, mind. I mean, not a fucking entity in the entire universe likes you. No, this new found liberation, I believe, will be your total undoing. And perhaps it's time to get things back in order and open the pits and once again cast the stones."

"And what do you think the Lord will make of you, Morris?"

"Ooh a bit of fight! I love it! Man will always stand higher, my dear, that's the way God meant it! For you are just a commodity, put on this earth to be fucked, until finally you can fuck no more and are replaced by another. Oh how I hanker for the days of old, and the pick and mix of the great harems!"

Sylvia twisted and kicked in rage. "I HATE YOU, I HATE YOU!"

Morris laughed. "Of course you do dear, why on earth wouldn't you? But enough of small talk. You know, of course, I'm going to kill you? Not here mind, hidden away in this little shop, people believing it was a common burglary gone wrong. Oh, how grubby! No my dear you are worth more than that, you see my dear, I believe death is the grandest theatre of all, the ultimate show. And you, Sylvia Bevan, shall have a fitting stage, an arena well worthy of your demise." Morris turned away and rummaged through the shop, Sylvia looked to the heavens and whispered. "Please wake Fitz, please!"

"Ah the very thing!" Said Morris, turning towards Sylvia with a length of rope in his hand. "And don't bother praying to your lover, when I hit, I hit hard, and she is, without doubt out for the final count." Morris looped the rope, twisted and pulled until he achieved the desired result. He smiled and waved the noose before Sylvia's eyes. "Any thoughts on tonight's curtain call?" Morris laughed, grabbed Sylvia and hoisted her off her feet. Sylvia screamed and, as she was slumped over his shoulder, she saw her chance and sunk her teeth into Morris's ear, and she tore and shook it, like a dog with a doll. Morris howled in agony and threw Sylvia from his shoulder. She gripped hard on the lobe and, as she fell, it severed in her mouth. Sylvia hit the floor and spat out Morris's flesh. Morris growled and screamed, clutching the wound as the blood poured. "YOU FUCKING BITCH!" The blows were hard and struck with lightning force. Sylvia could vaguely feel through the numbing haze, the gag being stuffed in her mouth and herself again being hoisted off her feet.

"Wake, wake up!" Fitz jolted back to life, "Martel?" She could have sworn she'd heard her voice. Slowly she got to her feet, then like a thunder bolt, the pain and realisation hit her; a flashback of a club and an echo of Sylvia's scream. "SYLVIA, SYLVIA!" Fitz stormed, and tumbled out of the bedroom and the world swayed and her vision rolled. She clung to the banister to steady her descent of the stairs, her head pounding with the slightest strain. Slowly she descended and entered the shop and all hope was crushed, the signs of struggle plainly evident, with toppled and broken furniture and scattered goods. Then Fitz noticed the damning trail of blood and her heart froze and her mind raced. "Oh God, no Syl, no!" Her thoughts locked in a panic of options and choices. She steadied herself with a deep breath. "Right, right. He could have killed her here, why didn't he? Where would he go? Think, think!" Fitz again looked at the blood on the floor and the horror of it gave hope, Fitz noticed the spill trailing through the open shop door, her mind clicked into action, there was still hope. Fitz rummaged under the counter till her hands fell upon the torch. She grabbed it and headed into the street to follow a trail of blood.

Not a soul, the town huddled in their beds, shutting out the world and its bogey men with a shield of blankets and lullabies. The law had again closed for the night, giving villains free reign of the twilight world. Morris bounded through the streets with the strength and stamina only madness and rage could fuel. Sylvia lay gagged and bound, slumped over her attacker's shoulder. She noticed the paving turning to green as they left the town and hit the meadow at the foot of Bell's Barrow Hill. Morris dumped Sylvia off his shoulder, he grabbed her hair and yanked her head back "See!" Morris pointed to the hill. "How fitting, don't you think, the old hanging tree given purpose once again? Romantic, don't you think? You will live in infamy my dear, the last witch ever to hang on Bell's Barrow Hill. Oh the poetry of it all...You can just imagine in the glorious days of old, line upon line of old wart-riddled hags, all waiting their turn to swing and kick, right into the grave and damnation! You know, it's a bit of a shame it's come to this, you were an awesome fuck in your day. Before, of course, you punched above your station and started denying me my little kinks. Oh well, enough of fruitless reminiscing, time to tackle the task at hand, so come on, up we go!"

As Fitz hit the meadow, the trail of blood dried up. She sobbed, her mind a spin with options. She looked to the river, and the thought of Sylvia drowning shook her rigid. She looked to the distant woods, but she could see no reason why Morris would head there. As she viewed Bells Barrow Hill, Fitz froze and the image of poor old Tom hanging off the bell tower flashed before her eyes. "The hanging tree!" Fitz knew right then, the thought stunk of Morris. "It has to be, just the thing the twisted bastard would get off on." Fitz ran, now sure of her purpose. "Please mother, please!"

    Beauty is a state of mind. Sylvia forced happy memories of Bell's Barrow Hill to still her fears, deciding to die with thoughts of better days. The mad mutterings of Morris Bevan were a constant challenge to her state of mind, but she was determined, in her final moments, not to be consumed by her twisted and sadistic spouse. She remembered the carefree days of her secret forbidden love, when she and Fitz foraged for wild herbs and mushrooms. She remembered the joy of being taught the gifts of nature by her adored tutor, and how they would sit for hours upon the hill and watch the beauty of the vale roll beneath them, and now, it all seemed a lifetime away. The clap and roar of triumph brought her out of her daydream. Sylvia stared at the hanging tree now bearing the fruit of the gallows. Morris stood below the noose, tugging the rope hard, to test its worth, Satisfied, he roared into the night. Sylvia sat, hands tied behind her back, still gagged into silence. Morris bounded towards her, happy as a sand boy in his castle of terror. He tore the gag from Sylvia's face. "There you are my dear, as I said I'm a bugger for nostalgia and theatre, and both demand the condemned their final words, a chance to beg the Lord for forgiveness."

    Sylvia's hate for the monster before her suppressed all fear, and her loathing took hold. "Oh I'm ready to die!" She spat the words. "I know there's better for me, and believe me Morris, I know what torment waits for you! There will be a reckoning, what, and who, do you think killed Cuthbert, the Hardy Brothers, it was…"

    Morris struck Sylvia hard across the mouth, drawing blood. "Oh, so you confess to your craft, and company of covens?"

"I confess to ridding the world of monsters, and you might take me, but she won't rest till you're rotting in your grave." Morris yanked Sylvia to her feet. "Hear now, Lord, the confession of this sinful crone; a wielder of spells destructive to man, a tongue that forks curses to raise the forces of famine and blight, a mutant of nature and partaker in the taboo of forbidden love. In your name and for my pleasure, I sentence the hag to hang by the neck, till she shuts the fuck up!"

Morris, with all the pomp of parade, marched Sylvia towards the hanging tree and its waiting gallows. Sylvia prayed; she prayed to all that's good and right in the world. She prayed for all the sisters that suffered in silence. She prayed for justice in the world and for a brighter day to dawn after her passing. She prayed for her soul, and for the lover she was leaving.

Morris placed the noose above Sylvia's head and sniggered with glee. "You know, I never suffered guilt, because I never suffered faith, and serving the Lord, sure beat working for a living. You see, my dear, manipulation is the greatest of gifts. Oh, if only your father could see us now, wouldn't he feel a fool! Your dear mother, mind, tried to tell him I was a cunt, but he just wouldn't have it, bless him. Oh well, enough of fanfare and teary goodbyes, time to rid the world of another troublesome free thinking bitch!"

"NOOO!" Fitz, with all her might, slammed the torch into Morris's temple. Morris reeled back in shock, put his hand to his temple, feeling the slightest trickle of blood and laughed. "Oh dear! Is that the best you can do?" The howl was from the gut, and fierce, as Morris lunged, talons and teeth bared. He sledge-hammered into Fitz and Sylvia, the force toppling them like skittles. Sylvia, bound, hits the ground hard. Fitz, though winded from the fall, quickly got to her feet, but even quicker was Morris Bevan, and in seconds the bone vice of his hands were around her neck, squeezing the life juice out of her throat. "YES, YES!" Morris drooled and gibbered in ecstasy. "OH THIS IS FUCKING LIVING, WATCHING LIFE DRAIN FROM THOSE...YOU DESPISE, BY MY OWN...AGHHH!"

Fitz, with all the force she could muster, rammed a finger deep into Morris's eye, and the vice gave. Fitz staggered backwards as Morris howled, clutching his eye. Fitz staggered towards Sylvia, gasping for breath. She reached down and yanked the gag off Sylvia's mouth. "Oh Fitz, lookout!" Fitz turned to face the glaring beast of Morris Bevan. He prowled towards her, the rock raised ready to strike. Fitz desperately felt through her jacket pockets, hoping the knife was still there, but all in vain. Morris was nearly upon her when her hand fell upon the leather pouch. She pulled it from her pocket, with really no idea what good it could do, as Morris readied for the strike. Fitz poured the remaining ashes into her hand and, with just seconds to spare, blew them into the face of Morris Bevan. The result was instant; Morris dropped the weapon and rubbed furiously at the ash that choked and blinded him. Fitz wasted no time and darted over to Sylvia, tearing into her bonds, tugging and pulling with all her might to free her lover.

The scream was that of a thousand tormented souls, sounding dungeon deep in the branding flame of torture.

And blind the monster formed, Fitz and Sylvia edged back as Morris Bevan cracked and mutated, his flesh alive with growths that boil and blister and ripple through his body, his face a mask of strained agony.

And In that instant, the world of Morris Bevan turned blood red, the moon pulsed above him, black as a killer's heart. It boomed, leaking its gore with every thump, deafening and all consuming. Morris looked each and every way for an exit from this land of nightmares, he made to run and the ground beneath him cracked and splintered, and he tumbled into a mire of bones. Morris heaved himself up and again the ground beneath his feet cracked once more. He scanned the land around, seeking a path to take him from this open graveyard. But as far as the eye could see was littered with bones, skulls gazed up, seeming to mock his attempt of escape and all the while the beat of the black heart above him. Morris screamed in frustration. "WHAT'S HAPPENING, WHERE AM I?"

"You are in the world you made!" The voice was a cold, deep echo. "You are where you belong, you are the bearer of the black heart that beats above you, the maker of the path you tread, you are the taker of blood and bone."

Morris turned to face the source of the voice that shimmered towards him. The girl child was draped in rags, her fair hair straggled a face as black as boiled blood. "What the hell!" Barked Morris. "I don't know you!"

"The little girl smiled. "You didn't have to know me, to kill me!" She lifted up her head, and the noose remained rotted, the knot that choked out her life was now part of her flesh. Morris struggled to his feet, turning away from the pitiful scene, again the bones cracked and Morris howled in rage. "WHAT IS THIS, WHAT IS THIS?"

Fitz untied the last of Sylvia's bonds and they embraced, while looking on bewildered at Morris Bevan as he thrashed and screamed at thin air. "He's gone mad; come on Fitz, let's run while we have the chance!"

Fitz shook her head. "No, he can't see us I'm sure. It's the ashes, Syl I do believe dear old Morris is being tormented by his crimes, and I'm not leaving till I see him dead!" They huddled close under the hanging tree, and lay witness to their tormentor's insanity.

The sound was of hissing geezers that blew up to the heavens, and as the bones under Morris's feet shattered and crumbled, they let off a discharge of ice cold steam that smothered and choked the horizon. Morris coughed and desperately fanned the air, trying to make a path of vision. He bellowed his hate and shook a fist at the heavens. "I WILL NOT BE DEFIED, I WILL KILL… YOU HEAR…KILL!"

"So many!" The voice rang clear as the air stilled, Morris's head cracked sharply, back and forth in search of the voice. "Who's there? Show yourself!" The mist dropped; it swirled and the swirls gathered and took shape. Then they appeared, the phantoms surrounded Morris, the dead, young and old baring eternal the scars that dug their graves. They pointed accusing fingers at Morris, and the wind wailed. "Murderer, murderer, eternal doom, hangman, torturer, taker of innocence, betrayer, liar, feeder, feeder…Maker of blood and bone, blood and bone."

"NOOOOO!" Morris swung his fists wildly and pounded thin air as his targets evaporated around him. He stumbled and clutched the ground grasping for breath, cursing the world as he did so, and the heavens boomed. Morris looked up to the sky as the heart of the black moon pounded and pumped blood. Just a trickle at first, a dripping that trickled down Morris's face and then the pulse increased, faster, faster, until a waterfall of gore washed over him. Furiously he rubbed the blood out of his eyes and stood; he howled at the blood moon. "WHERE ARE YOU…DAMN YOU! YOU FUCKING HAGS!"

"I am hear, Morris my love, come to me." Morris turned and there before him stood Pauline. His toy in life stood under the hanging tree, her arms spread to him in welcome, revealing the slash of her naval and the spill of her inners. She smiled at Morris, holding his noose in her hand. "Come play my love. Look, you can hang me, you know I can deny you nothing. Come, come play with me." Every bone and muscle in Morris's body tensed and the scream issued from the belly of his demon, he charged. "YOU'RE FUCKING DEAD!" He dived at the phantom before him, and a thud halted him in mid-air.

Fitz and Sylvia dragged down on the rope and pulled with all their might, the moment the noose looped around his neck. Morris's breath was cut from under his feet the instant the noose bit. His toes struggled to keep a grip on ground and life. And then he saw, as the ghost world, and the black heart moon vanished. Morris stared down at his adversaries, as they tugged with all their might to put him forever in the world of the dead. In desperation he swung, his hands clawing for grip under the rope that threatened to cut off his life.

Fitz glared up into the eyes of her hated foe, as she heaved her heart out to end his life. "Fucking die, you monster, fucking die!" With all their will and effort, the two dragged the rope for all they were worth and Morris swung, his eyes bulged and his face turned an ice cold blue, and for what seemed an eternity, they gripped hard on the rope, until the last breath of Morris Bevan rattled away from the land of the living into the realm of the cold black night.

SOLACE IN AMBER...

And so the weekend of joyous festivities reached its bloody conclusion, and all too soon the guilt and blame of the town was shrugged off people's shoulders. Some wept, some rejoiced and some really didn't give a fuck.

Missus Chuckles heard the devastating news of her husband's demise and threw a party, and her children skipped, danced and smiled, and ate ice cream for the very first time.

Nobody threw a party for Ethel Sledgewhick, as very few people knew her, but someone who didn't really know her, but nevertheless believed really not knowing her was about as familiar as you could get, said. "No fuss is the way she would have liked it." Which was just as well.

Peter Bellroy woke the happiest killer alive. He did not feel like a felon, far from it, Peter Bellroy felt free. He had shed the tail and bray of a donkey, and overnight had fledged the wings of an eagle and the roar of a lion. Peter Bellroy did not, that morning, get out of bed, oh no, he soared out of bed into a brave new world, unchained and free to rise as high as his desires could dream. In short Peter Bellroy shed the Lamb and woke a ram.

The Church stood hushed in its grounds, and it seemed God had stilled the call of bells and shunned the holy, turning his back in shame, and withholding all invites. The pomp of the Church stood curtained in shadow, the sin of its past, seeping through its bones, turning the temple of hope into a chamber of doom, and worshippers, henceforth would be viewed with suspicion.

Derek Huws would never play the Church organ again, for he knew, you needed smiles to play music, and Derek Huws would never smile again. With life's skip, lamed, Derek Huws would now drag himself through the grind of life. People, he found, were full of understanding when life made no sense at all, and sympathy, he soon discovered was just a mask of curiosity, a trap of pity to tear secrets from the heart. He felt a stranger in this land of the living, bare of substance, raped of will and barren of desire. He was an engine sapped of oil, a shell without a host, a man without a wife, a life without a soul. Friends promised him the World, alas for Derek, the world was long dead, along with his wife and Morris bloody Bevan.

The overcast mood of gloom lay over the town for days as folk shuffled and scowled about their business, dodging eyes and company. But time does indeed lick wounds and soon enough the busy bodies were swarming out of their hives, all on the scent of honey sweet gossip.

"It had been going on for years!" Growled Phillis White, hoisting her bosom up under her chin in a show of authority. She paused, making sure ears were on high alert to catch her startling revelations. "Oh I seen them once, in a very unholy position, and let's just say she was buffing something…And it wasn't a candle stick! Oh always been a boiler that one, hungry for a man's bit of beef."

"PHILLIS!" Gasped Doreen More. "Poor woman's dead, and in the most ghastly circumstances imaginable! We should show some respect."

"Oh but Phillis is right," butted in Janet Smith. "She was always in the Butchers." As normal, Janet baffled her company, and was quickly overlooked. Phillis ground her teeth and shook her head, unrepentant. "Mark my words, you play with fire…And Pauline Huws had been poked more times than any fire I know! Uh, she was the same in school, the boys swarmed to her like flies round…"

"I think we get the picture, Phillis," said Mabel Greenway, turning her nose up, to avoid it dipping in the gutter.

"And fancy the Vicar, hanging himself like thats" said Hillary Thomson.

Mary Robinson laughed. "Well, how else would you hang yourself? And good enough for him I say, after what he done! And to think we blamed his poor wife, oh, only God knows what she must have gone through."

"Well I still blame her!" Said Phillis White, elevating her bosom even higher. "The mind of a man is a fickle creature, ladies, and no doubt, her cavorting with a member of the sexual opposition is bound to dislodge a couple of screws."

"Huh!" Gasped Lorna Richards. "Come on! Are we to be blamed for every chink in a man's armour? Morris Bevan was an ambassador of the Lord, surely his faith should have got him through the crisis? I mean, you don't change from local Vicar to serial killer, overnight. Oh no ladies, you mark my words, Morris Bevan, was a devil in disguise!"

The cluck of hens looked at Lorna Richards in silent contempt, well aware the woman lacked the capability of dragging a good name through the mud, a disadvantage that made her a total disaster in the sacred art of gossip.

"Afternoon ladies," said Megan Small, breaking the stand-off and walking across the square towards them. "Oh damn, what a day!" She continued, placing down her bags of shopping. She waited for full attention before spilling her precious beans. "I've just come from Agatha Hardy's…Oh God, she's in a right old state!"

"Oh, upset is she? Missing Boris, I suppose" Chipped in Hilary Thomson.

"Well!" Megan smiled. "You know Agatha. Angry, I'd say, is more the word, and the poor thing is black and blue, says he done it, Boris, says he was a pig of a man! But she does admit she'll miss the income."

"Huh!" Sneered Phillis White. "Oh I bet she will, and the snobby bitch, will no doubt miss her standing in the community. And let's see her look down that barrel of a nose, when she's claiming the dole."

Mabel Greenway laughed. "Oh I think you'll wait a long time to see that, old Boris Hardy had his fingers in more pies than a baker! Ooh, I wouldn't mind hatching that little nest egg!"

"And the Brother!" Mary Robinson, knowingly nodded her head. "They reckon Brinmore had more fiddles than an Irish wake, *the bent note bobby,* they're calling him, reckon too, a lot more will tumble when they delve into the station's dirty washing."

"God what an age we live in." Tutted Olive Brooks. "Murder, hangings, fights to the death, and my husband tells me that Slug is out, you know the one who started the fire at the witches house."

"Well that's the thing," said Mary Robinson, "it's all to do with Brinmore Hardy, they say a load of convictions will be quashed, because of his dodgy dealings."

"Oh great!" Boomed Phillis White. "After all, we've been through they are now going to flood the town with every misfit this vale has to offer!"

"Phillis is right!" Agreed Olive brooks. "I don't care if that Slug is an arsonist or not, the fact is the man's a lice crawling drunk, who wouldn't know a toilet if it bumped into his backside!

Quarantined he should be, locked up for the health of the community. Ooh he makes my skin crawl."

Janet Smith giggled. "Eh, perhaps Gwyn will marry Slug, now Norm has gone."

"MARRY SLUG!" Howled Megan Small. "Well I can tell you now! I wouldn't marry the likes, not for all the soap in China! Ooh, the dirty smelly thing, and I'm surprised Gwyn didn't go before her husband, after…Ooh I can't bear to think about it!"

"For God's sake Janet!" Scolded Phillis. "You don't marry Slugs, you squish em! And I heard, within seconds of his freedom he was gulping em down at the Duck, bold as brass, and as shameless as a beggar, frothing with excitement and accosting decent folk on his way home, with his crude drunken, toilet antics! The man's a liability to good manners and hygiene. And mark my words ladies, if we don't make a stand against the filth of this community, we'll all be washed away in a tide of vomit!"

Elizabeth Procter hadn't smiled for days and she had no intention of breaking the habit any time soon. Her nose twitched constantly, irritated, no doubt, by the alien air that had polluted her godly Parish. She poured the tea, while her only two friends sipped in dutiful silence, sensing the souring curdle of their host's mood. The patio table, usually adorned with delightful, mouth-watering assorted fancies, limped drab with twig snapping, arid biscuits, reflecting in full the mood of the gathering.

Helen Nolan, always the first to twitch in an uncomfortable silence, took the deathly plunge into communication. "Ah, nice tea Elizabeth."

"HUH." Barked the host, piercing the communicator with an icy glare. "I don't think anything will ever be nice again."

Margret Mugford cleared her throat as a warning of her intentions to talk. "Well, I think, ladies..." She paused to suss the mood of her host, then with no verbal rebuke, she continued. "I think that, we the middle class pillars of the community, should..."

"Middle class!" quipped Elizabeth. "Can't you see, that the godly middle class of this vale are drowning in the open drain of working class mentality, a system derived to keep opinions and standards firmly embedded in the swill ideology of the gutter! Oh, mark my words my dears, they won't be happy till we are all harvesting lice in hovels and breaking wind for entertainment. Dragged us down with them, that's what they've done! Made a porn peep show of the whole town, and believe me ladies, if youth was still my companion, I'd take my company to Bells Garden and live happy and respectable for ever after, without the, without the, oh God!" The usually composed Elizabeth Proctor, broke down in tears, blowing her shame into her fine lace hanky. Helen Nolan placed down her tea and darted over to soothe her friend's woes, massaging the misery out of her shoulders. "Come now, dear, things will sort themselves out, they always do."

"What!" Choked Elizabeth. "Sort themselves out? Oh how stupid of me, of course they will, the world will soon enough forget that this parish had more gangsters than nineteen thirty's Chicago, not to mention, Jack the Vicar, who, after Sunday service liked to disembowel cleaners, and hang preachers from the Bell Tower! Oh you really do talk utter gibberish sometimes Helen!"

Helen removed her hands from Elizabeth's shoulders. "Well really! I do not have to stay here, just to be insulted!"

"Of course you don't! You can go anywhere in the vale and be accommodated with plenty of the same, I'm sure." Helen stormed around the table and swiped her coat off the back of the chair. "Well ladies, I shall bid you both a good day"

"Oh don't leave like this, Helen!" Pleaded Margaret. "I mean, were all friends!"

"Hmm, that's certainly what I thought, but I find the company to be like those biscuits, a tad stale."

"Huh!" Snorted Elizabeth. "That certainly didn't stop you dunking a waistline full in your mouth!"

"Well my dear, you can dunk the rest were the sun doesn't shine!" Said Helen, storming out of the garden. Elizabeth shot out of her seat and hollered behind her. "Oh don't worry dear, I did that before serving." Helen waved her arms in disgust then stormed and cursed out of the garden. Elizabeth sat back down and sipped her tea, while Margaret eyed her biscuit with suspicion, and placed it back down on her plate. Elizabeth looked at her and scowled. "Oh don't be so ridiculous Margaret, of course I didn't. But my wit, it would seem, is adapting to the gutter that now surrounds it."

LIFE'S TOO SHORT...

The Roast Duck Inn welcomed Slug back like a long lost puddle, and by the way he was drinking it would not belong before that puddle would again absorb too much and spill back on to the street, and resume its hobby of lamppost groping. It was before lunch and as the Roast Duck readied itself for dinner service, Slug propped up the bar and readied himself for his twelfth pint. He raised his glorious chalice of booze up to the heavens, and proclaimed. "Drunk before breakfast, that's freedom for you!" Slug then proceeded to hop on one leg, sloshing his pint all over the bar. "Eh, cut it out!" Yelled, Jane the barmaid. "If you don't simmer down you'll be free all right, free to bugger off home, we're expecting lunch trade any moment, decent working types, who won't take too kindly to a drunken idiot spilling drinks all over their pin stripes and prawn cocktails."

Slug halted mid hop. "Oh, sorry love, I'm just happy, you see I always thought, I didn't do it."

Jane put down her polished glass and laughed. "What you mean thought? Surely you knew if you done it or not?"

"They're all bloody guilty, every last breathing one of them, guilty as murder." The croaking voice creaked out of the alcove, and Ron the resurrection's Dai-capped head popped around the corner, seemingly still resurrecting, and using his grave as a half- way house. "Too many fingers pointing, that's the trouble. Back in my day, everyone blinded their eyes and no one was guilty. We looked after our own, and if they belonged to someone else!" Ron screwed up a bone fist. "We…"

"Ah, don't tell me cowboy," giggled Jane, "you ran them out of town."

"NO! We…" Ron coughed and spat on the floor. "No, no, we ran over the buggers, no bloody police or courts. Why, I remember once, aye, it was, uh, anyway …Oh fuck em!" Ron's head once again disappeared back into the crypt of his alcove, and his snores reassured all, that he still wasn't dead.

Jane pulled Slug his thirteenth pint. "Some things never change, eh Slug? And by the way, I didn't believe for one minute that you were guilty."

"Oh he's bloody guilty all right." Both heads turned to the door. The brawn and grim threat of John Bishop entered the bar. Slug gave an innocent, sloppy grin. "Hello John. Want a pint?"

"Huh!" Growled John Bishop. "Not off a murderer, I don't."

"Now don't start John!" Warned Jane. "Old Slug here has been through enough, and has been proved innocent, and no one died in that fire anyhow!"

"Pint if you please," said John, pointing to the pump. "And let's get one thing straight, I couldn't give a damn about the Vicar's wife and her whore, way I see it, burning's too good for the likes of them who go around flaunting their filth in front of decent folk and children." John poked his finger in Slug's chest. "It's the blood of my mate, Norman Stubs! That's the blood this fucking tramp has on his hands!"

Slug bowed his head, tears welling in his eyes. "I, I didn't mean to, he was my friend too."

"Bah, bollocks!" Spat John, picking up his pint.

"Now hold on!" Said Jane, tapping John's arm. "I was here that night, and Gwyn grabbed him ...Poor Slug didn't know what hit him!"

John grabbed Slug by the collar. "Oh believe me, he'll know what's hit him, soon enough. You see, I was there watching, as my mate fell to pieces, crushed by betrayal." John's hands tightened harder on Slug's collar, and his face squeezed into Slug's space. "I don't know what was harder for him to take, her being a slag, or who she chose to slag with. Oh yes, I was witness to a man drowning himself in shame." John screwed his fist into Slug's face.

"Right, I'm warning you John!" The Barmaid pointed to the door. "You've knocked enough teeth out in this bar, and God knows this town has had its fill of violence these last few weeks, so if it's a fight you've come out for, you can damn well take your money and custom up the social...And I mean it this time, you put the lad down you'll enjoy your last pint in this pub!"

John Bishop growled in the face of the trembling Slug. "Fair enough, I can wait." He loosened his grip on Slug's collar and smiled. Slug panted hard with relief. John Bishop took a huge gulp of his pint, wiped his mouth and pointed a finger. "Decent men this town has lost, and no bugger seems to give a damn, and we're stuck with the meddlers who made the mischief in the first place. Those two witches brewed all this bother, you mark my words...And this town of bloody sheep, welcomes them back with open bloody arms, and I'll tell you, if I had my way..." He pointed menacingly at Slug. "Him and those two crones, would be…"

"He without sin, eh John Bishop?" John Bishop swung round and looked into the smug, smiling face of the town's new Sergeant, the right and decent Nigel Hastings, an oddity in Sickle's Constabulary, known for his Christian values and fair play. "FUCK ME!" Gasped John. "What the hell are you doing in here, Constable? I thought church was more your thing, ain't you afraid you'll be struck by lightning?"

Sergeant Hastings was as neat as his uniform, well trimmed, of athletic build, as opposite to his predecessor as you could possibly get. He pointed to his stripes. "Sergeant Hastings, if you don't mind, Mister Bishop, and you seem to have dodged the bolts well, over the years, so I thought I'd try my luck."

"Well seems, today's your lucky day, so point proved, you can now fuck off back to your desk and finish your paperwork!"

Sergeant Hastings walked towards John Bishop. He arrived at breath's reach and smiled. "Or, I could do a spot of paperwork here, and arrest you for threatening behaviour, a breach of the peace, and intimidating an innocent member of the public."

"Huh! John Bishop cracked down his pint. "That's the first time I've heard Slug called a member of the public, never mind an innocent member of the public!"

"Oh, they're all innocent members of the public to me, John. That is as long they toe the line, of course."

John Bishop fidgeted, snared in a conversation, with no option of using his fists. "You'll never fill the boots of Sergeant Hardy. You knew where you was with him, none of this bloody namby bloody pamby policing!"

"Oh indeed, both the Hardy brothers, did have a certain way about them; a way of cracking skulls and picking pockets."

The Barmaid clapped her hands. "Hear, hear, Sergeant, I loathed the pair of them! Fat, horrible, pervy buggers. Ooh they'd make your skin crawl!"

John Bishop pounded the bar top. "Show some respect, you hear me? Not one of you would have the balls to lift a finger, if they were here now!"

"Oh, I lifted a finger, John!" Said Slug. "And Sergeant Hardy broke that, and a lot more!"

John Bishop laughed. "Oh, I remember, right old kicking he gave you!"

Sergeant Hastings placed a hand on John's Shoulder. "Well, I know you old men hanker for tradition, but I'm afraid there's change in the air. Why, just this morning I heard the strangest thing, Sylvia Bevan is running for Councillor! Huh, can you imagine a female representative in the borough of the infamous Lock Horns? Dear, dear, I've never heard the like!"

John Bishop turned a violent shade of purple; he banged his fist hard on the bar. "What? That whore and her witch friend…A COUNCILLOR? Over my dead body!"

Sergeant Hastings shook his head. "Oh I'd be careful what you say about those two if I was you, John. The way I see it, many who felt the same, did indeed end up dead."

John Bishop growled, his fists knotting with frustration. "FUCK THIS!" He belted down his pint and headed for the door.

Slug tugged on his collar, and sighed with relief as John Bishop left the bar. "Thank God for that!" He slurred.

Jane again clapped her hands. "Oh, bravo Sergeant, have a pint on me!"

The Sergeant raised his hand. "Never on duty, Madam. I'll have a lemonade if you don't mind."

Jane laughed. "My God, things really are changing!"

Sylvia gazed out of the flat window, watching the bustle of folk clutter through the square. The town had soon healed, as she knew it would and change, in no time, was harnessed and soon became a comfort of routine. "Councillor Sylvia Bevan; now there's change for you," she smiled and blushed at the very thought. It had not been her idea, she would have never imagined such a thing, it was the notion of young Peter Bellroy, the new, up and coming Peter Bellroy, the council chambers' rising new star. She had laughed it off at first, but Fitz, ever the fighter, immediately took up the war cry, and the campaign for Sylvia Bevan began. She could hear her lover in the background of her daydream, pushing forward in pursuit of their brave new world, a world of enterprise, made possible by her loathed, deceased spouse. She laughed at the thought of Morris furiously spinning in his grave as the bank signed over his ill-gotten gains, the very gains that had purchased her beloved shop. Fitz had wasted no time in planning its rebirth, and, what a birth it was going to be. Whether the town would like it, was totally beside the point. Sylvia judged the town's reaction to be torn, fifty-fifty. She smirked at the thought of the scandal, oh they had indeed walked out of shadows and into the light. Sylvia smiled smugly to herself, a smile that was stopped in its tracks, as she caught sight of Derek Huws. The florist and the graveyard had become Derek Huws routine, and as he passed the shop window clutching his floral totem of devotion, Sylvia's daydream shattered, and she was reminded that not everyone walked out of Morris Bevan's shadow. "Right!" Sylvia rose from her perch, the misery of poor Derek Huws reminding her of an old friend and loose ends.

Fitz was busy pulling the old shop apart when Sylvia entered the room. Sylvia placed a cup of tea on the one remaining shelf that had survived Fitz's furious crusade of destruction. "Morning dear," Silvia hollered above the clatters and bangs.

A very dusty Fitz placed down the crowbar, and picked up the hot brew. "Ah, decided to wake and give us a hand have you? Damn good of you, I thought councillor's stayed in bed until at least midday."

Sylvia laughed. "I'm not a councillor yet."

"Just a matter of time my dear. I mean, who could resist the beautiful and talented Sylvia Bevan?"

Sylvia kissed her lover. "Well, before all that, there's something I need to do."

"Ah, intrigue, I love it!"

"Well not quite, I need to see Gwyn."

Fitz took a sip of her tea. "Are you sure she'll want to see you? I mean, she's had plenty of opportunity to visit since her master and jailer's death."

Sylvia shook her head. "Oh Fitz, you really do have a single tracked mind concerning men! Gwyn, I don't think, will quite see it like that, she'll be mourning the loss of the man she loved."

"Loved? Well I suppose it works with dogs."

"Fitz! That's so unkind!"

"Well I'm sorry, Syl, but it baffles me! She spent most of her life moaning about the man, telling us how much of a swine he was, then she gets one taste of freedom and quickly decides she prefers the taste of his boots, and scurries back to the life she claimed to loathe!"

"She was, and I hope, still is our friend…And I need to see her."

Fitz shrugged her shoulders. "Of course. But just don't expect the welcome of the redeemer."

"She's out!" Said a very grubby and soiled Dave, as he dragged deep on his fag, flicking his ash at Sylvia's feet.

A light drizzle had started, but there was no sign of Dave permitting entry to the porch. "Oh…"

Sylvia paused as Dave unconcernedly broke wind, smirking as he did so. "Ah, I'm sorry to hear about your father, that's why I've called."

"Ah, no worries, life goes on dun it. He had a fair innings. Any how, me and the kids have moved in, you know, look after mam and all that. And of course, financially, it made a lot of sense, I mean one house is cheaper to run than two."

Sylvia forced a smile. "Of course. Do you know what time she'll be back?"

"Haven't a bloody clue! Better be soon though, kids haven't had breakfast yet!"

"Ah, of course. I don't suppose you'd know where I could find her?"

"Huh, that's easy, you'll find her where she always is these days, down the park feeding fucking ducks. Huh, makes you bloody laugh, there's her grandkids starving, and she's out feeding stupid bloody birds!"

Sylvia turned and walked away without another word; Dave hollered behind her. "Do us a favour, if you see her, tell her to hurry up home, the kids are starving! Ooh, and tell her to pick up a packet of ciggies on the way, I'm nearly bloody out!"

It took a while for Sylvia, a while for recognition to finally sink in. The lone figure seemed oblivious to the steady drizzle. The image radiated misery, its grief consumed the space it stood in, and the breaking of bread to feed the feathered creatures, seemed more ritual than pleasure. She had lost weight, and the loss of pounds had left her worn and sapped of life. Sylvia neared her old friend, who did not stir, look up, or falter, from her pendulum of duty. Sylvia placed a gentle hand on the stooped shoulder of her old friend. "Gwyn!" The head slowly turned. Gwyn straightened and dusted off the crumbs. "Oh, it's you."

Sylvia smiled. "How are you Gwyn?"

Gwyn's smile was a quiver of nerves. "Oh I'm fine, never bloody better. I heard you were back…You and her!"

"Yes, we're living above the old shop."

"Oh, very cosy!"

"We're going to re-open it, Gwyn, a new shop, perhaps you'd…"

"Huh, a new shop! And just what will you be selling? No, don't tell me. I can bloody well guess; potions and bloody mischief, and cures and spells for a better life, stuff and nonsense, if that lover of yours has got anything to do with it! A brew of bloody trouble that woman!" Gwyn picked through her bag of crumbs, turned and scattered them into the water. Sylvia waited a few moments, waiting for her old friend's mood to settle. "She means well, you know her, she just shoots headlong into a problem. To her things are black and white. She could see you and Sally were not happy, so she…"

"So she laced me with a potion that turned me into a raving sex maniac! Oh how helpful, how very considerate. Two men I've slept with, Syl! The one, my now late husband of forty years, and the other. The other a fucking disgusting, dirty, smelling wino called Slug! And you are telling me she was trying to help!"

"We were all unhappy with our lives when we met her, Gwyn. You, me and Sally…"

"Oh yes, thanks for reminding me, Syl. You know, of course, Sally's dead?"

"Of course I know she's dead!"

"Killed, it would seem, in very suspicious circumstances, almost supernatural, her and Cuthbert. Now, I wonder how that could have happened?"

"Cuthbert killed Sally, Gwyn!"

"Well that's strange, because the rest of the town believes it was a mysterious pot hole that swallowed them…And their entire house!"

"Well the rest of the town are wrong, Gwyn! He killed her, that freak! He could no longer control her, so he killed her!"

"Huh, and just how on earth would you know?"

"She told us."

"Oh! But of course, how silly of me, the marvellous Fitz is bound to talk to the dead."

"Well actually, she can. And do you know what else Sally said? She wished she had never gone back to him, and just who advised that Gwyn?"

"You can't blame me for that!"

"Oh I'm sorry, I don't want to blame anyone. Look Gwyn, we all have choices, and if your Norman's choice had been to treat you better, you would never have looked for an escape, or a change from the drudge and misery of your life. You came looking for change, adventure, because you'd run out of hope and you needed a life!"

"I LOVED HIM!" Gwyn shook with emotion. "I loved him."

"Oh I know you did Gwyn, but tell me, what did you get in return?"

The question stung and the tears rose and rolled. Gwyn took a deep breath. "A husband," she sighed.

Sylvia shook her head. "Then I'm truly sorry for you Gwyn, because I always believed you deserved a lot more."

FOUR MOONS HAVE PASSED...

Four moons, a score of changed hearts, and a belly full of death and misery had passed when the town's new store announced its grand opening. The folk of Sickle expected the unexpected, and Fitz knew they would not be disappointed. For a town that did not mind change, as long as everything stayed the same, the past few moons had proved to be quite a turbulent ride. Folk had discovered that what, and who, they thought they knew, was not always the way it was and that some fronts needed a look beyond the door. Change was all around; Bell's Barrow Hill, had become an even greater attraction for young love, after the hanging tree lived up to its name and earned its stripes. Morris Bevan soon became the cursed word, a deep stain of association, a reminder of what the dropped guard of apathy could allow to stalk free unchecked. Some in the town believed you could hear the howls of the Hardy brothers from beyond the grave, the day the keys of Stag Hall were handed to the Sickle Quilters, and the roar of the Lock Horn's was finally stilled. It was a proud day for Peter Bellroy, who had used his newly acquired council clout to push forward the motion, and he had an overwhelming feeling of pride the day he announced the society's accepted execution. And he smirked as certain Council colleagues growled in disbelief when sentence was passed, all bowing their heads, never to charge again.

Forty two and forty four Primrose Drive would never again border a forty three. The mysterious event had earned the now deserted plot an air of mystery and foreboding. Cuthbert Combs' once immaculate home had now become a lawn, a very well kept lawn, and was the only shrine and resting place Fitz and Sylvia had for their lost and beautiful friend. The inscription on the bench simply read. *'HERE LIES BEAUTY'*. And each and every day, beauty was adorned with flowers.

The new moons also brought forth the town's new hero. Tom the Placard had indeed found glory in death and his name in the town would at least reach eternity, his saving of the young boy scout and his defiance in the face of demons had ensured his legend, and Tom's plaque was placed with honour beside the town's famous bugler. The inscription read. *REACH THE GATES OF HEAVEN BY FAITH, BUT REACH THE HEARTS OF MEN BY DEEDS.*

And so the crowd gathered, whether it was to witness the grand opening of the town's new store or to indulge in the free plonk and fruit cake, mattered not To Fitz and Sylvia. For, all that mattered was that they had the town's attention. Sylvia cleared her throat and smiled politely at the crowd as they grazed and gulped down their freebies. "I'd like to thank you all," started Sylvia, nervously, "for turning out and showing support to our..." Sylvia turned, smiled and beckoned Fitz to join her. "Bold new venture." Sylvia paused, waiting for some sort of reaction, but the crowd just chewed on in silence. "Ah, anyway, without further ado, I shall leave it to my partner to unveil our brand new enterprise. Sylvia clapped and giggled as Fitz walked to the mounted plaque for the great unveiling, and the crowd munched on. Fitz took a deep breath, held her chin high and drew the veil. *THE LADIES LABYRINTH.* The bold letters announced, and just so there was no mistake of the shops intended custom and purpose, the small print proclaimed, *A PATH THROUGH THE MAZE AND MYSTERY OF A WOMAN'S NEEDS.*

The crowd had the look of all being simultaneously stung on the backside by a giant wasp; crumbs tumbling out of gaping gobs, and wine dribbling down chins. Sylvia smiled at the stunned reaction, for it was true to say her lover could not make a cup of tea without chucking a lump of revolution into the pot.

Fitz laughed, well prepared for the 'lost in limbo' reaction, and she was also prepared for male outrage. Herbert Greenway was the first to gather his wits. "So what exactly is it you sell? I mean, it is a shop after all?" He then laughed and shook his head, appealing for the crowd to join in with his rebuke.

Fitz pointed a finger at Herbert. "Nothing for you, I'm afraid. That is, unless you want to get in touch with your feminine side."

Herbert turned furnace red at the quip of his sexuality, he gripped tight his wife's arm. "Come on Mabel, that's quite enough of this stuff and nonsense!" And off he marched, dragging his wife behind him. Soon the implications are digested by every male in the crowd and a score of wives are manhandled and marched away to safer outlets that offer beer, fags and pork chops.

Sylvia threw her hands into the air in despair, as the grand opening was well and truly scuppered. Fitz clapped her hands and laughed. Sylvia looked at her, bewildered. "Well I don't see what's so funny?"

"Don't you Syl?"

"No! I would say that was a complete disaster as shop openings go!"

"Do you? Oh, I think it went quite swimmingly!"

The source of curiosity is the mere drip of a tap, a relentless drip that ever so slowly erodes into the mind, drumming at the brain and demanding attention. The taboo becomes a magnet, an attraction that will rip the skull out of your scalp if you so much as try to pull against it, until finally the drip builds to a torrent, the dam bursts open and we hurtle into the deluge, not caring whether we sink or swim.

And so drip by drip the customers came, to poke their nose in and see what this strange new world was all about. And strange indeed, the world of the Ladies Labyrinth turned out to be.

Fitz Had said from the beginning of the venture that the town would self-advertise... And self-advertise it did. Tongues rolled hotter and faster than any tabloid printer. Doors and windows were knocked and tapped, as oblivious canvassers spread the news from street to terrace and avenue. "Oh, the insight of the woman!" Announced Mabel Greenway, the first to be dragged out of harm's way by her husband and, it would seem, one of the first to return. "She looked in that ball and, I swear, straight into my soul," said Mabel. Every ear of the gathering clutch was peaked to high alert as the words of Mabel Greenway stirred deep desires and dreams. "She said there was a shadow!" The ladies all gasped with the drama of it all. "Yes, the shadow of a great big boot that has hovered above me all my married life, suppressing my flair and leadership abilities, and overcasting my dreams and desires."

"Ooh!" Butted in Janet Smith. "I bet that's your Herbert she's on about, hell of a foot on him!"

The ladies all turned to scold the dim witted Janet but were stilled by Mabel's hand. "For once Janet is right. And believe me, the mystic implications were not lost to me, for I have indeed spent my life under the shadow of a size ten. But ladies, no more!" Mabel let the bait hang in the air and in no time got a bite. "Ooh, what did you do?" Said Hilary Thomson, hopping with excitement.

Mabel Greenway built well the climax. "I put down the iron, stilled the kettle, binned the duster and stuck his size ten where, my dears, the sun seldom shines!"

The ladies all hooted and clapped in delight at the telling of this bold act of revolution, and Mabel became a hero, a figurehead, and had more pats than a field full of cows.

And so the pitch was made, without a penny spent, the shop hit the hot gossip front page and the trickle of curiosity became a flood.

Fitz and Sylvia's moods purred contented, with the still warm, clear night. Their roof terrace had proved to be perfect harbour for a herb garden, herbs that were now selling like hot cakes as the business grew quicker than the garden. Sylvia's green fingers cherished the space and she worked and tended with a labour of love. Life was sweet and the red wine flowed, and smoothed right into the flow and mood of the night, with the clatter and busy sounds of the square below them, making the space seem all the more prized and sacred.

"Fitz?" Sylvia whispered in her lover's ear. Fitz stirred and raised her head from her lover's bosom. "Do you think Gwyn will ever come out of her grief?"

Fitz took a few moments to ponder the question. "It depends…Some wither through grief, others take hold of their spirit and see life for what it is."

"And just what is life?"

"Oh that's easy, my dear, it's simply ours to live."

What was it about Friday's and fish and chips? Where was it written, and just when was it enforced by law? And why, on this particular Friday, did it prove the catalyst that broke the straw, the camel and its bloody back?!

The double yoked egg ran down a stunned David's face, chips lay strewn across the floor, and David's shirt was splattered in ketchup. Gwyn's grandchildren covered their mouths and giggled. "What the hell has got into you Mother?" Quivered, a bewildered Dave.

The temper, for the first time since her husband's death, had brought a furnace of colour back to Gwyn's face. "What's wrong with me?" Gwyn fumed. "Well, according to you, I am a worthless old trout, who has not got the sense to know that King Dave, like his Father before him, will only eat fish on a Friday, and…"

"Now hold on Mam!" Said Dave, snatching a tea towel and wiping the egg off his face. "I've the kids to think about, their growing boys and need proper food, not bloody egg and chips."

"Oh, you mean like the proper food you and your dear ex used to provide, on your giro, after fags and booze deductions of course. Poor mites were lucky to have chips, never mind eggs!"

Dave slammed down the tea towel. "I don't have to stand here and listen to this!"

"Good point Dave! Just why are you, standing there listening to this, when you could have stayed in your own home and not listened to anyone at all?"

"I did it for you…after dad!"

"Huh!" Gwyn folded her arms and shook her head. "Oh Dave, just because a mother's love is blind, it does not mean I don't see. All my life I strived to do nothing more than please and wait on your Father. One mistake I made in all those years, and God knows, I've got the rest of my life to pay for it!" Gwyn sobbed and paced the room in frustration. "And it would have been nice...It would have been nice for my kids to have forgiven and stood by me, instead of damning me to hell!"

Dave wore his best schoolboy pout, went into the hall, then returned with his kids coats. "Right boys...We are not staying to listen to this, come on, we'll be welcome at Aunt Sand's."

Dave headed for the door, Gwyn got up to follow. "Look, you don't have to leave..."

"Oh, I think we do!" Dave herded his children through the hall and out of the door, slamming it in protest.

Gwyn, for lost moments, sat numb and alone, until the stir of an old friend reintroduced itself through a tingling of the toes. The old friend; pins and needles up her legs, and quakes and rumbles in her belly. A long forgotten heat smouldered through her body, rising like a tempest through the channel of her throat. The scream was long suppressed thunder, with the force to shatter bars and chains. It howled its freedom to a lost world; the companion of passion returned, and the room exploded. The haze eventually cleared and Gwyn sat, exhausted, among the wreckage of her rage. She laughed and cried, but was held once more, in the world of anger, joy and sorrow.

THE REVOLT OF THE SILENT KETTLES...

And so the women who should know better arrived. At first, they came with alibis, and a feigned duty to help others, but with a dip of the toe, their own hearts and needs soon swam, and the Labyrinth quickly became a hot bed of revolution, a breeding ground for feminine ambition. And it was at this time that kettles became eerily silent, or simply did not whistle when they should. Meal times became erratic, and with grumbling bellies the mood of men soon soured. But the kettle at the Labyrinth was red hot and forever whistling, as the shop became a necessity for every ill or want of a woman's needs. Soon the sacred lore of herb and root became every lady's staple, quickly replacing the miracle haze of Valium and Gin.

Friday in the town became girls night out, orchestrated by Fitz of course, and was quickly labelled the day of cold suppers, a day when the hard graft of men was rewarded with pre-made sandwiches, chilled and left with hand written instructions. To the eyes of the Vale, this was revolution indeed and was the last straw for John Bishop. He left the Roast Duck for the Social Club, never to return, upon seeing his precious, male sanctuary flooded with wild unshackled women, all hijacking the reserved pleasures of men.

But it was spiritual guidance that became the shop's bible and main attraction, and Fitz soon found herself being more Agony Aunt than clairvoyant. Safe in the sanctuary of spirits, the problems of sisters soon flowed, and Fitz became embroiled in some very peculiar desires and needs. Victoria Walker was a blossom of virtue, or so the world supposed, so it was something of a shock to see the door open and a cautious Victoria smuggle herself in, teary eyed and pleading for counsel.

Fitz waited patiently for the sobs and handbag fidgeting to subside, before dropping the prompt. "Well now my dear, just what can I do for you?"

Victoria forced her head up and fought hard to gulp down the distress, and still her quaking chins. "It's...my..." She paused, blew her nose and took a deep breath. "My husband!"

Fitz laughed, she could not help herself. "Well my dear, join a very big club and don't worry. I'd be out of business if it was not for the failings of husbands. Now, just what burden has he put upon you?"

"Huh!" It was Victoria who now laughed. "Burden me? Oh God I wish! Oh, he's a saint, my Hugo...Never a voice raised in anger. God and family first, without exception. Ooh, a meticulous provider, not a bill or need goes unchecked, caring, considerate, a bloody gift from heaven, and, and... About, as romantic as an anti-feminist axe murderer!" And the tears flowed. Fitz reached over and grabbed the essential box of tissues, handing one to the now totally distressed Victoria. Fitz waited for the flow of emotion to pass without saying a word. Victoria finally took a deep breath, sat up straight and dived straight in. "BLOODY TRAINS! A grown man, mind you! Blowing his bloody whistle and playing with his fucking choo, choo's...Oh, forgive the language?"

"No problem," said Fitz, smiling at the absurdity. "I've received and given worse."

"Well, I'll get straight to the point. After all, I've made it this far. You see, he promised this Thursday; I'd cooked a pot roast, bought scented candles, spent hours making up and looking my best..." Victoria paused and again took a deep breath. "Seven thirty! That's the time supper was being served...And sure enough, at seven thirty I heard the attic door open and finally close on the great railway terminal in the loft. I heard him coming down the stairs, so I lit the candles. I'd waited a whole week for this, and the last time I had any romance, God only knows! And in he came, covered in oil, and cradling like a baby... a steam locomotive! And, do you know? There were tears in his eyes! Yes that's right, a man, full grown, blubbing like a baby! Look, he said, it derailed at Crewe, I think the chassis has cracked, I won't be a tick, he continued, just popping round to Fred's. And that is when I lost it. 'Put that fucking train down!' I screamed, 'and start sucking my tits, we're supposed to be having sex tonight...'"

Fitz laughed out loud. She could not help it, even if she tried. "Oh I'm sorry, it's just…"

"Oh don't worry, I saw the funny side after the pot roast bounced off his head, and he scampered through the door howling like a scolded child."

Fitz forced a straight face. "So, let me guess. You're looking for something to stir the beast…an aphrodisiac?"

"Oh dear me no! I despise him! And if you give him anything to arouse his sex drive he'll probably end up screwing one of his trains. Oh no my dear, hope for romance is long passed. No, it's poison I want. I mean to kill the pious little bastard!"

"I declined of course," said Fitz, putting her tea down on the counter. Sylvia roared with laughter, as Fitz told of the afternoon's encounter with Victoria Walker. "But," continued Fitz, "good to see some bite in the old girl, I must admit."

"You never know," said Sylvia, reaching into the till to count the day's takings, "she might just find a way to snuff him without your help, and…"

Sylvia was interrupted by the sound of door chimes. She looked up from her coins.

"We're closing…Gwyn?" Sylvia darted around the counter and the old friends embraced. Sylvia kept a firm hold on Gwyn's hands and looked her from head to toe. "You look well!"

Gwyn smiled. "I feel better, it's been…"

"Hmmm!" Fitz cleared her throat for attention. Gwyn turned, noticing her for the first time. "Ah, hello Fitz, I feel…"

"What are you doing here Gwyn?"

Gwyn fidgeted, for a moment stuck for words. "I was wondering if there were any jobs going, you see I've a bit of time on my hands."

Fitz folded her arms and glared. "What experience do you have?"

Gwyn looked down at her feet. "Well I…"

Fitz laughed and raced towards her friend. "Of course you can have a job Gwyn, and welcome to our brave new world!"

THE END

Printed in Great Britain
by Amazon